HEARTS IN THE WIND

HEARTS IN THE WIND

EMMA DREAMWEAVER

PROTAJ

CONTENTS

Disclaimer of Liability

The author and publisher of this book have made every effort to ensure the accuracy and completeness of the information presented. However, the information contained in this book is provided "as is," and the author and publisher make no warranties or representations regarding its accuracy or completeness. The author and publisher shall not be liable for any errors or omissions, or for any consequences arising from the use of this information.

Content Warning:

This novel contains themes of emotional distress, illness, and other mature content. Reader discretion is advised.

Legal Disclaimer:

This book is a work of fiction. Names, characters, businesses, places, events, and incidents are either the product of the author's imagination or used in a fictitious manner. Any resemblance to actual persons, living or dead, or actual events is purely coincidental.

Preface

In the quiet corners of our lives, where the mundane meets the magical, we often find stories waiting to be told—stories that reflect our innermost desires, our deepest fears, and our unspoken hopes. "Hearts in the Wind" is one such story, a journey of love, loss, and renewal set against the backdrop of a small, idyllic town where the past and present intertwine in the most unexpected ways.

As you embark on this journey with Mia Prescott and Ethan Miller, you will traverse the paths of Willow Creek—a place that, while fictional, resonates with the real-life emotions and experiences we all encounter. The story weaves through the complexities of rekindling old flames, confronting unresolved pasts, and discovering the strength to embrace new beginnings. At its heart, it is a tale about the enduring power of love and the courage it takes to rebuild and grow.

Inspired by the quiet strength found in everyday moments and the profound impact of personal transformation, "Hearts in the Wind" explores themes of family, personal growth, and the resilience of the human spirit. Mia's journey, marked by both the trials of facing a loved one's illness and the joys of newfound love, serves as a reminder that even in the face of uncertainty, there is beauty in hope and strength in vulnerability.

This novel is a tribute to those who have faced their own challenges with grace, to the relationships that have weathered storms and emerged stronger, and to the dreams that have guided us through the darkest of times. As you turn these pages, I hope you find solace, inspiration, and a connection to the characters and their stories. May Mia and Ethan's journey remind you that no matter where life's winds may carry us, the heart's true compass always leads us home.

Thank you for joining me on this journey. I am honored to share "Hearts in the Wind" with you, and I hope it resonates with you as deeply as it did with me during its creation.

Emma Dreamweaver

Chapter 1: The Return

The sound of gravel crunching under the tires was the first sign that Mia Thompson had truly come home. The long, winding road leading to her family's old farmhouse was still as familiar as the back of her hand, yet it felt strangely foreign after all these years. She slowed the car to a crawl, rolling down the window to let the crisp, autumn air flood the interior. It smelled of pine, damp earth, and the faint scent of wood smoke—reminders of a simpler time.

Mia hadn't planned to return to Willow Creek. The small town held too many memories, both good and bad, that she'd spent the last few years trying to forget. But when her mother had called, voice trembling with worry, and asked her to come back to help care for Grandma June, Mia couldn't say no. Family was family, after all, and despite everything, Willow Creek was still home.

As she pulled into the driveway, Mia's gaze settled on the house. The white paint had begun to peel, and the once-vibrant flowerbeds were now overrun with weeds. It looked as though time had stood still, and yet, everything had changed. She stepped out of the car, the cool breeze ruffling her chestnut-brown hair, and took a deep breath. The air was sharper than in the city, cleaner somehow, and it grounded her in a way she hadn't felt in years.

The front door creaked as she pushed it open, the familiar groan echoing through the silent house. "Mom? Grandma?" she called out, her voice hesitant, unsure of what to expect. The house seemed empty, but she knew better.

"In the kitchen, sweetheart!" her mother's voice floated back, warm and inviting.

Mia set her bags down in the hallway and made her way to the kitchen. As she rounded the corner, she saw her mother, a petite woman with graying hair tied back in a loose bun, bustling around the kitchen. Grandma June sat at the table, her once-vibrant eyes now dulled by age, but still sharp with recognition when they landed on Mia.

"There she is," Grandma June said with a smile that made the lines on her face deepen. "My little Mia."

Mia crossed the room in a few quick strides and enveloped her grandmother in a gentle hug, careful of her frail frame. "I've missed you, Grandma."

"And I've missed you, too," Grandma June replied, her voice soft but filled with warmth. "It's good to have you back, dear. The house has been too quiet without you."

Mia pulled back and smiled, though her heart ached at how much her grandmother had aged since she'd last seen her. "It's good to be back. I've missed this place."

Her mother set a kettle on the stove and turned to face Mia, her eyes filled with a mixture of relief and concern. "How was the drive? Not too tiring, I hope?"

"It was fine," Mia replied, though the exhaustion of the long drive still lingered in her bones. "The countryside is as beautiful as ever."

They chatted about the trip and the weather, the conversation easy and familiar, like slipping into an old, well-worn coat. But underneath it all, Mia could sense the unspoken worries that hung in the air—the reason she was really here.

As they sipped their tea, the doorbell rang, its chime echoing through the house. Mia's mother glanced up, a frown tugging at the corners of her mouth. "I wonder who that could be. We don't usually get visitors this late."

"I'll get it," Mia offered, setting down her cup and heading toward the front door. The boards creaked under her feet as she crossed the hallway, a reminder of just how long it had been since the house had been filled with life.

She opened the door, expecting a neighbor or perhaps the mailman, but her breath caught in her throat when she saw who was standing on the other side.

"Ethan," she whispered, her voice barely audible.

Ethan Parker stood there, tall and broad-shouldered, his dark hair tousled by the wind. He looked older, more rugged than she remembered, but those deep blue eyes were just as piercing as they'd been the last time she'd seen him. A wave of memories crashed over her—laughter, shared secrets, the heartache of their last goodbye.

"Mia," he replied, his voice rich and steady. "It's been a while."

She nodded, too stunned to speak for a moment. Of all the people she'd expected to see tonight, Ethan was the last on the list. "What... what are you doing here?"

He offered a small, tentative smile. "I heard you were back in town. Thought I'd come by and say hello."

Mia stepped aside, allowing him to enter. As he walked past her, she caught a hint of his familiar scent—woodsy, with a touch of something she couldn't quite place but had always associated with him. She closed the door and turned to face him, her mind racing.

"It's been a long time," she finally said, her voice steadying.

"Too long," he agreed, his gaze meeting hers with an intensity that made her heart skip a beat.

They stood there in silence, the weight of their shared past hanging between them like a tangible thing. Mia wanted to ask him so many questions, but she didn't know where to start. Why had he come back to Willow Creek? And why now, just as she was trying to piece her life back together?

"Are you... staying?" she asked, the question loaded with more meaning than she intended.

"For a while, yeah," Ethan replied. "I've got some things to take care of here."

Mia nodded, though her mind was still spinning. "Well, it's good to see you."

"You too, Mia," he said softly.

As they stood there, the sound of laughter drifted from the kitchen, reminding Mia that they weren't alone. She forced a smile and gestured toward the kitchen. "Mom and Grandma are in the kitchen. You should say hello."

Ethan smiled, a genuine one this time, and followed her into the warmth of the kitchen. As she watched him greet her family, Mia couldn't help but wonder if his return was just a coincidence, or if fate had decided to bring them back together for a reason.

But whatever the reason, one thing was clear—nothing in Willow Creek would be the same now that Ethan Parker was back.

Mia watched as Ethan and her grandmother exchanged pleasantries, the years of distance between them dissolving in an instant. Her mother, always the gracious host, quickly set another place at the table, filling a mug with steaming tea and placing it in front of Ethan as if it were the most natural thing in the world for him to be here.

As they settled into easy conversation, Mia felt a strange mix of comfort and unease. It was as if the past had come rushing back, uninvited, pulling her into a whirlwind of emotions she thought she had buried long ago. Ethan's presence stirred memories that were both sweet and painful, and she couldn't help but wonder what his return really meant.

"So, Ethan," her mother began, her tone curious but casual, "what brings you back to Willow Creek?"

Ethan took a sip of his tea, his gaze briefly meeting Mia's before he answered. "I've been away for too long. Figured it was time to come back and take care of some things I left unfinished."

Mia's heart skipped a beat at his words. She knew they weren't just talking about mundane matters—there was something deeper, something that involved the two of them.

Her mother nodded, seemingly satisfied with his vague response. "Well, it's good to see familiar faces around here. The town hasn't changed much, but it's always nice when old friends return."

"Thank you, Mrs. Thompson," Ethan replied with a smile that didn't quite reach his eyes. Mia noticed the slight tension in his posture, the way he kept glancing her way, as if trying to gauge her reaction.

The conversation drifted to safer topics—old town gossip, memories of school days, the latest news about the neighbors—but Mia's mind was elsewhere. She couldn't shake the feeling that Ethan's return was more than just a visit to his hometown. There was something unspoken between them, something that had been left unresolved when they'd parted ways all those years ago.

As the evening wore on, Grandma June began to tire, her eyelids drooping as she fought to stay awake. Mia's mother noticed and stood up, her voice gentle. "I think it's time we get you to bed, Mom. You've had a long day."

Grandma June nodded, her smile soft but weary. "Yes, I suppose it's time. But it was lovely to see you, Ethan. It's been too long."

Ethan rose from his seat and leaned down to give her a gentle hug. "It's good to see you too, Mrs. Prescott. Take care of yourself."

Mia watched as her mother helped Grandma June to her feet and led her toward the stairs. As they disappeared from view, the kitchen seemed to grow quieter, the ticking of the old clock on the wall suddenly much louder.

Ethan turned to Mia, his expression unreadable. "It's really good to see you, Mia. I've missed this place. I've missed... a lot of things."

Mia's heart tightened at his words, but she forced herself to stay composed. "It's good to see you too, Ethan. I just didn't expect..."

"Didn't expect me to come back?" he finished for her, his tone soft but laced with something that sounded like regret.

She nodded, unable to find the right words. The truth was, she didn't know how she felt about his return. Part of her was relieved, happy even, to see him again. But another part of her was wary, afraid that opening old wounds would only lead to more pain.

Ethan took a step closer, his gaze locking onto hers with an intensity that made her pulse quicken. "I know things ended badly between us, and I know I've got a lot to make up for. But I'm here now, and I want to make things right. If you'll let me."

Mia looked into his eyes, seeing the sincerity there, and for a moment, she let herself imagine what it would be like to let him back in, to give them another chance. But the scars of the past were still fresh, and she wasn't sure if she was ready to reopen that chapter of her life.

"Ethan, I..." she began, but the words caught in her throat.

Before she could finish, he reached out and gently took her hand, his touch warm and familiar. "You don't have to decide anything right now. Just... think about it. I'm not going anywhere."

Mia nodded, her heart racing as she pulled her hand away, the loss of his touch leaving her feeling cold. "I'll think about it," she promised, though she wasn't sure what she would do.

Ethan smiled, though it was tinged with sadness. "That's all I ask."

They stood there in silence for a moment longer before Ethan finally said goodnight and left, the door closing softly behind him. Mia stood in the hallway, her thoughts swirling like the autumn leaves outside, wondering what the future held now that Ethan Parker was back in her life.

As she made her way upstairs to her old bedroom, she couldn't help but feel that everything was about to change. And for the first time in a long time, she wasn't sure if that was a good thing or not.

Mia lingered in the hallway for a moment after Ethan left, her thoughts tangled in a web of uncertainty. The familiar hum of the house surrounded her, the ticking of the grandfather clock in the living room keeping time with her racing heart. She hadn't expected to see Ethan tonight, or perhaps ever again. But now that he was back, the emotions she had buried deep within herself began to resurface, swirling in a confusing mix of longing, regret, and hope.

Taking a deep breath, Mia turned and headed upstairs to her old bedroom. Each step on the creaking wooden stairs felt like she was retracing the path of her past, a journey she wasn't sure she was ready to make. Her hand grazed the banister, its smooth wood worn from years of use, as she ascended to the second floor.

When she reached her bedroom, she hesitated for a moment before pushing the door open. The room was just as she had left it—her childhood bed with its floral quilt, the oak dresser with a few old knick-knacks, and the window that overlooked the fields stretching out behind the house. It was as if time had stood still here, preserving the remnants of her youth like a time capsule.

Mia crossed the room and set her suitcase down at the foot of the bed. She glanced around, taking in the familiar surroundings, but her mind was elsewhere—back downstairs with Ethan. His sudden reappearance in her life had shaken her more than she wanted to admit. She had thought she had moved on, but now, she wasn't so sure.

She walked over to the window and pulled back the curtains. The night was clear, the sky a deep indigo dotted with stars. The fields beyond the house were bathed in the soft glow of the moonlight, the tall grasses swaying gently in the breeze. It was a peaceful scene, one that had always brought her comfort as a child. But tonight, it did little to calm the storm of emotions inside her.

Mia leaned her forehead against the cool glass, closing her eyes as she tried to make sense of everything. Ethan's return was unexpected, but what troubled her more was the way her heart had reacted to seeing him. The rush of emotions, the memories they had shared—it all felt too overwhelming, too soon.

She remembered the last time they had seen each other, the hurt in his eyes as they said their goodbyes. They had been so young, so full of dreams and hopes for the future. But life had pulled them in different directions, and they had parted ways, believing it was for the best. Mia had moved to the city, chasing a career that had taken her far from Willow Creek and the life she had once known. And now, here she was, back in the place she had once called home, confronted by the man she had never truly forgotten.

With a sigh, Mia pushed away from the window and sat down on the edge of the bed. She knew she had to focus on the present—on why she had come back to Willow Creek in the first place. Grandma June needed her, and that was what mattered most. But she couldn't ignore the fact that Ethan's return had stirred something deep within her, something she thought she had buried long ago.

As she lay back on the bed, staring up at the ceiling, Mia's thoughts drifted to what might happen now that Ethan was back in town. Could they pick up the pieces of their past, or was it too late to try? And did she even want to open that door again, knowing the pain it had caused the first time around?

The questions swirled in her mind as she drifted off to sleep, the cool autumn breeze whispering through the open window, carrying with it the scent of pine and wood smoke. Tomorrow would bring a new day, and with it, the chance to face the future—whatever that might hold.

But for now, Mia allowed herself to rest, the memories of the past fading into the background as sleep claimed her. The journey she had begun by returning to Willow Creek was only just beginning, and she had no idea where it would lead. But one thing was certain—nothing would ever be the same again.

The morning sun streamed through the window, casting a warm, golden light over Mia's room. She blinked awake, momentarily disoriented by the unfamiliar surroundings, before the events of the previous day came rushing back. Willow Creek. Grandma June. And Ethan. The memories stirred her from sleep, leaving a bittersweet taste in her mouth.

Mia stretched and pushed herself out of bed, the cool hardwood floor sending a shiver up her spine as she padded over to the dresser. She glanced in the mirror, taking in her reflection—the dark circles under her eyes, the tired lines etched around her mouth. She looked older, more worn than she remembered. City life had taken its toll, and the stress of the last few years was visible on her face.

She quickly pulled on a pair of jeans and a soft, oversized sweater before making her way downstairs. The house was quiet, the only sound the creak of the floorboards beneath her feet. When she reached the kitchen, she found her mother already up, her back turned as she stood at the stove, flipping pancakes.

"Morning, sweetheart," her mother greeted her, not turning around.

"Morning," Mia replied, her voice still heavy with sleep.

She poured herself a cup of coffee and took a seat at the kitchen table, inhaling the rich aroma. The warmth of the cup in her hands brought a small comfort, a grounding sensation amidst the whirlwind of emotions she was still trying to process.

Her mother placed a stack of pancakes on the table, along with a small pitcher of maple syrup. "I thought we'd have a nice breakfast together," she said, her voice cheerful, but with an undercurrent of something more—anxiety, perhaps, or concern. Mia couldn't quite tell.

"Thanks, Mom," Mia said, offering a small smile as she drizzled syrup over her plate.

They ate in companionable silence for a few minutes before her mother spoke again. "I saw Ethan last night," she said casually, though her eyes were watchful as they met Mia's.

Mia paused, her fork halfway to her mouth. "Yeah. He stopped by."

Her mother nodded, her expression neutral, though Mia could sense the questions bubbling just beneath the surface. "He's grown up, hasn't he?"

"He has," Mia agreed, though that was an understatement. The boy she had once known was now a man—a man who had clearly lived a life full of experiences that had shaped him in ways she couldn't begin to imagine.

Her mother didn't press the matter further, and for that, Mia was grateful. She wasn't ready to talk about Ethan, about the confusion and uncertainty his return had stirred within her. There would be time for that later, but for now, she just wanted to focus on the simple act of being home, surrounded by family.

After breakfast, Mia helped clear the table and wash the dishes, slipping easily back into the rhythm of life in Willow Creek. It was comforting, in a way, to be back in the routine of her childhood, even if it felt a bit like wearing an old pair of shoes that didn't quite fit anymore.

As they finished cleaning up, her mother turned to her, a thoughtful look on her face. "I'm going to head into town later to run a few errands. Do you want to come with me? It might be nice to get out, see some familiar faces."

Mia hesitated for a moment, considering the offer. Part of her wanted to stay home, to avoid the questions and the inevitable gossip that would follow her reappearance in town. But another part of her knew that she couldn't hide forever. If she was going to be here for a while, she might as well start facing the reality of her situation.

"Sure," she said finally. "I'll come with you."

Her mother smiled, a hint of relief in her eyes. "Great. We can leave in about an hour, if that works for you."

"Sounds good," Mia replied, though her stomach twisted with a mix of anticipation and dread.

As her mother headed upstairs to get ready, Mia walked out onto the front porch, the wooden boards creaking under her weight. She leaned against the railing, her eyes sweeping over the fields that stretched out before her. The leaves on the trees had begun to change, their vibrant reds and oranges a stark contrast against the clear blue sky.

It was beautiful here, in a way that was different from the city. The air was cleaner, the pace slower, and there was a sense of peace that she hadn't felt in a long time. But with that peace came a sense of unease, a feeling that she was standing on the edge of something she couldn't quite see, something that was just out of reach.

Mia took a deep breath, letting the crisp air fill her lungs. No matter how much she tried to ignore it, the truth was that being back in Willow Creek was bringing up emotions she wasn't sure she was ready to deal with. And the fact that Ethan was here only complicated things further.

But she had made the decision to come home, and now she would have to face whatever came next, one step at a time.

As she stood there, lost in thought, the sound of footsteps on the gravel driveway drew her attention. She turned, expecting to see her mother, but instead, her breath caught in her throat.

Ethan was walking toward her, his hands in his pockets, a tentative smile on his face. The morning sun glinted off his dark hair, and as he approached, Mia felt her heart begin to race.

"Morning," he said, his voice warm and familiar.

"Morning," Mia replied, her voice steady, though her heart was anything but.

Ethan stopped a few feet away from her, his eyes searching hers. "I was hoping I'd catch you before you left for town," he said.

"What's up?" she asked, trying to keep her tone casual, though she couldn't deny the flutter of anticipation in her chest.

"I was wondering if you'd like to go for a walk later," Ethan said, his gaze steady. "There's a spot I'd like to show you. It's changed a bit since you were last here."

Mia hesitated, a thousand thoughts running through her mind. She wasn't sure if she was ready for this—for the closeness, the memories, the possibility of reopening old wounds. But as she looked into Ethan's eyes, she saw something there that made her want to say yes. A connection, a thread that had never really been severed, no matter how much time had passed.

"Sure," she said finally, a small smile playing on her lips. "I'd like that."

Ethan's smile widened, and for a moment, it felt like they were teenagers again, standing on the precipice of something new and exciting. "Great. I'll come by this afternoon?"

"Okay," Mia agreed, her heart lifting slightly at the thought.

As Ethan turned to leave, Mia watched him go, a sense of calm settling over her. Maybe, just maybe, this return to Willow Creek was exactly what she needed. A chance to heal, to reconnect with her roots, and perhaps, to discover what her heart truly wanted.

And as she stood there on the porch, watching the man who had once been her everything walk away, Mia couldn't help but feel that this was just the beginning of a new chapter in her life—one that she was finally ready to embrace.

Chapter 2: Old Wounds

Later that evening, after dinner had been cleared away and Grandma June had retired to her room, Mia found herself sitting on the porch, wrapped in a woolen blanket. The night was cool, and the stars twinkled brightly above, undisturbed by the city lights she'd grown accustomed to. The silence of Willow Creek was a stark contrast to the constant hum of life in the city, and it left her with too much time to think.

Ethan's unexpected visit had stirred something in her—something she thought she had buried deep inside. She closed her eyes and let the memories wash over her, unbidden.

They had been inseparable once, two kids growing up in a town where everyone knew everyone. Ethan had been her first real friend, her first real everything. They'd spent countless summer nights lying on this very porch, whispering about their dreams, their fears, and everything in between. But life had a way of complicating even the purest of friendships.

It was the summer after they graduated high school when everything had changed. Mia had been accepted into an art school in the city, a dream she had nurtured for years. Ethan, on the other hand, had been set on joining the military, eager to see the world beyond Willow Creek. They had both known that their paths were about to diverge, but neither had been prepared for the heartbreak that followed.

The night before Ethan left for boot camp, they had argued—fiercely. Ethan had wanted her to wait for him, to keep their relationship alive despite the distance. But Mia, terrified of being left behind and unsure of what the future held, had refused. She had wanted to move forward, to chase her dreams without the weight of a long-distance relationship holding her back.

"I can't do this, Ethan," she had said, tears streaming down her face. "I can't wait around for something that might never happen."

"And I can't stay here, Mia," he had replied, his voice cracking with emotion. "I have to go. I need to do this."

They had parted ways that night with harsh words and broken hearts, both too stubborn to give in. Ethan had left the next morning without saying goodbye, and Mia had thrown herself into her studies, determined to forget the boy who had once meant everything to her.

But she never truly had. And now, all those old wounds were re-opening, fresh and raw as if no time had passed at all.

The creak of the porch door pulled Mia from her thoughts. She glanced over her shoulder to see Ethan stepping outside, his hands shoved into the pockets of his jacket. He hesitated for a moment, as if unsure whether to join her, before finally making his way over.

"Mind if I sit?" he asked, his voice low.

"Sure," she replied, pulling the blanket tighter around her as he took a seat beside her on the porch swing. The wooden slats groaned under the added weight, but the swing held, just like it always had.

They sat in silence for a while, the only sound the gentle creaking of the swing and the distant chirp of crickets. Mia could feel the tension between them, thick and suffocating, but she didn't know how to break it.

"I'm sorry for just showing up like that," Ethan said eventually, his gaze fixed on the dark horizon. "I didn't mean to catch you off guard."

"It's okay," Mia replied, though her heart was still racing from the surprise. "I just... wasn't expecting to see you, that's all."

"I wasn't sure if I should come," he admitted, his voice tinged with uncertainty. "But when I heard you were back in town, I couldn't stay away."

Mia swallowed hard, the emotions she'd been trying to keep at bay bubbling to the surface. "Why now, Ethan? After all these years, why come back now?"

Ethan sighed, running a hand through his hair. "I don't know, Mia. Maybe it's because I realized that I've been running for too long. From this place, from you... from everything. I needed to come back, to face what I left behind."

Mia's chest tightened at his words. Part of her wanted to believe him, to think that he was here to make amends, but the other part was still too wounded, too afraid of being hurt again.

"And what is it you think you left behind?" she asked, her voice barely above a whisper.

Ethan turned to look at her then, his blue eyes dark with emotion. "You, Mia. I left you behind. And I've regretted it every day since."

His words hit her like a punch to the gut, knocking the wind out of her. For so long, she had convinced herself that she was the one who had been left behind, that she was the one who had been abandoned. Hearing him admit that he had felt the same way was almost too much to bear.

"You walked away, Ethan," she said, her voice trembling. "You didn't even say goodbye."

"I know," he replied, his voice heavy with guilt. "I was young, and I was angry, and I thought it would be easier to just leave without facing you. But it wasn't. It never was."

Mia stared at him, her mind swirling with a thousand thoughts. She had dreamed of this moment for years, of the day when Ethan would finally return and apologize for everything that had happened between them. But now that it was here, she didn't know what to do with it.

"I don't know if I can just forgive and forget, Ethan," she said, her voice cracking. "So much has happened since then. We're different people now."

"I know we are," Ethan replied softly. "And I'm not asking you to forgive me right away. I just... I want a chance to make things right, Mia. To show you that I'm not the same person I was back then."

Mia felt tears prick at the corners of her eyes, but she blinked them away. She had spent so long building up walls around her heart, protecting herself from the pain of the past. Letting Ethan back in would mean tearing those walls down, exposing herself to the possibility of being hurt again.

But as she looked into his eyes, she saw something there that made her pause—hope. Hope that maybe, just maybe, they could find a way back to each other, despite everything that had happened.

"I don't know if we can ever go back to the way things were," she said, her voice trembling.

"I don't want to go back," Ethan replied, his gaze steady. "I want to start over. To build something new. Something better."

Mia's heart pounded in her chest as she considered his words. It would be a risk, letting him back into her life. But wasn't life all about taking risks? About opening yourself up to the possibility of something beautiful, even if it meant facing the pain that came with it?

"I'm not making any promises," she finally said, her voice barely above a whisper.

Ethan nodded, a small smile tugging at the corners of his mouth. "I wouldn't expect you to. But I'm here, Mia. And I'm not going anywhere this time."

They sat in silence after that, the weight of their conversation settling between them. But it wasn't the same heavy silence as before. This time, it was filled with the possibility of something new—something that could grow into something more, if they were both willing to take the chance.

As the night grew colder, Mia's resolve slowly began to thaw. Maybe, just maybe, there was a way forward for them after all. But only time would tell.

Later that evening, after dinner had been cleared away and Grandma June had retired to her room, Mia found herself sitting on the porch, wrapped in a woolen blanket. The night was cool, and the stars twinkled brightly above, undisturbed by the city lights she'd grown accustomed to. The silence of Willow Creek was a stark contrast to the constant hum of life in the city, and it left her with too much time to think.

Ethan's unexpected visit had stirred something in her—something she thought she had buried deep inside. She closed her eyes and let the memories wash over her, unbidden.

They had been inseparable once, two kids growing up in a town where everyone knew everyone. Ethan had been her first real friend, her first real everything. They'd spent countless summer nights lying on this very porch, whispering about their dreams, their fears, and everything in between. But life had a way of complicating even the purest of friendships.

It was the summer after they graduated high school when everything had changed. Mia had been accepted into an art school in the city, a dream she had nurtured for years. Ethan, on the other hand, had been set on joining the military, eager to see the world beyond Willow Creek. They had both known that their paths were about to diverge, but neither had been prepared for the heartbreak that followed.

The night before Ethan left for boot camp, they had argued—fiercely. Ethan had wanted her to wait for him, to keep their relationship alive despite the distance. But Mia, terrified of being left behind and unsure of what the future held, had refused. She had wanted to move forward, to chase her dreams without the weight of a long-distance relationship holding her back.

"I can't do this, Ethan," she had said, tears streaming down her face. "I can't wait around for something that might never happen."

"And I can't stay here, Mia," he had replied, his voice cracking with emotion. "I have to go. I need to do this."

They had parted ways that night with harsh words and broken hearts, both too stubborn to give in. Ethan had left the next morning without saying goodbye, and Mia had thrown herself into her studies, determined to forget the boy who had once meant everything to her.

But she never truly had. And now, all those old wounds were reopening, fresh and raw as if no time had passed at all.

The creak of the porch door pulled Mia from her thoughts. She glanced over her shoulder to see Ethan stepping outside, his hands shoved into the pockets of his jacket. He hesitated for a moment, as if unsure whether to join her, before finally making his way over.

"Mind if I sit?" he asked, his voice low.

"Sure," she replied, pulling the blanket tighter around her as he took a seat beside her on the porch swing. The wooden slats groaned under the added weight, but the swing held, just like it always had.

They sat in silence for a while, the only sound the gentle creaking of the swing and the distant chirp of crickets. Mia could feel the tension between them, thick and suffocating, but she didn't know how to break it.

"I'm sorry for just showing up like that," Ethan said eventually, his gaze fixed on the dark horizon. "I didn't mean to catch you off guard."

"It's okay," Mia replied, though her heart was still racing from the surprise. "I just... wasn't expecting to see you, that's all."

"I wasn't sure if I should come," he admitted, his voice tinged with uncertainty. "But when I heard you were back in town, I couldn't stay away."

Mia swallowed hard, the emotions she'd been trying to keep at bay bubbling to the surface. "Why now, Ethan? After all these years, why come back now?"

Ethan sighed, running a hand through his hair. "I don't know, Mia. Maybe it's because I realized that I've been running for too long. From this place, from you... from everything. I needed to come back, to face what I left behind."

Mia's chest tightened at his words. Part of her wanted to believe him, to think that he was here to make amends, but the other part was still too wounded, too afraid of being hurt again.

"And what is it you think you left behind?" she asked, her voice barely above a whisper.

Ethan turned to look at her then, his blue eyes dark with emotion. "You, Mia. I left you behind. And I've regretted it every day since."

His words hit her like a punch to the gut, knocking the wind out of her. For so long, she had convinced herself that she was the one who had been left behind, that she was the one who had been abandoned. Hearing him admit that he had felt the same way was almost too much to bear.

"You walked away, Ethan," she said, her voice trembling. "You didn't even say goodbye."

"I know," he replied, his voice heavy with guilt. "I was young, and I was angry, and I thought it would be easier to just leave without facing you. But it wasn't. It never was."

Mia stared at him, her mind swirling with a thousand thoughts. She had dreamed of this moment for years, of the day when Ethan would finally return and apologize for everything that had happened between them. But now that it was here, she didn't know what to do with it.

"I don't know if I can just forgive and forget, Ethan," she said, her voice cracking. "So much has happened since then. We're different people now."

"I know we are," Ethan replied softly. "And I'm not asking you to forgive me right away. I just... I want a chance to make things right, Mia. To show you that I'm not the same person I was back then."

Mia felt tears prick at the corners of her eyes, but she blinked them away. She had spent so long building up walls around her heart, protecting herself from the pain of the past. Letting Ethan back in would mean tearing those walls down, exposing herself to the possibility of being hurt again.

But as she looked into his eyes, she saw something there that made her pause—hope. Hope that maybe, just maybe, they could find a way back to each other, despite everything that had happened.

"I don't know if we can ever go back to the way things were," she said, her voice trembling.

"I don't want to go back," Ethan replied, his gaze steady. "I want to start over. To build something new. Something better."

Mia's heart pounded in her chest as she considered his words. It would be a risk, letting him back into her life. But wasn't life all about taking risks? About opening yourself up to the possibility of something beautiful, even if it meant facing the pain that came with it?

"I'm not making any promises," she finally said, her voice barely above a whisper.

Ethan nodded, a small smile tugging at the corners of his mouth. "I wouldn't expect you to. But I'm here, Mia. And I'm not going anywhere this time."

They sat in silence after that, the weight of their conversation settling between them. But it wasn't the same heavy silence as before. This time, it was filled with the possibility of something new—something that could grow into something more, if they were both willing to take the chance.

As the night grew colder, Mia's resolve slowly began to thaw. Maybe, just maybe, there was a way forward for them after all. But only time would tell.

Mia's breath caught as Ethan's words hung in the cool night air. The silence between them felt different now—charged with a mixture of hope, fear, and the unspoken question of whether they were truly ready to face the past.

Mia finally broke the silence, her voice barely above a whisper. "I don't even know where to start, Ethan. So much has happened, so much has changed."

Ethan leaned forward, resting his elbows on his knees as he looked out into the darkness. "I know, Mia. I'm not asking for everything to be fixed overnight. I just want to try. Maybe we start with small steps. We could talk... really talk, like we used to. No expectations, no pressure."

She nodded slowly, trying to absorb the weight of what he was saying. A part of her wanted to dive back into the safety of the walls she'd built around her heart. But another part, the part that remembered the warmth of Ethan's friendship and the depth of their bond, was tired of being alone.

"Maybe," she murmured, her fingers tightening around the edges of the blanket. "But I need time, Ethan. Time to figure out if I can let go of the past."

Ethan reached out, gently placing his hand over hers. The simple touch sent a shiver down her spine, stirring memories she'd long tried to forget. "Take all the time you need, Mia. I'm not going anywhere."

His sincerity struck a chord deep within her. She had been so focused on protecting herself from the potential of being hurt again that she had nearly forgotten what it felt like to be cared for, to be seen.

She hesitated, searching his face for any sign that this was just another fleeting moment. But all she saw was earnestness and the faintest glimmer of hope. "Okay," she said softly, almost to herself. "We'll start with talking."

Ethan's smile was small but genuine. "That's all I can ask for."

They fell into another silence, but this time it felt less daunting, more comfortable. The past still lingered between them, but it no longer felt like an insurmountable barrier.

Eventually, Ethan broke the silence. "Do you remember that time we snuck out to the lake in the middle of the night? We thought we'd catch fireflies, but all we ended up catching was a cold."

Mia couldn't help but laugh, the sound easing some of the tension in her chest. "I remember. We were so convinced that we'd get away with it, but Grandma June caught us sneaking back in and made us drink that awful ginger tea for days."

Ethan chuckled. "I can still taste it. But it was worth it, just to see the stars that night. I've never seen anything like it since."

The memory warmed her, reminding her of the simple joys they had shared before life became so complicated. "Yeah, it was worth it," she admitted.

They talked for a while longer, trading stories and memories, some sweet and others bittersweet. It was easy, natural, like slipping into a well-worn pair of shoes. But even as they laughed and reminisced, Mia knew they were only scratching the surface. The real conversation, the one that would determine whether they could truly move forward, still lay ahead.

Eventually, the chill in the air grew too sharp to ignore, and Mia shivered, pulling the blanket tighter around her shoulders. "I should probably get inside before I freeze," she said, standing up and stretching her stiff muscles.

Ethan stood as well, rubbing his hands together to ward off the cold. "Yeah, I should get going too. But... thanks, Mia. For letting me in tonight."

She offered him a small smile, the first genuine one she'd felt in a long time. "Thanks for showing up, Ethan."

He nodded, his expression softening as he took a step back. "Goodnight, Mia. I'll see you around."

"Goodnight," she replied, watching as he walked down the steps and disappeared into the night.

Mia stayed on the porch for a few more minutes, staring out into the darkness, her thoughts a jumble of emotions. Tonight had been unexpected, but it had also been necessary. She wasn't sure what the future held, but for the first time in a long while, she felt like she could face it without fear.

As she finally turned to go inside, a single thought crossed her mind: Maybe old wounds didn't have to stay open forever. Maybe, just maybe, they could heal.

Mia closed the door behind her, the warmth of the house enveloping her as she stepped inside. The quiet of the night outside gave way to the familiar creaks of the old farmhouse. As she made her way through the dimly lit hallway, she felt the weight of the evening's conversation settle over her like a heavy blanket. She wasn't quite sure how she felt—relieved, perhaps, that the initial confrontation with Ethan was over, but also anxious about what might come next.

She paused at the bottom of the stairs, her eyes drifting to the framed photos lining the walls. Pictures of her and Ethan as children, of Grandma June, and of her parents before things had become complicated. Each image told a story, a fragment of the life she had once known and, in many ways, had been trying to leave behind. Yet here she was, back where it all began, grappling with the very things she had thought she could outrun.

With a sigh, Mia ascended the stairs, her feet heavy on the worn wood. When she reached the landing, she paused again, her hand resting on the banister. Her father's old study was just down the hall, the door slightly ajar as if it were waiting for her. She hadn't stepped foot in that room since she had come back, avoiding it like a wound that hadn't fully healed.

Unable to resist the pull any longer, she walked towards the study. The door creaked as she pushed it open, the smell of old books and faded memories greeting her. The room was just as she remembered—shelves lined with dusty volumes, a cluttered desk strewn with papers, and her father's old armchair by the window.

Mia hesitated in the doorway, her heart pounding. This room had always been her father's sanctuary, a place where he could retreat from the world. As a child, she had often sat in the chair opposite his desk, watching him work, hoping for a moment of his attention. But those moments had been rare, overshadowed by his stern demeanor and the distance that had grown between them as she got older.

Slowly, she stepped inside, her fingers brushing over the books on the shelf. Many were classics, their spines cracked with age. She remembered her father reading from them to her when she was young, his deep voice bringing the stories to life. But those days had faded, replaced by years of silence and unspoken words.

Her eyes landed on a stack of letters tied with a faded ribbon, tucked away in the corner of the desk. Curious, she reached out and untied the bundle, the paper crackling as she unfolded the first one. The handwriting was familiar—her father's neat script, every word carefully chosen.

Mia sank into the armchair, her eyes scanning the words. The letter was addressed to her mother, dated just a few months before her mother had left. As she read, the walls she had built around her memories began to crumble, revealing the truth she had long tried to ignore.

The letter spoke of regret, of missed opportunities, and of a love that had been lost in the chaos of life. It was a confession of sorts, an acknowledgment of the pain her father had caused and the distance that had grown between them as a result. But it was also a plea—a desperate hope that somehow, they could find a way back to each other.

Tears blurred her vision as she reached the end of the letter. She hadn't known, hadn't realized how much her father had struggled, how much he had tried to keep their family together even as it was falling apart. She had always blamed him for the way things had turned out, for her mother's departure and the loneliness that had followed. But now, reading his words, she saw a different side of the story—a side she had never been willing to consider.

Mia carefully refolded the letter and placed it back on the desk, her hands trembling. She felt a wave of guilt wash over her, mingled with sorrow and a longing for the relationship she had never had with her father. But it was too late now. He was gone, and the chance to make amends had vanished with him.

Wiping her eyes, she stood and took one last look around the study. There was so much history here, so many memories tied to this place. But she couldn't stay in the past any longer. She had to move forward, to find a way to heal—even if that meant facing the pain she had buried for so long.

With a heavy heart, Mia left the study and made her way to her bedroom. She climbed into bed, pulling the covers up to her chin as she stared at the ceiling. The night had brought back so much, more than she had been prepared to deal with. But as she closed her eyes, she made a silent promise to herself: she would try. She would face the past, no matter how painful, and find a way to move on.

Outside, the stars continued to twinkle in the night sky, unaware of the turmoil brewing in the small town below. Willow Creek had always been a place of memories, of beginnings and endings. And now, as Mia drifted off to sleep, she couldn't help but wonder what the future held—if it was possible to find peace after so many years of running, and if the wounds of the past could ever truly heal.

The next morning, sunlight filtered through the lace curtains, casting soft patterns on the walls of Mia's bedroom. She woke slowly, her mind heavy with the remnants of yesterday's emotions. The conversation with Ethan, the old wounds it had reopened, and the discovery of her father's letter all swirled together in her thoughts. She lay there for a moment, staring at the ceiling, trying to make sense of it all.

After a few minutes, she pushed the covers aside and got out of bed. The floor was cool beneath her feet as she made her way to the window. She pushed the curtains aside, taking in the view of the backyard. The garden was overgrown, the flowers and plants a tangle of color and greenery, but it was beautiful in its own wild way. It reminded her of how things had been when she was a child, before life had become so complicated.

Mia turned away from the window and began to get ready for the day. She dressed quickly, pulling on a pair of jeans and a sweater, before heading downstairs. The house was quiet, the only sound the ticking of the old grandfather clock in the hallway. She paused at the bottom of the stairs, glancing towards the kitchen where she could hear the faint clinking of dishes.

When she entered the kitchen, she found Grandma June already at the table, a cup of tea in hand and the morning paper spread out before her. Her grandmother looked up as she walked in, a warm smile lighting up her face.

"Good morning, Mia," she said, her voice soft and comforting. "Did you sleep well?"

Mia nodded, though the truth was she hadn't slept much at all. Her mind had been too restless, turning over the events of the previous night again and again.

"Good enough," she replied, forcing a smile as she poured herself a cup of coffee. "How about you?"

"Oh, I always sleep well in this old house," Grandma June said with a chuckle. "There's something about it that's just so comforting."

Mia sat down across from her, cradling the warm mug in her hands. She took a sip of the coffee, savoring the bitter taste, and let out a small sigh. For a moment, they sat in companionable silence, the weight of the previous night hanging in the air between them.

"You had a visitor last night," Grandma June said after a while, her eyes twinkling with curiosity. "Ethan, wasn't it?"

Mia nodded, her stomach tightening at the mention of his name. "Yes, it was Ethan."

Her grandmother studied her for a moment, her expression thoughtful. "He's grown into a fine young man. Always was a good boy, even when he was little. I remember the two of you running around here like wild things."

A small smile tugged at the corners of Mia's mouth at the memory. "Yeah, we had some good times."

"But I imagine last night wasn't just about reminiscing," Grandma June said gently, her gaze steady. "There's a lot of history between you two."

Mia sighed, her shoulders slumping as she stared down into her coffee. "It's complicated, Grandma. We didn't part on good terms all those years ago. And now that he's back... I don't know what to do with it all."

Her grandmother reached across the table, placing a hand over Mia's. "You don't have to figure it all out right away, Mia. Sometimes, things take time to work themselves out. Just take it one step at a time."

Mia nodded, appreciating the comfort her grandmother's words brought. But deep down, she knew it wasn't going to be that simple. There was so much pain between her and Ethan, so many things left unsaid. And then there was her father—his presence still lingered in the house, in her heart, despite his absence.

"I found some letters last night," Mia said quietly, her voice barely above a whisper. "In Dad's study. They were written to Mom, just before she left."

Grandma June's expression softened, a flicker of sadness passing through her eyes. "I wondered if you'd find those. Your father... he had a lot of regrets, Mia. More than he ever let on."

Mia's chest tightened at her grandmother's words. "I didn't know, Grandma. I didn't know he felt that way. I always thought… I thought he didn't care."

"Oh, he cared," Grandma June said, her voice thick with emotion. "He cared deeply, more than you'll ever know. But he had a hard time showing it. He wasn't perfect, Mia, but he loved you and your mother in his own way."

Tears pricked at the corners of Mia's eyes, and she blinked them away, not wanting to cry in front of her grandmother. "I wish things had been different. I wish I had known."

Her grandmother squeezed her hand, offering silent support. "We all have regrets, sweetheart. But you can't change the past. All you can do is learn from it and try to do better moving forward."

Mia nodded, knowing her grandmother was right. She couldn't change what had happened, but she could choose how to move forward. It wouldn't be easy, facing the pain of the past and trying to find a way to heal. But maybe, with time, she could start to mend the broken pieces of her heart.

As they sat together in the quiet kitchen, the sun continued to rise, filling the room with soft, golden light. It was a new day, and with it came the possibility of new beginnings—if Mia was brave enough to embrace them.

Chapter 3: New Beginnings

The days that followed Ethan's visit passed in a blur of activity. Mia found herself falling into the rhythm of small-town life, a rhythm she had once known so well but had long since forgotten. Each morning, she would wake early to help her mother tend to Grandma June, preparing meals and keeping the house in order. In the afternoons, she would take long walks through the fields surrounding the farmhouse, letting the quiet serenity of nature soothe the worries that buzzed incessantly in her mind.

But no matter how busy she kept herself, thoughts of Ethan were never far away. He seemed to be everywhere she looked—in the old photo albums that her mother kept on the living room shelf, in the familiar haunts around town, and most of all, in her memories. Memories that were now tinged with a mix of nostalgia and uncertainty.

Ethan had kept his word; he didn't push her for more than she was ready to give. He would stop by the farmhouse occasionally, usually under the pretense of checking on Grandma June or dropping off something he thought they might need. Their interactions were polite, sometimes even a bit awkward, as if they were both trying to navigate the unfamiliar territory of being in each other's lives again.

But despite the initial discomfort, Mia couldn't deny that something between them had shifted. The wounds of the past were still there, but they no longer felt as raw as they once had. And though she was hesitant to admit it, there was a part of her that wanted to see where this new path with Ethan might lead.

One crisp Saturday morning, Mia found herself standing on the front porch, a basket of freshly picked apples in hand, when she spotted Ethan's truck coming up the driveway. Her heart gave a little flutter, as it always did when she saw him, but she pushed the feeling aside. They were just friends, after all—at least for now.

Ethan stepped out of the truck, a smile tugging at his lips as he approached. "Morning, Mia. Looks like you've been busy."

She nodded, gesturing to the basket. "Mom wants to make apple pies for the church bake sale tomorrow, so I thought I'd help out. You know how much she loves showing off her baking skills."

Ethan chuckled. "She's the best baker in Willow Creek, hands down. Those pies won't last five minutes once they hit the table."

Mia smiled, feeling a warmth spread through her chest at the familiar banter. "Do you want to come in? I'm sure Mom would love to see you."

"Actually," Ethan said, his tone suddenly more serious, "I was wondering if you'd like to take a drive with me. There's something I want to show you."

Mia hesitated for a moment, caught off guard by the invitation. She had spent so much time trying to keep her distance, unsure if she was ready to let Ethan back into her life in a meaningful way. But the look in his eyes was genuine, hopeful, and she found herself unable to say no.

"Sure," she finally agreed, setting the basket down on the porch. "Let me just tell Mom I'm heading out."

A few minutes later, they were driving down the narrow country roads, the golden leaves of autumn swirling in the breeze around them. The radio played softly in the background, but neither of them spoke, content to let the comfortable silence fill the space between them.

Mia watched the landscape roll by, her mind wandering to the countless times she and Ethan had taken drives like this when they were younger. Back then, the future had seemed so bright, so full of promise. They had spent hours talking about their dreams, making plans for the lives they wanted to build. It felt strange to think about those conversations now, after everything that had happened.

"Where are we going?" Mia asked after a while, curiosity getting the better of her.

Ethan glanced over at her, a mysterious smile playing on his lips. "You'll see."

They drove for another ten minutes before Ethan turned off the main road and onto a dirt path that led into the woods. Mia frowned in confusion but didn't say anything, trusting that he knew where he was going. The truck bounced over the uneven ground, the trees closing in around them, until finally, they emerged into a small clearing.

Mia gasped as she took in the sight before her. The clearing was bordered by tall oak trees, their leaves a riot of reds and oranges, and in the center stood an old, weathered barn, its wooden beams worn but sturdy. The sunlight filtered through the trees, casting dappled shadows on the ground and giving the entire scene an almost magical quality.

"What is this place?" she asked, her voice filled with awe.

Ethan cut the engine and turned to face her, his expression serious. "This used to belong to my grandparents. They lived here when I was a kid. I used to spend every summer playing in that barn, dreaming up all kinds of adventures."

Mia looked at the barn with new eyes, imagining a younger Ethan running through the fields, his laughter echoing in the air. "It's beautiful," she said softly.

Ethan nodded, his gaze distant as he looked at the barn. "After they passed, the place fell into disrepair. No one's really been here in years. But when I came back to Willow Creek, I found myself drawn to it again. It's like... I don't know, a part of me still belongs here."

Mia felt a pang of understanding. She had left Willow Creek to chase her dreams, but there had always been a part of her that missed the simplicity, the sense of belonging that came with being in a place where everyone knew your name.

Ethan turned back to her, his eyes searching hers. "I've been thinking about fixing it up. Maybe turning it into something... new. A place where people can come together, create something meaningful. But I can't do it alone."

Mia's heart skipped a beat at the implication in his words. He wasn't just talking about the barn—he was talking about them, about starting over, building something new together.

"Ethan..." she began, but he cut her off, holding up a hand.

"You don't have to decide anything right now," he said gently. "I just wanted to show you this place, to let you know that I'm serious about making things right. About finding a way back to each other, if that's what you want."

Mia swallowed hard, emotions swirling inside her. She had spent so long guarding her heart, afraid of getting hurt again, but standing here with Ethan, in this place filled with so many memories, she felt a flicker of hope. Maybe they could start over. Maybe this time, things would be different.

She took a deep breath and looked into Ethan's eyes, seeing the sincerity, the vulnerability there. "I don't know what the future holds," she said honestly. "But I'm willing to try."

Ethan's face lit up with a smile, the kind that reached his eyes and made her heart swell with warmth. "That's all I'm asking for, Mia."

They stood there for a moment, the crisp autumn air swirling around them, the promise of new beginnings hanging in the air. And for the first time in a long time, Mia felt like she was exactly where she was meant to be.

As they walked toward the barn, side by side, Mia couldn't help but think that maybe, just maybe, the best parts of their story were still ahead of them.

As they approached the barn, Mia's mind was buzzing with a mix of excitement and apprehension. The idea of starting something new with Ethan was both thrilling and terrifying. She had spent so many years running from her past, from the hurt and the regrets that came with it, and now here she was, standing on the precipice of a new chapter with the one person who had always been a part of her story.

The barn's doors creaked as Ethan pushed them open, revealing the dim interior. Sunlight streamed through the gaps in the weathered wood, casting a warm, golden glow over the dust-covered floor. The air was thick with the scent of aged timber and memories, and Mia couldn't help but feel a sense of nostalgia as she stepped inside.

"This place has so much potential," Ethan said, his voice echoing softly in the spacious barn. "I can see it as a community space—maybe a workshop, or a gallery where people can showcase their work. A place where folks can come together, like they used to."

Mia nodded, her imagination beginning to run wild with possibilities. "It could be amazing," she agreed, her voice filled with a newfound sense of purpose. "We could bring in local artists, craftsmen... it could be a real hub for the community."

Ethan smiled, clearly pleased that she was on board with the idea. "Exactly. I've already talked to a few people in town, and they're interested in getting involved. But it's going to take a lot of work."

Mia glanced around the barn, taking in the worn beams and the layers of dust that had settled over the years. It was a daunting task, but one that filled her with a sense of excitement. She could feel the stirrings of a passion she hadn't felt in years, the desire to create something meaningful, something that could make a difference.

"I'm in," she said, her voice steady with determination. "Whatever you need, I'm here to help."

Ethan's smile grew wider, his eyes sparkling with a mix of relief and gratitude. "I knew I could count on you, Mia."

For a moment, they stood there in the middle of the barn, the weight of their shared history hanging between them. There was still so much they needed to talk about, so much they needed to work through, but for now, they were united by a common goal—a new beginning, not just for the barn, but for themselves as well.

"Let's get started, then," Ethan said, rolling up his sleeves. "We've got a lot of work to do."

Mia nodded, a sense of purpose filling her heart. Together, they began to clear the space, sweeping away the dust and debris, and as they worked side by side, a new rhythm began to take shape. It wasn't the same rhythm they had once known, but it was one that felt right, one that felt like it could lead them to something better.

As the sun began to set, casting long shadows across the barn, Mia looked over at Ethan, his face streaked with sweat and dust, and felt a warmth spread through her chest. Maybe this was what she had been searching for all along—a place where she could belong, where she could build something lasting, with someone who truly understood her.

And as they stood there, watching the first stars appear in the twilight sky, Mia knew that this was just the beginning of their journey. There would be challenges ahead, no doubt, but for the first time in a long time, she felt ready to face them—together.

Over the next few weeks, the barn became a sanctuary for Mia and Ethan, a place where they could both escape from the pressures of their lives and focus on something tangible. They worked tirelessly, clearing out debris, repairing the structure, and slowly transforming the old, forgotten space into something new.

The project brought them closer together, their shared efforts weaving a new kind of connection between them. Each day, as they hammered nails, painted walls, and cleaned the remnants of the past, they found themselves talking about things they hadn't discussed in years.

One afternoon, while they were sanding down a weathered old door they had found buried under a pile of broken boards, Ethan paused, looking over at Mia with a thoughtful expression.

"You know, I was thinking... we should name this place," he said, his voice carrying a mix of seriousness and excitement. "Something that captures what we're trying to do here."

Mia smiled, leaning back to consider his suggestion. "That's a great idea. It should be something that reflects both the history and the future we want to build."

They spent the rest of the day tossing around ideas, laughing as they came up with increasingly ridiculous suggestions, but nothing seemed quite right. It wasn't until later that evening, as they sat on the front steps of the barn, watching the sun set over the fields, that inspiration struck.

"What about 'The Haven'?" Mia suggested softly, the name coming to her as she watched the last rays of sunlight disappear behind the horizon. "A place where people can come together, find solace, and create something meaningful."

Ethan's eyes lit up as he considered the name, a slow smile spreading across his face. "The Haven... I like it. It feels right."

With the name decided, they threw themselves even more fully into the project, their vision for The Haven becoming clearer with each passing day. Word began to spread around Willow Creek about what they were doing, and soon, they found themselves with more help than they had expected. Neighbors, old friends, and even a few curious strangers stopped by to lend a hand, each person contributing something unique to the evolving space.

As the barn took shape, so did the relationship between Mia and Ethan. The awkwardness that had once lingered between them slowly dissolved, replaced by a sense of ease and familiarity that felt both comforting and new. They still had their moments of uncertainty, times when the past threatened to intrude, but they faced those moments together, finding strength in the bond they were rebuilding.

One chilly evening, after a long day of work, they sat together on an old, refurbished bench outside the barn, wrapped in blankets to ward off the cold. The stars were out, shining brightly in the clear night sky, and for a while, they simply sat in companionable silence, enjoying the peace of the moment.

"You know," Ethan said eventually, his voice low and contemplative, "I never thought I'd be back here, doing something like this. But I'm glad I am. I'm glad we're doing this together."

Mia looked over at him, her heart swelling with emotion. "Me too," she replied softly, feeling the weight of her words. "It feels like...

like we're finding our way back to something we lost a long time ago."

Ethan reached out, taking her hand in his. "We are. And this time, I don't want to let it slip away."

They sat there for a long time, holding hands under the starry sky, both of them knowing that The Haven was more than just a barn—it was a symbol of their journey, of the new beginnings they were carving out together. And as they stared out at the horizon, they both knew that the future was full of possibilities, and that they were ready to face whatever came next, side by side.

As the festivities of The Haven's grand opening continued, Mia found herself swept up in the celebration. The barn was alive with the sounds of laughter and music, and the warm glow of lanterns and fairy lights created a magical atmosphere. The sense of community was palpable, and Mia felt a deep sense of satisfaction seeing how their efforts had brought people together.

She wandered through the barn, taking in the various displays and activities. Local artists had set up booths showcasing their crafts, children were participating in art workshops, and adults were engaged in lively conversations about the future of The Haven. The space was bustling with energy and creativity, and Mia couldn't help but feel a sense of pride in what they had accomplished.

As she was admiring a display of handmade pottery, she noticed Ethan standing near the entrance, speaking with a group of local business owners. His face was lit up with enthusiasm, and he looked every bit the proud visionary who had seen this project through from start to finish. Mia's heart swelled with admiration for him, and she felt a renewed sense of connection between them.

After a while, Ethan caught her eye and made his way over to her. "Hey," he said, a broad smile on his face. "How's everything going?"

"It's amazing," Mia replied, her eyes shining with excitement. "I can't believe how well it's all come together."

Ethan took her hand and led her outside, where they found a quieter spot under the stars. The night air was crisp, and the sounds of the celebration seemed to fade into the background. They stood together in the silence, looking out at the twinkling lights that decorated the barn.

"I wanted to talk to you about something," Ethan said, his tone more serious now.

Mia turned to him, curiosity piqued. "What's up?"

"I've been thinking a lot about what's next for us," Ethan began. "This project has been incredible, but it's also made me realize how much I want to keep building on this—on what we have."

Mia's heart skipped a beat. "Building on what we have?"

Ethan nodded, his gaze steady and sincere. "I'm talking about more than just The Haven. I mean us—our future together. I know we've had our ups and downs, and there's still a lot we need to figure out. But I want to explore where this can go. I want to see if we can create something lasting, not just with The Haven, but in our lives as well."

Mia felt a mix of emotions wash over her. She had been so focused on the immediate task of getting The Haven up and running that she hadn't fully allowed herself to think about the future. But now, standing here with Ethan, she could see the potential for something more.

"I'd like that," she said softly, her voice filled with emotion. "I want to explore that too. But we need to take it one step at a time. We need to be honest with each other and ourselves about what we want."

Ethan's eyes softened as he looked at her. "Absolutely. We'll take it slow and figure it out together. I'm just glad that we're on this journey, whatever it may bring."

They stood there, holding each other close, the promise of new beginnings enveloping them. The stars above seemed to sparkle with possibility, and Mia felt a sense of hope and excitement for the future.

As the night wore on, the celebration began to wind down. Guests started to say their goodbyes, and the barn, once filled with energy and laughter, gradually became quieter. Mia and Ethan remained behind, taking in the last of the festivities and reflecting on the night's success.

With the crowd gone and the barn bathed in the soft glow of moonlight, they began to tidy up, their movements reflecting a sense of accomplishment and contentment. Ethan picked up a stray piece of confetti and glanced over at Mia, who was carefully folding up a tablecloth.

"Tonight was perfect," he said, his voice full of warmth. "Thank you for being a part of it all, for believing in this."

Mia looked up at him, her heart full. "Thank you for giving me the chance to be a part of it. For believing in us."

They shared a tender smile, and for a moment, the world seemed to stand still. The barn, now a symbol of their shared dreams and efforts, stood as a testament to their journey and their commitment to one another.

As they walked out of The Haven, hand in hand, Mia felt a sense of excitement for the future. There were still many unknowns ahead, but with Ethan by her side and The Haven as a new foundation, she felt ready to face whatever came next. Together, they would navigate the challenges and embrace the possibilities, building a life that was truly their own.

The barn, once an old relic of the past, now stood as a beacon of hope and renewal, reflecting the new chapter that Mia and Ethan were beginning to write together. And as they looked up at the starry sky, they knew that their story was only just beginning.

Chapter 4: A Leap of Faith

The days that followed felt like a whirlwind of change, and yet, a strange calm settled over Mia as she found herself spending more and more time with Ethan. The old barn became their shared project, a symbol of everything they were trying to rebuild. They spent hours cleaning out the debris, repairing the walls, and planning what the space could become. It was hard work, but it was also therapeutic—a way to channel their emotions into something tangible.

Mia found herself opening up to Ethan in ways she hadn't expected. They talked about their lives, their dreams, and even the mistakes they had made along the way. It wasn't always easy, especially when old wounds resurfaced, but each conversation felt like another brick being laid in the foundation of something new.

One crisp afternoon, as the sun dipped low in the sky, casting long shadows over the clearing, Ethan and Mia sat on a makeshift bench outside the barn, sipping cold lemonade that Mia's mom had packed for them. The air was filled with the scent of freshly cut wood, and the sound of birds chirping in the distance provided a soothing backdrop.

Ethan glanced over at Mia, his eyes thoughtful. "You know, I've been thinking a lot about what we're doing here."

Mia looked at him, sensing the seriousness in his tone. "What about it?"

"I'm not just talking about the barn," he said, running a hand through his hair. "I mean... us. What we're trying to rebuild. It's been good, right?"

Mia nodded, her heart fluttering. "Yeah, it has. It's been really good."

Ethan smiled, but it was a small, tentative smile. "I know we've been taking things slow, and I think that's been the right choice. But I can't help but wonder... where do we go from here?"

Mia felt a lump form in her throat. She had been wondering the same thing. They had been dancing around the possibility of rekindling their relationship, but neither had dared to take that final step. It was as if they were both afraid of what might happen if they leaped too soon.

"I don't know, Ethan," she said honestly, her voice barely above a whisper. "I'm scared. I'm scared of what might happen if we try and it doesn't work out. I don't want to lose you again."

Ethan reached out and took her hand, his touch warm and reassuring. "I'm scared too, Mia. But I think that's a good thing. It means we care about this. About each other."

Mia looked down at their joined hands, her heart racing. She wanted to believe him, to believe that they could make this work. But the fear of getting hurt again was so strong, it threatened to paralyze her.

"I want to try, Ethan," she said, her voice trembling. "But I don't know if I'm ready to jump in with both feet. Not yet."

Ethan squeezed her hand gently, his gaze soft and understanding. "Then let's take it one step at a time. We don't have to have all the answers right now. We just have to be willing to take the next step, whatever that might be."

Mia looked up at him, her heart swelling with gratitude for his patience, his understanding. She knew that not everyone would be so willing to take things slow, to allow her the time she needed to heal. But Ethan wasn't just anyone—he was the boy she had once loved, the man she was slowly coming to care for again.

"Okay," she said, a small smile tugging at her lips. "One step at a time."

Ethan smiled back, relief evident in his eyes. "That's all I need to hear."

They sat there in comfortable silence for a while, watching the sun dip lower in the sky, casting the clearing in a warm golden glow. The barn, still a work in progress, stood as a testament to the new beginning they were forging together. It wasn't perfect, but it was theirs, and that was enough.

As they packed up their tools and prepared to head back to the farmhouse, Ethan suddenly stopped and turned to Mia, his expression serious. "There's something I want to show you tomorrow. Something important."

Mia raised an eyebrow, intrigued. "What is it?"

Ethan hesitated for a moment before answering. "It's a surprise. But I think it'll help us figure out where we're headed."

Mia's curiosity was piqued, but she knew better than to press him. Ethan had always loved surprises, and she had learned long ago that it was best to let him reveal things in his own time.

"Okay," she said with a smile. "I'll be ready."

Ethan grinned, a boyish excitement lighting up his face. "Good. I think you'll like it."

As they drove back to the farmhouse, Mia couldn't help but feel a sense of anticipation building inside her. Whatever Ethan had planned, she had a feeling it would be a turning point—a moment that would define the direction of their relationship moving forward.

The next morning, Ethan arrived at the farmhouse just after breakfast, a mysterious smile on his lips as he helped Mia into his truck. The drive was familiar—down the same country roads they had traveled the day before—but instead of turning off toward the barn, Ethan took a different route, one that led them deeper into the heart of Willow Creek.

After about twenty minutes, they pulled up to a small, picturesque lake surrounded by towering pine trees. The water was crystal clear, reflecting the bright blue sky above. A narrow dock extended out into the lake, and a small rowboat was tied to it, bobbing gently in the water.

Mia's breath caught as she took in the scene. "Ethan... this place is beautiful."

Ethan smiled, clearly pleased by her reaction. "This is one of my favorite spots in Willow Creek. My dad used to bring me here to fish when I was a kid. I thought it would be the perfect place to talk."

Mia nodded, her heart pounding with a mix of excitement and nervousness. She wasn't sure what Ethan had planned, but she had a feeling it was something big.

They walked down to the dock and climbed into the rowboat, Ethan taking the oars while Mia settled in at the front. The boat glided smoothly across the water, the only sounds the soft splash of the oars and the distant call of birds.

After a few minutes, Ethan stopped rowing and let the boat drift, turning to face Mia with a serious expression. "Mia, I brought you here because I wanted to talk about us. About where we're going."

Mia's heart raced as she looked into his eyes, seeing the vulnerability there. She knew how much this conversation meant to him, and to her.

"I care about you, Mia," Ethan continued, his voice steady but filled with emotion. "I've always cared about you, even when we were apart. And being back here, working on the barn together, it's made me realize that I don't want to lose you again. I want us to have a future, but I know that future has to be built on trust and honesty."

Mia swallowed hard, her throat tight with emotion. "I care about you too, Ethan. But I'm scared. Scared of making the same mistakes we made before."

Ethan nodded, his gaze never leaving hers. "I'm scared too. But I think the difference this time is that we're older, wiser. We know what we want, and we know what we don't want. And I don't want to rush you into anything you're not ready for."

Mia felt tears prick at the corners of her eyes, but she blinked them away. "I don't want to lose you either, Ethan. But I need time. Time to figure out what I want, and what we could be."

Ethan reached out and took her hand, his touch warm and reassuring. "Then we'll take that time. We'll take it slow, one day at a time. And whatever happens, we'll face it together."

Mia smiled through her tears, her heart swelling with a mix of relief and hope. "Thank you, Ethan. For being patient with me."

Ethan smiled back, his eyes filled with warmth. "You're worth the wait, Mia."

They sat there in the boat, hand in hand, the gentle sway of the water lulling them into a sense of peace. The sun was beginning to dip lower in the sky, casting a golden glow over the lake, and Mia felt a sense of calm settle over her.

She didn't know what the future held, but for the first time in a long time, she felt like she was on the right path. With Ethan by her side, she was ready to take that leap of faith, one step at a time.

As the sun continued its descent, painting the sky with hues of pink and orange, Mia and Ethan sat in the rowboat, the serene lake providing a perfect backdrop for their heartfelt conversation. The gentle ripples on the water seemed to echo the quiet emotions that swirled between them.

Ethan looked out over the lake, taking in the peaceful surroundings. "You know," he said softly, "this place has always felt like a sanctuary to me. It's where I come to think things through, to find clarity. And now, sharing it with you, it feels even more special."

Mia squeezed his hand, feeling a deep sense of connection. "I'm glad you brought me here. It's beautiful, and it's given me a lot to think about."

They drifted in silence for a few moments, each lost in their own thoughts. The gentle sway of the boat and the sounds of nature created a tranquil atmosphere that seemed to ease their worries.

Finally, Ethan spoke up, his voice thoughtful. "There's something else I wanted to tell you. Something that might help us both see things more clearly."

Mia turned to him, her curiosity piqued. "What is it?"

Ethan took a deep breath, as if gathering his thoughts. "I've been working on a new project—something that's been on my mind for a while now. It's a way to combine my passion for community with the things I've learned from The Haven. I'm thinking of starting a non-profit organization that focuses on local development and support for small businesses and artisans."

Mia's eyes widened in surprise and admiration. "That sounds incredible, Ethan. I can see how passionate you are about it."

Ethan smiled, his eyes bright with enthusiasm. "I am passionate about it. And I want you to be a part of it. I think your skills, your vision, and your experience would be invaluable to the project. It's something that could really make a difference in Willow Creek and beyond."

Mia felt a rush of emotions—excitement, pride, and a bit of apprehension. "I'd love to help, Ethan. It sounds like a wonderful idea. But what does this mean for us, for our relationship?"

Ethan looked at her with a mixture of hope and uncertainty. "It means that we have a chance to build something meaningful together, both professionally and personally. It's a way for us to channel our energies into something positive and to continue growing as a couple. But it also means we need to communicate openly and honestly about our goals and our fears."

Mia nodded, taking in his words. "I agree. I want us to build something together, but we have to be prepared for the challenges that come with it. It won't always be easy."

Ethan squeezed her hand gently. "I know it won't be easy, but I believe we're strong enough to face those challenges. We've already come so far, and we've proven that we can overcome obstacles when we work together."

Mia smiled, feeling a renewed sense of determination. "You're right. We've already shown that we can navigate difficult situations. And I'm willing to give this a try, to explore what we can create together."

Ethan's face lit up with relief and joy. "That's all I needed to hear. Thank you for being open to this."

They sat there for a while longer, enjoying the peaceful evening and the promise of new beginnings. The sun continued its slow descent, casting a warm, golden glow over the lake and the surrounding trees.

As they rowed back to the dock, Mia felt a sense of excitement for the future. The possibilities seemed endless, and with Ethan by her side, she felt ready to embrace whatever came next. Their shared project and their relationship were both stepping into a new chapter, one that held the potential for growth and fulfillment.

Back on solid ground, they made their way to the truck, their spirits high. Ethan's surprise had not only solidified their commitment to each other but had also given them a tangible goal to work toward. It was a leap of faith, but one that they were both willing to take.

As they drove back to the farmhouse, hand in hand, Mia felt a profound sense of peace. The journey ahead would undoubtedly be challenging, but with Ethan's support and their shared vision, she was ready to face it with hope and determination. Together, they were embarking on a new adventure, one that promised to bring them closer and to create a meaningful impact on their lives and their community.

With each mile that passed, Mia's confidence grew, and she knew that whatever the future held, she and Ethan were ready to tackle it together—one step at a time.

The drive back to the farmhouse was filled with a comfortable silence, each of them lost in their own thoughts but connected by the shared excitement of their new project. The sun was just beginning to set, casting a soft twilight over Willow Creek, and the sky was awash with colors that mirrored the emotions swirling inside Mia.

As they arrived at the farmhouse, the warm glow of the lights spilling out from the windows created a welcoming ambiance. They stepped inside, greeted by the delicious aroma of a home-cooked meal. Mia's mom had prepared a special dinner to celebrate the progress they had made on the barn, and the table was set with a spread of comfort food.

Mia's mom, always the gracious host, greeted them with a warm smile. "You two look like you've had a productive day. How was the lake?"

"It was wonderful," Mia said, her eyes shining with the afterglow of their conversation. "Ethan showed me a place that's really special to him. It was the perfect setting for our talk."

Her mom raised an eyebrow playfully. "A talk, huh? Sounds serious."

Ethan chuckled. "It was. We were discussing our future and some exciting plans we have."

As they sat down to eat, the conversation naturally flowed from their barn project to Ethan's new idea and their vision for the future. Mia's mom was genuinely interested and supportive, asking thoughtful questions and offering her own insights.

"It sounds like you two are on the brink of something amazing," she said, her eyes twinkling with pride. "Just remember to keep communication open and make time for each other amidst all the planning and work."

Mia nodded, appreciating her mom's wise words. "We'll definitely keep that in mind. It's important to balance everything and make sure we're both on the same page."

After dinner, they all gathered in the cozy living room, where the soft crackle of the fireplace provided a comforting backdrop. Mia's mom excused herself to clean up, leaving Mia and Ethan to enjoy some quiet time together.

Ethan took a deep breath, looking around at the familiar surroundings. "It feels nice to be here, to be with you and your family. It's like coming home."

Mia smiled, leaning against him as they sat on the sofa. "It does feel like home. And having you here with me makes it even more special."

They spent the evening talking, sharing stories and dreams, and enjoying each other's company. The conversation eventually turned to their plans for the non-profit. Mia was eager to dive into the details and start brainstorming ideas, and Ethan was equally enthusiastic about involving her in every step of the process.

As the night grew late, Ethan looked at Mia with a thoughtful expression. "I've been thinking about how we can really make a difference with this project. It's not just about helping local businesses, but also about bringing the community together. We could organize workshops, events, and even mentorship programs."

Mia's eyes sparkled with excitement. "That sounds incredible. We could use the barn as a community space, host events, and create opportunities for people to connect and support each other."

Ethan nodded. "Exactly. And we can start small, see what works, and build from there. It's going to take time and effort, but I believe it's worth it."

Mia felt a surge of determination. "I believe that too. And with you by my side, I know we can make it happen."

Ethan leaned in and kissed her forehead gently. "I'm so glad we're in this together."

Mia smiled, feeling a deep sense of contentment. "Me too."

As they said goodnight and headed to their separate rooms, Mia felt a renewed sense of purpose and excitement. The journey ahead was still uncertain, but with Ethan's support and their shared vision, she felt ready to face whatever challenges lay ahead.

She lay in bed, reflecting on the day's events and the promises of the future. The barn, the non-profit, and their relationship were all interwoven into a tapestry of hope and possibility. Mia knew that they were building something meaningful, not just for themselves but for their entire community.

As she drifted off to sleep, a smile tugged at her lips. She felt a profound sense of peace and anticipation, knowing that she was embarking on a new chapter of her life—one that held the promise of growth, love, and shared dreams.

The next morning, the sun rose with a crisp clarity that seemed to signal the start of a new beginning. Mia awoke feeling refreshed, eager to dive into the plans for the barn and the non-profit project. She met Ethan in the kitchen, where her mom was already preparing breakfast.

"Morning!" Mia's mom greeted them with a cheerful smile. "I thought we could start the day with a hearty breakfast. We've got a lot ahead of us!"

"Sounds perfect," Ethan said, giving Mia a warm look that made her heart flutter.

Over breakfast, they discussed the plans for the day. Ethan was particularly excited about the upcoming task of transforming the barn into a community space, and Mia shared his enthusiasm. After the meal, they gathered their tools and supplies and headed to the barn.

The work was a mix of hard labor and creative brainstorming. They tackled the structural repairs with determination, and whenever they needed a break, they would sit and sketch out ideas for how to best use the space. It was during these moments that their visions for the non-profit began to take shape.

"What if we set up a small café area here?" Ethan suggested, pointing to one corner of the barn. "It could be a place for people to gather, grab a coffee, and network."

Mia nodded thoughtfully. "And we could have a section for local artists to display their work. It would be great to support the arts and provide a venue for the community."

As they worked, their conversations flowed effortlessly, filled with excitement about the possibilities. They shared stories of their childhoods, their dreams, and their hopes for the future. Each shared moment felt like another layer being added to their growing bond.

By late afternoon, they decided to take a break and enjoy the cool breeze outside. Ethan brought out a thermos of lemonade, and they settled on the grass, enjoying the tranquility of the countryside.

"This place really is coming together," Mia said, looking around at the barn. "I can't wait to see it all finished."

Ethan took a sip of lemonade and nodded. "Me too. It's going to be something special, I can feel it."

Mia glanced at him, her eyes soft with affection. "I'm so grateful for your support and for being here with me. It means a lot."

Ethan reached out and took her hand, giving it a gentle squeeze. "I wouldn't want to be anywhere else. This project, this place—it's all part of something bigger. And being with you, working on this together, it feels like we're building something really meaningful."

The conversation shifted to their plans for the non-profit. They discussed potential partnerships with local businesses and organizations, and how they could leverage their network to make a greater impact. It was clear that both were deeply committed to the success of the project and to each other.

As the sun began to set, casting a golden hue over the landscape, Ethan stood up and dusted off his hands. "I've got one more surprise for you," he said, his eyes twinkling with mischief.

Mia's curiosity was immediately piqued. "Another surprise?"

"Yep," Ethan said with a grin. "I thought we'd celebrate our progress with something a bit more fun."

He led her to a small clearing near the barn where a makeshift outdoor movie setup awaited them. A projector was set up against a backdrop of hay bales, and a cozy arrangement of blankets and pillows covered the grass.

Mia's eyes widened in delight. "This is amazing! How did you set this up so quickly?"

Ethan shrugged, looking pleased with himself. "I had a little help from a few friends. I figured after all the hard work, we deserved a night under the stars."

They settled into their makeshift seats, and Ethan started the projector. As the opening credits of their favorite movie began to roll, Mia felt a deep sense of contentment. The day had been a whirlwind of activity and emotions, but this simple, intimate moment was exactly what she needed.

Throughout the movie, they snuggled close together, sharing popcorn and stealing glances at each other. The light from the projector flickered softly on their faces, and the night sky above was dotted with stars, adding to the magic of the evening.

As the movie ended, Ethan turned to Mia with a serious expression. "I know things have been moving fast, and there's still a lot to figure out. But I want you to know that I'm committed to this. To us."

Mia smiled, her heart full. "I'm committed too. I may not have all the answers right now, but I'm excited about the journey we're on together."

Ethan leaned in and kissed her softly, the warmth of the moment filling her with a profound sense of connection. "One step at a time, right?"

"Exactly," Mia agreed, resting her head on his shoulder. "One step at a time."

As they lay there under the stars, the future felt full of promise and possibility. The barn, their project, and their relationship were all intertwined in a beautiful tapestry of hope and dedication. Mia knew that whatever challenges lay ahead, they would face them together, building something truly remarkable, one step at a time.

The following morning, the air was crisp and filled with the promise of a new day. The peaceful quiet of the farmhouse was punctuated only by the soft clinking of dishes as Mia's mom prepared breakfast. Mia and Ethan, refreshed from their movie night, joined her at the table, their conversations filled with the excitement of their recent progress.

After breakfast, they headed back to the barn, eager to continue their work. The barn was slowly transforming, and their vision was beginning to take shape. The sunlight streamed through the open doors, casting a warm glow over the space as they worked together, laughter and banter punctuating their efforts.

Ethan was focused on installing some new light fixtures while Mia was organizing materials and planning the layout for the community space. The energy between them was palpable, a blend of teamwork and shared purpose that made every task feel lighter.

As they took a break for lunch, Mia glanced over at Ethan, who was wiping sweat from his brow. "You know, we've made a lot of progress. It's really coming together."

Ethan looked up, his eyes sparkling with enthusiasm. "I couldn't have done it without you. Your ideas and energy are what's driving this project forward."

Mia felt a blush creep up her cheeks, warmed by his compliment. "Well, I have to admit, it's been more enjoyable than I expected. And having you here makes all the difference."

They shared a comfortable silence, enjoying the simplicity of their picnic on the grass. After lunch, Ethan glanced at his watch and then turned to Mia with a grin. "Ready for part two of your surprise?"

Mia's curiosity was immediately piqued. "Another surprise? You're really outdoing yourself."

Ethan chuckled. "I thought it might be nice to take a break from work and do something a little different. Follow me."

He led her to a nearby trail that meandered through the woods, the path shaded by tall trees and dappled with sunlight. The walk was peaceful, and the sounds of nature provided a soothing soundtrack. Ethan seemed to have a purpose in mind, guiding her through the trees until they reached a small clearing with a breathtaking view of the valley below.

Mia's eyes widened in amazement. "Wow, Ethan, this view is incredible!"

Ethan nodded, clearly pleased with her reaction. "I thought you'd like it. It's one of my favorite spots to come and clear my head. I thought it might be nice for us to spend a few quiet moments here."

They sat together on a large rock, taking in the view. The valley stretched out below them, lush and green, with the distant hills rolling gently. It was a stark contrast to the busy, hands-on work of the barn but equally beautiful in its own way.

"So," Ethan began, breaking the silence, "how are you feeling about everything? About the project, about us?"

Mia took a deep breath, feeling a sense of calm settle over her. "I'm feeling good. Better than I have in a long time. The project is coming along, and I'm excited about what it can become. And us... well, I'm hopeful. I feel like we're on the right track."

Ethan reached over and took her hand, his gaze earnest. "I'm glad to hear that. I know we've had our share of challenges, but I really believe in what we're building here—both with the barn and with our relationship."

Mia squeezed his hand, her heart swelling with affection. "I do too. It's been a journey, and it's not always easy, but I'm grateful for every step we're taking together."

Ethan smiled, his eyes reflecting the warmth of the moment. "Me too. And I want you to know that I'm here for the long haul. Whatever happens, I'm committed to making this work."

They sat there for a while longer, enjoying the serenity of the moment. The conversation drifted to lighter topics—favorite memories, future dreams, and silly anecdotes from their past. The laughter that followed was a testament to the deepening connection between them.

As the sun began to lower in the sky, casting long shadows across the valley, Ethan stood up and offered his hand to Mia. "Ready to head back?"

Mia took his hand, rising gracefully. "Absolutely. I'm looking forward to seeing how much more we can accomplish."

They made their way back to the barn, the warmth of the day giving way to the coolness of the evening. The barn was illuminated with a soft, golden light as they arrived, and the sight of their hard work so far filled Mia with a sense of pride.

They resumed their tasks with renewed energy, working until the stars began to appear in the night sky. As they finished up for the day, Ethan looked over at Mia with a thoughtful expression.

"You know," he said, "I've been thinking about what you said the other night—about taking things one step at a time."

Mia met his gaze, her heart fluttering with anticipation. "And?"

Ethan smiled, a mixture of excitement and nervousness in his eyes. "I think we've taken some pretty great steps already. And I want to keep moving forward, not just with the barn but with us. So, I've been thinking about how we can make our next steps even more meaningful."

Mia's curiosity was piqued. "What do you have in mind?"

Ethan hesitated for a moment, then took a deep breath. "I was thinking that maybe we should start planning some future milestones. Not just for the barn, but for us—things we want to achieve together, both personally and professionally."

Mia's eyes lit up with excitement. "I love that idea. It's like setting goals for our journey together."

"Exactly," Ethan said, looking relieved and hopeful. "And I want us to keep dreaming and growing, together."

As they finished their work and prepared to head inside, Mia felt a renewed sense of purpose and excitement. The future was filled with possibilities, and with Ethan by her side, she felt ready to embrace whatever came next. One step at a time, they were building something beautiful—both the barn and their relationship. And for the first time in a long time, Mia felt truly hopeful about the journey ahead.

Chapter 5: The First Step

The days after their conversation on the lake passed in a blur of activity, but the air between Mia and Ethan had changed. There was a new sense of understanding, an unspoken agreement that they were in this together, no matter how slowly they needed to move. Every moment they spent in each other's company felt more meaningful, and even the smallest gestures carried a weight that Mia hadn't realized she'd missed.

One Saturday, as autumn leaves began to blanket the ground in rich shades of red and gold, Mia found herself at the town square for the annual Harvest Festival. It was a Willow Creek tradition, one she had attended every year as a child, and though she hadn't been in years, the familiar sights and sounds brought a rush of nostalgia.

The square was alive with activity. Stalls lined the streets, selling everything from homemade jams to hand-knit scarves, and the air was filled with the scent of caramel apples and freshly baked pies. Children ran between the booths, their laughter ringing out above the chatter of townsfolk catching up with old friends. A small band played lively folk tunes, adding to the festive atmosphere.

Mia wandered through the crowd, stopping at various stalls to admire the wares. She bought a jar of honey from Mrs. Carter, who still ran the same stand she had as long as Mia could remember, and picked up a small, hand-painted ornament from a local artist. Everywhere she looked, she saw familiar faces—people she had grown up with, people who had watched her grow. It was comforting, in a way she hadn't expected.

"Mia! Over here!"

Mia turned at the sound of her name and saw Ethan waving to her from a booth near the edge of the square. He was standing with a group of people she recognized from high school—old friends who had stayed in Willow Creek, who had built their lives here. She hesitated for a moment, suddenly self-conscious, but then Ethan's warm smile drew her in, and she made her way over.

"Hey, you made it," Ethan said as she approached, his voice filled with genuine pleasure.

"I wouldn't miss it," Mia replied, returning his smile. "It's been years since I've been to the Harvest Festival. It's just as I remember it."

"Some things never change," Ethan said with a chuckle. He introduced her to the group, who greeted her with the kind of easy familiarity that comes from shared history. They talked for a while, reminiscing about old times, and Mia found herself relaxing, enjoying the sense of community that she had missed while living in the city.

As the afternoon wore on, Ethan suggested they take a walk around the square. The crowd had thinned slightly as people drifted toward the stage where the evening's main event, a barn dance, was set to take place. Mia and Ethan strolled through the streets, the setting sun casting a warm glow over the town.

"I'm glad you came today," Ethan said after a while. "It's nice, isn't it? Being part of something like this."

Mia nodded, her heart full. "It is. I didn't realize how much I missed it until now."

They walked in comfortable silence for a few more minutes before Ethan stopped and turned to face her. "You know, there's something I've been meaning to ask you."

Mia looked up at him, curiosity piqued. "What is it?"

Ethan hesitated, a small, nervous smile playing on his lips. "Would you like to go to the barn dance with me tonight? As, you know... more than just friends?"

Mia's heart skipped a beat at his words. She had expected their relationship to move slowly, but this felt like a big step. And yet, as she looked into Ethan's eyes, she felt a surge of excitement. She wanted to say yes, to take that leap, even if it was just a small one.

"I'd love to," she said, her voice steady but her heart racing.

Ethan's smile widened, relief evident in his eyes. "Great. I'll pick you up at seven?"

Mia nodded, feeling a flutter of nerves mixed with anticipation. "Seven sounds perfect."

The rest of the afternoon passed in a blur. Mia found herself both excited and anxious about the evening ahead. She knew it was just a dance, just a small step, but it felt like so much more. It felt like the beginning of something real, something that could be the foundation of the future they had both been cautiously building.

By the time Ethan arrived to pick her up, Mia had changed outfits three times, finally settling on a simple but elegant dress that made her feel both comfortable and confident. When she opened the door and saw Ethan standing there, looking handsome and a little nervous himself, her heart swelled with warmth.

"You look beautiful," Ethan said, his voice soft and sincere.

Mia blushed, feeling a rush of affection for the boy she had once known and the man he had become. "Thank you. You don't look too bad yourself."

They drove to the dance in Ethan's truck, the familiar hum of the engine and the quiet country roads adding to the sense of anticipation. When they arrived at the barn, it was already filled with people—couples dancing, children running around, and groups of friends laughing and talking. The band was playing a lively tune, and the air was filled with the sweet smell of hay and the distant sound of crickets chirping in the night.

Ethan took Mia's hand as they entered, leading her to the center of the barn where the dancing was in full swing. For a moment, Mia felt a rush of nerves, but then Ethan pulled her close, his hand resting gently on her waist, and all her worries melted away.

The music picked up, and they fell into an easy rhythm, moving together as if they had been dancing like this for years. Mia laughed as Ethan spun her around, the joy of the moment bubbling up inside her. It felt like everything had fallen into place, like all the doubts and fears that had held her back were nothing compared to the happiness she felt right now.

As the song slowed, Ethan pulled her even closer, their movements becoming more intimate, more connected. Mia looked up at him, her heart pounding in her chest, and for a moment, everything else faded away. It was just the two of them, surrounded by the warmth and love of the community, and for the first time, Mia allowed herself to believe that maybe, just maybe, they could have a future together.

The song ended, but Ethan didn't let go. Instead, he leaned down, his forehead resting gently against hers. "Mia," he whispered, his voice filled with emotion. "I know we're taking things slow, but I want you to know that I'm all in. Whatever happens, whatever you need, I'm here. I'm not going anywhere."

Mia felt tears prick at the corners of her eyes, but they were happy tears, tears of relief and gratitude. She had spent so long guarding her heart, so afraid of getting hurt again, but in this moment, she knew she was ready. Ready to take that leap, to trust in what they were building together.

"I'm all in too," she whispered back, her voice trembling with emotion. "I'm ready, Ethan. I'm ready to see where this takes us."

Ethan smiled, a look of pure happiness spreading across his face, and in that moment, Mia knew that she had made the right choice. They were taking the first step, and whatever challenges lay ahead, they would face them together.

As the night wore on, they danced and laughed, surrounded by the warmth and joy of the community they had both come to cherish. And as they swayed to the music, lost in each other's embrace, Mia couldn't help but think that this was just the beginning of something truly special—something that, with time and patience, could grow into the love they had both been searching for.

And for the first time in a long time, Mia felt like she was exactly where she was meant to be.

As the night deepened and the barn dance continued, Mia and Ethan found themselves in a bubble of shared joy and newfound commitment. The vibrant lights strung across the barn flickered softly, casting a warm glow over the room. The lively tunes of the band gave way to slower, more romantic melodies, perfect for moments like this.

Mia rested her head against Ethan's shoulder, feeling the steady beat of his heart. The rhythmic sway of their bodies and the soft hum of the music created a soothing backdrop, making her feel as though she was floating on a cloud. It was a rare moment of complete contentment, and she savored every second.

"You know," Ethan murmured, breaking the comfortable silence, "I used to think these dances were just about having a good time. But tonight, it feels like so much more."

Mia tilted her head up to look at him, her eyes reflecting the soft glow of the barn lights. "I know what you mean. It feels like we're creating something new here, something really special."

Ethan's gaze was intense, filled with sincerity. "I've been thinking a lot about the future lately. About what we could build together, not just with the barn but with our lives. And I'm excited. I know we're taking it slow, but I believe that's the right way. It feels like we're setting a strong foundation."

Mia nodded, her heart swelling with affection. "I've been thinking about that too. I'm starting to feel more confident about where we're headed. I know it won't be perfect, but I believe in what we're building."

Ethan's smile was both reassuring and hopeful. "Me too. I'm grateful for every step we're taking together, and I'm looking forward to the future."

As the night went on, Mia and Ethan continued to dance and enjoy the festivities. They shared laughter and stories with friends and family, their connection growing stronger with each shared moment. It was as if the entire town was celebrating their new beginning, and Mia couldn't help but feel overwhelmed by the sense of community and belonging.

When the last song of the evening was played, Ethan led Mia outside to the cool, crisp night air. The sky was a blanket of stars, and the moon cast a silvery sheen over the landscape. They walked hand in hand to a quiet spot near the edge of the field, away from the noise and bustle of the festival.

Ethan turned to Mia, his expression tender and filled with affection. "I've been wanting to show you something. It's a little secret spot of mine."

Mia's curiosity was piqued as they followed a narrow path leading to a small hill. At the top, they found a cozy nook surrounded by a few large rocks and soft grass. The view from this spot was breathtaking, offering a panoramic look at the twinkling lights of Willow Creek below.

"This is incredible," Mia said softly, her voice filled with awe. "I never knew there was a place like this."

Ethan smiled, clearly pleased with her reaction. "It's my favorite spot to come and think. It's peaceful, and the view always puts things into perspective."

They settled onto the grass, leaning back against the rocks and gazing up at the stars. The air was filled with the faint sounds of the festival in the distance, but here, it was just the two of them, enveloped in the tranquility of the night.

Mia turned to Ethan, her heart full. "Tonight has been perfect. Thank you for sharing this with me."

Ethan reached over and took her hand, his touch warm and reassuring. "I'm glad you enjoyed it. I wanted to share something special with you, something that represents how much you mean to me."

Mia's eyes met his, and she felt a surge of emotion. "Ethan, I feel the same way. I'm really grateful for you and for everything we're building together."

Ethan's gaze was tender as he leaned in, his forehead resting gently against hers. "I know we've got a long road ahead of us, but I believe in us. I believe that we're on the right path."

Mia nodded, her heart swelling with hope and love. "I believe that too. And I'm ready to face whatever comes next, with you by my side."

They sat there for a while, wrapped in the warmth of each other's presence and the beauty of the night. The stars above seemed to shine a little brighter, as if reflecting the promise and potential of their future.

As the evening grew colder, Ethan and Mia made their way back to the truck, their hands intertwined. The drive back to the farmhouse was quiet but filled with an unspoken understanding. They knew that they were taking the first step toward something meaningful, and it felt right.

When they arrived at the farmhouse, Ethan turned to Mia with a soft smile. "I'll see you tomorrow?"

Mia smiled back, her heart full of warmth. "Definitely."

With a final, tender kiss goodnight, Mia watched as Ethan drove away, feeling a deep sense of contentment. She knew that the journey ahead would have its challenges, but with Ethan by her side, she felt ready to embrace whatever came next.

As she walked inside and headed to bed, Mia felt a renewed sense of hope and excitement for the future. The first step had been taken, and it was only the beginning of a journey that promised to be filled with love, growth, and endless possibilities.

The following days unfolded with a gentle rhythm, as Mia and Ethan continued to nurture the budding connection they had rekindled. The Harvest Festival had marked a significant step in their journey, but it was the small, everyday moments that truly deepened their bond.

As autumn progressed, the air grew cooler and the leaves painted the town in shades of amber and crimson. Mia found solace in these changing seasons, mirroring the changes in her own life. Each morning, she walked to the barn, enjoying the crisp air and the crunch of fallen leaves underfoot. Ethan was always there, ready with a warm smile and a shared sense of purpose.

One bright, chilly morning, Mia arrived at the barn to find Ethan already at work. He was sanding down a piece of wood, his focus evident in the way he moved with deliberate care. The barn had transformed from a cluttered, abandoned structure into a place full of promise, and it was becoming more than just a project—it was a symbol of their evolving relationship.

"Good morning," Mia greeted, her voice carrying a hint of excitement.

Ethan looked up, his eyes lighting up at the sight of her. "Morning! Ready to tackle today's list?"

"Absolutely," Mia said, stepping into the barn and surveying their progress. "What's on the agenda?"

Ethan handed her a blueprint they had been working from, detailing the layout and design for the barn's interior. "Today, we're focusing on installing the new shelving and finishing the paint job. I thought we could make a start on the community board we talked about."

Mia took the blueprint with a grin. "Sounds like a plan. Let's get to it."

The day passed quickly as they worked side by side, their movements synchronized as they tackled tasks together. The conversation flowed easily, punctuated by shared laughter and comfortable silence. Each task completed seemed to bring them closer, their teamwork reinforcing the sense of partnership they were building.

By mid-afternoon, as the sun began its slow descent, painting the sky in hues of pink and orange, they took a break outside. They sat on the edge of the barn's porch, sipping hot cocoa from the thermos Mia had brought along.

"You know," Mia began, her gaze drifting over the landscape, "I've been thinking about the future a lot lately. About what we're creating here."

Ethan looked over at her, curiosity in his eyes. "What about it?"

Mia hesitated for a moment before speaking. "I know we're taking things one step at a time, but I'm starting to see this barn not just as a project, but as a place where we could bring people together. A place for community events, workshops, maybe even small gatherings."

Ethan's eyes widened with admiration. "I love that idea. It's exactly what I've been hoping for—to make this a place that brings people together. We could start planning some events, maybe get the word out to the community."

Mia's heart swelled with excitement. "That sounds amazing. I think it would be a great way to give back to the town, and it would make the barn even more special."

They spent the rest of the afternoon brainstorming ideas, their discussion fueled by enthusiasm and shared dreams. The more they talked, the more they realized how much they wanted this vision to become a reality. It wasn't just about the barn—it was about creating something meaningful together, something that would leave a lasting impact on their community.

As the sun set and they packed up their tools, Ethan took Mia's hand, his expression serious but filled with hope. "Mia, I want you to know how much this means to me. Working on this barn with you, dreaming about the future—it's been incredible. I can't wait to see where this journey takes us."

Mia squeezed his hand, her heart full. "Me too, Ethan. I'm really excited about what's to come. And I'm grateful for every step we're taking together."

They shared a quiet moment, their eyes locked in understanding. The barn, now a symbol of their hard work and commitment, stood as a testament to the future they were building together.

That evening, as they sat by the fire in the farmhouse, wrapped in blankets and sharing stories, Mia felt a profound sense of peace. The path ahead was still uncertain, but with Ethan by her side and a shared vision for the future, she knew they were on the right track.

As they prepared for bed, Ethan turned to Mia with a thoughtful expression. "There's something else I've been meaning to ask you."

Mia raised an eyebrow, curious. "What is it?"

Ethan took a deep breath, his gaze steady. "I've been thinking about how much we've accomplished together and how much more we can do. I was wondering if you'd consider making this journey a more permanent part of your life. I mean... if you'd consider staying in Willow Creek for good."

Mia's heart skipped a beat at his words. The question hung in the air, filled with the weight of their shared experiences and the promise of a future together. She looked into Ethan's eyes, seeing the sincerity and hope there, and realized that she had been contemplating the same thing.

"I... I hadn't really thought about it in those terms," Mia said, her voice trembling slightly. "But the more I think about it, the more it feels like the right place for me. For us."

Ethan's face broke into a relieved smile. "I'm glad to hear that. I know it's a big step, but I believe in what we're building here. And I want you to be a part of it, every step of the way."

Mia reached out and took his hand, her heart filled with warmth. "I want that too. I want to be here, to build a life with you and be a part of this community."

As they embraced, the future seemed to unfold with new possibilities. The barn, the town, and their shared dreams all felt like pieces of a larger, beautiful mosaic. And as they faced the challenges and joys ahead, Mia knew that she was ready to embrace it all, with Ethan by her side.

The first step had been taken, and with each new day, they would continue to build their future, one moment at a time.

The next few weeks flew by in a flurry of activity and excitement. The barn, now more than halfway completed, began to take shape as a vibrant community hub. Mia and Ethan, driven by their shared vision, worked tirelessly to get everything ready for their first big event: the Barn's Grand Opening.

Mia spent her days finalizing the community board and coordinating with local vendors and volunteers. The barn, once a symbol of uncertainty, was now a beacon of hope and connection. Each day, as she saw the progress, her heart swelled with pride and anticipation. She felt a profound sense of belonging in Willow Creek, a feeling she hadn't experienced in a long time.

One crisp Saturday morning, as the sun cast a golden glow over the town, Mia and Ethan stood at the entrance of the barn, surveying their work. The walls were freshly painted, the new shelving was in place, and a stage had been set up for local performances. The barn had been transformed into a warm, welcoming space, ready to host the community's first gathering in years.

"This looks amazing," Mia said, her voice filled with awe. "I can't believe how far we've come."

Ethan squeezed her hand, a proud smile on his face. "It really does look incredible. I couldn't have done it without you."

Mia's heart fluttered at his words. Their shared effort had not only rejuvenated the barn but had also deepened their relationship. She glanced around, taking in the final touches they had added, from string lights to colorful banners. It was perfect.

As they made their final preparations, the excitement in Willow Creek was palpable. The town had embraced the idea of the barn as a gathering place, and the opening event had become a highly anticipated occasion. The smell of freshly baked goods and the sound of cheerful chatter filled the air as locals began to arrive, each person eager to see the transformation for themselves.

When the clock struck seven, the barn was filled with people. The space buzzed with laughter and conversation as old friends reunited and new connections were made. The stage was alive with local musicians playing upbeat tunes, and a variety of food stalls offered everything from homemade pies to savory treats.

Mia and Ethan moved through the crowd, greeting guests and ensuring everything ran smoothly. As they worked together, Mia couldn't help but feel a deep sense of satisfaction. This wasn't just an event; it was a testament to their hard work and their commitment to Willow Creek.

Around eight o'clock, Ethan tapped a glass to get everyone's attention. The barn quieted down, and all eyes were on him. He stood next to Mia, his face glowing with pride.

"Thank you all for coming tonight," Ethan began, his voice filled with gratitude. "This barn has always been a part of Willow Creek's history, but tonight it marks a new beginning. Mia and I have been working hard to create a space where we can come together as a community, and we couldn't have done it without your support."

The crowd erupted into applause, and Mia felt a rush of warmth at the outpouring of appreciation. Ethan continued, his gaze shifting to Mia.

"I want to especially thank Mia for all her hard work and dedication. She's brought so much to this project and to my life. Without her, none of this would be possible."

Mia's cheeks flushed with a mix of embarrassment and joy. She looked at Ethan, her heart swelling with love and admiration. The sincerity in his words was a reminder of how much they had accomplished together and how far they had come.

After Ethan's speech, the evening continued with dancing and merriment. Mia and Ethan joined in, moving together to the rhythm of the music. The barn was alive with energy, and Mia felt a sense of belonging that she hadn't felt in years.

Later, as the night began to wind down and the crowd started to thin, Mia and Ethan found a quiet corner of the barn. They stood together, watching the last of the guests leave, their hands intertwined.

"This has been incredible," Mia said softly, her voice filled with emotion. "I never imagined we'd make something like this happen."

Ethan turned to her, his eyes reflecting the warm glow of the string lights overhead. "It's been a dream come true. And it's just the beginning."

Mia smiled, feeling a deep sense of contentment. "I'm so glad we're doing this together. I feel like we've created something really special here."

Ethan pulled her close, wrapping his arms around her in a tender embrace. "We have. And we're just getting started. There's so much more we can do, so many more dreams to chase."

As they held each other, Mia felt a profound sense of hope for the future. The barn was more than just a physical space; it was a symbol of their shared journey and the possibilities that lay ahead. With Ethan by her side, she felt ready to face whatever challenges and joys the future might bring.

The Grand Opening had been a resounding success, but for Mia and Ethan, it was only the beginning. As they looked out at the barn, now quiet and still after the excitement of the evening, they knew that their journey together was just starting. And with each step they took, they would continue to build not only their future but also a vibrant, connected community in Willow Creek.

The next few weeks were a whirlwind of activity and reflection. The barn continued to buzz with activity as it became a central hub for community events. Mia and Ethan hosted various gatherings, from book clubs to craft fairs, each event reinforcing the barn's role as a cornerstone of Willow Creek's social life.

One crisp November evening, as the first hints of winter began to chill the air, Mia and Ethan found themselves sitting on the porch of the farmhouse, wrapped in blankets and sipping hot cider. The barn, now fully operational, had become a beloved fixture in town, but the work wasn't done yet. They were in the midst of planning their next big project: a winter festival to celebrate the season and bring the community together.

Mia looked over at Ethan, who was intently sketching out plans for the festival. The soft glow of the porch light illuminated his face, and Mia felt a deep sense of contentment as she watched him work. Their shared vision for the barn and the town had become a reality, and it had strengthened their bond in ways she hadn't anticipated.

"Looks like you've got everything under control," Mia said with a smile, breaking the comfortable silence.

Ethan glanced up, his eyes bright with enthusiasm. "I hope so. I want this festival to be something special—something that everyone will remember. What do you think of the idea of a bonfire and storytelling session?"

Mia's eyes lit up at the suggestion. "That sounds amazing. I think the townspeople would love it. It'll be a great way to celebrate the season and bring everyone together."

Ethan nodded, clearly pleased with her response. "I was thinking we could also have some local musicians and maybe even a hot cocoa stand. Something to keep everyone warm and cozy."

Mia grinned. "I love it. We should also think about some activities for the kids—maybe a craft station or a small petting zoo."

As they continued to brainstorm, the conversation turned to other aspects of their lives. They talked about their hopes for the future, their plans for the barn, and their dreams beyond Willow Creek. The discussion flowed easily, each topic adding another layer to their deepening connection.

When the conversation lulled, Ethan looked over at Mia with a thoughtful expression. "You know, Mia, I've been thinking about something lately. About us."

Mia's heart skipped a beat. "What's on your mind?"

Ethan took a deep breath, his gaze steady. "I know we've been taking things slowly, and that's been important. But I can't help but feel that we're ready for the next step. I want to build a future with you, not just for the barn or the town, but for us."

Mia's pulse quickened, a mix of excitement and apprehension coursing through her. She had been feeling the same way, but hearing Ethan articulate it so clearly made her heart swell. "I've been thinking about that too," she admitted. "I feel like we're in a really good place, and I want to explore what that means for us."

Ethan's eyes softened, and he reached out to take her hand. "So, what do you think? Are you ready to talk about what the future might hold for us?"

Mia looked down at their joined hands, her heart full. She had spent so much time guarded and uncertain, but now she felt ready to embrace the possibilities. "Yes, I'm ready. I want to see where this can go, to really build something together."

Ethan's face broke into a wide, genuine smile. "I'm so glad to hear that."

They spent the rest of the evening talking about their dreams and aspirations, not just for the barn but for their lives together. It was a conversation filled with hope and possibility, and Mia felt a profound sense of excitement about the future.

As the night grew colder, they wrapped up in their blankets and sat in comfortable silence, watching the stars twinkle in the clear, crisp sky. The warmth of their shared conversation and the cozy comfort of the porch created a sense of peace and anticipation.

When Ethan finally stood to go inside, he turned to Mia with a soft smile. "I think this winter festival is going to be amazing. And I think our future is looking pretty bright too."

Mia's heart swelled with affection. "I agree. I'm excited for what's to come, both for the festival and for us."

They went inside, their hearts full of hope and their minds buzzing with plans. The barn, the festival, and their future together were all coming into focus, and for the first time in a long time, Mia felt certain about the path she was on. With Ethan by her side, she was ready to face whatever challenges and joys the future might bring.

As November progressed, the excitement for the winter festival grew, and the whole town seemed to be buzzing with anticipation. Mia and Ethan threw themselves into preparations with renewed energy, their shared enthusiasm evident in every detail they worked on.

One chilly Saturday morning, Mia arrived at the barn to find Ethan already hard at work. He was busy hanging strings of twinkling lights around the rafters, and the warm glow of the lights created a cozy atmosphere amidst the cold outside.

"Good morning!" Mia called out as she stepped inside, shaking off the chill from the crisp air. "Looks like you've been busy."

Ethan looked up, his face lighting up with a smile. "Morning! Yeah, I figured I'd get a head start on the decorations. These lights are going to look amazing once we're done."

Mia walked over and began helping him with the lights. They worked side by side, their movements synchronized as they chatted about the festival and their plans for the future. The air inside the barn was filled with laughter and the soft hum of Christmas music playing in the background, adding to the festive spirit.

As they worked, Ethan took a moment to look over at Mia with a thoughtful expression. "You know, I've been thinking about something. We've been so focused on the festival and everything we've been building here, but I wanted to make sure we're taking time for ourselves too. I know things have been moving quickly."

Mia paused, considering his words. "You're right. We've been so caught up in everything that we haven't had much time just for us. Maybe we should plan something special, just the two of us."

Ethan's eyes brightened with interest. "That sounds like a great idea. How about a quiet evening out? We could have dinner at that little café in town that you mentioned—there's always something cozy about it."

Mia smiled, touched by his thoughtfulness. "I'd love that. It sounds perfect."

They finished decorating the barn and made plans for their dinner date. The anticipation for the evening added a new layer of excitement to their already busy days.

That evening, Mia and Ethan dressed up for their date, a rare and cherished opportunity to enjoy each other's company without the pressures of the festival preparations. Mia wore a simple but elegant dress, and Ethan looked sharp in a button-down shirt and jacket.

As they arrived at the café, the warm glow from the windows and the smell of fresh bread and coffee welcomed them inside. They were shown to a cozy table near the fireplace, and as they settled in, Mia couldn't help but feel a sense of contentment.

The meal was delightful, filled with delicious food and engaging conversation. They talked about their favorite memories from the past year, their dreams for the future, and everything in between. The evening felt like a perfect balance to their busy lives—a chance to reconnect and enjoy the simple pleasure of being together.

After dinner, they took a leisurely walk through the town square, now beautifully adorned with holiday decorations. The sight of the twinkling lights and the festive atmosphere created a magical backdrop for their stroll.

"I'm really glad we did this," Mia said, leaning into Ethan as they walked. "It's nice to have a moment to just enjoy each other's company."

Ethan squeezed her hand gently. "Me too. It's moments like these that remind me of why we're doing all this. It's not just about the barn or the festival—it's about building a life together."

Mia looked up at him, her heart full. "You're right. It's about creating something meaningful and sharing it with the people we care about."

They stopped for a moment near the fountain in the center of the square, its gentle flow of water sparkling under the lights. Ethan turned to Mia, his eyes filled with emotion.

"Mia," he began, "I want you to know how much you mean to me. These past few months have been some of the happiest of my life, and I can't imagine the future without you in it."

Mia's heart skipped a beat. She had been feeling the same way, but hearing Ethan's words made it all the more real. "I feel the same way, Ethan. I'm so grateful for everything we've built together, and I'm excited about what's to come."

They shared a tender kiss, their connection deepening in the quiet moment. As they pulled away, Ethan took Mia's hand in his, a smile on his face.

"Let's make a promise," he said softly. "No matter how busy things get, we'll always find time for each other. We'll keep building this life together, step by step."

Mia nodded, her heart swelling with love. "I promise."

As they continued their walk, hand in hand, Mia felt a renewed sense of optimism and excitement for the future. The festival was just around the corner, and their plans were coming together beautifully. But more importantly, she felt a deep sense of fulfillment and joy in the relationship she was nurturing with Ethan.

The first step had been taken, and it had led them to a place of shared dreams and mutual support. With each passing day, they were building something special—something that would continue to grow and flourish, just like the winter festival they were about to celebrate. And as the first snowflakes began to fall gently from the sky, Mia knew that they were on the brink of something truly magical.

Chapter 6: Echoes of the Past

The following weeks brought a steady rhythm to Mia and Ethan's lives. They spent their days working on the barn, sharing quiet moments, and deepening their connection. Each day felt like a new step forward, a further solidification of the path they were slowly but surely walking together.

But with every step forward, the past continued to cast its shadow.

One crisp morning, as Mia was finishing her coffee on the porch, she noticed a familiar car pulling up the driveway. Her heart skipped a beat as she recognized the sleek, black sedan. It was her father's car. The sight of it stirred up a mix of emotions—relief, anxiety, and a touch of resentment.

She hadn't seen her father, William Prescott, since she returned to Willow Creek. Their relationship had always been complicated. Growing up, he had been more focused on his work, traveling frequently, and often distant, leaving Mia feeling neglected. She had spent years trying to win his approval, to make him proud, but it had never felt like enough.

As the car came to a stop, Mia stood up, smoothing her hands over her jeans as she watched her father step out. He was impeccably dressed, as always, in a tailored suit, his graying hair neatly combed back. He looked out of place against the rustic backdrop of the farmhouse, a man who belonged to boardrooms and city lights, not quiet country mornings.

"Mia," he said as he approached, his voice warm but with a formal edge that always made her feel like a little girl again.

"Dad," Mia replied, forcing a smile as she met him halfway.

They embraced briefly, the hug stiff and a bit awkward, as it always was. When they pulled apart, Mia noticed her father's eyes sweeping over the farmhouse, the barn in the distance, and the fields stretching out beyond. She couldn't quite read his expression—part approval, part concern, and something else she couldn't place.

"This place looks... different," William said, his tone carefully neutral.

"It's home," Mia replied, a hint of defensiveness creeping into her voice. She wasn't sure what she expected—criticism, perhaps, or some thinly veiled comment about how she had left behind a promising career in the city. But she wasn't about to let him make her feel small in her own home.

William nodded slowly. "I can see that. It's good to see you, Mia. I was starting to wonder if you were planning to stay in Willow Creek for good."

"I haven't decided yet," Mia said, choosing her words carefully. "But I'm happy here for now."

Her father studied her for a moment, his eyes narrowing slightly. "And Ethan? How does he fit into all of this?"

Mia felt a pang of discomfort at the question. "He's... we're working things out."

William's gaze softened, and for a moment, the formal mask slipped, revealing a flicker of concern. "Mia, I know I haven't always been the most supportive father, and I know we've had our differences. But I want what's best for you. I don't want to see you get hurt."

Mia looked down, her throat tightening with emotion. It was rare for her father to speak so openly, to show any kind of vulnerability. She knew he meant well, but his words brought up all the old fears she had been trying to push aside—the fear of making the same mistakes, of getting hurt again.

"I know, Dad," she said quietly. "But I have to figure this out for myself. I can't keep running from the past."

William sighed, running a hand through his hair as he looked out at the fields. "I suppose you're right. But just know that if you ever need anything—help, advice, or even just someone to talk to—I'm here."

Mia felt a surge of warmth at his words. It wasn't exactly an apology for the years of distance, but it was as close as her father could come. "Thanks, Dad. I appreciate that."

They stood in silence for a moment, the sounds of the farm filling the space between them. It wasn't a perfect moment, but it was a start—an olive branch extended, and one that Mia was willing to accept.

Eventually, her father cleared his throat, breaking the silence. "Well, I should be getting back to the city. I just wanted to check on you, make sure you were okay."

"I'm okay," Mia said, offering him a small smile. "And you don't have to worry so much. I'm not a little girl anymore."

William smiled faintly, a hint of sadness in his eyes. "I know that. But you'll always be my daughter."

With that, they embraced again, and this time, the hug was a little less stiff, a little more genuine. As her father got back into his car and drove away, Mia felt a strange mix of emotions—relief, sadness, and a lingering sense of uncertainty.

Her father's visit had stirred up old memories, old fears, and as much as she wanted to focus on the present, the past still had a way of creeping in when she least expected it.

Later that day, as Mia and Ethan were working in the barn, she found herself distracted, her thoughts drifting back to her father's words. Ethan noticed her quiet mood and paused what he was doing, wiping his hands on a rag before walking over to her.

"Hey, you okay?" he asked, concern etched on his face.

Mia looked up at him, feeling the weight of everything she had been holding inside. "My dad came by this morning."

Ethan's eyebrows rose in surprise. "Really? How did it go?"

Mia shrugged, leaning against the workbench. "It was... fine, I guess. He was just checking in, but it brought up a lot of stuff I thought I'd put behind me."

Ethan nodded, his expression understanding. "Family has a way of doing that."

Mia sighed, running a hand through her hair. "I don't know, Ethan. Sometimes I feel like I'm still trying to prove something to him, even though I know I don't have to."

Ethan reached out and took her hand, squeezing it gently. "You don't have to prove anything to anyone, Mia. Not to your dad, and not to me. You're enough, just as you are."

Mia felt tears prick at her eyes, but she blinked them away, grateful for Ethan's support. "I just wish I could stop feeling like I'm going to mess everything up again."

Ethan stepped closer, cupping her face in his hands, his touch warm and reassuring. "You're not going to mess anything up. We're in this together, remember? One step at a time."

Mia looked into his eyes, seeing the sincerity there, and she felt some of the tension ease from her shoulders. "Thank you, Ethan. For always being here for me."

"Always," he said softly, brushing a kiss against her forehead.

They stood there for a moment, wrapped in each other's warmth, and Mia felt a sense of peace settle over her. The past was still there, lurking in the shadows, but it didn't feel as overwhelming anymore. With Ethan by her side, she knew she could face whatever came her way.

The day ended with a sense of calm, the two of them working side by side in the barn, the late afternoon light streaming through the windows, casting everything in a golden glow. The quiet companionship they shared was enough for now, a reminder that they didn't have to have everything figured out all at once.

As the sun dipped below the horizon, casting the farm in soft twilight, Mia realized that this was what she had been searching for all along—not perfection, not a life free of complications, but a place where she could be herself, with all her flaws and fears, and still be loved.

And in that moment, she knew that she had finally found it.

As the weeks wore on, the preparations for the winter festival became a central focus for the town and for Mia and Ethan. The barn was transformed into a magical space, with sparkling lights and festive decorations bringing a sense of cheer to the crisp winter air.

One evening, as Mia was hanging up the last of the garlands, Ethan approached her with a grin. "I think we're finally done," he said, surveying their work with satisfaction. "The barn looks incredible."

Mia stepped back and admired their handiwork. "It does look amazing. I'm really proud of what we've accomplished."

Ethan's eyes softened as he looked at her. "Me too. And I'm proud of you—of us. We've come a long way."

Mia felt a swell of emotion at his words. "We really have. It feels like everything is falling into place."

They shared a quiet moment of contentment, standing in the glow of the lights they had worked so hard to put up. The barn, once a simple structure, had been transformed into a warm and inviting space that felt like home.

The night of the winter festival arrived, and the barn was filled with the buzz of excited chatter and the warmth of community. Mia and Ethan welcomed guests, their faces lighting up as they saw familiar faces and new friends alike.

The festival was a success, with laughter and joy filling the air. The barn was alive with the sounds of music and celebration, and Mia felt a deep sense of fulfillment as she watched the community come together.

As the evening drew to a close, Mia and Ethan found a quiet spot away from the crowd. The barn, now dimly lit and decorated with twinkling lights, provided a serene backdrop for their conversation.

"I can't believe how well everything turned out," Mia said, leaning against the wall. "This has been such a wonderful experience."

Ethan took her hand, his eyes filled with warmth. "It has. And it's been amazing to share it with you. You've really made a difference here."

Mia smiled, feeling a sense of pride and happiness. "I couldn't have done it without you. You've been my rock through all of this."

Ethan squeezed her hand gently. "And you've been mine. I think we've proven that we can handle anything together."

They stood there in comfortable silence, the festive lights casting a gentle glow around them. For the first time in a long time, Mia felt a sense of complete peace and belonging. She was surrounded by the people she cared about, doing something she loved, and with someone who made her feel cherished and supported.

As they made their way back to the main area of the barn, the music shifted to a slow, romantic tune. Ethan looked at Mia with a playful smile. "Care for a dance?"

Mia's heart fluttered at the thought. "I'd love to."

They moved to the center of the barn, where the crowd had begun to thin out. Ethan pulled her close, his arms wrapping around her as they swayed to the music. Mia rested her head on his shoulder, feeling the steady beat of his heart.

"This feels perfect," she whispered, closing her eyes.

Ethan's voice was soft and tender as he spoke. "It does. And I want us to keep making moments like this. Together."

Mia looked up at him, her eyes shining with emotion. "I want that too. More than anything."

They danced slowly, lost in the moment, their hearts in sync as they held each other close. The barn, now quiet and filled with the gentle hum of the music, felt like a haven—a place where they could be themselves and find solace in each other.

As the song came to an end, Ethan leaned down and kissed Mia softly, their connection deepening with each touch. When they finally pulled away, their faces were lit with happiness and a shared understanding of what they meant to each other.

The festival had been a success, but it was the quiet, intimate moments like this that truly made it special. Mia knew that no matter what challenges lay ahead, she and Ethan would face them together, supported by their love and the community they had come to cherish.

As they walked hand in hand through the barn, the winter festival lights casting a soft glow around them, Mia felt a renewed sense of hope and anticipation for the future. She had found a place where she could be herself, where she was loved and supported, and where she felt truly at home.

In the warmth of the barn, surrounded by the echoes of the past and the promise of the future, Mia knew that she had finally found the happiness she had been searching for all along. And as she and Ethan continued to build their life together, she was ready to embrace whatever came next, one step at a time.

As the winter festival drew to a close, the barn slowly emptied, leaving Mia and Ethan alone amid the twinkling lights and the remnants of a successful evening. The last notes of the final song lingered in the air as they picked up discarded cups and plates, their earlier dance still fresh in their minds.

"I can't believe it's over already," Mia said, her voice tinged with both satisfaction and a hint of sadness. "It feels like the night just started."

Ethan smiled, his eyes crinkling at the corners. "It's been a perfect night. But you know, I've been thinking..."

Mia raised an eyebrow, curiosity piqued. "Oh? What have you been thinking about?"

Ethan hesitated for a moment, then took her hand in his, his expression serious but gentle. "I've been thinking about us, about what we've built together here. And I want us to keep building, not just here in Willow Creek, but in our future."

Mia felt a flutter of anticipation. "What are you saying, Ethan?"

He took a deep breath, as if gathering his thoughts. "I know things have been moving slowly, and I'm grateful for every step we've taken. But I want to take the next step. I want to make this—us—a permanent part of my life. I want to build a future with you."

Mia's heart raced, her emotions a mix of excitement and nervousness. "Are you saying...?"

Ethan nodded, his eyes never leaving hers. "Yes, I'm saying that I want to marry you, Mia. I want us to build a life together, here or wherever life takes us."

The words hung in the air, and for a moment, Mia was overwhelmed by a wave of emotion. She had dreamed of this, of finding someone who truly understood her and wanted to build a future together, but hearing it from Ethan made it feel all the more real.

She looked at him, her eyes filled with tears of joy. "Ethan, I... I don't know what to say."

Ethan's gaze was steady, filled with hope and sincerity. "You don't have to say anything right now. I just wanted you to know how I feel and what I want for us. Take all the time you need."

Mia squeezed his hand, her heart swelling with love and affection. "Ethan, I've never been more sure of anything in my life. I want that too. I want to spend my life with you, to build our future together."

Ethan's face lit up with a radiant smile. "Really?"

Mia nodded, her voice trembling with emotion. "Yes, really. I've never been more certain of anything."

Ethan pulled her into a tight embrace, his arms warm and reassuring around her. "I'm so glad to hear that."

They held each other for a long moment, the noise of the festival fading into the background as they savored their shared happiness. The future felt more vivid and hopeful than ever before, and Mia knew that whatever challenges lay ahead, they would face them together.

As they finished tidying up the barn, Ethan took Mia's hand and led her outside, where the winter sky was clear and the stars twinkled brightly above. The world seemed to be holding its breath, as if waiting for them to make their next move.

"Let's take a walk," Ethan suggested, his voice soft and inviting.

Mia nodded, feeling a sense of peace as they strolled hand in hand through the snow-covered fields. The cold air was invigorating, and the crunch of snow beneath their boots was a soothing rhythm that matched the beat of their hearts.

They walked in silence for a while, each lost in their thoughts, until they reached a small hill overlooking the town. From there, they could see the lights of Willow Creek twinkling in the distance, a symbol of the community they had come to love.

Ethan stopped and turned to face Mia, his expression filled with a mix of hope and determination. "I know it won't always be easy. We'll face challenges and obstacles, just like everyone does. But I promise you, no matter what happens, I'll always be here for you. We'll get through it together."

Mia looked up at him, her heart full of love and trust. "I believe that. I trust you, Ethan. And I'm ready to face whatever comes next, as long as we're together."

Ethan smiled, leaning in to kiss her gently. The kiss was tender and full of promise, a seal on their commitment to each other and the future they were building.

As they stood there, wrapped in each other's arms, the stars shining above and the quiet of the winter night surrounding them, Mia felt a deep sense of contentment. She had found her place, her purpose, and the person she wanted to share her life with.

The echoes of the past were still there, but they no longer held the same power over her. With Ethan by her side, she was ready to embrace the future, to build a life filled with love, joy, and the shared dreams they had begun to weave together.

And as the night wore on, Mia knew that this was only the beginning of their journey—one filled with hope, love, and the promise of a future that they would create together.

As the cold wind gently brushed against their faces, Mia and Ethan remained on the hill, taking in the serene beauty of the night. The sight of Willow Creek, illuminated by the soft glow of streetlights and festive decorations, felt like a perfect backdrop to the new chapter they were about to begin.

After a while, Ethan broke the silence, his voice thoughtful and calm. "I've been thinking about the wedding and what we want for our future. There's so much to plan, but I want it to be something special—something that reflects who we are and what we've been through."

Mia nodded, her thoughts mirroring his. "I've been thinking about that too. I want it to be something meaningful, something that feels like home."

Ethan smiled, a hint of mischief in his eyes. "What if we had a wedding right here, in Willow Creek? With the barn as the backdrop, and a celebration that feels like a true reflection of our journey?"

Mia's eyes lit up at the idea. "I love that! It would be so personal and unique. It would feel like a real celebration of everything we've built here."

Ethan squeezed her hand, clearly pleased with her reaction. "I'm glad you think so. We could have the ceremony in the barn, decorated with fairy lights and flowers, and then have the reception outside under the stars. It could be just as magical as we've imagined."

Mia leaned her head against his shoulder, feeling a deep sense of contentment. "That sounds perfect. It would be a true celebration of our life here and the community we've come to love."

As they continued their walk, they began to talk about the details of their wedding, their voices filled with excitement and anticipation. They envisioned a day filled with laughter, love, and the warmth of their friends and family. The idea of starting their new life together in a place that had become so meaningful to them made everything feel even more special.

When they finally made their way back to the farmhouse, the cold air had invigorated them, and they were ready to tackle the next steps in their journey. They had a plan, a vision for their future, and the unwavering support of each other.

Inside, as they settled in front of the fireplace with mugs of hot cocoa, Mia felt a wave of gratitude. The past weeks had been transformative—she had faced her fears, rebuilt connections, and discovered a deep, enduring love with Ethan. She knew that their path forward wouldn't always be easy, but with Ethan by her side, she felt more prepared than ever to face whatever challenges might come their way.

As they sipped their cocoa and talked about their plans for the wedding, Mia reflected on how far she had come. She had come to terms with her past, embraced her present, and was now looking forward to a future filled with hope and promise.

Ethan's hand found hers again, and he looked at her with a mixture of affection and determination. "No matter what happens, Mia, I want you to know that you're everything to me. I'm so grateful for this life we're building together."

Mia smiled, her heart full. "And I'm grateful for you, Ethan. For your patience, your love, and the way you've always been there for me."

They sat together in comfortable silence, the crackling of the fire and the soft glow of the lights creating a cozy and intimate atmosphere. The future was still uncertain, but with each other, they felt ready to embrace it with open hearts.

The echoes of the past had not disappeared entirely, but they no longer held the same power over Mia. Instead, they had become part of the tapestry of her life—a reminder of how far she had come and how much she had grown.

As the night wore on, Mia and Ethan made their way to bed, their hearts light and their minds buzzing with the possibilities of the future. The love they shared felt like a guiding star, illuminating their path and giving them the strength to face whatever lay ahead.

With Ethan by her side, Mia knew she had found her place, her purpose, and the person she wanted to spend her life with. And as she drifted off to sleep, she felt a deep sense of peace, knowing that they were embarking on a new chapter—one filled with love, hope, and the promise of a beautiful future together.

The days leading up to the wedding were a whirlwind of activity and excitement. Mia and Ethan threw themselves into preparations, transforming the barn into a magical venue and planning every detail with care. Their friends and family were eager to help, bringing their own touches to the event and creating an atmosphere filled with warmth and community.

One afternoon, as Mia and her closest friends—Sarah, Emily, and Lucy—were setting up floral arrangements in the barn, the conversation turned to the past and how it had shaped them all. They were arranging delicate white roses and greenery, laughter and chatter mingling with the scent of fresh flowers.

"I can't believe how quickly this day has come," Sarah said, securing a bouquet with a ribbon. "It feels like just yesterday we were talking about how Mia was trying to figure out what she wanted to do with her life."

Emily grinned. "And now look at her. She's about to marry the love of her life and create a home in Willow Creek."

Lucy nodded in agreement. "It's amazing how life can change in ways you never expect. Mia, you've come such a long way."

Mia felt a swell of emotion at her friends' words. "I couldn't have done it without all of you. Your support has meant everything to me."

Sarah reached over and squeezed her hand. "We've always been here for you, Mia. And we're so happy to see you find your place and your happiness."

As they continued to work, the conversation shifted to the future. They discussed their dreams and aspirations, their hopes for their own lives. Mia found solace in the shared understanding and the bond she had with her friends.

Later, Ethan joined her in the barn, his face lighting up at the sight of the progress they had made. "This place looks incredible," he said, his voice filled with admiration. "You and your friends have done an amazing job."

Mia smiled, her heart swelling with pride. "We've been working hard to make it perfect. I want this day to be everything we've dreamed of."

Ethan took her hand and pulled her into a warm embrace. "It will be. And no matter what, it's going to be perfect because it's our day."

As the sun began to set, casting a golden hue over the barn, Mia and Ethan took a moment to themselves, stepping outside to enjoy the peaceful evening. The stars were starting to appear, their twinkling light creating a magical atmosphere.

"This is going to be one of the best nights of our lives," Ethan said, his arm around Mia's shoulders. "I can't wait to see you walk down the aisle."

Mia leaned into him, feeling a sense of contentment. "I'm excited too. And a little nervous. But I know that with you by my side, everything will be alright."

Ethan kissed her forehead, his touch tender and reassuring. "We've come so far, Mia. We've faced challenges and grown stronger together. I have no doubt that our future will be just as amazing."

The night before the wedding, Mia found it difficult to sleep. Her mind was filled with a whirlwind of thoughts and emotions. She lay in bed, the soft rustle of the wind outside and the distant sounds of the farm soothing her restless mind. Despite the excitement and anticipation, she couldn't help but reflect on the journey that had brought her to this point.

She thought about her father's visit, the mixed feelings it had stirred up, and the progress she had made in healing old wounds. She thought about Ethan and how his love had transformed her life, giving her the courage to embrace her past and look forward to the future.

As she lay there, her thoughts were interrupted by a soft knock on her door. It was Sarah, carrying a small gift wrapped in a delicate ribbon.

"Hey," Sarah said quietly, stepping inside. "I thought you might like this."

Mia sat up, intrigued. "What is it?"

Sarah handed her the gift with a smile. "Open it and see."

Mia carefully unwrapped the ribbon and opened the box to find a beautiful locket inside. It was engraved with intricate patterns and had a small photo of her and Ethan inside.

"It's lovely," Mia said, her voice filled with emotion. "Thank you, Sarah. It means a lot to me."

Sarah hugged her tightly. "I wanted you to have something special to remember this day by. You've come such a long way, and I'm so proud of you."

Mia hugged her back, feeling a deep sense of gratitude. "Thank you for everything. For being here and for your support."

As Sarah left, Mia held the locket close, feeling a sense of peace wash over her. She knew that the day ahead would be filled with joy and celebration, but it would also be a poignant reminder of how far she had come and how much she had grown.

With a deep breath, she finally closed her eyes and drifted off to sleep, the locket clutched in her hand. The next day would mark the beginning of a new chapter, one filled with love, hope, and the promise of a future that was finally within reach.

As dawn broke and the first light of the day began to filter through the windows, Mia awoke with a renewed sense of purpose and excitement. She knew that the wedding would be a beautiful celebration of her journey, and she couldn't wait to share it with the people who mattered most to her.

And as she prepared for the day ahead, she felt a profound sense of gratitude for the love and support she had received and for the life she was about to begin with Ethan.

Chapter 7: Shadows and Light

The days following her father's visit were filled with an unexpected sense of calm for Mia. It was as if confronting those old wounds had released some of the weight she had been carrying for years. Still, the echoes of her past lingered in the back of her mind, reminding her that healing wasn't a straight path—it was a winding road, with unexpected turns and shadows that needed to be faced.

As autumn deepened, Willow Creek's colors grew more vibrant, the town embracing the season's chill with warmth and tradition. The Harvest Festival had marked the beginning of a series of community events that brought everyone together—baking contests, pumpkin carving, and eventually, the annual Fall Fair, a celebration that drew people from nearby towns to join in the fun.

Mia had always loved the Fall Fair. As a child, it had been her favorite time of year—a place where she could forget her worries and immerse herself in the joy of the moment. This year, however, she approached it with mixed emotions. The town had been nothing but welcoming since her return, but she couldn't shake the feeling that she was still an outsider, someone who had left and wasn't sure if she truly belonged anymore.

Ethan, as if sensing her hesitation, was by her side every step of the way. His quiet support was a constant, steady and unwavering, reminding her that she wasn't alone. They spent their days preparing for the fair—decorating the barn, helping neighbors set up their booths, and even volunteering to run a few games.

One crisp afternoon, as they were putting the finishing touches on the barn decorations, Ethan glanced over at Mia, who was lost in thought as she arranged a bouquet of dried flowers.

"Penny for your thoughts?" he asked, his tone light but his eyes filled with concern.

Mia looked up, her fingers stilling as she met his gaze. "Just thinking about the fair. It's bringing up a lot of memories."

Ethan nodded, understanding in his expression. "Good ones, I hope?"

"Mostly," Mia admitted, a small smile tugging at her lips. "But also... I don't know. It's hard to explain. I feel like I'm still figuring out where I fit in all of this. Like I'm not quite the same person who used to love this fair so much."

Ethan walked over to her, his presence grounding. "You're not the same person, Mia. You've grown, changed. But that doesn't mean you don't belong here. You're a part of this town, and more importantly, you're a part of my life."

Mia felt her heart warm at his words, the sincerity in his voice soothing some of her lingering doubts. "Thank you, Ethan. I just need to keep reminding myself of that."

He smiled, leaning down to press a gentle kiss to her forehead. "We'll figure it out together. One step at a time, remember?"

Mia nodded, her spirits lifting. "One step at a time."

The day of the Fall Fair arrived with clear skies and a crisp breeze, the perfect backdrop for the festivities. The town square was bustling with activity, the sounds of laughter and music filling the air. Stalls were set up along the streets, selling everything from hand-made crafts to baked goods, and the scent of cinnamon and apple cider wafted through the crowd.

Mia and Ethan arrived early, eager to immerse themselves in the day's events. They walked hand in hand through the fair, stopping at various booths and chatting with neighbors. Mia felt a sense of nostalgia mixed with contentment as she took in the familiar sights—the same caramel apple stand she had frequented as a child, the games she had played with friends, the warmth of the community that had always been the heart of Willow Creek.

As the afternoon wore on, they found themselves at the edge of the square, near a small stage where a local band was setting up for the evening's performance. The area was quieter, away from the hustle and bustle, and Mia found herself drawn to the peacefulness of it.

"Let's sit for a while," Ethan suggested, leading her to a bench beneath a large oak tree. They sat down, and Mia leaned into Ethan's side, enjoying the closeness and the sense of safety it brought.

For a while, they simply watched the crowd, content to be in each other's company. But as the band began to play, a slow, soulful tune that seemed to resonate with the mood of the day, Mia felt a familiar ache in her chest—one she hadn't felt in a long time.

"Ethan," she began, her voice soft and hesitant. "Do you ever think about... what could have been? If things had been different between us back then?"

Ethan was silent for a moment, his expression thoughtful as he considered her question. "I used to," he admitted finally. "A lot, actually. I wondered what I could have done differently, what we could have been if we hadn't gone our separate ways."

Mia looked up at him, her heart tightening at the vulnerability in his eyes. "And now?"

"Now, I think about what we can be," he said, his voice steady. "I've made my peace with the past, Mia. I've accepted that we can't change what happened. But we have a second chance now, and I don't want to waste it."

Mia felt tears well up in her eyes, but they were tears of gratitude, not sadness. "I don't want to waste it either," she whispered, her voice thick with emotion.

Ethan reached out, gently brushing a tear from her cheek. "Then let's not. Let's keep moving forward, together."

Mia nodded, a sense of resolve settling in her chest. The past was still there, a part of her, but it didn't have to define her future. She had a chance to build something new, something real, with Ethan by her side. And she was ready to take that chance.

As the sun began to set, casting a warm golden light over the town, Mia and Ethan stood up, their hands still intertwined. They walked back into the heart of the fair, ready to embrace whatever the future held—one step at a time.

As the sun set and the first stars began to twinkle in the evening sky, the Fall Fair came alive with vibrant colors and joyous sounds. The music from the local band filled the air, and the soft glow of lanterns and fairy lights illuminated the town square, creating a magical atmosphere that made the day even more special.

Mia and Ethan rejoined the festivities, their hearts lighter and their spirits high. They continued to explore the fair, indulging in caramel apples and freshly baked cookies, and even trying their luck at a few of the carnival games. The playful competition between them brought laughter and joy, a reminder of the simple pleasures that made their relationship so special.

As the evening wore on, the crowd began to gather around the stage for the main event of the night—a talent show featuring local performers. Mia and Ethan found a cozy spot near the stage, where they could enjoy the show and the company of their friends and neighbors.

The first act was a group of children performing a cheerful dance routine, their energy and enthusiasm drawing cheers and applause from the audience. Mia watched with a smile, feeling a sense of community and belonging that she had been yearning for since her return to Willow Creek.

As the night progressed, the talent show featured a variety of acts—singers, musicians, and even a local comedian who had everyone in stitches. Each performance was a testament to the talent and creativity within the town, and Mia felt a deep appreciation for the people who made Willow Creek such a unique and special place.

When the final act, a soulful singer with a powerful voice, took the stage, Mia and Ethan held each other close, swaying to the music. The singer's rendition of a classic love song resonated with Mia, reminding her of the journey she had been on and the love she had found with Ethan.

As the song came to an end, Ethan turned to Mia, his expression tender. "This song—it feels like it was meant for us tonight."

Mia nodded, her eyes glistening with emotion. "It really does. It's like it's capturing everything we've been through and everything we're looking forward to."

Ethan took her hand, his gaze steady and sincere. "No matter what challenges we face, we have each other. And that's what matters most."

Mia squeezed his hand, feeling a deep sense of gratitude and love. "I couldn't agree more. I'm so glad we're here together, sharing this moment."

As the night drew to a close, the crowd began to disperse, and the lights of the fair slowly dimmed. Mia and Ethan walked back to the barn, their hearts full and their spirits uplifted by the day's events.

When they arrived at the barn, they paused to take in the beautiful decorations they had worked so hard on. The barn looked stunning, with its twinkling lights and autumnal accents creating a warm and inviting atmosphere.

Mia and Ethan stood together, their arms around each other, as they took in the peaceful scene. The barn was a symbol of their journey, a place where they had faced challenges, celebrated milestones, and built a future together.

"This place," Mia said softly, her voice filled with emotion, "it feels like home now. And I'm so grateful for everything we've built here."

Ethan kissed her forehead, his touch gentle and reassuring. "It is home, Mia. And it will always be a reminder of how far we've come and how much we've grown."

They stood in silence for a moment, their hearts full of love and contentment. The past had its shadows, but the light of their present and future was bright and hopeful.

As they headed inside, ready to relax and unwind after the day's festivities, Mia felt a deep sense of peace. She knew that while the shadows of her past might always be a part of her, the light of her present and future was something she could embrace with open arms.

With Ethan by her side and the support of the community around her, Mia was ready to face whatever came next, knowing that together, they could overcome any obstacle and build a life filled with love, joy, and endless possibilities.

As Mia and Ethan settled into their evening routine, the barn's cozy interior offered a comforting respite from the day's excitement. The soft glow of a few strategically placed lamps cast a warm, inviting light over the room, and the scent of cinnamon from the day's fair lingered in the air, blending with the earthy aroma of the barn.

Mia wrapped herself in a knitted blanket, sinking into a comfortable armchair by the fireplace. Ethan, ever attentive, made his way to the kitchen to prepare some hot cider, a tradition they had started to enjoy together. The crackling of the fire and the gentle clinking of mugs filled the space with a sense of calm and contentment.

Ethan returned with two steaming mugs, handing one to Mia before sitting down beside her. "Here you go. A little something to help us wind down after a busy day."

"Thank you," Mia said, her voice warm with appreciation. She took a sip of the cider, savoring its spiced sweetness. "This is perfect."

They sat in comfortable silence for a moment, simply enjoying each other's company. Mia's thoughts drifted back to the fair, the way the town had come alive with energy and joy, and the way Ethan had been her rock throughout the day. It was a day she would remember fondly, a reminder of the love and support that surrounded her.

Eventually, Ethan broke the silence, his voice soft but serious. "Mia, I've been thinking about something."

She turned to him, her curiosity piqued. "What is it?"

Ethan hesitated for a moment, his brow furrowing as he chose his words carefully. "I know we've been focusing on the present and the future, but I think it's important that we also take a moment to address the past—specifically, the things we still need to work through, both individually and together."

Mia's heart skipped a beat. She knew that the past was something they both carried with them, but hearing Ethan bring it up so directly made it feel more immediate. "What do you have in mind?"

Ethan set his mug down and took her hands in his, his gaze steady and earnest. "I think we need to talk about what we've been through—both the good and the difficult. We need to make sure we're on the same page about where we've been and where we want to go. It's not about dwelling on the past but about understanding it so we can move forward with clarity."

Mia nodded slowly, appreciating Ethan's honesty and the thoughtfulness behind his words. "I agree. It's important for us to be open and honest with each other. We've both had our share of struggles and experiences that have shaped us, and it's crucial that we acknowledge and understand them."

Ethan squeezed her hands gently, his touch reassuring. "Exactly. I want us to be strong together, and that means being willing to face our fears and insecurities, no matter how difficult it may be."

Mia took a deep breath, her mind racing with the weight of their shared history. "Okay. Let's talk about it. We don't have to go through everything all at once, but I think it's important that we start somewhere."

They spent the next hour talking about their pasts—sharing memories, regrets, and hopes. Mia spoke about her complicated relationship with her father, the challenges she had faced in the city, and the fears she had about her future. Ethan opened up about his own struggles, his past heartbreaks, and his journey to find his place in the world.

As they spoke, they found solace in each other's understanding and empathy. It wasn't always easy to revisit old wounds, but the act of sharing and listening brought them closer together, strengthening their bond.

By the time they finished their conversation, the fire had died down to a gentle glow, and the barn was enveloped in a peaceful silence. Mia felt a sense of relief and clarity, as if a weight had been lifted from her shoulders. The past was still a part of her, but it no longer felt as burdensome.

Ethan wrapped an arm around her, pulling her close. "Thank you for being so open and honest with me. I know it wasn't easy, but I think it was necessary."

Mia leaned into him, her heart full. "Thank you for initiating the conversation. I feel like we're in a better place now, and I'm grateful for your support."

They sat together in the quiet, the warmth of the fire and each other's presence creating a sense of comfort and safety. The night was a reminder that while their pasts would always be a part of them, their future was something they could shape together.

As they prepared for bed, Mia felt a renewed sense of hope and determination. The journey ahead might still have its challenges, but with Ethan by her side, she felt ready to face them.

They climbed into bed, the soft rustling of the sheets and the gentle hum of the night creating a soothing backdrop. As Mia closed her eyes, she whispered a silent promise to herself and to Ethan—that they would continue to face their fears, embrace their past, and build a future filled with love and understanding.

The shadows of their past might always linger, but in the light of their shared commitment and love, Mia knew that they could overcome anything and find their way to a bright and fulfilling future.

As the days of autumn unfolded, Mia and Ethan grew even closer, their relationship deepening with each shared experience and honest conversation. The Fall Fair had been a turning point, a celebration of their renewed connection and a reminder of the community that had always been a part of Mia's life.

One chilly morning, with frost glistening on the fields, Mia awoke with a sense of anticipation. Today marked the beginning of a new project—one she and Ethan had been discussing for weeks. They were going to start a community garden, an idea that had been inspired by their love for the land and their desire to contribute something meaningful to Willow Creek.

Mia made her way to the kitchen, where Ethan was already at work, preparing breakfast. The smell of freshly brewed coffee and sizzling bacon filled the air, adding a cozy touch to the crisp morning.

"Good morning," Mia said, sliding into a chair at the kitchen table.

"Morning," Ethan replied with a smile. "I figured you'd be up early today. Are you excited about the garden?"

"Absolutely," Mia said, her eyes lighting up. "I've been thinking about it a lot. It feels like a way to give back to the community and make a difference, even in a small way."

Ethan set a plate of bacon and eggs in front of her, his gaze filled with warmth. "I think it's a great idea. And it'll be a fun project for us to work on together."

They enjoyed their breakfast together, discussing their plans for the garden. The vision was simple but ambitious—a shared space where community members could grow their own fruits, vegetables, and flowers. They hoped it would foster a sense of camaraderie and provide a tangible way for people to connect with the land and each other.

After breakfast, they bundled up in warm jackets and gloves, ready to tackle the day's tasks. The first step was to clear the designated area—a plot of land adjacent to the barn that had once been a small, overgrown field.

With shovels and rakes in hand, they set to work. The crisp air and physical labor were invigorating, and they found themselves laughing and chatting as they dug and cleared the debris. The work was hard but satisfying, and they made significant progress by midday.

As they took a break, sitting on a nearby log and sipping from their water bottles, Mia looked around at the cleared space with a sense of accomplishment. "I can already picture it," she said, her voice filled with excitement. "Rows of plants, vibrant colors, and a lot of hard work paying off."

Ethan smiled, his eyes reflecting the same enthusiasm. "It's going to be amazing. And it's going to bring a lot of joy to the community. I can't wait to see it all come together."

They spent the rest of the day working on the garden, their efforts fueled by the shared vision of what it could become. As the sun began to set, casting a warm glow over the land, they took a moment to stand back and admire their progress.

"Not bad for one day's work," Ethan said, wrapping an arm around Mia's shoulders.

"Not bad at all," Mia agreed, leaning into him. "I'm really proud of what we've accomplished today."

As they made their way back to the barn, the evening chill began to set in, and they enjoyed the peaceful quiet of the twilight. They were tired but satisfied, their sense of accomplishment enhancing their already deep connection.

Later that evening, as they prepared dinner together, the kitchen was filled with laughter and the aroma of a hearty meal. The day's hard work had only strengthened their bond, and they relished the simple joy of being together, sharing their hopes and dreams for the future.

As they sat down to eat, Ethan took Mia's hand across the table. "I've been thinking about us, about where we're headed. I know we've made great strides, but I want to make sure we're both on the same page about our future."

Mia looked at him, her heart full. "What do you mean?"

Ethan's expression was thoughtful as he spoke. "I want us to continue building something meaningful together. The garden is just the beginning. I see so much potential in our future—our life here, our relationship, and our contributions to the community. I want to make sure we're both committed to that vision."

Mia smiled, her eyes shining with affection. "I am committed. I want to build a life here with you, to be part of this community and create something lasting. I'm excited about our future and everything we can achieve together."

Ethan's face lit up with a broad smile, his eyes reflecting the same excitement. "Me too. I think we're creating something really special, and I'm grateful for every step we take together."

They spent the rest of the evening discussing their plans and dreams, their conversation filled with laughter and love. As they settled into bed that night, Mia felt a deep sense of contentment and anticipation for what lay ahead.

The journey they had embarked on was far from over, but with each passing day, they were building a foundation for a future filled with hope and possibility. The shadows of the past might still linger, but they were learning to navigate them with grace and strength, guided by the light of their shared commitment and love.

As Mia closed her eyes, she whispered a silent thanks for the journey they were on, for the love they shared, and for the promise of a bright and fulfilling future. With Ethan by her side, she knew that they could face whatever came their way, one step at a time.

The days continued to blend seamlessly into one another, with the garden project becoming a focal point of Mia and Ethan's lives. Each morning, they awoke with a sense of purpose, ready to tackle the next stage of their endeavor. The garden was steadily taking shape, and the community's excitement was palpable. Neighbors were stopping by to offer their support, and some had even volunteered to help with planting and maintenance.

One particularly crisp afternoon, as they were planting rows of seedlings, Mia noticed a group of children from the local elementary school watching from the edge of the garden. Their faces were pressed against the fence, eyes wide with curiosity.

Ethan glanced up and saw them too. "Looks like we have some young admirers," he said with a chuckle.

Mia smiled and waved at the children. "Why don't we invite them in to help? It could be a fun learning experience for them."

Ethan agreed, and they made their way over to the fence. "Hey there, would you all like to come help us with the garden?"

The children's faces lit up with excitement as they clamored to get closer. A teacher, who had been standing with them, approached with a smile. "I think that's a wonderful idea. The kids have been eager to learn more about gardening."

Mia and Ethan set up small gardening stations for the children, teaching them how to plant seeds and explaining the importance of taking care of plants. The kids were enthusiastic and eager to get their hands dirty, their laughter and chatter filling the air.

As they worked alongside the children, Mia felt a renewed sense of purpose. The garden was becoming more than just a project—it was a way to connect with the community, to share knowledge, and to foster a sense of collective effort.

As the afternoon wore on, the children's teacher thanked Mia and Ethan for the opportunity, and the kids waved goodbye, their hands smeared with soil but their smiles bright and cheerful.

"That was a lot of fun," Ethan said as they watched the children leave. "It's amazing how a simple project can bring so much joy."

Mia nodded, her heart warmed by the experience. "It really is. I'm glad we decided to do this. It's more than just planting a garden—it's about creating something meaningful and sharing it with others."

The weeks continued to pass with a steady rhythm, the garden flourishing under their care. Mia and Ethan were spending more time together, finding joy in the little things and appreciating the progress they were making.

One evening, as they were finishing up for the day, Mia received a call from her mother, who had been visiting relatives in another state. Her mother's voice was tinged with excitement as she spoke.

"Mia, I have some news," she said. "Your father called me earlier today. He's planning to come back to Willow Creek for a while. He wants to reconnect with you."

Mia's heart skipped a beat at the news. The thought of her father returning stirred up a mix of emotions—apprehension, hope, and a lingering sense of uncertainty.

"I'm not sure how I feel about it," Mia admitted. "We've made some progress, but it's still a lot to process."

Her mother's voice was reassuring. "I understand. Just remember that people change, and sometimes, second chances can lead to something wonderful. Keep an open mind, and try to see it as an opportunity."

Mia nodded, even though her mother couldn't see her. "I'll try. Thanks for letting me know."

As she hung up, she turned to Ethan, who had been listening quietly. "My dad is coming back to Willow Creek. He wants to reconnect."

Ethan reached out and took her hand, his expression supportive. "How do you feel about it?"

Mia sighed, her emotions swirling. "I don't know. I want to be open to the possibility, but I'm also afraid of being hurt again."

Ethan squeezed her hand gently. "Whatever happens, I'm here for you. We'll face it together."

Mia smiled, grateful for Ethan's unwavering support. "Thank you. I really appreciate that."

The days leading up to her father's arrival were a whirlwind of preparation and reflection. Mia found herself thinking a lot about their past, the moments of joy and pain, and the potential for healing. She wanted to approach the situation with an open heart, but the uncertainty lingered.

When the day finally arrived, Mia stood at the edge of the driveway, her heart pounding as she watched her father's car pull up. The same sleek, black sedan that had always seemed so out of place in Willow Creek. As the car came to a stop, her father stepped out, looking as composed and polished as ever.

He approached Mia with a tentative smile, his eyes filled with a mix of emotions. "Mia," he said, his voice soft. "It's good to see you."

Mia swallowed hard, her throat dry. "Hi, Dad."

They embraced briefly, and for a moment, everything felt strangely familiar and distant all at once. As they stood together on the porch, Mia could feel the weight of the past pressing in on them, but there was also a glimmer of hope—a chance for something new, something better.

With Ethan by her side, ready to support her, Mia felt a sense of resolve. The past might still cast its shadows, but she was determined to face them with courage and openness. As she prepared to navigate this new chapter with her father, she knew that she had the strength and the support to embrace whatever came next.

Together, Mia and Ethan continued their journey, step by step, finding joy in the simple moments and strength in their shared commitment. The garden, the community, and the promise of a renewed connection with her father were all part of the evolving tapestry of their lives, each thread weaving together to create a future full of possibility and hope.

Chapter 8: Unspoken Truths

The Fall Fair continued into the evening, the festive atmosphere becoming even more vibrant as twilight descended upon Willow Creek. Lanterns lit up the town square, casting a soft, golden glow over the bustling crowd. The local band played upbeat tunes, and couples danced under the stars, their laughter echoing through the night.

Mia and Ethan wandered through the fair, enjoying the lively atmosphere. But as the night wore on, Mia felt a subtle tension building between them—a tension she couldn't quite place but knew she needed to address.

They eventually found themselves near the old oak tree at the edge of the square, the same tree where they had shared so many childhood memories. It was quieter here, away from the noise and excitement of the fair, and Mia felt a familiar sense of peace as they sat down beneath the tree.

Ethan leaned against the trunk, gazing up at the stars, his expression thoughtful. Mia watched him for a moment, studying the lines of his face, the way his eyes reflected the light of the lanterns. She had always loved this about him—his quiet strength, his ability to find calm in the midst of chaos.

But tonight, there was something different in his demeanor, a weight in his silence that made her heart ache.

"Ethan," she began softly, breaking the silence. "Is something on your mind?"

He looked at her then, his eyes filled with an emotion she couldn't quite decipher. "Mia, there's something I need to tell you. Something I've been holding back."

Mia's heart skipped a beat, a sense of unease settling in her chest. "What is it?"

Ethan took a deep breath, his gaze never leaving hers. "It's about why I stayed in Willow Creek all these years, why I never left after you did."

Mia frowned, confusion mixing with curiosity. "I always thought it was because of your family, your love for this town."

"That's part of it," Ethan admitted, his voice tinged with a sadness that Mia hadn't heard before. "But it's not the whole story. The truth is... I stayed because of you."

Mia's breath caught in her throat, a rush of emotions flooding her senses. "Because of me? What do you mean?"

Ethan looked away, his jaw tightening as he struggled to find the right words. "When you left, Mia, it broke me. I didn't know how to move on, how to let go of everything we had. I thought that if I stayed here, if I kept the memories of us alive, maybe one day you'd come back, and we could pick up where we left off."

Mia felt tears prick at her eyes, her heart breaking at the pain in his voice. She had never realized how much her departure had affected him, how deeply he had held onto the hope of their reunion.

"I'm so sorry, Ethan," she whispered, her voice trembling. "I never wanted to hurt you."

"I know," Ethan said, his tone gentle but firm. "And I don't blame you for leaving. You had your reasons, and I respect that. But what I didn't realize until recently was that by holding onto the past, I was stopping myself from moving forward, from finding happiness again."

Mia's tears began to fall, but she didn't try to stop them. She reached out, taking Ethan's hand in hers, her grip firm and reassuring. "We both made mistakes, Ethan. We both held onto things we should have let go of. But we're here now, and we have a chance to start over."

Ethan's eyes softened, and he squeezed her hand in return. "I want that, Mia. I want to start over, with you. But I need you to know that I'm not the same person I was back then. I've changed, and I know you have too."

Mia nodded, understanding the weight of his words. "I've changed a lot, Ethan. I'm still figuring out who I am, what I want. But I know one thing for sure—I want to be with you. I want to see where this goes, whatever it takes."

Ethan's expression lightened, a small smile playing at the corners of his mouth. "Then let's take that leap, together."

Mia smiled through her tears, feeling a surge of hope and determination. The road ahead wasn't going to be easy—there were still so many unspoken truths, so many wounds that needed healing. But for the first time in a long time, she felt ready to face it all, with Ethan by her side.

They sat there for a while longer, their hands intertwined, the sounds of the fair fading into the background as they talked about their hopes, their fears, and the future they wanted to build together. It was a conversation they had needed for a long time, one that opened the door to a deeper understanding of each other.

As the night grew darker and the fair began to wind down, Mia and Ethan made their way back to the heart of the square. The crowd had thinned, and the lanterns cast long shadows on the cobblestone streets. But the warmth of the evening remained, wrapping around them like a comforting embrace.

When they reached Mia's house, Ethan walked her to the door, their steps slow and unhurried, as if they were reluctant to end the night. They stood on the porch, the night air cool against their skin, the silence between them filled with unspoken promises.

"I'll see you tomorrow?" Ethan asked, his voice gentle, his eyes searching hers.

Mia nodded, her heart full. "Definitely."

Ethan leaned down, pressing a soft, lingering kiss to her lips. It was a kiss filled with hope, with the promise of new beginnings, and it left Mia feeling breathless and alive.

"Goodnight, Mia," he whispered as he pulled away, his thumb brushing lightly over her cheek.

"Goodnight, Ethan," she replied, her voice barely above a whisper.

She watched as he walked down the steps and into the night, his figure gradually fading into the shadows. But as she turned to go inside, Mia knew that the darkness no longer held the same fear it once did. There was light ahead—uncertain, yes, but warm and welcoming, and she was ready to embrace it.

For the first time in years, Mia felt a sense of peace as she closed the door behind her, the promise of tomorrow bright in her mind.

Mia's heart still fluttered with the remnants of their conversation as she prepared for bed. The words Ethan had shared, the vulnerability in his eyes, had opened a new chapter in their relationship—one filled with the potential for healing and growth.

In the quiet of her room, Mia replayed their conversation in her mind. The revelations, the shared emotions, and the newfound understanding between them created a mosaic of hope and possibility. She felt a mixture of relief and anticipation, knowing that they had both taken a significant step toward building something meaningful together.

As she lay in bed, her thoughts wandered to the future—what it might hold for her and Ethan. They had both experienced pain and loss, but their willingness to confront their past and embrace the future together was a testament to their strength and commitment.

The next morning, the sun rose with a golden hue, casting a warm glow over Willow Creek. Mia awoke with a sense of optimism, the events of the previous night fresh in her mind. She had planned to meet Ethan later in the day, but for now, she wanted to start the day with a sense of purpose.

She spent the morning in her garden, tending to the plants and enjoying the peace that came with nature. The garden had become a symbol of renewal and growth for her, a place where she could find solace and clarity. As she worked, she thought about the conversation with Ethan and the path they were forging together.

By late morning, Mia headed into town to run some errands and prepare for her meeting with Ethan. The Fall Fair had left the town buzzing with excitement, and she found herself caught up in the festive spirit. The streets were adorned with colorful decorations, and the scent of freshly baked goods filled the air.

She stopped by the local bakery to pick up some pastries for their meeting, the warm, inviting aroma of cinnamon and sugar making her smile. As she was about to leave, she ran into Sarah, who was browsing through the store's selection.

"Mia! Good to see you," Sarah said, her face lighting up with a friendly smile.

"Hi, Sarah," Mia replied, returning the smile. "I'm just grabbing some treats for Ethan and me. We're going to spend some time together later."

Sarah's eyes sparkled with curiosity. "That sounds lovely. How are things going between you two?"

Mia hesitated for a moment, then said, "We've had some important conversations recently. We're trying to navigate our past and figure out how to move forward together."

Sarah nodded, her expression thoughtful. "That sounds like a significant step. Relationships can be complicated, but it's good to hear that you're working through things. If you ever need someone to talk to, I'm here."

Mia appreciated Sarah's offer, feeling grateful for the support. "Thank you, Sarah. I might take you up on that."

With the pastries in hand, Mia made her way to the café where she and Ethan had agreed to meet. It was a charming little spot with cozy tables and a welcoming atmosphere. As she arrived, she saw Ethan already seated at a table near the window, his eyes scanning the room until they landed on her.

He stood up, his smile broadening as she approached. "Good morning, Mia."

"Good morning, Ethan," she replied, her heart fluttering at the sight of him. She placed the pastries on the table and sat down across from him.

Ethan looked at the treats with a grin. "I see you've come prepared. What do we have here?"

"Just some pastries from the bakery," Mia said, returning his smile. "I thought it would be a nice touch for our meeting."

They chatted as they enjoyed their pastries, the conversation flowing easily. Ethan was attentive, his focus entirely on Mia, and she found herself opening up about her feelings and the changes she had been experiencing. The connection between them was stronger than ever, the walls they had once built slowly coming down.

As they finished their treats, Ethan took a deep breath, his expression turning serious. "There's something else I've been thinking about, Mia. It's about the future."

Mia's heart skipped a beat, a mixture of excitement and apprehension filling her. "What do you mean?"

Ethan reached across the table, taking her hand in his. "I know we've been focusing on our past and working through things, but I want to talk about what comes next. I want us to plan for our future, not just for the moment."

Mia looked into his eyes, seeing the sincerity and determination there. "I want that too, Ethan. I want us to build a future together, whatever it may look like."

Ethan's smile was warm and reassuring. "Then let's start talking about it. Let's think about what we want, what we're both hoping for."

Mia nodded, feeling a surge of excitement. "I'd like that. Let's take the time to really plan and dream about our future."

They spent the rest of the afternoon discussing their hopes and aspirations, talking about their dreams for the future and how they envisioned their life together. It was a conversation filled with possibility, and as they spoke, Mia felt a renewed sense of clarity and purpose.

When the time came to part ways, they both felt a sense of fulfillment and anticipation. The journey ahead was still uncertain, but the commitment they had made to each other was a source of strength and hope.

As Mia walked home, she felt a deep sense of gratitude for the path she was on. The unspoken truths had been shared, and their relationship had grown stronger as a result. The future was now a canvas waiting to be painted, and she was ready to embrace it, step by step, with Ethan by her side.

As Mia made her way home, the afternoon sun cast long shadows across the town, creating a warm and serene atmosphere. The conversations she and Ethan had shared felt like a new beginning, a promise of growth and mutual understanding. Despite the uncertainties that lay ahead, Mia was filled with a sense of optimism and excitement about their future.

She decided to take a stroll through Willow Creek before heading back to her house. The town had a way of calming her, its familiar sights and sounds reminding her of the deep connections she had with this place and its people. As she walked along the tree-lined streets, she couldn't help but think about the journey she and Ethan had embarked upon.

The path leading to the old library, a favorite childhood spot of hers, caught her eye. The library, with its quaint brick exterior and ivy-clad walls, had always been a refuge for Mia. On a whim, she decided to stop by, hoping the serenity of the library's reading nook would offer her a moment of reflection.

Inside, the library was a haven of quiet and calm. The soft rustling of pages and the faint scent of old books filled the air. Mia made her way to her favorite reading corner by the large window, where sunlight streamed in, casting a gentle glow over the cozy chairs and shelves lined with books.

She sank into a comfortable chair, letting out a contented sigh as she gazed out at the sun-drenched garden outside. Her thoughts drifted back to Ethan, and she felt a pang of longing mixed with hope. Their conversation had opened her eyes to the depth of his feelings and the potential for their relationship to evolve in meaningful ways.

As she sat in reflective silence, she noticed Mrs. Thompson, the library's longtime librarian, approaching with a warm smile. Mrs. Thompson had been a staple in Mia's life growing up, and Mia had always admired her kindness and wisdom.

"Mia, dear! It's so nice to see you," Mrs. Thompson greeted her, her voice carrying the familiar comfort of home.

"Hi, Mrs. Thompson," Mia replied, returning the smile. "I was just taking a moment to reflect. It's been a busy day."

Mrs. Thompson nodded understandingly. "Sometimes, a quiet spot in the library is just what we need. Is there something on your mind?"

Mia hesitated, then decided to share a bit about her recent experiences. "Actually, yes. I've been reconnecting with someone from my past, and we've been having some important conversations about our future."

Mrs. Thompson's eyes twinkled with curiosity. "Ah, the journey of the heart can be both challenging and rewarding. It sounds like you're making some significant strides."

Mia nodded, feeling a sense of relief in sharing her thoughts. "Yes, it's been both. We've talked about our past and what we want for the future. It feels like we're building something real together, but there's still so much to navigate."

Mrs. Thompson offered a comforting smile. "Love and relationships are like a garden, Mia. They require care, patience, and understanding. Sometimes, the most beautiful blooms come from the seeds we plant with intention and hope."

Mia considered Mrs. Thompson's words, finding solace in the analogy. "That's a lovely way to put it. I guess I'm just trying to be intentional about how we move forward."

"You're on the right path," Mrs. Thompson assured her. "Trust in the process and in each other. The journey may have its bumps, but it can also lead to something truly wonderful."

With a grateful heart, Mia thanked Mrs. Thompson and left the library, feeling a renewed sense of clarity. The wisdom of the library and its people had given her a fresh perspective on her relationship with Ethan.

As she walked back home, the setting sun painted the sky in shades of orange and pink, casting a warm glow over Willow Creek. The town seemed to embrace her with a sense of reassurance, reminding her that she was part of something larger, something meaningful.

When she arrived at her house, Mia took a moment to appreciate the quiet evening, the soft rustling of leaves outside, and the gentle hum of life in the town. She knew that the path ahead wouldn't always be smooth, but she felt prepared to face it with Ethan by her side.

Later that evening, as she sat at her kitchen table with a cup of tea, Mia decided to write in her journal. She wanted to capture her thoughts and feelings, a personal record of this pivotal moment in her life.

August 31, 2024

Today was a day of new beginnings. Ethan and I had a heart-to-heart about our past and our future, and it felt like a significant step forward. There's still so much to navigate, but the conversations we had gave me hope and clarity. I feel ready to embrace whatever comes next, knowing that we're in this together.

Mrs. Thompson reminded me that relationships, like gardens, require patience and care. Her words resonated deeply with me, and I feel more confident about our journey. I'm excited and a bit apprehensive about the future, but I know that with Ethan, I'm not alone.

Here's to new beginnings and the promise of what's to come.

As Mia closed her journal and set it aside, she felt a sense of peace settle over her. The night was still and quiet, and the promise of tomorrow seemed bright and full of possibility. With Ethan by her side, she was ready to face whatever challenges lay ahead, knowing that their journey together was just beginning.

The days following the Fall Fair were filled with a quiet, steady rhythm for Mia. Each morning, she woke to the soft sunlight filtering through her curtains, a reminder of the new chapter she was embarking on with Ethan. The conversations they had shared had deepened their connection, but Mia was also keenly aware that there were still unspoken truths and unresolved feelings to address.

One crisp morning, as the town prepared for the upcoming Harvest Festival, Mia decided to take a walk through the woods near her home. The forest had always been her sanctuary, a place where she could think and reflect without interruption. She hoped that the solitude would help her process her thoughts and emotions.

The forest trail was dappled with sunlight, the leaves crunching softly underfoot as Mia made her way deeper into the woods. She found a familiar clearing, where a small stream trickled gently over smooth stones, and settled onto a large rock at the edge of the water.

She closed her eyes for a moment, letting the sounds of the forest envelop her. The gentle murmur of the stream, the rustling of leaves, and the distant call of birds created a soothing backdrop for her thoughts.

Her mind drifted back to her conversation with Ethan under the old oak tree. It had been a turning point, but Mia knew that true healing and understanding required more than just shared words. It required facing the shadows of their past and acknowledging the pain they both carried.

Mia thought about her father's visit and the conversations they'd had. It had been a cathartic experience, but it had also brought up emotions she wasn't fully prepared to deal with. Her relationship with her father was still a source of inner conflict, and she knew that it would take time to resolve.

As she sat in contemplation, her phone buzzed with a message from Ethan. She glanced at the screen, a smile forming on her lips as she read his message:

Ethan: *Hey Mia, just wanted to check in and see how you're doing. I've been thinking about our conversation and wanted to make sure you're okay. Let me know if you'd like to talk or if you just want some company.*

Mia's heart warmed at the thoughtfulness of his message. She appreciated his support and his willingness to be there for her. She quickly typed a response:

Mia: *Hi Ethan, I'm doing okay. Just needed some time to myself to think things through. I'd love to see you later if you're free. Maybe we can talk more then?*

A few moments later, Ethan's reply came through:

Ethan: *Sounds good. How about we meet at the café this afternoon? I'll be there at 3. Looking forward to it.*

Mia felt a sense of relief and anticipation. The café had always been a special place for them, a spot where they had shared many conversations and memories. It seemed fitting that they would continue their journey of understanding there.

After her walk, Mia returned home and prepared for her meeting with Ethan. She took a moment to reflect on their relationship, acknowledging both the joy and the challenges they had faced. She wanted to be honest with him, to share her thoughts and feelings openly.

When the time came, Mia headed to the café, her heart fluttering with a mix of excitement and nervousness. The small, cozy space was filled with the aroma of freshly brewed coffee and baked goods. The soft chatter of patrons and the soothing music created a warm ambiance that felt comforting.

As Mia entered, she spotted Ethan at their usual table by the window. He looked up and smiled warmly, and Mia felt a wave of relief wash over her. She made her way to the table, her heart lightening at the sight of him.

"Hey," Mia said as she took her seat, her smile matching his.

"Hey," Ethan replied, his eyes reflecting his concern. "How are you really doing?"

Mia took a deep breath, gathering her thoughts. "I'm okay. I've been doing a lot of thinking, and I've realized that there are still some things I need to work through. It's not just about us; it's about my past and how it affects my present."

Ethan nodded, his expression serious. "I understand. I've been thinking a lot too. I want to support you, but I also need to be honest about my own feelings. I know we've made progress, but I feel like there's more we need to talk about."

Mia felt a lump in her throat, but she managed a nod. "I agree. I think we need to be open about our fears and hopes. I want us to build something strong and lasting, but I also want to make sure we're on the same page."

Ethan reached across the table, taking her hand in his. "I want that too, Mia. I want us to be honest with each other, to face our fears together. I'm here for you, no matter what."

Mia's eyes filled with tears, but she smiled through them. "Thank you, Ethan. It means a lot to me. I know this journey won't be easy, but I'm committed to it. I'm committed to us."

As they talked, they delved into their hopes and fears, their dreams for the future, and their commitment to facing their challenges together. It was a conversation that brought them closer, deepening their connection and reinforcing their bond.

When they finally left the café, the sun was beginning to set, casting a golden glow over Willow Creek. Mia and Ethan walked side by side, their hands intertwined, feeling a renewed sense of unity and purpose.

As they reached Mia's house, Ethan paused, turning to face her with a serious but hopeful expression. "I know we have a lot to work through, but I believe in us. I believe in our future."

Mia nodded, her heart full of gratitude and hope. "I believe in us too, Ethan. Let's take it one step at a time and build the future we want."

They shared a tender kiss, a promise of their commitment to each other, and as Ethan walked away, Mia felt a profound sense of peace. She knew that the path ahead would have its challenges, but with Ethan by her side, she was ready to face whatever came their way.

As she closed the door behind her and prepared for the evening, Mia felt a renewed sense of purpose and excitement. The journey was far from over, but she was ready to embrace it with open arms, knowing that she and Ethan were building something truly special together.

Mia spent the evening reflecting on her conversation with Ethan, feeling a renewed sense of optimism. Their talk at the café had brought clarity and reassurance. She was grateful for Ethan's unwavering support and his willingness to work through their challenges together.

The next morning, as the sun began to warm Willow Creek, Mia decided to visit the town's library. The library had always been a haven for her—a place of solace and discovery. She felt it would be the perfect setting to clear her mind and maybe even gain some new insights into her ongoing journey of self-discovery.

The library was quiet, the kind of tranquility that only a space filled with books could offer. Mia made her way to a cozy corner, nestled between tall shelves of novels and old manuscripts. She picked out a few books on personal growth and relationships, hoping to find some guidance and perspective.

As she settled into a comfortable armchair, she began reading a book on emotional healing. The words resonated deeply with her, offering new perspectives on dealing with past traumas and building a healthy, fulfilling relationship. She highlighted passages and made notes, feeling a sense of empowerment with each page.

Just as she was getting lost in her reading, she heard the soft rustle of someone approaching. Looking up, she saw Sarah standing at the end of the aisle, a friendly smile on her face.

"Mia! I didn't expect to see you here," Sarah said, walking over to her. "I was just dropping off some books. Mind if I join you?"

Mia smiled back, feeling a warm sense of familiarity. "Of course, Sarah. I'd love the company."

Sarah settled into the chair opposite Mia, glancing curiously at the book she was reading. "What's got you so engrossed?"

Mia closed the book and looked at Sarah, her expression thoughtful. "I've been doing a lot of thinking lately—about my past, my future, and my relationship with Ethan. I'm trying to understand myself better and figure out how to move forward."

Sarah nodded, her eyes reflecting understanding. "That sounds like an important journey. If you ever want to talk or need support, I'm here for you."

Mia's heart warmed at Sarah's offer. "Thank you, Sarah. That means a lot to me."

They spent the next hour chatting about everything from Mia's personal reflections to the upcoming Harvest Festival. Sarah's presence was comforting, a reminder that she wasn't alone in her journey.

As they left the library, Sarah suggested grabbing lunch at the local diner. "I've heard they have some new dishes on the menu. What do you say?"

Mia agreed, appreciating the chance to spend more time with Sarah and enjoy a change of scenery. They headed to the diner, where they indulged in hearty sandwiches and shared stories of their recent experiences.

Over lunch, Sarah mentioned that she had been working on a community project aimed at revitalizing the town's historical landmarks. "We're trying to preserve some of the old buildings and create a space for local events and gatherings. I think it could be a great addition to Willow Creek."

Mia's interest was piqued. "That sounds amazing. I'd love to help out if there's anything I can do."

Sarah's eyes lit up. "That would be fantastic! We're always looking for volunteers. I'll send you the details."

As they finished their meal and parted ways, Mia felt a renewed sense of purpose. Her conversation with Ethan and her time with Sarah had given her a clearer sense of direction and a deeper connection to the community she had returned to.

Later that afternoon, as Mia walked back to her house, she noticed a small crowd gathering in front of the town hall. Curious, she approached and found that the town was holding a meeting to discuss the upcoming Harvest Festival and other community events.

She joined the gathering, listening to the discussions and feeling a sense of belonging. The people of Willow Creek were passionate and dedicated to making their town a vibrant and welcoming place.

Mia felt a growing desire to be an active part of this community and contribute in any way she could.

As the meeting wrapped up, Mia caught sight of Ethan, who had also been attending. He came over to her with a smile. "I didn't know you were coming to the meeting."

Mia returned his smile, feeling a sense of warmth and connection. "I just wanted to see what's going on and get involved. There's so much happening, and I want to be a part of it."

Ethan's eyes shone with approval. "I'm glad to hear that. It's great to see you so engaged. How about we grab a coffee and talk about our plans for the festival?"

Mia agreed, and they walked together to a nearby café. As they sipped their coffee and discussed their ideas for the festival, Mia felt a deep sense of contentment. She was building something meaningful in Willow Creek, not just with Ethan, but with the community that had welcomed her back.

As the sun began to set, casting a golden hue over the town, Mia knew that her journey was far from over. But she was ready to face whatever challenges lay ahead, with Ethan by her side and the support of her friends and community. For the first time in a long time, she felt truly at home.

With a renewed sense of purpose and excitement, Mia embraced the future, knowing that it held the promise of new beginnings and the opportunity to create a life filled with love, connection, and fulfillment.

Chapter 9: A Shift in the Wind

The next morning, the crisp autumn air greeted Mia as she stepped outside onto her porch. The remnants of last night's fair were being cleared away by early risers, the town slowly returning to its quiet rhythm. She wrapped her arms around herself, the warmth of Ethan's kiss still lingering on her lips.

Mia had always loved mornings in Willow Creek. The town had a way of waking up slowly, as if it knew there was no need to rush. She could hear the faint chatter of her neighbors, the sound of birdsong in the distance, and the rustle of leaves in the breeze. It was peaceful, almost idyllic, but today it felt different—like the calm before a storm.

She made her way to the diner, hoping to grab a coffee and maybe some time to think. The bell above the door chimed as she entered, and she was immediately greeted by the warm scent of freshly brewed coffee and the sight of familiar faces. It was a place where everyone knew everyone, and that sense of community had always made her feel at home.

"Mia! Over here!"

She turned to see Liz waving from a corner booth. Liz had been one of her closest friends growing up, and their friendship had rekindled since Mia's return. With her bright smile and infectious energy, Liz was a force of nature, always bringing light to any situation.

Mia smiled and walked over, sliding into the booth across from Liz. "Morning," she greeted.

"Morning! You look... different today. Like you're glowing or something. What happened?"

Mia chuckled, feeling a slight blush creep up her cheeks. "Nothing much, just had a good night, that's all."

Liz raised an eyebrow, a mischievous grin spreading across her face. "Uh-huh. A good night with a certain someone, perhaps?"

Mia rolled her eyes but couldn't suppress her smile. "Maybe."

"Come on, spill the details! It's about time something exciting happened around here."

Mia hesitated, the memory of last night still fresh in her mind. She wanted to share everything with Liz, but part of her wanted to keep those moments between her and Ethan, at least for now. "We just talked," she said finally. "Really talked, you know? About the past, about where we're headed. It felt... important."

Liz's expression softened, and she reached across the table to squeeze Mia's hand. "I'm happy for you, Mia. You deserve to be happy."

"Thanks, Liz," Mia replied, feeling a warmth spread through her chest. "It's still a work in progress, but I think we're getting there."

They spent the next hour catching up, their conversation flowing easily as they discussed everything from the fair to the latest town gossip. But even as they talked, Mia couldn't shake the feeling that something was brewing just beneath the surface, something that would soon demand her attention.

After leaving the diner, Mia decided to take a walk through town. She needed to clear her head, to process everything that had happened in the last few days. The streets were quiet, the leaves crunching beneath her boots as she walked, her thoughts swirling.

As she turned down Main Street, she spotted a figure standing in front of the town's old library. It was William, her father. He was leaning against the stone steps, his hands in his pockets, looking out at the town with a contemplative expression.

Mia felt a pang of emotion at the sight of him. Their last conversation had been heavy, filled with unresolved tension and unspoken words. She had hoped for a little more time before facing him again, but it seemed that life had other plans.

Taking a deep breath, she approached him. "Dad?"

William turned to her, his face lighting up with a small, but genuine smile. "Mia. I was hoping I'd run into you."

"What are you doing here?" she asked, trying to keep her tone neutral.

"Just thinking," he said, looking back at the town. "This place holds a lot of memories. Some good, some not so much."

Mia nodded, understanding all too well what he meant. "Do you want to talk about it?"

He sighed, his shoulders sagging slightly. "I don't know. There's a lot to say, but I'm not sure where to start."

Mia felt her heart clench. She knew that whatever her father needed to say would be difficult, but she also knew that it was necessary. "Start wherever you need to, Dad. I'm here to listen."

William looked at her, his eyes filled with a mix of regret and resolve. "I've made a lot of mistakes, Mia. I know that. I wasn't the father you needed, and I wasn't there for you when it mattered most. I was too wrapped up in my own world, in my own pain, to see what I was doing to you and your mother."

Mia felt a lump form in her throat. This was the conversation she had been dreading, yet also hoping for. "We all made mistakes," she said quietly. "But we can't change the past. We can only try to move forward."

"I know," William replied, his voice thick with emotion. "And I want to move forward, Mia. I want to make things right between us, but I don't know how. I'm scared that I've lost you for good."

Mia took a deep breath, the weight of his words settling over her. She had spent so many years harboring resentment, anger, and sadness toward her father, but in that moment, she realized that she didn't want to carry that burden anymore. She wanted to heal, to let go of the past, and to find a way to rebuild their relationship.

"You haven't lost me," she said softly. "But it's going to take time, Dad. We can't fix everything overnight, but we can try. We can take it one step at a time, just like I'm doing with everything else."

William's eyes glistened with unshed tears, and he nodded, a look of relief washing over him. "I'd like that, Mia. I'd like that a lot."

They stood there for a while, side by side, as the town of Willow Creek continued to move around them. It was a small step, but it was a step in the right direction, and for the first time in a long time, Mia felt a sense of hope when it came to her relationship with her father.

As they parted ways, Mia felt a shift within herself—a sense that things were finally starting to change, to move forward. She knew there would be more challenges ahead, more difficult conversations and moments of doubt, but she also knew that she wasn't alone. She had Ethan, she had Liz, and now, perhaps, she was starting to have her father again.

The wind picked up slightly as she walked back home, rustling the leaves around her, as if the town itself was whispering promises of new beginnings. Mia smiled to herself, feeling that promise in her heart. Whatever storms lay ahead, she was ready to face them—with the people she loved by her side.

The next few days brought a flurry of activity to Willow Creek as preparations for the Harvest Festival ramped up. Mia threw herself into helping with the festival preparations, her days filled with decorating, organizing events, and coordinating with volunteers. The bustling energy of the town was infectious, and she found herself enjoying the camaraderie and sense of purpose that came with working alongside her neighbors.

Ethan was a constant presence during the preparations, his enthusiasm and dedication evident in every task he took on. They spent long hours together, sometimes working side by side, other times discussing plans and ideas over coffee or during brief breaks. Their renewed connection was palpable, their conversations filled with a blend of shared goals and personal revelations.

One afternoon, as they were setting up booths for the festival, Ethan took a moment to look around and then turned to Mia. "You know, this festival has always been a big deal for the town, but it feels even more special this year. Maybe it's because it's our first big event together."

Mia smiled, her heart swelling at his words. "I think you're right. There's something magical about this year. It feels like everything is falling into place."

Ethan nodded, his expression thoughtful. "I've been thinking a lot about what we talked about—the future and everything we want. I want us to have a real chance, Mia. I want us to build something lasting together."

Mia's heart skipped a beat at his words. "I want that too, Ethan. I want us to be a part of each other's lives in a meaningful way. I know it won't always be easy, but I'm ready to face it all with you."

Ethan reached out and took her hand, giving it a reassuring squeeze. "I'm glad we're on the same page. I think we've both learned a lot about ourselves and each other. And I'm excited about what's next."

Their conversation was interrupted by a call from Liz, who was standing by the festival stage, waving energetically. "Mia, Ethan! We need your help with the stage decorations!"

They hurried over to help, their tasks involving hanging lights and arranging flowers. As they worked, the sun began to dip toward the horizon, casting a warm golden glow over the town. The festival was starting to take shape, and the excitement in the air was palpable.

Later that evening, as the final touches were being added and the first festival-goers began to arrive, Mia took a moment to step back and admire the transformation. The town square had been transformed into a festive wonderland, with colorful banners, twinkling lights, and the smell of delicious food wafting through the air.

As she stood there, she noticed her father approaching, looking a bit nervous but determined. He had been helping out with the festival's setup, and Mia had seen him working alongside other townsfolk. It was a small but significant step toward reconnecting with him.

"Hey, Dad," Mia said, approaching him with a warm smile. "You've done a great job with the decorations."

William looked at her with a mix of gratitude and apprehension. "Thanks, Mia. I've been trying to do my part. I hope it's okay that I'm here."

"It's more than okay," Mia replied, her heart swelling with a mix of emotions. "I'm really glad you're here. It means a lot to me."

They spent the evening together, mingling with the other townsfolk and enjoying the festival. Mia felt a sense of contentment as she watched her father interact with her friends and neighbors, his presence a symbol of the progress they were making in their relationship.

As the night wore on, Ethan joined Mia and her father at a small table near the stage. The festival's festivities were in full swing, with music, laughter, and the glow of lanterns illuminating the square.

"You know," Ethan said, glancing around at the lively scene, "this town has a way of making everything feel right. It's like the magic of the Harvest Festival brings out the best in all of us."

Mia nodded, feeling the warmth of the evening and the connections around her. "I think you're right. It's moments like these that remind us of what really matters—community, love, and the chance to start fresh."

As they sat there, enjoying the festival and each other's company, Mia felt a profound sense of peace. The past was still a part of her, but it no longer held the same power over her. She was ready to embrace the future, to build a life filled with hope and possibility.

The Harvest Festival was a celebration of the season, but for Mia, it was also a celebration of new beginnings and the strength of the connections she was rebuilding. The town's vibrant energy mirrored her own sense of renewal, and as she looked around at the smiling faces and the joyful atmosphere, she knew that Willow Creek was where she belonged.

With Ethan by her side, her father beginning to reconnect with her, and her friends surrounding her, Mia felt that she was finally on the right path. Whatever challenges lay ahead, she was ready to face them with an open heart and a hopeful spirit.

As the festival continued into the night, Mia danced with Ethan under the stars, their laughter mingling with the music. The wind carried away the remnants of doubt and uncertainty, leaving behind a sense of optimism and possibility.

For the first time in a long while, Mia felt truly at home, surrounded by the people she loved and a future filled with promise.

As the evening wore on, the festival continued to buzz with energy. The laughter of children playing games, the hum of conversations, and the sweet melodies from the local band created a vibrant tapestry of sound. Mia and Ethan found themselves caught up in the joy of the night, dancing and mingling with friends, their earlier conversation about the future lingering in their minds.

The night sky was clear, the stars twinkling brightly above them. The cool autumn air felt refreshing against their skin, a perfect complement to the warmth of the festival atmosphere. The lanterns hanging from the trees and the strings of lights overhead added a magical glow to the scene, making everything seem just a little bit more enchanting.

At one point, Mia noticed Liz approaching with a mischievous grin. "Mia, Ethan! We've got something special planned for tonight. You have to come see!"

Curious, Mia and Ethan followed Liz to a makeshift stage where the community talent show was about to begin. The stage was decorated with autumn leaves and fairy lights, and the crowd gathered in anticipation.

Liz turned to them, her eyes twinkling with excitement. "We're going to start the evening with a special performance from a local band, and then we have a surprise act. I promise you won't want to miss it!"

As the band began to play, the crowd erupted in applause, their excitement palpable. The music was lively, and people began to dance and sing along. Mia felt a sense of euphoria as she joined in, her worries momentarily forgotten in the rhythm of the evening.

The surprise act turned out to be a group of local kids performing a charming rendition of a classic song. Their enthusiasm and energy were infectious, and the crowd cheered them on with enthusiasm. Mia watched with a smile, her heart swelling with pride for her town.

As the night progressed, Ethan pulled Mia aside, leading her to a quieter corner of the festival grounds. "I have something I've been meaning to give you," he said, his voice soft.

Mia looked at him, her curiosity piqued. "What is it?"

Ethan reached into his pocket and pulled out a small, velvet box. He opened it to reveal a delicate locket, intricately designed with a small photograph inside.

"This was my grandmother's," Ethan explained, his eyes meeting hers. "I've had it for years, and I wanted to give it to you. It's a symbol of the past, but also of the future I hope we can build together."

Mia's breath caught in her throat as she took the locket in her hands. The gesture was incredibly touching, and she could feel the weight of its significance. "It's beautiful, Ethan. Thank you."

Ethan smiled, his expression tender. "I know we've had our ups and downs, but I believe in us. I believe in what we have and what we can build together. I wanted you to have something that represents that."

Mia looked down at the locket, her heart full of emotion. She could see herself wearing it, a tangible reminder of their journey and the promise of their future. "I'll treasure it always," she said softly.

As they stood there, the festival lights casting a warm glow around them, Mia felt a deep sense of contentment. The night had been filled with moments of joy, reflection, and connection, and she felt more certain than ever about the path she was on.

The sound of the band's final song floated through the air, and Mia and Ethan joined the crowd for one last dance. As they moved together, Mia realized how much had changed in her life since returning to Willow Creek. The town had embraced her with open arms, and she had found healing and hope in unexpected places.

When the festival finally began to wind down, Mia and Ethan walked back to the heart of the square, where the crowd had started to disperse. The lanterns were dimming, and the cool night air felt crisp and invigorating.

"Tonight was amazing," Ethan said, his voice filled with warmth. "Thank you for being a part of it with me."

Mia smiled, her heart swelling with gratitude. "Thank you for everything, Ethan. For the locket, for the support, and for reminding me of what truly matters."

They reached the edge of the square, where the first hints of dawn were beginning to appear on the horizon. The quiet of the early morning was a stark contrast to the lively festival, and it felt like a new beginning.

As they said their goodbyes and Ethan walked her home, Mia felt a renewed sense of hope and purpose. The festival had been a celebration of more than just the season—it had been a celebration of new beginnings, of healing, and of the deep connections that made life meaningful.

Mia closed her door behind her and leaned against it, her mind still buzzing from the night's events. The festival had been a reminder of the beauty of life's simple moments and the power of community.

She walked to her window and looked out at the quiet streets of Willow Creek, the first rays of sunlight beginning to cast a soft glow over the town. The promise of a new day was filled with endless possibilities, and Mia felt ready to embrace whatever lay ahead.

With the support of Ethan, the rekindling of her relationship with her father, and the strength of her community, Mia knew she was on the right path. The road ahead would be filled with challenges and uncertainties, but she was prepared to face them with courage and hope.

As she turned away from the window and prepared for the day ahead, Mia felt a profound sense of peace. Whatever storms might come, she knew she had the strength to weather them and the love to guide her through.

And with that thought, Mia embraced the new day, ready to continue her journey with an open heart and a hopeful spirit.

The sun rose over Willow Creek with a gentle, golden light that promised a beautiful day. Mia woke up feeling refreshed, her heart lighter than it had been in a long time. She stretched, taking a deep breath as she gazed out the window at the serene morning. The crisp autumn air seemed to carry the echoes of last night's festival, mingling with the faint scent of freshly baked bread from the nearby bakery.

After a quick breakfast, Mia decided to take a walk through town, hoping to clear her mind and enjoy the tranquility of the early morning. The streets were still quiet, the town's hustle and bustle not yet in full swing. As she wandered past the charming storefronts and flower boxes bursting with color, she felt a renewed sense of connection to her hometown.

She found herself drawn toward the park at the edge of town, a place she used to visit often as a child. The park was bathed in the soft light of morning, the trees casting long, dappled shadows across the grass. Mia sat on a bench near the pond, watching the ducks glide across the water, and allowed herself to simply be in the moment.

As she sat there, lost in her thoughts, her phone buzzed with a message. It was from Liz.

Liz: *"Hey Mia! Just wanted to check in and see how you're doing this morning. Any chance you're up for a brunch date? I have some news to share!"*

Mia's curiosity was piqued. She quickly replied, agreeing to meet Liz at their favorite café. As she made her way there, her mind wandered to the events of the previous evening. The festival, the heartfelt conversation with Ethan, and the meaningful moment with her father had all left her feeling optimistic about the future.

The café was bustling with activity when Mia arrived. Liz was already seated at a corner table, a look of excitement on her face. She waved eagerly as Mia approached.

"Good morning!" Liz greeted her with a bright smile. "I'm so glad you could make it."

"Morning!" Mia replied, taking a seat across from Liz. "What's the news?"

Liz's eyes sparkled with enthusiasm. "You remember how I was talking about starting a new project? Well, I've finally decided to open my own art studio here in Willow Creek!"

Mia's eyes widened in surprise and delight. "That's incredible, Liz! Congratulations!"

"Thanks!" Liz said, beaming. "I've been working on the plans for a while, and everything's finally falling into place. The studio will be a place for local artists to showcase their work, hold workshops, and just have a space to create. I'm really excited about it."

Mia could see the passion in Liz's eyes and felt a surge of pride for her friend. "That's such a fantastic idea. Willow Creek is going to benefit so much from having a place like that."

Liz nodded, her excitement palpable. "I think so too. And I want you to be involved, Mia. I've been thinking about having a small section of the studio dedicated to community events and gatherings. Maybe you could help with organizing some of them."

Mia felt a warm glow at the thought. "I'd love to help. It sounds like a wonderful opportunity to give back to the community and bring people together."

They spent the next hour discussing Liz's plans and brainstorming ideas for the studio. The conversation flowed easily, filled with laughter and excitement. It was a welcome distraction from Mia's recent emotional turmoil and a reminder of the supportive friendships she had in Willow Creek.

As they finished their brunch and prepared to part ways, Liz gave Mia a heartfelt hug. "Thanks for being so supportive, Mia. I really appreciate it."

"Anytime," Mia replied, her smile genuine. "I'm looking forward to seeing the studio come to life."

After saying their goodbyes, Mia felt a renewed sense of purpose and optimism. The morning had been a reminder of the importance of following one's passions and supporting friends in their endeavors.

On her way back home, Mia passed by the town square where the remnants of the festival were being cleaned up. The square looked different in the daylight—less magical but still charming. She noticed a few people setting up for a community meeting that would take place later in the day.

Mia's thoughts turned to her father and their recent conversation. She knew there was still a long way to go in rebuilding their relationship, but the fact that they had taken the first step together gave her hope. The day's events had reinforced her belief in the power of community and the importance of facing challenges with an open heart.

When she returned home, she found a message from Ethan, inviting her to join him for a walk in the park later that afternoon.

She eagerly accepted, looking forward to spending more time with him and continuing their journey together.

The rest of the day was spent preparing for the community meeting and taking care of small tasks around the house. As the afternoon approached, Mia felt a sense of anticipation. She was excited to catch up with Ethan and see where their relationship would lead next.

When the time came, Mia met Ethan at the park. The sun was beginning to set, casting a golden hue over the landscape. They walked side by side, enjoying the peacefulness of the park and the beauty of the autumn scenery.

As they reached a secluded spot by the pond, Ethan turned to her, his expression thoughtful. "I've been thinking a lot about what we talked about the other night. About our future and where we're headed."

Mia looked at him, her heart fluttering with a mix of hope and uncertainty. "Me too. I think we're both ready to move forward, but it's going to take time and effort."

Ethan nodded, taking her hand in his. "I'm willing to put in that effort, Mia. I believe in what we have, and I want to build a future together, one step at a time."

Mia squeezed his hand, feeling a surge of warmth. "I believe in us too. Let's take it slow and enjoy the journey."

As they stood there, hand in hand, the sun dipped below the horizon, casting a soft, golden light over the park. The moment felt perfect—a quiet pause in the midst of their busy lives, a chance to reflect on their progress and look forward to the future.

With a deep sense of contentment, Mia and Ethan continued their walk, savoring the tranquility of the evening and the promise of new beginnings. The road ahead might be uncertain, but they were ready to face it together, with hope in their hearts and a shared vision for the future.

As the sky darkened and the stars began to emerge, Mia and Ethan continued their walk through the park, the evening air crisp and invigorating. They talked about their dreams and hopes for the future, sharing their fears and the things they were excited about. The conversation flowed easily, their connection deepening with each passing moment.

Ethan eventually steered them toward a small gazebo nestled among the trees. It was a favorite spot of theirs from when they were younger, a place where they had shared countless conversations and stolen moments. The gazebo was now illuminated by a few string lights that twinkled like stars, casting a soft, romantic glow.

They stepped inside and took a seat on the wooden bench, the gentle rustling of leaves and distant sounds of the town providing a soothing backdrop. Ethan turned to Mia, his expression serious yet tender.

"I've been thinking a lot about us," he began, his voice soft. "And I want to make sure we're on the same page. We both know there's a lot we need to work through, but I also want to make sure we're building something real, something that will last."

Mia looked at him, her heart swelling with affection. "I feel the same way, Ethan. I want us to be honest with each other and to keep working on our relationship. We've both changed, and it's important that we understand each other's needs and expectations."

Ethan nodded, taking a deep breath. "There's something I've been meaning to tell you, something I've been holding back because I wasn't sure how to say it."

Mia's curiosity was piqued, and she gave him her full attention. "What is it?"

Ethan hesitated for a moment before continuing. "I've been offered a job opportunity. It's a great position with a company I've always admired. But it's in another city, and I'm torn about what to do. I want to pursue this chance, but I also don't want to jeopardize what we're building together."

Mia's heart sank at the news. She had hoped for a future where they would be together in Willow Creek, but she understood the significance of Ethan's opportunity. "That's a big decision, Ethan. Have you had a chance to think about what you really want?"

Ethan sighed, his eyes filled with a mix of hope and uncertainty. "I have. And while the job is a fantastic opportunity, I keep coming back to the idea of being with you. I don't want to make any decisions that would put our relationship at risk."

Mia felt a surge of emotion, a mix of sadness and hope. She reached out and took Ethan's hand, squeezing it gently. "I want you to follow your dreams, Ethan. I want you to be happy and fulfilled. But I also want us to find a way to make our relationship work, no matter where life takes us."

Ethan looked at her with gratitude and admiration. "I'm so lucky to have you in my life, Mia. Your support means everything to me. I want to work through this together, to find a balance between our individual dreams and our relationship."

They sat in silence for a moment, each lost in their thoughts. The soft glow of the lights and the peaceful surroundings provided a comforting backdrop to their conversation.

Mia finally broke the silence. "How about we take some time to think things through? We can both consider what we want and what we're willing to compromise on. We don't have to make any decisions right away."

Ethan nodded, a look of relief on his face. "That sounds like a good plan. I appreciate your understanding, Mia. It means a lot to me."

They shared a tender kiss, the warmth of their connection providing comfort and reassurance. As they pulled away, Mia felt a renewed sense of determination. They were facing a significant challenge, but they were facing it together, and that made all the difference.

The evening continued with gentle conversation and moments of shared laughter. As they walked back through the park, hand in hand, Mia felt a deep sense of peace. She knew that the path ahead would be filled with uncertainties, but she also knew that they had the strength and love to navigate whatever came their way.

When they reached the edge of the park, Ethan turned to Mia, his eyes filled with affection. "Thank you for being so understanding. I'm looking forward to figuring things out with you."

Mia smiled, her heart full. "Me too, Ethan. We'll get through this, together."

They parted ways at the entrance to the park, their steps light and hopeful. As Mia walked home, she reflected on the evening and the important conversations they had shared. She felt a sense of clarity and determination, knowing that whatever challenges lay ahead, she and Ethan would face them with love and commitment.

The night air was cool and refreshing as she arrived at her doorstep. She took one last look at the peaceful town, feeling a renewed sense of hope and optimism. The future was uncertain, but it was filled with possibilities, and Mia was ready to embrace it all with open arms.

Chapter 10: Echoes of the Past

The next few days passed in a blur of routine and quiet moments. Mia found herself settling into a rhythm in Willow Creek that felt almost natural, as if the town itself was slowly welcoming her back. She spent her mornings writing at the kitchen table, the sunlight streaming through the window as she poured her thoughts onto the page. The afternoons were for wandering the familiar streets, reconnecting with old friends, and rediscovering the little nooks and crannies of the town she had once called home.

Ethan was a constant presence in her life, but they didn't rush things. After their heart-to-heart under the oak tree, they both seemed to understand that they needed to take their time, to rebuild their relationship piece by piece. They went on quiet walks, shared meals, and simply enjoyed each other's company without the pressure of defining what they were just yet.

But even in the midst of this newfound peace, there were moments when Mia couldn't escape the echoes of her past. One afternoon, as she was walking along the edge of Willow Creek's small lake, she caught sight of a figure she hadn't seen in years. Her heart skipped a beat as she recognized Sarah Jennings, her best friend from high school.

Sarah had always been the life of the party, with a laugh that could light up a room and a spirit that refused to be tamed. They had been inseparable once, sharing secrets, dreams, and heartaches during those formative years. But after Mia left town, they had drifted apart, their lives taking them in different directions.

Mia hesitated, unsure whether to approach Sarah or keep walking. But Sarah had already spotted her, and a bright smile spread across her face as she waved.

"Mia Prescott! Is that really you?"

Mia couldn't help but smile back, the familiarity of Sarah's voice tugging at something deep within her. "Sarah Jennings, in the flesh."

They met halfway, hugging each other tightly as if the years hadn't passed at all. When they pulled back, Sarah studied Mia with a look of genuine surprise.

"You look amazing," Sarah said, her tone filled with warmth. "What brings you back to Willow Creek?"

Mia shrugged, trying to keep her voice light. "A little soul-searching, I guess. I needed to reconnect with this place, and with myself."

Sarah nodded, understanding flashing in her eyes. "I get it. A lot's changed since you left, but some things stay the same, you know?"

They walked along the lake, falling into an easy conversation. Sarah updated Mia on the latest town gossip, the new shops that had opened, and the people who had come and gone. Mia found herself laughing at Sarah's stories, the sense of familiarity and connection bringing a comfort she hadn't realized she missed.

But as they walked, the conversation inevitably turned to the past.

"Do you ever think about those days?" Sarah asked quietly, her gaze fixed on the shimmering surface of the lake. "The things we did, the plans we made?"

Mia nodded, a bittersweet smile tugging at her lips. "All the time. It feels like a lifetime ago, but also like it was just yesterday."

Sarah sighed, a wistful look in her eyes. "I miss it sometimes. The simplicity of it all, before life got so complicated."

"Yeah," Mia agreed, her thoughts drifting to those carefree days of youth, when the future had seemed wide open and full of promise. "But we can't go back, can we? We've all changed."

Sarah looked at her then, a serious expression on her face. "You've really changed, Mia. I can see it. You're not the same girl who left Willow Creek all those years ago."

Mia met her gaze, feeling a mix of emotions. "Neither are you, Sarah. We've both grown up, faced our own challenges. But that doesn't mean we can't find new ways to be in each other's lives."

Sarah smiled, her eyes softening. "I'd like that. I've missed having you around, Mia."

"I've missed you too," Mia admitted, feeling a warmth spread through her chest. "Maybe we can start over, just like everything else."

They walked in silence for a while, the sounds of nature filling the space between them. It was a comfortable silence, one that spoke of understanding and a shared history. For the first time since her return, Mia felt like she was truly reconnecting with her past, finding a way to blend it with her present.

As the sun began to dip toward the horizon, casting a golden glow over the lake, Mia felt a sense of peace settle over her. The echoes of the past were still there, but they no longer haunted her. Instead, they felt like gentle reminders of where she had come from, and how far she had come.

When they finally parted ways, Mia felt lighter, as if a weight she hadn't realized she was carrying had been lifted. Reconnecting with Sarah had been more than just a walk down memory lane—it had been a reminder that she didn't have to leave her past behind to move forward. She could carry it with her, shaping her present and future in ways she had never imagined.

As she walked home, the evening air cool against her skin, Mia's thoughts turned to Ethan, to her father, to the life she was slowly rebuilding in Willow Creek. There was still so much work to be done, so many conversations to be had, but for the first time, she felt ready to face it all.

That night, as she settled into bed, Mia reflected on the day's events. She had come back to Willow Creek in search of something she couldn't quite name, but now, she felt like she was starting to find it. It wasn't just about healing old wounds or rekindling old relationships—it was about finding herself again, and allowing herself to grow into the person she was always meant to be.

With that thought, Mia drifted off to sleep, a contented smile on her lips. For the first time in a long time, she felt like she was exactly where she was supposed to be.

The days following her reunion with Sarah felt like a turning point for Mia. She embraced the routine of her life in Willow Creek with a new sense of purpose. Each morning, she found herself more attuned to the subtle changes in the town, the way the seasons were shifting, and the rhythm of her own heart.

One afternoon, as she sat in her favorite spot at the local café, working on her novel, her phone buzzed with a message from Ethan. It was a simple, but heartfelt note: *"Thinking of you. Can we meet at our spot tonight?"* Her heart fluttered at the thought of their special place, the old oak tree that had witnessed many of their shared moments.

Later that evening, Mia made her way to the park. The sun was setting, casting a warm, golden light over the landscape. She felt a mixture of excitement and nervousness as she approached the oak tree. Ethan was already there, standing beneath the sprawling branches, his silhouette framed by the fading light.

"Hey," Mia greeted softly as she walked up to him.

Ethan turned, a smile spreading across his face. "Hi, Mia."

They settled onto the blanket he had laid out, a picnic of sorts prepared with simple, yet thoughtful touches. The soft glow of lanterns he had strung up around the tree added to the intimate atmosphere. Ethan poured them each a glass of wine, and they clinked glasses in a quiet toast.

"I wanted to talk," Ethan began after a few moments of comfortable silence. "About what we discussed the other night."

Mia looked at him, her heart racing. "Okay. What's on your mind?"

Ethan took a deep breath, his gaze meeting hers with sincerity. "I've been thinking a lot about my job offer. It's a fantastic opportunity, but it's clear that it's pulling me away from Willow Creek. And it's pulling me away from us."

Mia felt a pang of uncertainty but maintained a hopeful expression. "What are you thinking about doing?"

"I've realized that no matter how great the job is, it's not worth losing what we have," Ethan said, his voice filled with conviction. "I want to make this work with you, Mia. I want us to build a future together, here, in Willow Creek."

Mia's eyes softened, and she felt tears prickling at the corners. "Are you saying you're going to turn down the job?"

Ethan nodded. "Yes. I've decided that I want to stay here, to be with you. I'm not sure what that means for my career in the long run, but right now, this—being with you—is what matters most."

Mia was overwhelmed with emotion. She reached out and took Ethan's hand, her voice trembling slightly. "That means so much to me, Ethan. I've been struggling with the idea of losing you, but hearing you say this... it gives me hope."

Ethan squeezed her hand, his own emotions evident. "I'm committed to making this work, Mia. I want to build a life with you, to face whatever comes our way together."

They spent the rest of the evening wrapped in each other's arms, talking about their dreams and the life they wanted to build. The future was still uncertain, but the promise of facing it together made everything feel possible.

As they walked back to the edge of the park, Ethan pulled Mia close and kissed her gently. It was a kiss filled with promise and love, a symbol of their renewed commitment to each other.

The next morning, Mia woke up with a sense of excitement and anticipation. The path ahead might still be filled with challenges, but she felt more prepared than ever to face them. Her relationship with Ethan was stronger than it had been before, and she had found a way to reconnect with her past and bring it into her present.

As she looked out the window at the sun rising over Willow Creek, Mia felt a deep sense of contentment. She was ready to embrace the future, to continue her journey of self-discovery and growth, and to cherish the love and connections she had in her life.

With a hopeful heart, Mia prepared for the day ahead, knowing that whatever came next, she would face it with strength and grace, surrounded by the people she loved and the town that had always been a part of her.

The days following Ethan's decision to stay in Willow Creek were filled with a renewed sense of energy for Mia. They found themselves immersing in the town's activities, embracing the small joys that came with life in Willow Creek. Their bond deepened with each passing day, and the future they were beginning to build together felt more tangible and promising.

One crisp autumn morning, Mia decided to visit the town's historical society. She had always been curious about the town's history, and now seemed like the perfect time to explore it. The small, brick building housed a collection of old photographs, artifacts, and documents that chronicled the town's past.

As Mia walked through the exhibits, she marveled at how much history lay beneath the surface of the quaint town she had come to love again. It was fascinating to see old photographs of Willow Creek, its streets bustling with people and life that seemed so different from the quiet town she now knew.

In one corner of the museum, Mia found an old photograph of her grandparents' bookstore, a place she remembered fondly from her childhood. It was a comforting sight, and she felt a wave of nostalgia wash over her.

As she studied the photo, a voice interrupted her reverie. "You've found one of the hidden gems, I see."

Mia turned to find Mr. Thompson, the town historian, standing nearby. He was a kind-faced man with a passion for local history that was contagious.

"Yes," Mia replied, her eyes still on the photograph. "I didn't realize how much history this town has."

Mr. Thompson smiled warmly. "Oh, Willow Creek has a rich history. And it's wonderful to see someone new, or rather returning, taking an interest in it."

Mia chuckled. "I suppose I'm a bit of both—new and returning. It's been a while since I've been back, but this place feels like home."

Mr. Thompson's eyes twinkled with understanding. "Home has a way of calling us back, doesn't it? If you're interested, we're having a community event next week, showcasing some of our most treasured artifacts and sharing stories from the past. It would be wonderful to have you join us."

Mia's interest was piqued. "I'd love to. I think it would be a great way to connect more with the town."

As she left the historical society, Mia felt a renewed sense of purpose. The thought of participating in the community event excited her, and she began to envision how she could contribute, perhaps by sharing her own experiences and memories of Willow Creek.

That evening, as Mia and Ethan enjoyed a quiet dinner at their favorite café, Mia shared her plans with him. Ethan was enthusiastic about the idea and offered to help her prepare for the event.

"I think it's great that you're diving into the history of the town," Ethan said, his eyes shining with pride. "It's a wonderful way to connect with the community and honor the past."

Mia smiled, feeling grateful for his support. "I'm really looking forward to it. It feels like a way to bring all the pieces of my life together."

In the days leading up to the event, Mia and Ethan worked side by side, organizing their contributions and preparing their own personal stories. They spent their evenings discussing their plans, and their conversations often drifted to their dreams for the future.

When the day of the community event arrived, Willow Creek was abuzz with excitement. The town square was adorned with banners and displays, and the air was filled with the scent of freshly baked goods from the local bakery. Mia and Ethan arrived early to help set up, and the atmosphere was vibrant with anticipation.

The event was a success, with many townsfolk attending and sharing their own stories. Mia found herself immersed in conversations about Willow Creek's past, discovering new facets of the town's history and connecting with people in a meaningful way.

As the day drew to a close, Mia and Ethan took a moment to re-flect on the event. They stood together, watching the sunset cast a warm glow over the town, their hearts full of contentment.

"This has been amazing," Mia said, leaning into Ethan's side. "I feel like I'm truly part of this place now, like I've come full circle."

Ethan kissed the top of her head. "You've done more than just be-come part of the town. You've brought something special to it. And I'm so proud of you."

Mia looked up at him, her heart full. "Thank you for being by my side through all of this. I couldn't have done it without you."

They stood there in comfortable silence, taking in the beauty of the evening and the quiet promise of the future. The echoes of the past, once haunting, now seemed like gentle reminders of how far Mia had come and the new path she was forging.

As they walked hand in hand back to their home, Mia felt a pro-found sense of peace. The past had shaped her, but it was the present and the future that were now guiding her forward. And with Ethan by her side, she knew that whatever came next, she was ready to face it with courage and love.

As the community event wound down and the last of the guests began to leave, Mia and Ethan lingered, helping with the final clean-up. The energy of the day lingered in the air, a tangible reminder of how vibrant Willow Creek could be when its people came together.

Mia was busy packing up the remaining artifacts when she no-ticed Sarah approaching. Sarah had stayed through most of the event, and she now walked up with a thoughtful expression.

"Hey," Sarah said, joining Mia at the table where they were fold-ing up tablecloths. "I just wanted to say how great everything was. You did an amazing job today."

Mia smiled, brushing a strand of hair from her face. "Thanks, Sarah. It was a lot of work, but it was worth it. I'm glad you could be here."

Sarah's eyes sparkled with a mix of admiration and curiosity. "You know, I've been thinking about something. We've both been reconnecting with the past lately, but I feel like there's still so much we don't know about each other's lives now."

Mia raised an eyebrow. "What do you mean?"

"Well," Sarah began, a hint of excitement in her voice, "I was thinking it might be nice to catch up properly. We should have dinner sometime, just the two of us, and really talk about where life has taken us."

Mia felt a surge of warmth at the idea. "I'd like that. It feels like there's so much to share, and it would be nice to reconnect in a more personal way."

Sarah grinned. "Great! How about tomorrow evening? We could meet at that new bistro on Elm Street. I've heard good things about it."

"It's a date," Mia agreed. "I'll see you there."

As the evening drew to a close, Mia and Ethan finished tidying up and headed home. The quiet of their small house was a stark contrast to the lively event, but it was a welcome calm. They sat together on the porch, wrapped in blankets as the temperature dropped.

"This has been quite a day," Ethan said, his voice filled with contentment. "I'm really proud of everything you've accomplished."

Mia leaned her head against his shoulder. "Thank you. I couldn't have done it without you. It feels like we're really starting to build something here, something meaningful."

Ethan nodded, his arm around her. "We are. And it's not just about the town or the event. It's about us finding our place in each other's lives again and building our future together."

Mia looked up at him, her heart full. "I know. And I'm excited about it. There's so much we can do, so much we can be together."

As they sat there, the night growing colder around them, Mia felt a deep sense of peace. The past was no longer a weight around her neck but a series of experiences that had shaped her into who she was today. And as she looked at Ethan, she knew that her future was filled with possibilities, all of which she wanted to explore with him by her side.

The next day, as Mia prepared for her dinner with Sarah, she reflected on the progress she had made. Reconnecting with her past, repairing her relationships, and embracing the future had been challenging but rewarding. She felt more centered and hopeful than she had in years.

Dressed in a cozy sweater and jeans, Mia arrived at the bistro, the warm glow of the interior inviting her in. Sarah was already there, waiting with a bright smile.

"Hey, Mia!" Sarah called out, waving her over. "You look great!"

"Thanks, Sarah," Mia replied, taking a seat. "So do you. I'm really looking forward to catching up."

The two friends chatted over a delicious meal, sharing stories about their lives since they last saw each other. Sarah talked about her career changes, her family, and her travels, while Mia shared her experiences from the city and her journey back to Willow Creek.

As they spoke, Mia felt a sense of connection and understanding with Sarah that had been missing for so long. Their conversation flowed easily, filled with laughter, nostalgia, and a genuine interest in each other's lives.

By the end of the evening, as they parted ways, Mia felt a renewed sense of gratitude for her friendships and the life she was building in Willow Creek. The echoes of the past had become a gentle hum, guiding her forward rather than holding her back.

Walking home under the starlit sky, Mia thought about all that had transpired. She was finding her way, piece by piece, and with each step, she was more certain that she was exactly where she was meant to be.

As she entered her house and prepared for bed, Mia reflected on her journey. The past, present, and future were intertwining in a beautiful tapestry, and she was ready to embrace whatever came next. With Ethan's support, her renewed friendships, and her own inner strength, Mia felt a profound sense of hope and excitement for the future.

Drifting off to sleep, she knew that tomorrow would bring new challenges and opportunities, but she was ready to face them with an open heart and a sense of purpose. For the first time in a long while, Mia felt truly at home in Willow Creek, and she couldn't wait to see what the future held.

The following morning, the soft golden light of dawn filtered through the curtains of Mia's bedroom, gently waking her from sleep. She stretched and smiled, feeling a quiet sense of anticipation for the day ahead. There was something invigorating about the new routines she was establishing in Willow Creek, and she was eager to embrace whatever came next.

After a leisurely breakfast, Mia decided to spend the morning working on her writing. She had found a comfortable nook in the corner of her living room, where the sunlight cast a warm glow on her desk. With her cup of coffee nearby and her laptop open, she began to type, her thoughts flowing freely as she worked on her latest piece.

The sound of her phone vibrating on the desk interrupted her concentration. She glanced at the screen and saw a text from Ethan.

Ethan: Hey! I'm thinking of checking out the old barn on the outskirts of town today. Want to join me?

Mia's curiosity was piqued. The old barn had been a fixture of local legend, a place of both nostalgia and mystery. It was rumored to hold hidden treasures from the past, and the thought of exploring it with Ethan sounded like a fun adventure.

Mia: That sounds like a great idea! What time were you thinking?

Ethan: How about noon? I'll meet you at the edge of town.

Mia: Perfect! See you then.

With her plans set, Mia returned to her writing, her thoughts now infused with excitement for the day's exploration. As the clock inched toward noon, she finished her work and prepared to head out.

Arriving at the edge of town, Mia saw Ethan waiting by his truck, his face lighting up when he spotted her. He waved and motioned for her to join him.

"Ready for an adventure?" Ethan asked with a grin.

"Absolutely," Mia replied, matching his enthusiasm. "I've heard so many stories about this place. I'm excited to see it for myself."

They drove along a dusty road that led to the barn. As they approached, Mia could see the large, weathered structure emerging from behind a cluster of trees. It looked as though it had been standing for decades, its wood darkened by the elements and its roof sagging under the weight of time.

Ethan parked the truck and they got out, the crunch of gravel under their feet as they approached the barn. The air was filled with the scent of earth and old wood, adding to the sense of adventure.

"Are you ready?" Ethan asked, holding the door open.

"Let's do it," Mia said, stepping inside.

The interior of the barn was dimly lit by slivers of sunlight streaming through cracks in the walls. Dust motes danced in the air, and the space was filled with the remnants of a bygone era—old farming tools, stacks of faded newspapers, and forgotten pieces of furniture.

Mia wandered through the space, her eyes scanning the old relics. She picked up a rusted tool, examining it with curiosity. "I can't believe how much history is packed into this place."

Ethan nodded, his eyes focused on a corner of the barn where an old trunk sat partially hidden by a pile of discarded blankets. "Look at that. It's like something out of a story."

They approached the trunk, and Ethan knelt down to open it. The lid creaked as it lifted, revealing a collection of vintage clothing, old letters, and various knick-knacks.

"Wow," Mia said, peering inside. "This is incredible."

Ethan carefully pulled out a bundle of letters, their edges yellowed with age. "These look like they were written a long time ago. I wonder what stories they hold."

Mia's heart raced with excitement. "Let's read them. Maybe we'll uncover some hidden history of Willow Creek."

They found a spot on the floor and began to read through the letters, their contents revealing glimpses into the lives of people from the past. The letters spoke of love, loss, and the everyday struggles of a bygone era. It was a poignant reminder of the lives that had shaped the town before them.

As they read, Mia felt a deep connection to the past, understanding more about the history of Willow Creek and the people who had lived there before her. Each letter seemed to weave a tapestry of emotions and experiences, bringing the past to life in a way she hadn't expected.

After they finished reading the letters, Ethan closed the trunk and looked at Mia with a smile. "This was amazing. I'm glad we did this together."

"Me too," Mia said, her voice filled with warmth. "It's moments like these that make me realize how much I love being back here. There's something so special about reconnecting with the past and discovering new layers of this place."

As they made their way back to the truck, Mia felt a renewed sense of appreciation for Willow Creek. The town was more than just a backdrop to her life; it was a living, breathing entity with its own stories and secrets.

The afternoon sun cast a golden glow over the landscape as they drove back to town. Mia and Ethan chatted about their discoveries, their laughter filling the truck as they reminisced about the day's adventure.

When they arrived back in town, Mia felt a sense of contentment and fulfillment. The exploration of the barn had been a reminder of the rich history that surrounded her, and it had deepened her connection to Willow Creek.

As she prepared for another evening at home, Mia reflected on the events of the day. The barn had been a tangible link to the past, and spending time with Ethan had made the experience even more meaningful. She felt a growing sense of belonging and a renewed commitment to her life in Willow Creek.

That night, as Mia settled into bed, she thought about the future. She was finding her place in the town, reconnecting with old friends, and exploring new possibilities. It was a journey of rediscovery and growth, and she was ready to embrace it all.

With a contented sigh, Mia drifted off to sleep, her dreams filled with the echoes of the past and the promise of a bright future.

The next morning, Mia awoke with a renewed sense of purpose. The thrill of discovering the old barn had left her energized and eager to continue exploring the connections she was rebuilding in Willow

Creek. She started her day with a brisk walk around the town, taking in the crisp morning air and the peaceful surroundings.

As she passed by the local market, she spotted a flyer on the community board advertising the upcoming Fall Harvest Festival. The festival was a cherished tradition in Willow Creek, celebrating the season's bounty with food, crafts, and games. It promised to be a lively event, and Mia couldn't help but feel excited about the prospect of participating.

Back at home, she decided to call Liz to see if she was interested in attending the festival together. The phone rang a few times before Liz answered, her cheerful voice greeting Mia.

"Hey, Mia! What's up?"

"Hi, Liz. I just saw the flyer for the Fall Harvest Festival. I was thinking it might be fun to go together. What do you think?"

"That sounds like a blast!" Liz responded enthusiastically. "I haven't been to the festival in ages. Count me in!"

They made plans to meet up at the festival that afternoon, and Mia spent the rest of the morning preparing. She wanted to make the most of the event, so she decided to wear something that felt festive and comfortable.

When Mia arrived at the festival grounds, the scene was vibrant with activity. Colorful booths and tents were set up, each offering a variety of local goods and treats. The aroma of freshly baked pies and roasted corn filled the air, mixing with the sounds of laughter and music.

Liz was waiting for her near the entrance, looking radiant in a cozy sweater and jeans. She waved excitedly when she saw Mia, and they quickly fell into step, their conversation flowing easily as they explored the festival.

They wandered from booth to booth, sampling homemade pastries, browsing handmade crafts, and enjoying the festive atmosphere. Mia felt a sense of joy in the simple pleasures of the day, surrounded by the community and the warmth of the season.

At one booth, they came across a local artist selling watercolor paintings of Willow Creek's landmarks. Mia paused to admire a piece depicting the old barn they had explored with Ethan. The artist, a friendly woman with a kind smile, noticed Mia's interest.

"I'm glad you like that one," the artist said. "It's one of my favorites. The barn has so much character, don't you think?"

"It does," Mia agreed. "I actually just visited it recently. It was amazing to see it up close."

The artist's eyes brightened. "That's wonderful to hear! It's a place with a lot of history. I'm always inspired by its story."

Mia and Liz continued to explore, enjoying the various activities and chatting with friends they encountered along the way. As the afternoon wore on, they found themselves near the stage where a local band was setting up for a performance.

"This is going to be great," Liz said, her eyes sparkling with anticipation. "I love live music."

Mia smiled, feeling a deep sense of contentment. The festival was everything she had hoped for and more—a perfect blend of community spirit and personal joy.

As the sun began to set, casting a golden hue over the festival, Mia's thoughts turned to Ethan. She had been looking forward to sharing this experience with him and was hoping he could join them later in the evening.

Just as the band started playing, Mia's phone buzzed with a text from Ethan.

Ethan: Hey! I just finished up some work. I'm on my way to the festival now. Can't wait to see you!

Mia's heart fluttered with excitement. **Mia: Great! I'm here with Liz. We're by the stage. See you soon!**

A short while later, Ethan arrived, his face lighting up when he spotted Mia and Liz. He greeted them with a warm hug and a smile that made Mia's heart skip a beat.

"I'm so glad I could make it," Ethan said, joining them by the stage. "This place looks incredible."

Liz gave him a playful nudge. "We're about to enjoy some live music. You're just in time for the best part."

They settled in, enjoying the music and the lively atmosphere. As they sang along and danced to the band's energetic tunes, Mia felt a deep sense of belonging. The festival had been a perfect way to immerse herself in the community and to celebrate the connections she was rekindling.

As the night wore on, the festival began to wind down. The crowd started to thin, and the lights began to dim, casting a soft glow over the remaining revelers. Mia, Ethan, and Liz decided to take a stroll around the festival grounds, savoring the last moments of the evening.

They found a quiet spot near the edge of the festival, where the sounds of the music were faint and the stars shone brightly overhead. Mia leaned against Ethan, feeling his warmth and comfort.

"This has been such a wonderful day," Mia said softly. "I'm really grateful for all of this."

Ethan kissed the top of her head. "Me too. It's been perfect."

Liz, ever the enthusiastic friend, added with a grin, "I'm glad we all had such a great time. We should make this a tradition."

As they walked back to their cars, Mia reflected on the day's events. The festival had been a celebration of community and connection, and it had been a reminder of how much she had come to appreciate Willow Creek.

The evening had also been a chance to strengthen her bond with Ethan and to enjoy the company of friends. It was moments like these that made her feel truly at home.

As she headed back to her cozy house, Mia felt a sense of peace and contentment. The echoes of the past were fading into the background, replaced by the vibrant present she was building. She knew that there would be challenges ahead, but she felt ready to face them with the support of the people she loved.

With a heart full of gratitude and a smile on her lips, Mia settled into bed, ready to embrace whatever new adventures awaited her in Willow Creek.

Chapter 11: The Road Less Traveled

Mia woke the next morning with a sense of purpose. The sunlight streamed through her bedroom window, casting a warm glow over the room, and for the first time in weeks, she didn't feel weighed down by uncertainty. The conversation with Sarah had stirred something in her—an understanding that her past didn't have to be a burden. Instead, it could be a guide, helping her navigate the present and future.

After breakfast, she decided to visit Willow Creek's old bookstore. It had been one of her favorite places growing up, a quiet sanctuary filled with the scent of worn pages and stories waiting to be discovered. She hadn't been back since returning to town, and today felt like the perfect time to reconnect with another piece of her past.

The bookstore was nestled between a bakery and a flower shop on Main Street. Its faded sign, "Pages of Time," hung above the door, and the windows were filled with displays of both new releases and beloved classics. Mia pushed the door open, the familiar chime of the bell greeting her.

Inside, the store was just as she remembered—shelves lined with books from floor to ceiling, cozy reading nooks scattered throughout, and the soft hum of quiet conversations. The smell of coffee from the small café at the back of the store wafted through the air, adding to the comforting atmosphere.

As she wandered through the aisles, running her fingers along the spines of books, Mia felt a sense of nostalgia wash over her. This place had been her refuge during those tumultuous teenage years, a place where she could escape into different worlds and forget about her troubles, even if just for a little while.

"Can I help you find something?"

Mia turned to see a woman standing behind the counter, smiling warmly at her. She was in her mid-thirties, with dark hair pulled back into a ponytail and a pair of glasses perched on her nose. There was something familiar about her, and it took Mia a moment to realize that she had gone to high school with this woman.

"Riley? Riley Matthews?"

The woman's eyes widened in recognition, and a bright smile spread across her face. "Mia Prescott! I can't believe it's you!"

They hugged, the years melting away in an instant. Riley had been a few grades ahead of Mia in school, and they had shared a few classes together. Mia remembered her as the quiet, bookish girl who always had her nose in a novel, much like herself.

"What are you doing back in Willow Creek?" Riley asked as they pulled apart.

Mia smiled, a little embarrassed. "Trying to find my way, I guess. It's been a while since I've been here, and I needed to reconnect with everything."

"Well, I'm glad you did," Riley said, her eyes shining with genuine happiness. "It's so good to see you. What have you been up to all these years?"

They spent the next hour catching up, sitting in one of the bookstore's cozy nooks with cups of coffee in hand. Riley shared how she had returned to Willow Creek after college to take over the bookstore from her parents. She had always dreamed of running it one day, and now she was living that dream.

Mia found herself sharing more about her life in the city, her struggles to find a sense of belonging, and the reasons she had returned to Willow Creek. It felt good to talk about it all, to share her story with someone who understood the unique pull of this small town.

"So, what's next for you?" Riley asked after a while, her gaze curious but kind.

Mia hesitated, the question echoing in her mind. It was something she had been asking herself every day since she arrived. But now, after reconnecting with Ethan, her father, and old friends like Sarah and Riley, she felt like she was beginning to find some answers.

"I'm not entirely sure," Mia admitted, sipping her coffee. "But I do know that I want to stay here, at least for a while. I need to figure out what this place means to me now, and how I can build a life here that feels right."

Riley nodded, understanding. "I think that's a good place to start. Willow Creek has a way of surprising you, you know? Sometimes, the answers you're looking for show up when you least expect them."

Mia smiled, feeling a sense of comfort in Riley's words. "I hope so. I'm starting to realize that coming back here was the right decision, even if I didn't know it at the time."

As they chatted, a thought began to form in Mia's mind. She had always loved writing, but she had put that passion on hold when life became too overwhelming. Being back in Willow Creek, surrounded by the familiar sights and sounds of her childhood, had rekindled that creative spark. Maybe, just maybe, it was time to start writing again—not just for herself, but as a way to connect with others.

"I've been thinking about writing," Mia said, almost to herself. "About using my experiences to create something that could help others. I don't know what it would look like yet, but I feel like it's something I need to do."

Riley's eyes lit up. "That sounds amazing, Mia. You've always had a way with words—I remember how much you loved writing in school. Maybe this is the next chapter in your story."

Mia considered the idea, feeling a sense of excitement she hadn't felt in a long time. Could she really turn her experiences into something meaningful? The thought of writing again, of pouring her heart into a project that could reach others, filled her with a sense of purpose.

"Maybe it is," Mia said, smiling. "Maybe it's time to start a new chapter."

As they finished their coffee and said their goodbyes, Mia left the bookstore with a sense of determination. The road ahead was still uncertain, but for the first time in a long while, she felt like she was on the right path. The idea of writing again filled her with a sense of excitement and hope—a way to take everything she had been through and turn it into something beautiful.

The rest of the day passed in a blur as Mia mulled over the possibilities. She spent the afternoon jotting down ideas, letting her thoughts flow freely onto the pages of a notebook she found tucked away in a drawer. It felt good to write again, to let her emotions take shape in words.

That evening, as she sat on the porch, watching the sun dip below the horizon, Mia felt a sense of peace settle over her. The future was still uncertain, but she no longer felt lost. She was finding her way, one step at a time, and that was enough for now.

As the first stars began to twinkle in the sky, Mia made a silent promise to herself—to embrace the journey ahead, to trust in the process, and to allow herself to be open to whatever life had in store. She was ready to take the road less traveled, and wherever it led, she knew she wouldn't be walking it alone.

Mia woke the next morning with a sense of purpose. The sunlight streamed through her bedroom window, casting a warm glow over the room. For the first time in weeks, she felt unburdened by uncertainty. The conversation with Sarah had sparked a realization—her past could be a guide, not a burden. It could help her navigate the present and future.

After breakfast, Mia decided to visit Willow Creek's old bookstore. It had been a sanctuary for her growing up, a quiet haven filled with the scent of worn pages and stories waiting to be discovered. She hadn't been back since returning to town, and today seemed like the perfect time to reconnect with a cherished piece of her past.

The bookstore, nestled between a bakery and a flower shop on Main Street, had a faded sign that read "Pages of Time." Mia pushed open the door, greeted by the familiar chime of the bell.

Inside, the store was as she remembered—shelves lined with books from floor to ceiling, cozy reading nooks scattered throughout, and the soft hum of quiet conversations. The smell of coffee from the small café at the back of the store added to the comforting atmosphere.

As she wandered through the aisles, running her fingers along the spines of the books, Mia felt a wave of nostalgia. This place had been her refuge during those turbulent teenage years, a place where she could escape into different worlds and forget her troubles, if only for a little while.

"Can I help you find something?"

Mia turned to see a woman standing behind the counter, smiling warmly. She was in her mid-thirties, with dark hair pulled back into a ponytail and glasses perched on her nose. Mia realized with a start that she had gone to high school with this woman.

"Riley? Riley Matthews?"

Riley's eyes widened in recognition, and a bright smile spread across her face. "Mia Prescott! I can't believe it's you!"

They hugged, the years melting away in an instant. Riley had been a few grades ahead of Mia in school, a quiet, bookish girl who had always had her nose in a novel, much like Mia.

"What are you doing back in Willow Creek?" Riley asked, pulling back to study Mia with curiosity.

Mia smiled, feeling a bit shy. "Trying to find my way, I guess. It's been a while since I've been here, and I needed to reconnect with everything."

"Well, I'm glad you did," Riley said, her eyes shining with genuine happiness. "It's so good to see you. What have you been up to all these years?"

They spent the next hour catching up in one of the bookstore's cozy nooks, each with a cup of coffee in hand. Riley shared how she had returned to Willow Creek after college to take over the bookstore from her parents. It had always been her dream, and now she was living it.

Mia talked about her life in the city, her struggles, and the reasons for her return to Willow Creek. It was comforting to share her story with someone who understood the town's unique pull.

"So, what's next for you?" Riley asked after a while, her gaze kind but probing.

Mia hesitated, the question resonating deeply within her. It was something she had been asking herself daily since her return. But after reconnecting with Ethan, her father, Sarah, and Riley, she felt like she was beginning to find some answers.

"I'm not entirely sure," Mia admitted, sipping her coffee. "But I do know that I want to stay here, at least for a while. I need to figure out what this place means to me now and how I can build a life here that feels right."

Riley nodded, understanding. "I think that's a good place to start. Willow Creek has a way of surprising you. Sometimes, the answers you're looking for show up when you least expect them."

Mia smiled, feeling comforted by Riley's words. "I hope so. I'm starting to realize that coming back here was the right decision, even if I didn't know it at the time."

As they chatted, a thought began to form in Mia's mind. She had always loved writing but had put that passion on hold when life became overwhelming. Being back in Willow Creek, surrounded by familiar sights and sounds, had rekindled that creative spark. Maybe it was time to start writing again—not just for herself, but as a way to connect with others.

"I've been thinking about writing," Mia said, almost to herself. "About using my experiences to create something that could help others. I don't know what it would look like yet, but I feel like it's something I need to do."

Riley's eyes lit up. "That sounds amazing, Mia. You've always had a way with words—I remember how much you loved writing in school. Maybe this is the next chapter in your story."

Mia considered the idea, feeling a surge of excitement. Could she turn her experiences into something meaningful? The thought of writing again, of pouring her heart into a project that could reach others, filled her with purpose.

"Maybe it is," Mia said, smiling. "Maybe it's time to start a new chapter."

As they finished their coffee and said their goodbyes, Mia left the bookstore with a renewed sense of determination. The road ahead was still uncertain, but for the first time in a long while, she felt like she was on the right path. The idea of writing again brought her a sense of excitement and hope—a way to channel her experiences into something beautiful.

The rest of the day flew by as Mia mulled over the possibilities. She spent the afternoon jotting down ideas, letting her thoughts flow freely onto the pages of a notebook she found tucked away in a drawer. It felt invigorating to write again, to let her emotions take shape in words.

That evening, as she sat on the porch, watching the sun dip below the horizon, Mia felt a deep sense of peace. The future was still uncertain, but she no longer felt lost. She was finding her way, one step at a time, and that was enough for now.

As the first stars began to twinkle in the sky, Mia made a silent promise to herself—to embrace the journey ahead, to trust in the process, and to remain open to whatever life had in store. She was ready to take the road less traveled, and wherever it led, she knew she wouldn't be walking it alone.

Mia woke the next morning with a sense of purpose. The sunlight streamed through her bedroom window, casting a warm glow over the room. For the first time in weeks, she felt unburdened by uncertainty. The conversation with Sarah had sparked a realization—her past could be a guide, not a burden. It could help her navigate the present and future.

After breakfast, Mia decided to visit Willow Creek's old bookstore. It had been a sanctuary for her growing up, a quiet haven filled with the scent of worn pages and stories waiting to be discovered. She hadn't been back since returning to town, and today seemed like the perfect time to reconnect with a cherished piece of her past.

The bookstore, nestled between a bakery and a flower shop on Main Street, had a faded sign that read "Pages of Time." Mia pushed open the door, greeted by the familiar chime of the bell.

Inside, the store was as she remembered—shelves lined with books from floor to ceiling, cozy reading nooks scattered throughout, and the soft hum of quiet conversations. The smell of coffee from the small café at the back of the store added to the comforting atmosphere.

As she wandered through the aisles, running her fingers along the spines of the books, Mia felt a wave of nostalgia. This place had been her refuge during those turbulent teenage years, a place where she could escape into different worlds and forget her troubles, if only for a little while.

"Can I help you find something?"

Mia turned to see a woman standing behind the counter, smiling warmly. She was in her mid-thirties, with dark hair pulled back into a ponytail and glasses perched on her nose. Mia realized with a start that she had gone to high school with this woman.

"Riley? Riley Matthews?"

Riley's eyes widened in recognition, and a bright smile spread across her face. "Mia Prescott! I can't believe it's you!"

They hugged, the years melting away in an instant. Riley had been a few grades ahead of Mia in school, a quiet, bookish girl who had always had her nose in a novel, much like Mia.

"What are you doing back in Willow Creek?" Riley asked, pulling back to study Mia with curiosity.

Mia smiled, feeling a bit shy. "Trying to find my way, I guess. It's been a while since I've been here, and I needed to reconnect with everything."

"Well, I'm glad you did," Riley said, her eyes shining with genuine happiness. "It's so good to see you. What have you been up to all these years?"

They spent the next hour catching up in one of the bookstore's cozy nooks, each with a cup of coffee in hand. Riley shared how she had returned to Willow Creek after college to take over the bookstore from her parents. It had always been her dream, and now she was living it.

Mia talked about her life in the city, her struggles, and the reasons for her return to Willow Creek. It was comforting to share her story with someone who understood the town's unique pull.

"So, what's next for you?" Riley asked after a while, her gaze kind but probing.

Mia hesitated, the question resonating deeply within her. It was something she had been asking herself daily since her return. But after reconnecting with Ethan, her father, Sarah, and Riley, she felt like she was beginning to find some answers.

"I'm not entirely sure," Mia admitted, sipping her coffee. "But I do know that I want to stay here, at least for a while. I need to figure out what this place means to me now and how I can build a life here that feels right."

Riley nodded, understanding. "I think that's a good place to start. Willow Creek has a way of surprising you. Sometimes, the answers you're looking for show up when you least expect them."

Mia smiled, feeling comforted by Riley's words. "I hope so. I'm starting to realize that coming back here was the right decision, even if I didn't know it at the time."

As they chatted, a thought began to form in Mia's mind. She had always loved writing but had put that passion on hold when life became overwhelming. Being back in Willow Creek, surrounded by familiar sights and sounds, had rekindled that creative spark. Maybe it

was time to start writing again—not just for herself, but as a way to connect with others.

"I've been thinking about writing," Mia said, almost to herself. "About using my experiences to create something that could help others. I don't know what it would look like yet, but I feel like it's something I need to do."

Riley's eyes lit up. "That sounds amazing, Mia. You've always had a way with words—I remember how much you loved writing in school. Maybe this is the next chapter in your story."

Mia considered the idea, feeling a surge of excitement. Could she turn her experiences into something meaningful? The thought of writing again, of pouring her heart into a project that could reach others, filled her with purpose.

"Maybe it is," Mia said, smiling. "Maybe it's time to start a new chapter."

As they finished their coffee and said their goodbyes, Mia left the bookstore with a renewed sense of determination. The road ahead was still uncertain, but for the first time in a long while, she felt like she was on the right path. The idea of writing again brought her a sense of excitement and hope—a way to channel her experiences into something beautiful.

The rest of the day flew by as Mia mulled over the possibilities. She spent the afternoon jotting down ideas, letting her thoughts flow freely onto the pages of a notebook she found tucked away in a drawer. It felt invigorating to write again, to let her emotions take shape in words.

That evening, as she sat on the porch, watching the sun dip below the horizon, Mia felt a deep sense of peace. The future was still uncertain, but she no longer felt lost. She was finding her way, one step at a time, and that was enough for now.

As the first stars began to twinkle in the sky, Mia made a silent promise to herself—to embrace the journey ahead, to trust in the process, and to remain open to whatever life had in store. She was ready to take the road less traveled, and wherever it led, she knew she wouldn't be walking it alone.

The next few days were filled with a new rhythm for Mia. Her mornings began with a burst of creativity, as she wrote and brainstormed ideas for her new project. The quiet of the house and the serene backdrop of Willow Creek provided the perfect setting for her thoughts to flow.

In the afternoons, Mia explored different aspects of her life in Willow Creek. She visited local landmarks, engaged in conversations with the townspeople, and found herself rediscovering the charms of the town she had once called home. Each encounter seemed to weave a new thread into the tapestry of her life, adding color and depth to her understanding of what it meant to return.

Ethan remained a steadfast presence. Their relationship continued to grow organically, with shared moments of laughter, quiet conversations, and the occasional spontaneous adventure. They would walk the trails around Willow Creek, talk about their dreams and fears, and support each other in their individual journeys.

One sunny afternoon, as Mia and Ethan strolled through the town's central park, Mia shared her recent revelations with him. She told him about her newfound inspiration to write and how reconnecting with her past had given her a sense of clarity.

"That sounds amazing, Mia," Ethan said, his voice filled with encouragement. "I've always believed you had a gift with words. It's great to see you embracing it again."

Mia smiled, feeling a surge of gratitude for Ethan's support. "Thanks, Ethan. It feels like a fresh start, like I'm finally aligning my past experiences with my present."

As they walked hand in hand, the afternoon sun casting a warm glow over the park, Mia couldn't help but reflect on how much had changed since her return to Willow Creek. The road less traveled had not only led her back to her roots but had also opened up new possibilities she had never imagined.

The next step in her journey was clear—she would continue to write, explore her creative passions, and build connections with the people around her. The road ahead was still filled with uncertainties, but Mia felt equipped to face whatever came her way.

That evening, as Mia sat by her writing desk, the soft glow of the lamp illuminating her notebook, she felt a deep sense of contentment. She was ready to embrace her journey, knowing that each step, no matter how uncertain, was a step toward discovering who she truly was.

With a renewed sense of purpose and a heart full of hope, Mia continued to write, her words flowing like a river of dreams and possibilities. The road less traveled had led her to a place of self-discovery and growth, and she was excited to see where it would take her next.

Mia woke the next morning with a sense of purpose. The sunlight streamed through her bedroom window, casting a warm glow over the room. For the first time in weeks, she felt unburdened by uncertainty. The conversation with Sarah had sparked a realization—her past could be a guide, not a burden. It could help her navigate the present and future.

After breakfast, Mia decided to visit Willow Creek's old bookstore. It had been a sanctuary for her growing up, a quiet haven filled with the scent of worn pages and stories waiting to be discovered. She hadn't been back since returning to town, and today seemed like the perfect time to reconnect with a cherished piece of her past.

The bookstore, nestled between a bakery and a flower shop on Main Street, had a faded sign that read "Pages of Time." Mia pushed open the door, greeted by the familiar chime of the bell.

Inside, the store was as she remembered—shelves lined with books from floor to ceiling, cozy reading nooks scattered throughout, and the soft hum of quiet conversations. The smell of coffee from the small café at the back of the store added to the comforting atmosphere.

As she wandered through the aisles, running her fingers along the spines of the books, Mia felt a wave of nostalgia. This place had been her refuge during those turbulent teenage years, a place where she could escape into different worlds and forget her troubles, if only for a little while.

"Can I help you find something?"

Mia turned to see a woman standing behind the counter, smiling warmly. She was in her mid-thirties, with dark hair pulled back into a ponytail and glasses perched on her nose. Mia realized with a start that she had gone to high school with this woman.

"Riley? Riley Matthews?"

Riley's eyes widened in recognition, and a bright smile spread across her face. "Mia Prescott! I can't believe it's you!"

They hugged, the years melting away in an instant. Riley had been a few grades ahead of Mia in school, a quiet, bookish girl who had always had her nose in a novel, much like Mia.

"What are you doing back in Willow Creek?" Riley asked, pulling back to study Mia with curiosity.

Mia smiled, feeling a bit shy. "Trying to find my way, I guess. It's been a while since I've been here, and I needed to reconnect with everything."

"Well, I'm glad you did," Riley said, her eyes shining with genuine happiness. "It's so good to see you. What have you been up to all these years?"

They spent the next hour catching up in one of the bookstore's cozy nooks, each with a cup of coffee in hand. Riley shared how she had returned to Willow Creek after college to take over the bookstore from her parents. It had always been her dream, and now she was living it.

Mia talked about her life in the city, her struggles, and the reasons for her return to Willow Creek. It was comforting to share her story with someone who understood the town's unique pull.

"So, what's next for you?" Riley asked after a while, her gaze kind but probing.

Mia hesitated, the question resonating deeply within her. It was something she had been asking herself daily since her return. But after reconnecting with Ethan, her father, Sarah, and Riley, she felt like she was beginning to find some answers.

"I'm not entirely sure," Mia admitted, sipping her coffee. "But I do know that I want to stay here, at least for a while. I need to figure out what this place means to me now and how I can build a life here that feels right."

Riley nodded, understanding. "I think that's a good place to start. Willow Creek has a way of surprising you. Sometimes, the answers you're looking for show up when you least expect them."

Mia smiled, feeling comforted by Riley's words. "I hope so. I'm starting to realize that coming back here was the right decision, even if I didn't know it at the time."

As they chatted, a thought began to form in Mia's mind. She had always loved writing but had put that passion on hold when life became overwhelming. Being back in Willow Creek, surrounded by familiar sights and sounds, had rekindled that creative spark. Maybe it

was time to start writing again—not just for herself, but as a way to connect with others.

"I've been thinking about writing," Mia said, almost to herself. "About using my experiences to create something that could help others. I don't know what it would look like yet, but I feel like it's something I need to do."

Riley's eyes lit up. "That sounds amazing, Mia. You've always had a way with words—I remember how much you loved writing in school. Maybe this is the next chapter in your story."

Mia considered the idea, feeling a surge of excitement. Could she turn her experiences into something meaningful? The thought of writing again, of pouring her heart into a project that could reach others, filled her with purpose.

"Maybe it is," Mia said, smiling. "Maybe it's time to start a new chapter."

As they finished their coffee and said their goodbyes, Mia left the bookstore with a renewed sense of determination. The road ahead was still uncertain, but for the first time in a long while, she felt like she was on the right path. The idea of writing again brought her a sense of excitement and hope—a way to channel her experiences into something beautiful.

The rest of the day flew by as Mia mulled over the possibilities. She spent the afternoon jotting down ideas, letting her thoughts flow freely onto the pages of a notebook she found tucked away in a drawer. It felt invigorating to write again, to let her emotions take shape in words.

That evening, as she sat on the porch, watching the sun dip below the horizon, Mia felt a deep sense of peace. The future was still uncertain, but she no longer felt lost. She was finding her way, one step at a time, and that was enough for now.

As the first stars began to twinkle in the sky, Mia made a silent promise to herself—to embrace the journey ahead, to trust in the process, and to remain open to whatever life had in store. She was ready to take the road less traveled, and wherever it led, she knew she wouldn't be walking it alone.

The next few days unfolded with a new rhythm. Mia's mornings began with bursts of creativity as she wrote and brainstormed ideas for her project. The tranquility of the house and the picturesque backdrop of Willow Creek provided the perfect setting for her thoughts to flow.

In the afternoons, Mia explored different facets of her life in Willow Creek. She visited local landmarks, engaged in conversations with townspeople, and rediscovered the charms of her childhood home. Each encounter seemed to weave a new thread into the tapestry of her life, adding depth and color to her understanding of her return.

Ethan remained a constant, supportive presence. Their relationship continued to grow organically, with shared moments of laughter, quiet conversations, and the occasional spontaneous adventure. They would stroll through the trails around Willow Creek, discuss their dreams and fears, and support each other's journeys.

One sunny afternoon, as Mia and Ethan walked through the town's central park, Mia shared her recent revelations with him. She told him about her inspiration to write and how reconnecting with her past had given her a sense of clarity.

"That sounds amazing, Mia," Ethan said, his voice filled with encouragement. "I've always believed you had a gift with words. It's great to see you embracing it again."

Mia smiled, feeling a surge of gratitude for Ethan's support. "Thanks, Ethan. It feels like a fresh start, like I'm finally aligning my past experiences with my present."

As they walked hand in hand, the afternoon sun casting a warm glow over the park, Mia couldn't help but reflect on how much had changed since her return to Willow Creek. The road less traveled had not only led her back to her roots but had also opened up new possibilities she had never imagined.

The next step in her journey was clear—she would continue to write, explore her creative passions, and build connections with the people around her. The road ahead was still filled with uncertainties, but Mia felt equipped to face whatever came her way.

That evening, as Mia sat by her writing desk, the soft glow of the lamp illuminating her notebook, she felt a deep sense of contentment. She was ready to embrace her journey, knowing that each step, no matter how uncertain, was a step toward discovering who she truly was.

With a renewed sense of purpose and a heart full of hope, Mia continued to write, her words flowing like a river of dreams and possibilities. The road less traveled had led her to a place of self-discovery and growth, and she was excited to see where it would take her next.

Mia woke the next morning with a sense of purpose. The sunlight streamed through her bedroom window, casting a warm glow over the room. For the first time in weeks, she felt unburdened by uncertainty. The conversation with Sarah had sparked a realization—her past could be a guide, not a burden. It could help her navigate the present and future.

After breakfast, Mia decided to visit Willow Creek's old bookstore. It had been a sanctuary for her growing up, a quiet haven filled with the scent of worn pages and stories waiting to be discovered. She hadn't been back since returning to town, and today seemed like the perfect time to reconnect with a cherished piece of her past.

The bookstore, nestled between a bakery and a flower shop on Main Street, had a faded sign that read "Pages of Time." Mia pushed open the door, greeted by the familiar chime of the bell.

Inside, the store was as she remembered—shelves lined with books from floor to ceiling, cozy reading nooks scattered throughout, and the soft hum of quiet conversations. The smell of coffee from the small café at the back of the store added to the comforting atmosphere.

As she wandered through the aisles, running her fingers along the spines of the books, Mia felt a wave of nostalgia. This place had been her refuge during those turbulent teenage years, a place where she could escape into different worlds and forget her troubles, if only for a little while.

"Can I help you find something?"

Mia turned to see a woman standing behind the counter, smiling warmly. She was in her mid-thirties, with dark hair pulled back into a ponytail and glasses perched on her nose. Mia realized with a start that she had gone to high school with this woman.

"Riley? Riley Matthews?"

Riley's eyes widened in recognition, and a bright smile spread across her face. "Mia Prescott! I can't believe it's you!"

They hugged, the years melting away in an instant. Riley had been a few grades ahead of Mia in school, a quiet, bookish girl who had always had her nose in a novel, much like Mia.

"What are you doing back in Willow Creek?" Riley asked, pulling back to study Mia with curiosity.

Mia smiled, feeling a bit shy. "Trying to find my way, I guess. It's been a while since I've been here, and I needed to reconnect with everything."

"Well, I'm glad you did," Riley said, her eyes shining with genuine happiness. "It's so good to see you. What have you been up to all these years?"

They spent the next hour catching up in one of the bookstore's cozy nooks, each with a cup of coffee in hand. Riley shared how she had returned to Willow Creek after college to take over the bookstore from her parents. It had always been her dream, and now she was living it.

Mia talked about her life in the city, her struggles, and the reasons for her return to Willow Creek. It was comforting to share her story with someone who understood the town's unique pull.

"So, what's next for you?" Riley asked after a while, her gaze kind but probing.

Mia hesitated, the question resonating deeply within her. It was something she had been asking herself daily since her return. But after reconnecting with Ethan, her father, Sarah, and Riley, she felt like she was beginning to find some answers.

"I'm not entirely sure," Mia admitted, sipping her coffee. "But I do know that I want to stay here, at least for a while. I need to figure out what this place means to me now and how I can build a life here that feels right."

Riley nodded, understanding. "I think that's a good place to start. Willow Creek has a way of surprising you. Sometimes, the answers you're looking for show up when you least expect them."

Mia smiled, feeling comforted by Riley's words. "I hope so. I'm starting to realize that coming back here was the right decision, even if I didn't know it at the time."

As they chatted, a thought began to form in Mia's mind. She had always loved writing but had put that passion on hold when life became overwhelming. Being back in Willow Creek, surrounded by familiar sights and sounds, had rekindled that creative spark. Maybe it

was time to start writing again—not just for herself, but as a way to connect with others.

"I've been thinking about writing," Mia said, almost to herself. "About using my experiences to create something that could help others. I don't know what it would look like yet, but I feel like it's something I need to do."

Riley's eyes lit up. "That sounds amazing, Mia. You've always had a way with words—I remember how much you loved writing in school. Maybe this is the next chapter in your story."

Mia considered the idea, feeling a surge of excitement. Could she turn her experiences into something meaningful? The thought of writing again, of pouring her heart into a project that could reach others, filled her with purpose.

"Maybe it is," Mia said, smiling. "Maybe it's time to start a new chapter."

As they finished their coffee and said their goodbyes, Mia left the bookstore with a renewed sense of determination. The road ahead was still uncertain, but for the first time in a long while, she felt like she was on the right path. The idea of writing again brought her a sense of excitement and hope—a way to channel her experiences into something beautiful.

The rest of the day flew by as Mia mulled over the possibilities. She spent the afternoon jotting down ideas, letting her thoughts flow freely onto the pages of a notebook she found tucked away in a drawer. It felt invigorating to write again, to let her emotions take shape in words.

That evening, as Mia sat on the porch, watching the sun dip below the horizon, she felt a deep sense of peace. The future was still uncertain, but she no longer felt lost. She was finding her way, one step at a time, and that was enough for now.

As the first stars began to twinkle in the sky, Mia made a silent promise to herself—to embrace the journey ahead, to trust in the process, and to remain open to whatever life had in store. She was ready to take the road less traveled, and wherever it led, she knew she wouldn't be walking it alone.

The following morning, Mia met with Ethan at the park for their usual walk. The crisp autumn air was invigorating, and the vibrant colors of the leaves added a touch of magic to their surroundings. As they strolled along the path, Mia shared her thoughts about writing and how it felt like a new beginning.

"It sounds like you've really found something that resonates with you," Ethan said, his voice warm and encouraging. "I'm really glad for you. I think it's great that you're following your passion."

Mia smiled, feeling a surge of gratitude for Ethan's unwavering support. "Thanks, Ethan. It means a lot to me to have you in my corner."

They continued their walk, discussing their dreams and hopes for the future. Mia found herself opening up more than she ever had before, sharing her fears and aspirations with Ethan. His presence was a grounding force, helping her navigate the uncertainties of her journey.

As the days turned into weeks, Mia found herself embracing her new routine. She dedicated her mornings to writing, pouring her heart into her work with renewed vigor. The afternoons were spent exploring Willow Creek, reconnecting with its charm and its people. And the evenings were for quiet moments with Ethan, where they would talk, laugh, and support each other through the challenges of life.

One chilly afternoon, as Mia sat by the fireplace with a cup of tea and her notebook, she felt a deep sense of contentment. The road less traveled had brought her to a place of self-discovery and growth, and she was grateful for every step of the journey.

With a heart full of hope and a mind brimming with creativity, Mia knew that the future was filled with possibilities. She was ready to face whatever came her way, knowing that she was not alone. The road ahead might be uncertain, but it was a road she was eager to travel—one step at a time.

Chapter 12: New Beginnings

Mia woke up with a sense of determination she hadn't felt in years. The conversations she had with Sarah, Ethan, and Riley had stirred something deep within her—a longing to make sense of her past, not just for herself but for others who might be struggling to find their way. She realized that her experiences, as painful and confusing as they had been, could serve a greater purpose. And that purpose was writing.

She spent the morning at the kitchen table, notebook open, pen in hand. The words didn't flow easily at first, but she forced herself to start. She wrote about her return to Willow Creek, her complex feelings about her father, and the unresolved emotions that had driven her away in the first place. The more she wrote, the more she began to see patterns—ways in which her past had shaped her, both positively and negatively.

Mia knew she had only scratched the surface, but even this initial effort gave her a sense of clarity. Writing was more than just a way to process her emotions; it was a way to make sense of her life, to draw connections between her experiences and the person she had become. And maybe, just maybe, it could help her find a path forward.

After a few hours, Mia set down her pen and stretched, feeling a mix of satisfaction and exhaustion. She looked at the pages filled with her handwriting and felt a surge of pride. It wasn't perfect, but it was a start—a tangible step toward something she had been avoiding for far too long.

Later that day, she decided to visit the town's library. It had been years since she'd stepped foot inside, but she remembered it as a place of quiet reflection, where she could lose herself in the pages of a book or simply sit and think. As she walked through the familiar streets of Willow Creek, she couldn't help but notice how much the town had changed—and how much it hadn't. The old buildings were still there, but there were new shops, new faces, and a new energy that seemed to pulse through the town.

When she arrived at the library, Mia was struck by a wave of nostalgia. The building was just as she remembered it—sturdy brick walls, large wooden doors, and windows that let in the perfect amount of natural light. She pushed open the door and stepped inside, immediately enveloped by the comforting scent of old books and polished wood.

Mia spent the next few hours browsing the shelves, pulling down books that caught her interest and flipping through their pages. She wasn't sure what she was looking for, but she knew she would find it here—somewhere in the quiet corners of this familiar place.

As she wandered through the aisles, she found herself drawn to the section on local history. Willow Creek had a rich past, filled with stories of the people who had lived and worked here over the centuries. She picked up a book about the town's founding and settled into one of the cozy reading nooks to explore its pages.

The stories of Willow Creek's early settlers fascinated her—their struggles, their triumphs, and the way they had built this town from the ground up. As she read, Mia realized that these stories weren't so different from her own. The settlers had faced hardships, made mistakes, and struggled to find their place in the world, just as she had. But they had also found strength in their community and in each other, something Mia had been missing for a long time.

Lost in thought, Mia didn't notice the older woman approaching until she spoke. "You're Mia Prescott, aren't you?"

Mia looked up, startled. The woman had kind eyes and a gentle smile, her gray hair neatly pulled back in a bun. Mia recognized her immediately—Mrs. Thompson, the librarian who had been a fixture at the library for as long as she could remember.

"Yes, that's me," Mia said, returning the smile. "It's been a long time, Mrs. Thompson."

The librarian nodded, her smile widening. "It certainly has. I remember when you were just a little girl, always in here with your nose in a book. It's good to see you back in town."

Mia felt a warm flush of nostalgia. "It's good to be back, though it's been an adjustment."

Mrs. Thompson settled into the chair across from Mia, her expression thoughtful. "Coming back to a place you once called home can be difficult, especially when you've been away for so long. But Willow Creek is a good place to find yourself again."

Mia nodded, feeling the truth of those words. "I'm starting to see that."

They talked for a while longer, discussing the changes in the town, the people who had come and gone, and the way Willow Creek had evolved over the years. Mrs. Thompson spoke with the kind of wisdom that comes from a life well-lived, and Mia found herself comforted by the conversation.

As they talked, an idea began to form in Mia's mind. The stories she had read about Willow Creek's history, combined with the personal stories she was now writing, could come together into something larger—a project that not only told her story but also connected it to the history and spirit of the town. It would be a way to honor both her past and the place that had shaped her.

When she left the library that afternoon, Mia felt a renewed sense of purpose. She had a lot of work ahead of her—writing, researching, and piecing together the stories that would form her project—but for the first time, she felt ready to face it.

As she walked home, the sun setting behind her, Mia realized that she was no longer running from her past. Instead, she was embracing it, using it as a foundation for the future she was beginning to build. And as she looked around at the familiar streets of Willow Creek, she knew that she was exactly where she needed to be.

Mia woke up with a sense of determination she hadn't felt in years. The conversations with Sarah, Ethan, and Riley had stirred something deep within her—a longing to make sense of her past, not just for herself but for others who might be struggling to find their way. She realized that her experiences, as painful and confusing as they had been, could serve a greater purpose. And that purpose was writing.

She spent the morning at the kitchen table, her notebook open, pen in hand. The words didn't flow easily at first, but she forced herself to start. She wrote about her return to Willow Creek, her complex feelings about her father, and the unresolved emotions that had driven her away in the first place. The more she wrote, the more she began to see patterns—ways in which her past had shaped her, both positively and negatively.

Mia knew she had only scratched the surface, but even this initial effort gave her a sense of clarity. Writing was more than just a way to process her emotions; it was a means to make sense of her life, to draw connections between her experiences and the person she had become. And maybe, just maybe, it could help her find a path forward.

After a few hours, Mia set down her pen and stretched, feeling a mix of satisfaction and exhaustion. She looked at the pages filled with her handwriting and felt a surge of pride. It wasn't perfect, but it was a start—a tangible step toward something she had been avoiding for far too long.

Later that day, Mia decided to visit the town's library. It had been years since she'd stepped foot inside, but she remembered it as a place of quiet reflection, where she could lose herself in the pages of a book or simply sit and think. As she walked through the familiar streets of Willow Creek, she couldn't help but notice how much the town had changed—and how much it hadn't. The old buildings were still there, but there were new shops, new faces, and a new energy that seemed to pulse through the town.

When she arrived at the library, Mia was struck by a wave of nostalgia. The building was just as she remembered it—sturdy brick walls, large wooden doors, and windows that let in the perfect amount of natural light. She pushed open the door and stepped inside, immediately enveloped by the comforting scent of old books and polished wood.

Mia spent the next few hours browsing the shelves, pulling down books that caught her interest and flipping through their pages. She wasn't sure what she was looking for, but she knew she would find it here—somewhere in the quiet corners of this familiar place.

As she wandered through the aisles, she found herself drawn to the section on local history. Willow Creek had a rich past, filled with stories of the people who had lived and worked here over the centuries. She picked up a book about the town's founding and settled into one of the cozy reading nooks to explore its pages.

The stories of Willow Creek's early settlers fascinated her—their struggles, their triumphs, and the way they had built this town from the ground up. As she read, Mia realized that these stories weren't so different from her own. The settlers had faced hardships, made mistakes, and struggled to find their place in the world, just as she had. But they had also found strength in their community and in each other, something Mia had been missing for a long time.

Lost in thought, Mia didn't notice the older woman approaching until she spoke. "You're Mia Prescott, aren't you?"

Mia looked up, startled. The woman had kind eyes and a gentle smile, her gray hair neatly pulled back in a bun. Mia recognized her immediately—Mrs. Thompson, the librarian who had been a fixture at the library for as long as she could remember.

"Yes, that's me," Mia said, returning the smile. "It's been a long time, Mrs. Thompson."

The librarian nodded, her smile widening. "It certainly has. I remember when you were just a little girl, always in here with your nose in a book. It's good to see you back in town."

Mia felt a warm flush of nostalgia. "It's good to be back, though it's been an adjustment."

Mrs. Thompson settled into the chair across from Mia, her expression thoughtful. "Coming back to a place you once called home can be difficult, especially when you've been away for so long. But Willow Creek is a good place to find yourself again."

Mia nodded, feeling the truth of those words. "I'm starting to see that."

They talked for a while longer, discussing the changes in the town, the people who had come and gone, and the way Willow Creek had evolved over the years. Mrs. Thompson spoke with the kind of wisdom that comes from a life well-lived, and Mia found herself comforted by the conversation.

As they talked, an idea began to form in Mia's mind. The stories she had read about Willow Creek's history, combined with the personal stories she was now writing, could come together into something larger—a project that not only told her story but also connected it to the history and spirit of the town. It would be a way to honor both her past and the place that had shaped her.

When she left the library that afternoon, Mia felt a renewed sense of purpose. She had a lot of work ahead of her—writing, researching, and piecing together the stories that would form her project—but for the first time, she felt ready to face it.

As she walked home, the sun setting behind her, Mia realized that she was no longer running from her past. Instead, she was embracing it, using it as a foundation for the future she was beginning to build. And as she looked around at the familiar streets of Willow Creek, she knew that she was exactly where she needed to be.

In the weeks that followed, Mia threw herself into her new project with fervor. She spent her days at the library, poring over historical documents and interviewing long-time residents. She wrote diligently in the evenings, weaving together her personal experiences with the rich tapestry of Willow Creek's history.

Ethan, ever supportive, encouraged her efforts and provided feedback on her drafts. He even helped her organize some of her research, and together they explored the town, uncovering hidden stories and forgotten corners that would enrich her project.

As autumn deepened, Mia felt a profound connection to Willow Creek—both its past and its present. The project was transforming from a personal journey into a shared narrative that she hoped would resonate with others. It was more than just a book; it was a tribute to the resilience of the human spirit and the strength found in community.

One crisp morning, as Mia reviewed her latest draft, she glanced out the window and saw the first hints of snow on the ground. The sight filled her with a sense of peace and completion. She had come full circle, finding solace and purpose in the very place that had once felt like a burden.

With each chapter she wrote, Mia felt her heart lighter and her path clearer. She was no longer defined by her past but by how she chose to shape her future. The road ahead was still uncertain, but she was confident that she was on the right path.

As the year came to a close, Mia prepared for the next steps in her journey—finalizing her manuscript and preparing for the possibility of sharing her work with the world. And as she reflected on her experiences, she realized that every challenge, every twist in the road had led her to this moment of new beginnings.

Mia woke up with a sense of determination she hadn't felt in years. The conversations with Sarah, Ethan, and Riley had stirred something deep within her—a longing to make sense of her past, not just for herself but for others who might be struggling to find their way. She realized that her experiences, as painful and confusing as they had been, could serve a greater purpose. And that purpose was writing.

She spent the morning at the kitchen table, her notebook open, pen in hand. The words didn't flow easily at first, but she forced herself to start. She wrote about her return to Willow Creek, her complex feelings about her father, and the unresolved emotions that had driven her away in the first place. The more she wrote, the more she began to see patterns—ways in which her past had shaped her, both positively and negatively.

Mia knew she had only scratched the surface, but even this initial effort gave her a sense of clarity. Writing was more than just a way to process her emotions; it was a means to make sense of her life, to draw connections between her experiences and the person she had become. And maybe, just maybe, it could help her find a path forward.

After a few hours, Mia set down her pen and stretched, feeling a mix of satisfaction and exhaustion. She looked at the pages filled with her handwriting and felt a surge of pride. It wasn't perfect, but it was a start—a tangible step toward something she had been avoiding for far too long.

Later that day, Mia decided to visit the town's library. It had been years since she'd stepped foot inside, but she remembered it as a place of quiet reflection, where she could lose herself in the pages of a book or simply sit and think. As she walked through the familiar streets of Willow Creek, she couldn't help but notice how much the town had changed—and how much it hadn't. The old buildings were still there, but there were new shops, new faces, and a new energy that seemed to pulse through the town.

When she arrived at the library, Mia was struck by a wave of nostalgia. The building was just as she remembered it—sturdy brick walls, large wooden doors, and windows that let in the perfect amount of natural light. She pushed open the door and stepped inside, immediately enveloped by the comforting scent of old books and polished wood.

Mia spent the next few hours browsing the shelves, pulling down books that caught her interest and flipping through their pages. She wasn't sure what she was looking for, but she knew she would find it here—somewhere in the quiet corners of this familiar place.

As she wandered through the aisles, she found herself drawn to the section on local history. Willow Creek had a rich past, filled with stories of the people who had lived and worked here over the centuries. She picked up a book about the town's founding and settled into one of the cozy reading nooks to explore its pages.

The stories of Willow Creek's early settlers fascinated her—their struggles, their triumphs, and the way they had built this town from the ground up. As she read, Mia realized that these stories weren't so different from her own. The settlers had faced hardships, made mistakes, and struggled to find their place in the world, just as she had. But they had also found strength in their community and in each other, something Mia had been missing for a long time.

Lost in thought, Mia didn't notice the older woman approaching until she spoke. "You're Mia Prescott, aren't you?"

Mia looked up, startled. The woman had kind eyes and a gentle smile, her gray hair neatly pulled back in a bun. Mia recognized her immediately—Mrs. Thompson, the librarian who had been a fixture at the library for as long as she could remember.

"Yes, that's me," Mia said, returning the smile. "It's been a long time, Mrs. Thompson."

The librarian nodded, her smile widening. "It certainly has. I remember when you were just a little girl, always in here with your nose in a book. It's good to see you back in town."

Mia felt a warm flush of nostalgia. "It's good to be back, though it's been an adjustment."

Mrs. Thompson settled into the chair across from Mia, her expression thoughtful. "Coming back to a place you once called home can be difficult, especially when you've been away for so long. But Willow Creek is a good place to find yourself again."

Mia nodded, feeling the truth of those words. "I'm starting to see that."

They talked for a while longer, discussing the changes in the town, the people who had come and gone, and the way Willow

Creek had evolved over the years. Mrs. Thompson spoke with the kind of wisdom that comes from a life well-lived, and Mia found herself comforted by the conversation.

As they talked, an idea began to form in Mia's mind. The stories she had read about Willow Creek's history, combined with the personal stories she was now writing, could come together into something larger—a project that not only told her story but also connected it to the history and spirit of the town. It would be a way to honor both her past and the place that had shaped her.

When she left the library that afternoon, Mia felt a renewed sense of purpose. She had a lot of work ahead of her—writing, researching, and piecing together the stories that would form her project—but for the first time, she felt ready to face it.

As she walked home, the sun setting behind her, Mia realized that she was no longer running from her past. Instead, she was embracing it, using it as a foundation for the future she was beginning to build. And as she looked around at the familiar streets of Willow Creek, she knew that she was exactly where she needed to be.

In the weeks that followed, Mia threw herself into her new project with fervor. She spent her days at the library, poring over historical documents and interviewing long-time residents. She wrote diligently in the evenings, weaving together her personal experiences with the rich tapestry of Willow Creek's history.

Ethan, ever supportive, encouraged her efforts and provided feedback on her drafts. He even helped her organize some of her research, and together they explored the town, uncovering hidden stories and forgotten corners that would enrich her project.

One crisp morning, Mia and Ethan walked hand in hand through the snow-covered streets of Willow Creek. The town looked magical, with twinkling lights and a blanket of white that seemed to enhance its charm. They stopped at a small café for hot chocolate, their breath visible in the cold air.

As they sat by the window, Mia felt a sense of contentment wash over her. Ethan's presence was a comforting constant in her life, and their growing relationship added a layer of warmth to her new beginnings. She shared her latest progress with him, her eyes sparkling with excitement.

"I think this project is really coming together," Mia said, stirring her hot chocolate. "I'm starting to see how my story and the town's history fit together. It's like they're intertwining, creating something beautiful."

Ethan smiled, his eyes full of admiration. "I'm proud of you, Mia. You've found a way to turn your experiences into something meaningful, and it's inspiring to see you so passionate about it."

Mia squeezed his hand, feeling a deep sense of gratitude. "Thank you for all your support. It means the world to me."

As they finished their drinks and prepared to head out into the cold, Mia felt a renewed sense of excitement for the future. Her project was more than just a book; it was a testament to her journey and the way she had embraced her past to shape her future.

With each step she took, Mia felt more grounded and more hopeful. The road ahead was still filled with unknowns, but she was ready to face them with an open heart and a clear sense of purpose. The road less traveled had led her back to Willow Creek, where she was beginning to build a life that was not only meaningful but also full of promise.

As the first stars began to appear in the evening sky, Mia walked alongside Ethan, feeling a deep sense of peace. She knew that the journey was far from over, but for the first time in a long while, she felt that she was exactly where she was meant to be. And as she looked up at the starry sky, she couldn't help but smile, ready to embrace whatever new beginnings awaited her.

Mia woke up with a sense of determination she hadn't felt in years. The conversations with Sarah, Ethan, and Riley had stirred something deep within her—a longing to make sense of her past, not just for herself but for others who might be struggling to find their way. She realized that her experiences, as painful and confusing as they had been, could serve a greater purpose. And that purpose was writing.

She spent the morning at the kitchen table, her notebook open, pen in hand. The words didn't flow easily at first, but she forced herself to start. She wrote about her return to Willow Creek, her complex feelings about her father, and the unresolved emotions that had driven her away in the first place. The more she wrote, the more she began to see patterns—ways in which her past had shaped her, both positively and negatively.

Mia knew she had only scratched the surface, but even this initial effort gave her a sense of clarity. Writing was more than just a way to process her emotions; it was a means to make sense of her life, to draw connections between her experiences and the person she had become. And maybe, just maybe, it could help her find a path forward.

After a few hours, Mia set down her pen and stretched, feeling a mix of satisfaction and exhaustion. She looked at the pages filled with her handwriting and felt a surge of pride. It wasn't perfect, but it was a start—a tangible step toward something she had been avoiding for far too long.

Later that day, Mia decided to visit the town's library. It had been years since she'd stepped foot inside, but she remembered it as a place of quiet reflection, where she could lose herself in the pages of a book or simply sit and think. As she walked through the familiar streets of Willow Creek, she couldn't help but notice how much the town had changed—and how much it hadn't. The old buildings were still there, but there were new shops, new faces, and a new energy that seemed to pulse through the town.

When she arrived at the library, Mia was struck by a wave of nostalgia. The building was just as she remembered it—sturdy brick walls, large wooden doors, and windows that let in the perfect amount of natural light. She pushed open the door and stepped inside, immediately enveloped by the comforting scent of old books and polished wood.

Mia spent the next few hours browsing the shelves, pulling down books that caught her interest and flipping through their pages. She wasn't sure what she was looking for, but she knew she would find it here—somewhere in the quiet corners of this familiar place.

As she wandered through the aisles, she found herself drawn to the section on local history. Willow Creek had a rich past, filled with stories of the people who had lived and worked here over the centuries. She picked up a book about the town's founding and settled into one of the cozy reading nooks to explore its pages.

The stories of Willow Creek's early settlers fascinated her—their struggles, their triumphs, and the way they had built this town from the ground up. As she read, Mia realized that these stories weren't so different from her own. The settlers had faced hardships, made mistakes, and struggled to find their place in the world, just as she had. But they had also found strength in their community and in each other, something Mia had been missing for a long time.

Lost in thought, Mia didn't notice the older woman approaching until she spoke. "You're Mia Prescott, aren't you?"

Mia looked up, startled. The woman had kind eyes and a gentle smile, her gray hair neatly pulled back in a bun. Mia recognized her immediately—Mrs. Thompson, the librarian who had been a fixture at the library for as long as she could remember.

"Yes, that's me," Mia said, returning the smile. "It's been a long time, Mrs. Thompson."

The librarian nodded, her smile widening. "It certainly has. I remember when you were just a little girl, always in here with your nose in a book. It's good to see you back in town."

Mia felt a warm flush of nostalgia. "It's good to be back, though it's been an adjustment."

Mrs. Thompson settled into the chair across from Mia, her expression thoughtful. "Coming back to a place you once called home can be difficult, especially when you've been away for so long. But Willow Creek is a good place to find yourself again."

Mia nodded, feeling the truth of those words. "I'm starting to see that."

They talked for a while longer, discussing the changes in the town, the people who had come and gone, and the way Willow Creek had evolved over the years. Mrs. Thompson spoke with the kind of wisdom that comes from a life well-lived, and Mia found herself comforted by the conversation.

As they talked, an idea began to form in Mia's mind. The stories she had read about Willow Creek's history, combined with the personal stories she was now writing, could come together into something larger—a project that not only told her story but also connected it to the history and spirit of the town. It would be a way to honor both her past and the place that had shaped her.

When she left the library that afternoon, Mia felt a renewed sense of purpose. She had a lot of work ahead of her—writing, researching, and piecing together the stories that would form her project—but for the first time, she felt ready to face it.

As she walked home, the sun setting behind her, Mia realized that she was no longer running from her past. Instead, she was embracing it, using it as a foundation for the future she was beginning to build. And as she looked around at the familiar streets of Willow Creek, she knew that she was exactly where she needed to be.

In the weeks that followed, Mia threw herself into her new project with fervor. She spent her days at the library, poring over historical documents and interviewing long-time residents. She wrote diligently in the evenings, weaving together her personal experiences with the rich tapestry of Willow Creek's history.

Ethan, ever supportive, encouraged her efforts and provided feedback on her drafts. He even helped her organize some of her research, and together they explored the town, uncovering hidden stories and forgotten corners that would enrich her project.

One crisp morning, Mia and Ethan walked hand in hand through the snow-covered streets of Willow Creek. The town looked magical, with twinkling lights and a blanket of white that seemed to enhance its charm. They stopped at a small café for hot chocolate, their breath visible in the cold air.

As they sat by the window, Mia felt a sense of contentment wash over her. Ethan's presence was a comforting constant in her life, and their growing relationship added a layer of warmth to her new beginnings. She shared her latest progress with him, her eyes sparkling with excitement.

"I think this project is really coming together," Mia said, stirring her hot chocolate. "I'm starting to see how my story and the town's history fit together. It's like they're intertwining, creating something beautiful."

Ethan smiled, his eyes full of admiration. "I'm proud of you, Mia. You've found a way to turn your experiences into something meaningful, and it's inspiring to see you so passionate about it."

Mia squeezed his hand, feeling a deep sense of gratitude. "Thank you for all your support. It means the world to me."

As they finished their drinks and prepared to head out into the cold, Mia felt a renewed sense of excitement for the future. Her project was more than just a book; it was a testament to her journey and the way she had embraced her past to shape her future.

With each step she took, Mia felt more grounded and more hopeful. The road ahead was still filled with unknowns, but she was ready to face them with an open heart and a clear sense of purpose. The road less traveled had led her back to Willow Creek, where she was beginning to build a life that was not only meaningful but also full of promise.

As the first stars began to appear in the evening sky, Mia walked alongside Ethan, feeling a deep sense of peace. She knew that the journey was far from over, but for the first time in a long while, she felt that she was exactly where she was meant to be. And as she looked up at the starry sky, she couldn't help but smile, ready to embrace whatever new beginnings awaited her.

The future felt like a vast, open canvas, and Mia was eager to paint it with the colors of her experiences, hopes, and dreams. Each day, she took small steps toward her goals, and with each step, she felt herself growing stronger and more confident. She had found her way back to Willow Creek, and in doing so, had rediscovered a part of herself she thought she had lost.

As winter slowly gave way to spring, the town of Willow Creek transformed before Mia's eyes. The snow melted away, revealing the vibrant greens and blooming flowers of the season. The town seemed to come alive with new energy, and Mia felt that same vitality coursing through her. It was as if the town's renewal mirrored her own.

One bright morning, Mia stood on the porch of her small house, watching the sunrise. The world was awash in golden light, and she took a deep breath, feeling a profound sense of gratitude for the journey she had been on. Her project was taking shape, and she was excited to see where it would lead. She had found a new purpose and a renewed sense of self.

As she looked out over the blossoming landscape of Willow Creek, Mia knew that this was just the beginning of a new chapter in her life. The future was full of possibilities, and she was ready to embrace them with an open heart and a hopeful spirit.

And so, with the warmth of the sun on her face and the promise of new beginnings on the horizon, Mia stepped forward into the life she had always dreamed of—a life filled with love, purpose, and endless possibilities.

Mia woke up with a sense of determination she hadn't felt in years. The conversations with Sarah, Ethan, and Riley had stirred something deep within her—a longing to make sense of her past, not just for herself but for others who might be struggling to find their way. She realized that her experiences, as painful and confusing as they had been, could serve a greater purpose. And that purpose was writing.

She spent the morning at the kitchen table, her notebook open, pen in hand. The words didn't flow easily at first, but she forced herself to start. She wrote about her return to Willow Creek, her complex feelings about her father, and the unresolved emotions that had driven her away in the first place. The more she wrote, the more she began to see patterns—ways in which her past had shaped her, both positively and negatively.

Mia knew she had only scratched the surface, but even this initial effort gave her a sense of clarity. Writing was more than just a way to process her emotions; it was a means to make sense of her life, to draw connections between her experiences and the person she had become. And maybe, just maybe, it could help her find a path forward.

After a few hours, Mia set down her pen and stretched, feeling a mix of satisfaction and exhaustion. She looked at the pages filled with her handwriting and felt a surge of pride. It wasn't perfect, but it was a start—a tangible step toward something she had been avoiding for far too long.

Later that day, Mia decided to visit the town's library. It had been years since she'd stepped foot inside, but she remembered it as a place of quiet reflection, where she could lose herself in the pages of a book or simply sit and think. As she walked through the familiar streets of Willow Creek, she couldn't help but notice how much the town had changed—and how much it hadn't. The old buildings were still there, but there were new shops, new faces, and a new energy that seemed to pulse through the town.

When she arrived at the library, Mia was struck by a wave of nostalgia. The building was just as she remembered it—sturdy brick walls, large wooden doors, and windows that let in the perfect amount of natural light. She pushed open the door and stepped inside, immediately enveloped by the comforting scent of old books and polished wood.

Mia spent the next few hours browsing the shelves, pulling down books that caught her interest and flipping through their pages. She wasn't sure what she was looking for, but she knew she would find it here—somewhere in the quiet corners of this familiar place.

As she wandered through the aisles, she found herself drawn to the section on local history. Willow Creek had a rich past, filled with stories of the people who had lived and worked here over the centuries. She picked up a book about the town's founding and settled into one of the cozy reading nooks to explore its pages.

The stories of Willow Creek's early settlers fascinated her—their struggles, their triumphs, and the way they had built this town from the ground up. As she read, Mia realized that these stories weren't so different from her own. The settlers had faced hardships, made mistakes, and struggled to find their place in the world, just as she had. But they had also found strength in their community and in each other, something Mia had been missing for a long time.

Lost in thought, Mia didn't notice the older woman approaching until she spoke. "You're Mia Prescott, aren't you?"

Mia looked up, startled. The woman had kind eyes and a gentle smile, her gray hair neatly pulled back in a bun. Mia recognized her immediately—Mrs. Thompson, the librarian who had been a fixture at the library for as long as she could remember.

"Yes, that's me," Mia said, returning the smile. "It's been a long time, Mrs. Thompson."

The librarian nodded, her smile widening. "It certainly has. I remember when you were just a little girl, always in here with your nose in a book. It's good to see you back in town."

Mia felt a warm flush of nostalgia. "It's good to be back, though it's been an adjustment."

Mrs. Thompson settled into the chair across from Mia, her expression thoughtful. "Coming back to a place you once called home can be difficult, especially when you've been away for so long. But Willow Creek is a good place to find yourself again."

Mia nodded, feeling the truth of those words. "I'm starting to see that."

They talked for a while longer, discussing the changes in the town, the people who had come and gone, and the way Willow Creek had evolved over the years. Mrs. Thompson spoke with the kind of wisdom that comes from a life well-lived, and Mia found herself comforted by the conversation.

As they talked, an idea began to form in Mia's mind. The stories she had read about Willow Creek's history, combined with the personal stories she was now writing, could come together into something larger—a project that not only told her story but also connected it to the history and spirit of the town. It would be a way to honor both her past and the place that had shaped her.

When she left the library that afternoon, Mia felt a renewed sense of purpose. She had a lot of work ahead of her—writing, researching, and piecing together the stories that would form her project—but for the first time, she felt ready to face it.

As she walked home, the sun setting behind her, Mia realized that she was no longer running from her past. Instead, she was embracing it, using it as a foundation for the future she was beginning to build. And as she looked around at the familiar streets of Willow Creek, she knew that she was exactly where she needed to be.

In the weeks that followed, Mia threw herself into her new project with fervor. She spent her days at the library, poring over historical documents and interviewing long-time residents. She wrote diligently in the evenings, weaving together her personal experiences with the rich tapestry of Willow Creek's history.

Ethan, ever supportive, encouraged her efforts and provided feedback on her drafts. He even helped her organize some of her research, and together they explored the town, uncovering hidden stories and forgotten corners that would enrich her project.

One crisp morning, Mia and Ethan walked hand in hand through the snow-covered streets of Willow Creek. The town looked magical, with twinkling lights and a blanket of white that seemed to enhance its charm. They stopped at a small café for hot chocolate, their breath visible in the cold air.

As they sat by the window, Mia felt a sense of contentment wash over her. Ethan's presence was a comforting constant in her life, and their growing relationship added a layer of warmth to her new beginnings. She shared her latest progress with him, her eyes sparkling with excitement.

"I think this project is really coming together," Mia said, stirring her hot chocolate. "I'm starting to see how my story and the town's history fit together. It's like they're intertwining, creating something beautiful."

Ethan smiled, his eyes full of admiration. "I'm proud of you, Mia. You've found a way to turn your experiences into something meaningful, and it's inspiring to see you so passionate about it."

Mia squeezed his hand, feeling a deep sense of gratitude. "Thank you for all your support. It means the world to me."

As they finished their drinks and prepared to head out into the cold, Mia felt a renewed sense of excitement for the future. Her project was more than just a book; it was a testament to her journey and the way she had embraced her past to shape her future.

With each step she took, Mia felt more grounded and more hopeful. The road ahead was still filled with unknowns, but she was ready to face them with an open heart and a clear sense of purpose. The road less traveled had led her back to Willow Creek, where she was beginning to build a life that was not only meaningful but also full of promise.

As winter slowly gave way to spring, the town of Willow Creek transformed before Mia's eyes. The snow melted away, revealing the vibrant greens and blooming flowers of the season. The town seemed to come alive with new energy, and Mia felt that same vitality coursing through her. It was as if the town's renewal mirrored her own.

One bright morning, Mia stood on the porch of her small house, watching the sunrise. The world was awash in golden light, and she took a deep breath, feeling a profound sense of gratitude for the journey she had been on. Her project was taking shape, and she was excited to see where it would lead. She had found a new purpose and a renewed sense of self.

As she looked out over the blossoming landscape of Willow Creek, Mia knew that this was just the beginning of a new chapter in her life. The future was full of possibilities, and she was ready to embrace them with an open heart and a hopeful spirit.

With the warmth of the sun on her face and the promise of new beginnings on the horizon, Mia stepped forward into the life she had always dreamed of—a life filled with love, purpose, and endless possibilities. She had taken the road less traveled and, in doing so, had discovered a place where she truly belonged.

Chapter 13: The Festival

The annual Willow Creek Festival was a tradition that had been around for as long as anyone could remember. It was the highlight of the year—a time when the entire town came together to celebrate their community, their history, and each other. There were food stalls, games, music, and parades, all set against the backdrop of the town's picturesque streets.

Mia had almost forgotten how lively the festival could be. As she made her way through the crowded streets, she felt a surge of excitement. This was Willow Creek at its best—vibrant, welcoming, and full of life.

She had agreed to meet Ethan at the festival, and as she weaved through the crowd, she spotted him standing by one of the food stalls, a smile on his face as he waved to her. She waved back, feeling a flutter of anticipation in her chest.

"Hey," Ethan said as she approached, his eyes lighting up at the sight of her. "Glad you made it."

"Wouldn't miss it," Mia replied, returning his smile. "It's been a while since I've been to the festival."

"It's still the same as ever," Ethan said, handing her a cup of lemonade. "A few new faces, maybe, but the spirit's the same."

They spent the next hour wandering through the festival together, sampling food from the stalls, playing games, and watching the parade. It felt easy, natural, and Mia found herself relaxing in Ethan's company. They laughed, reminisced about old times, and talked about the changes in the town.

At one point, they stopped to watch a group of children performing a play about Willow Creek's history. The play was simple but charming, with the children dressed in costumes representing the town's early settlers. As they watched, Mia felt a deep sense of connection to the town and its history—a history that she was now a part of.

"I've been thinking about something," Mia said as the play came to an end. "About how much this town means to me, and how much it's shaped who I am."

Ethan turned to her, his expression serious. "What do you mean?"

"I've started writing again," Mia explained, feeling a mixture of excitement and nervousness. "But this time, I want to write something that's not just about me, but about Willow Creek—about the people who've lived here, the history, and the way this town has shaped all of us."

Ethan's eyes softened, and he reached out to take her hand. "That sounds incredible, Mia. I think it's exactly what you need to do."

Mia smiled, feeling a surge of gratitude for Ethan's support. "It's still just an idea, but it feels right. Like it's something I'm meant to do."

As they continued to explore the festival, Mia felt a sense of contentment that she hadn't felt in a long time. Being back in Willow Creek, reconnecting with her roots, and finding a new sense of purpose in her writing—it all felt like pieces of a puzzle falling into place.

That evening, as the festival began to wind down, Ethan walked Mia home. The streets were quieter now, the sky darkening as the stars began to appear. They walked in comfortable silence, the night air cool and refreshing.

When they reached Mia's porch, Ethan hesitated, his gaze lingering on her. "Mia, I—" He stopped, seeming to struggle with his words.

Mia looked at him, sensing the weight of whatever he was about to say. "What is it, Ethan?"

He took a deep breath, then met her eyes with a look of determination. "I just wanted to say that I'm glad you came back. And not just because of the festival, or because you're writing again. I'm glad you're here, Mia. It feels like things are finally starting to make sense again."

Mia felt her heart swell at his words, a warmth spreading through her. She reached out, taking his hand in hers. "I'm glad I'm here too, Ethan. More than I can put into words."

They stood there for a moment, the quiet of the night wrapping around them. And in that moment, Mia knew that whatever the future held, she was ready to face it—with Ethan by her side, and with the town of Willow Creek as her anchor.

The annual Willow Creek Festival was a tradition that had been around for as long as anyone could remember. It was the highlight of the year—a time when the entire town came together to celebrate their community, their history, and each other. There were food stalls, games, music, and parades, all set against the backdrop of the town's picturesque streets.

Mia had almost forgotten how lively the festival could be. As she made her way through the crowded streets, she felt a surge of excitement. This was Willow Creek at its best—vibrant, welcoming, and full of life.

She had agreed to meet Ethan at the festival, and as she weaved through the crowd, she spotted him standing by one of the food stalls, a smile on his face as he waved to her. She waved back, feeling a flutter of anticipation in her chest.

"Hey," Ethan said as she approached, his eyes lighting up at the sight of her. "Glad you made it."

"Wouldn't miss it," Mia replied, returning his smile. "It's been a while since I've been to the festival."

"It's still the same as ever," Ethan said, handing her a cup of lemonade. "A few new faces, maybe, but the spirit's the same."

They spent the next hour wandering through the festival together, sampling food from the stalls, playing games, and watching the parade. It felt easy, natural, and Mia found herself relaxing in Ethan's company. They laughed, reminisced about old times, and talked about the changes in the town.

At one point, they stopped to watch a group of children performing a play about Willow Creek's history. The play was simple but charming, with the children dressed in costumes representing the town's early settlers. As they watched, Mia felt a deep sense of connection to the town and its history—a history that she was now a part of.

"I've been thinking about something," Mia said as the play came to an end. "About how much this town means to me, and how much it's shaped who I am."

Ethan turned to her, his expression serious. "What do you mean?"

"I've started writing again," Mia explained, feeling a mixture of excitement and nervousness. "But this time, I want to write something that's not just about me, but about Willow Creek—about the people who've lived here, the history, and the way this town has shaped all of us."

Ethan's eyes softened, and he reached out to take her hand. "That sounds incredible, Mia. I think it's exactly what you need to do."

Mia smiled, feeling a surge of gratitude for Ethan's support. "It's still just an idea, but it feels right. Like it's something I'm meant to do."

As they continued to explore the festival, Mia felt a sense of contentment that she hadn't felt in a long time. Being back in Willow Creek, reconnecting with her roots, and finding a new sense of purpose in her writing—it all felt like pieces of a puzzle falling into place.

That evening, as the festival began to wind down, Ethan walked Mia home. The streets were quieter now, the sky darkening as the stars began to appear. They walked in comfortable silence, the night air cool and refreshing.

When they reached Mia's porch, Ethan hesitated, his gaze lingering on her. "Mia, I—" He stopped, seeming to struggle with his words.

Mia looked at him, sensing the weight of whatever he was about to say. "What is it, Ethan?"

He took a deep breath, then met her eyes with a look of determination. "I just wanted to say that I'm glad you came back. And not just because of the festival, or because you're writing again. I'm glad you're here, Mia. It feels like things are finally starting to make sense again."

Mia felt her heart swell at his words, a warmth spreading through her. She reached out, taking his hand in hers. "I'm glad I'm here too, Ethan. More than I can put into words."

They stood there for a moment, the quiet of the night wrapping around them. The soft hum of distant music from the festival lingered in the background, blending with the sounds of the night. Mia could see the stars shining brightly above, reflecting the clarity and peace she felt inside.

Ethan leaned closer, his expression tender. "Mia, I've been think-ing about us, about what we have here. I know it's been a whirlwind since you came back, but I can't imagine my life without you now. I want to be here with you, not just for the festival or the moment, but for everything that comes next."

Mia's heart raced at his words, and she felt a deep, genuine smile spreading across her face. "Ethan, I feel the same way. Being here with you, in this town that means so much to me, it's like everything is falling into place. I'm ready for whatever comes next too."

They stood there for a few more moments, savoring the stillness and the shared sense of certainty. The porch light cast a soft glow over them, and Mia felt an overwhelming sense of rightness about the direction her life was taking.

Eventually, Ethan reluctantly pulled away, his eyes holding hers with an intensity that made Mia's heart flutter. "I should go," he said softly. "But I'll see you soon, right?"

"Absolutely," Mia replied, feeling a rush of anticipation for their future together. "I'll be looking forward to it."

Ethan leaned in and kissed her gently on the cheek before turning to leave. Mia watched him walk down the path, feeling a deep sense of happiness and contentment.

As she closed the door behind her, Mia took one last look at the festival lights twinkling in the distance. She felt a renewed sense of hope and excitement for the future. Willow Creek was no longer just a place from her past—it was her present and her future, filled with possibilities and the promise of new beginnings.

In the days that followed, Mia continued to immerse herself in her writing and in her growing relationship with Ethan. The project she had started was taking shape, and she felt more connected to Wil-low Creek than ever before. The town's history, intertwined with her own experiences, was becoming a reflection of her journey and the path she was forging for herself.

With each passing day, Mia grew more confident and excited about the future. The festival had been a turning point, a reminder of the community and support that surrounded her. And as she moved forward, she did so with a heart full of gratitude and a spirit ready to embrace all that lay ahead.

The annual Willow Creek Festival was a tradition that had been around for as long as anyone could remember. It was the highlight of the year—a time when the entire town came together to celebrate their community, their history, and each other. There were food stalls, games, music, and parades, all set against the backdrop of the town's picturesque streets.

Mia had almost forgotten how lively the festival could be. As she made her way through the crowded streets, she felt a surge of excitement. This was Willow Creek at its best—vibrant, welcoming, and full of life.

She had agreed to meet Ethan at the festival, and as she weaved through the crowd, she spotted him standing by one of the food stalls, a smile on his face as he waved to her. She waved back, feeling a flutter of anticipation in her chest.

"Hey," Ethan said as she approached, his eyes lighting up at the sight of her. "Glad you made it."

"Wouldn't miss it," Mia replied, returning his smile. "It's been a while since I've been to the festival."

"It's still the same as ever," Ethan said, handing her a cup of lemonade. "A few new faces, maybe, but the spirit's the same."

They spent the next hour wandering through the festival together, sampling food from the stalls, playing games, and watching the parade. It felt easy, natural, and Mia found herself relaxing in

Ethan's company. They laughed, reminisced about old times, and talked about the changes in the town.

At one point, they stopped to watch a group of children performing a play about Willow Creek's history. The play was simple but charming, with the children dressed in costumes representing the town's early settlers. As they watched, Mia felt a deep sense of connection to the town and its history—a history that she was now a part of.

"I've been thinking about something," Mia said as the play came to an end. "About how much this town means to me, and how much it's shaped who I am."

Ethan turned to her, his expression serious. "What do you mean?"

"I've started writing again," Mia explained, feeling a mixture of excitement and nervousness. "But this time, I want to write something that's not just about me, but about Willow Creek—about the people who've lived here, the history, and the way this town has shaped all of us."

Ethan's eyes softened, and he reached out to take her hand. "That sounds incredible, Mia. I think it's exactly what you need to do."

Mia smiled, feeling a surge of gratitude for Ethan's support. "It's still just an idea, but it feels right. Like it's something I'm meant to do."

As they continued to explore the festival, Mia felt a sense of contentment that she hadn't felt in a long time. Being back in Willow Creek, reconnecting with her roots, and finding a new sense of purpose in her writing—it all felt like pieces of a puzzle falling into place.

That evening, as the festival began to wind down, Ethan walked Mia home. The streets were quieter now, the sky darkening as the stars began to appear. They walked in comfortable silence, the night air cool and refreshing.

When they reached Mia's porch, Ethan hesitated, his gaze lingering on her. "Mia, I—" He stopped, seeming to struggle with his words.

Mia looked at him, sensing the weight of whatever he was about to say. "What is it, Ethan?"

He took a deep breath, then met her eyes with a look of determination. "I just wanted to say that I'm glad you came back. And not just because of the festival, or because you're writing again. I'm glad you're here, Mia. It feels like things are finally starting to make sense again."

Mia felt her heart swell at his words, a warmth spreading through her. She reached out, taking his hand in hers. "I'm glad I'm here too, Ethan. More than I can put into words."

They stood there for a moment, the quiet of the night wrapping around them. The soft hum of distant music from the festival lingered in the background, blending with the sounds of the night. Mia could see the stars shining brightly above, reflecting the clarity and peace she felt inside.

Ethan leaned closer, his expression tender. "Mia, I've been thinking about us, about what we have here. I know it's been a whirlwind since you came back, but I can't imagine my life without you now. I want to be here with you, not just for the festival or the moment, but for everything that comes next."

Mia's heart raced at his words, and she felt a deep, genuine smile spreading across her face. "Ethan, I feel the same way. Being here with you, in this town that means so much to me, it's like everything is falling into place. I'm ready for whatever comes next too."

They stood there for a few more moments, savoring the stillness and the shared sense of certainty. The porch light cast a soft glow over them, and Mia felt an overwhelming sense of rightness about the direction her life was taking.

Eventually, Ethan reluctantly pulled away, his eyes holding hers with an intensity that made Mia's heart flutter. "I should go," he said softly. "But I'll see you soon, right?"

"Absolutely," Mia replied, feeling a rush of anticipation for their future together. "I'll be looking forward to it."

Ethan leaned in and kissed her gently on the cheek before turning to leave. Mia watched him walk down the path, feeling a deep sense of happiness and contentment.

As she closed the door behind her, Mia took one last look at the festival lights twinkling in the distance. The joy and vibrancy of the evening were still with her, filling her with a sense of hope and possibility.

She walked through the house, her thoughts swirling with the conversations she'd had and the future she was now embracing. Her project was taking shape, her connection with Ethan deepened, and her place in Willow Creek felt more solid than ever.

Sitting at her desk, she glanced at the stack of notes she had compiled for her writing. The festival had been a reminder of the community she was a part of, and it had sparked a new energy in her. With a renewed sense of purpose, she picked up her pen and began to write, letting the inspiration from the festival flow onto the pages.

As the words took shape, Mia felt a profound sense of fulfillment. The festival had not only celebrated the past but had also illuminated the path forward. Willow Creek, with its rich history and vibrant community, was now more than just a backdrop to her life—it was a key part of her story.

Mia's heart was full as she continued writing into the night, knowing that each word brought her closer to understanding herself and her place in the world. The festival had been a turning point, and she was ready to embrace the new chapters of her life with hope and excitement.

The annual Willow Creek Festival was a tradition that had been around for as long as anyone could remember. It was the highlight of the year—a time when the entire town came together to celebrate their community, their history, and each other. There were food stalls, games, music, and parades, all set against the backdrop of the town's picturesque streets.

Mia had almost forgotten how lively the festival could be. As she made her way through the crowded streets, she felt a surge of excitement. This was Willow Creek at its best—vibrant, welcoming, and full of life.

She had agreed to meet Ethan at the festival, and as she weaved through the crowd, she spotted him standing by one of the food stalls, a smile on his face as he waved to her. She waved back, feeling a flutter of anticipation in her chest.

"Hey," Ethan said as she approached, his eyes lighting up at the sight of her. "Glad you made it."

"Wouldn't miss it," Mia replied, returning his smile. "It's been a while since I've been to the festival."

"It's still the same as ever," Ethan said, handing her a cup of lemonade. "A few new faces, maybe, but the spirit's the same."

They spent the next hour wandering through the festival together, sampling food from the stalls, playing games, and watching the parade. It felt easy, natural, and Mia found herself relaxing in Ethan's company. They laughed, reminisced about old times, and talked about the changes in the town.

At one point, they stopped to watch a group of children performing a play about Willow Creek's history. The play was simple but charming, with the children dressed in costumes representing the town's early settlers. As they watched, Mia felt a deep sense of connection to the town and its history—a history that she was now a part of.

"I've been thinking about something," Mia said as the play came to an end. "About how much this town means to me, and how much it's shaped who I am."

Ethan turned to her, his expression serious. "What do you mean?"

"I've started writing again," Mia explained, feeling a mixture of excitement and nervousness. "But this time, I want to write something that's not just about me, but about Willow Creek—about the people who've lived here, the history, and the way this town has shaped all of us."

Ethan's eyes softened, and he reached out to take her hand. "That sounds incredible, Mia. I think it's exactly what you need to do."

Mia smiled, feeling a surge of gratitude for Ethan's support. "It's still just an idea, but it feels right. Like it's something I'm meant to do."

As they continued to explore the festival, Mia felt a sense of contentment that she hadn't felt in a long time. Being back in Willow Creek, reconnecting with her roots, and finding a new sense of purpose in her writing—it all felt like pieces of a puzzle falling into place.

That evening, as the festival began to wind down, Ethan walked Mia home. The streets were quieter now, the sky darkening as the stars began to appear. They walked in comfortable silence, the night air cool and refreshing.

When they reached Mia's porch, Ethan hesitated, his gaze lingering on her. "Mia, I—" He stopped, seeming to struggle with his words.

Mia looked at him, sensing the weight of whatever he was about to say. "What is it, Ethan?"

He took a deep breath, then met her eyes with a look of determination. "I just wanted to say that I'm glad you came back. And not just because of the festival, or because you're writing again. I'm glad you're here, Mia. It feels like things are finally starting to make sense again."

Mia felt her heart swell at his words, a warmth spreading through her. She reached out, taking his hand in hers. "I'm glad I'm here too, Ethan. More than I can put into words."

They stood there for a moment, the quiet of the night wrapping around them. The soft hum of distant music from the festival lingered in the background, blending with the sounds of the night. Mia could see the stars shining brightly above, reflecting the clarity and peace she felt inside.

Ethan leaned closer, his expression tender. "Mia, I've been thinking about us, about what we have here. I know it's been a whirlwind since you came back, but I can't imagine my life without you now. I want to be here with you, not just for the festival or the moment, but for everything that comes next."

Mia's heart raced at his words, and she felt a deep, genuine smile spreading across her face. "Ethan, I feel the same way. Being here with you, in this town that means so much to me, it's like everything is falling into place. I'm ready for whatever comes next too."

Ethan nodded, a look of relief and happiness on his face. "That means a lot to me, Mia. I know there are still things we need to figure out, but I'm excited to do that together."

Mia felt a thrill of anticipation at the thought. "Me too. I think we have something special here, and I'm eager to see where it takes us."

Ethan's gaze was unwavering as he leaned in and kissed her softly on the lips. The kiss was gentle and full of promise, a reaffirmation of the feelings they had for each other.

When they finally parted, Ethan's hand lingered on Mia's cheek, his thumb brushing softly against her skin. "I should go," he said softly, his voice tinged with reluctance. "But I'll be thinking about you."

"I'll be thinking about you too," Mia replied, her voice equally soft.

Ethan gave her one last, lingering smile before turning to leave. Mia watched him walk down the path, her heart full and her mind buzzing with the possibilities of their future together.

As she closed the door behind her, Mia felt a sense of profound satisfaction. The festival had been a reminder of everything she loved about Willow Creek—the community, the history, and the sense of belonging. And it had solidified her feelings for Ethan, reaffirming that she was exactly where she needed to be.

The evening was drawing to a close, but Mia wasn't ready to go to bed just yet. She felt inspired and invigorated by the day's events. She walked to her desk and sat down, her mind racing with ideas for her writing project. The festival had given her new insights into Willow Creek's history and its impact on its residents, and she was eager to incorporate these into her work.

Mia picked up her pen and began to write, the words flowing more easily than they had in days. She wrote about the festival, the people she had seen, and the way the town had come alive. She wrote about Ethan and their conversation, capturing the depth of her feelings and the promise of their future.

As the night wore on, Mia's writing took shape, each word a reflection of her renewed sense of purpose and connection to Willow Creek. The festival had been more than just a celebration—it had been a turning point, a moment of clarity that set the stage for the next chapter of her life.

When she finally put down her pen, the first light of dawn was beginning to seep through the window. Mia felt a deep sense of accomplishment and peace. The future was still uncertain, but for the first time in a long time, she was excited about what lay ahead. With Ethan by her side and Willow Creek as her foundation, she knew she was ready to face whatever came next.

The annual Willow Creek Festival was a tradition that had been around for as long as anyone could remember. It was the highlight of the year—a time when the entire town came together to celebrate their community, their history, and each other. There were food stalls, games, music, and parades, all set against the backdrop of the town's picturesque streets.

Mia had almost forgotten how lively the festival could be. As she made her way through the crowded streets, she felt a surge of excitement. This was Willow Creek at its best—vibrant, welcoming, and full of life.

She had agreed to meet Ethan at the festival, and as she weaved through the crowd, she spotted him standing by one of the food stalls, a smile on his face as he waved to her. She waved back, feeling a flutter of anticipation in her chest.

"Hey," Ethan said as she approached, his eyes lighting up at the sight of her. "Glad you made it."

"Wouldn't miss it," Mia replied, returning his smile. "It's been a while since I've been to the festival."

"It's still the same as ever," Ethan said, handing her a cup of lemonade. "A few new faces, maybe, but the spirit's the same."

They spent the next hour wandering through the festival together, sampling food from the stalls, playing games, and watching the parade. It felt easy, natural, and Mia found herself relaxing in Ethan's company. They laughed, reminisced about old times, and talked about the changes in the town.

At one point, they stopped to watch a group of children performing a play about Willow Creek's history. The play was simple but charming, with the children dressed in costumes representing the town's early settlers. As they watched, Mia felt a deep sense of connection to the town and its history—a history that she was now a part of.

"I've been thinking about something," Mia said as the play came to an end. "About how much this town means to me, and how much it's shaped who I am."

Ethan turned to her, his expression serious. "What do you mean?"

"I've started writing again," Mia explained, feeling a mixture of excitement and nervousness. "But this time, I want to write something that's not just about me, but about Willow Creek—about the people who've lived here, the history, and the way this town has shaped all of us."

Ethan's eyes softened, and he reached out to take her hand. "That sounds incredible, Mia. I think it's exactly what you need to do."

Mia smiled, feeling a surge of gratitude for Ethan's support. "It's still just an idea, but it feels right. Like it's something I'm meant to do."

As they continued to explore the festival, Mia felt a sense of contentment that she hadn't felt in a long time. Being back in Willow Creek, reconnecting with her roots, and finding a new sense of purpose in her writing—it all felt like pieces of a puzzle falling into place.

They came upon a booth where local artisans were displaying their crafts. Mia admired the handmade pottery and woven baskets, feeling inspired by the creativity and skill on display. Ethan seemed to sense her appreciation and suggested they pick out something to commemorate the day.

"How about this?" Ethan said, holding up a small, intricately carved wooden box. "It's beautiful and would make a great keepsake."

Mia took the box from him, running her fingers over the smooth surface. "It's perfect. It'll be a reminder of today."

They continued to wander, stopping at various stalls and enjoying the festival's lively atmosphere. The sun began to set, casting a warm glow over the town. The lights from the festival stalls flickered on, creating a magical ambiance.

As the evening wore on, the festival's main event—the fireworks display—began. Mia and Ethan found a spot on a grassy hill overlooking the town square. They sat close together, sharing a blanket and enjoying the view. The first fireworks exploded in the sky, filling it with vibrant colors and patterns.

Mia leaned her head on Ethan's shoulder, feeling a sense of peace and happiness. The fireworks mirrored her emotions—bright, joyful, and full of possibilities. As she watched the sky light up, she felt a deep connection to Ethan and to Willow Creek.

"This is incredible," Mia said, her voice soft.

Ethan turned to her, his expression tender. "It is. But what makes it even better is sharing it with you."

Mia smiled, her heart swelling with affection. "I'm really glad to be here with you, Ethan. This is exactly what I needed."

Ethan took her hand, his gaze earnest. "I'm here for you, Mia. Whatever you need, whatever you want to do, I'm with you."

The fireworks continued to burst overhead, casting a shimmering light over the town. Mia felt a profound sense of gratitude and love. The festival had brought a renewed sense of hope and clarity into her life. With Ethan by her side and the support of her community, she was ready to embrace the future and pursue her dreams.

As the last of the fireworks faded from the sky, Ethan gently squeezed Mia's hand. "How about we make a promise?"

Mia looked at him curiously. "A promise?"

"Yeah," Ethan said, his eyes sincere. "Let's promise to keep moving forward together, to keep supporting each other and chasing our dreams. No matter what challenges come our way."

Mia's heart fluttered at the thought. "I promise," she said, squeezing his hand back. "Together."

They sat there for a while longer, watching the last remnants of the fireworks and enjoying the peaceful night. The festival had been a celebration of their town and their connection, and Mia knew it marked the beginning of a new chapter in her life.

With the stars shining brightly above and Ethan beside her, Mia felt a renewed sense of purpose and excitement for the future. Whatever challenges lay ahead, she was ready to face them with a heart full of hope and a spirit ready to embrace the possibilities.

Chapter 14: Doubts and Decisions

The morning after the festival, Mia woke up feeling a mix of contentment and unease. The night before had been magical—Ethan's words, the feeling of connection, the sense that she was exactly where she needed to be. But as she lay in bed, staring at the ceiling, doubts began to creep in.

Her writing project was taking shape, but it also felt daunting. She wasn't just writing about her own experiences anymore; she was trying to capture the essence of Willow Creek, a place that meant so much to so many people. What if she couldn't do it justice? What if her words fell short, leaving the story incomplete?

Mia got out of bed and made her way to the kitchen, where she brewed a cup of coffee and sat down at the table, staring at the blank page in her notebook. The doubts weighed heavily on her, making it hard to focus.

As she sipped her coffee, her phone buzzed with a message. It was from her former colleague in the city, offering her a chance to return to her old job. The position was a step up from where she'd been before—a promotion, with better pay and more responsibility. It was the kind of opportunity she'd once dreamed of, back when her career had been everything to her.

Mia stared at the message, her heart sinking. She hadn't expected this, and it threw her into a whirlwind of confusion. Returning to the city meant leaving Willow Creek behind, abandoning her writing project, and giving up the new life she was starting to build. But it also meant security, stability, and a chance to reclaim the career she'd worked so hard for.

She spent the rest of the morning wrestling with the decision, the pros and cons spinning in her mind. The offer was tempting, but every time she thought about leaving Willow Creek, a pang of sadness hit her. This town had become more than just a place to escape—it had become home again. And then there was Ethan. The thought of leaving him behind, of walking away from the connection they were building, felt unbearable.

By the afternoon, Mia was no closer to making a decision. She decided to take a walk to clear her head, hoping that the familiar streets of Willow Creek would help her find some clarity.

As she walked, she found herself heading toward the bookstore, where she knew she'd find Sarah. When Mia entered, the bell above the door chimed, and Sarah looked up from behind the counter with a smile.

"Mia! What a surprise. How are you doing?"

Mia forced a smile, trying to hide the turmoil she was feeling. "I'm okay, I guess. I just needed to get out and clear my head."

Sarah's smile faded as she studied Mia's face. "You look like you have something on your mind. Want to talk about it?"

Mia hesitated for a moment, then nodded. She needed to talk to someone, and Sarah was one of the few people who understood her.

They moved to the small seating area at the back of the store, where they settled into the cozy armchairs. Sarah waited patiently as Mia gathered her thoughts, sipping her tea as she watched her friend.

"I got an offer to go back to the city," Mia finally said, her voice tinged with uncertainty. "A promotion, better pay—it's everything I thought I wanted."

Sarah's eyebrows rose in surprise. "Wow, that's... big. What are you going to do?"

"I don't know," Mia admitted, feeling the weight of the decision pressing down on her. "I've been thinking about it all day, and I'm torn. Part of me wants to go back, to pick up where I left off. But the other part... the other part doesn't want to leave Willow Creek."

Sarah nodded, her expression thoughtful. "You've built something here, Mia. It's not just about the town or your writing—it's about the connections you've made, the growth you've experienced. Going back to the city might mean leaving all of that behind."

"That's what scares me," Mia said quietly. "I don't want to lose what I've found here. But I also don't want to pass up an opportunity like this. What if I regret staying?"

Sarah leaned forward, her eyes kind but firm. "What if you regret leaving? Opportunities come and go, but the things that really matter—the people, the relationships, the sense of belonging—those are harder to find. And from what I've seen, you've found all of that here in Willow Creek."

Mia felt a lump form in her throat. Sarah's words struck a chord deep within her, resonating with the feelings she'd been trying to ignore. She had found something special in Willow Creek—something that went beyond a job or a career. But was it enough to keep her here?

"I don't know what to do," Mia whispered, her voice shaky. "I'm so scared of making the wrong choice."

Sarah reached out and took Mia's hand, giving it a reassuring squeeze. "Whatever choice you make, it will be the right one for you. But don't make it out of fear. Make it out of love—love for yourself, love for this town, love for the people who matter to you."

Mia nodded, tears stinging her eyes. "Thank you, Sarah. I needed to hear that."

They sat in silence for a few moments, Mia absorbing Sarah's words. She still didn't have all the answers, but she felt a little more at peace. The decision was hers to make, and whatever path she chose, she would face it with courage and love.

Later that evening, Mia found herself sitting on her porch, watching the sun dip below the horizon. The air was cool, the sky painted in shades of pink and orange. Willow Creek was quiet, the town settling into the peaceful rhythm of the night.

As she sat there, lost in thought, she heard footsteps on the path. She looked up to see Ethan approaching, his expression warm and familiar.

"Hey," he said, sitting down beside her. "Mind if I join you?"

Mia shook her head, a small smile playing on her lips. "Not at all. I could use the company."

They sat in companionable silence for a while, the only sounds the rustling of the leaves and the distant chirping of crickets. Mia felt a sense of calm settle over her, the doubts of the day fading into the background.

Eventually, Ethan spoke, his voice soft. "You've got something on your mind, don't you?"

Mia sighed, leaning back in her chair. "I got an offer to go back to the city. A good offer."

Ethan was quiet for a moment, his expression unreadable. "And how do you feel about that?"

"Conflicted," Mia admitted. "Part of me wants to go back, to take the job and pick up where I left off. But another part of me... doesn't want to leave. Doesn't want to leave Willow Creek, or you."

Ethan looked at her, his eyes searching hers. "Mia, I want you to be happy. Whether that means staying here or going back to the city, I'll support whatever decision you make. But I'll be honest—I don't want you to leave."

His words hung in the air between them, heavy with meaning. Mia felt her heart ache with the weight of it all—the choices she had to make, the paths she had to choose between.

"I don't want to leave either," Mia whispered, her voice barely audible. "But I'm scared. Scared of making the wrong choice, of giving up something that could be good for me."

Ethan reached out, taking her hand in his. His touch was warm, grounding her in the moment. "There's no right or wrong choice here, Mia. There's only what feels right to you. And whatever you decide, you'll figure it out. We'll figure it out."

Mia looked at him, her heart full of emotion. Ethan had been her anchor, her constant, ever since she returned to Willow Creek. The thought of leaving him behind, of walking away from what they were building together, felt unbearable. But the city, her career, the life she once knew—it all felt so far away now, like a distant memory she wasn't sure she wanted to revisit.

As they sat there, hand in hand, Mia realized that the answer wasn't going to come easily. But for now, she was content to be here, with Ethan, in the place that had become home. And whatever the future held, she knew she would face it with the strength and courage she had found in Willow Creek.

The morning after the festival, Mia woke up feeling a mix of contentment and unease. The night before had been magical—Ethan's words, the feeling of connection, the sense that she was exactly where she needed to be. But as she lay in bed, staring at the ceiling, doubts began to creep in.

Her writing project was taking shape, but it also felt daunting. She wasn't just writing about her own experiences anymore; she was trying to capture the essence of Willow Creek, a place that meant so much to so many people. What if she couldn't do it justice? What if her words fell short, leaving the story incomplete?

Mia got out of bed and made her way to the kitchen, where she brewed a cup of coffee and sat down at the table, staring at the blank page in her notebook. The doubts weighed heavily on her, making it hard to focus.

As she sipped her coffee, her phone buzzed with a message. It was from her former colleague in the city, offering her a chance to return to her old job. The position was a step up from where she'd been before—a promotion, with better pay and more responsibility. It was the kind of opportunity she'd once dreamed of, back when her career had been everything to her.

Mia stared at the message, her heart sinking. She hadn't expected this, and it threw her into a whirlwind of confusion. Returning to the city meant leaving Willow Creek behind, abandoning her writing project, and giving up the new life she was starting to build. But it also meant security, stability, and a chance to reclaim the career she'd worked so hard for.

She spent the rest of the morning wrestling with the decision, the pros and cons spinning in her mind. The offer was tempting, but every time she thought about leaving Willow Creek, a pang of sadness hit her. This town had become more than just a place to escape—it had become home again. And then there was Ethan. The thought of leaving him behind, of walking away from the connection they were building, felt unbearable.

By the afternoon, Mia was no closer to making a decision. She decided to take a walk to clear her head, hoping that the familiar streets of Willow Creek would help her find some clarity.

As she walked, she found herself heading toward the bookstore, where she knew she'd find Sarah. When Mia entered, the bell above the door chimed, and Sarah looked up from behind the counter with a smile.

"Mia! What a surprise. How are you doing?"

Mia forced a smile, trying to hide the turmoil she was feeling. "I'm okay, I guess. I just needed to get out and clear my head."

Sarah's smile faded as she studied Mia's face. "You look like you have something on your mind. Want to talk about it?"

Mia hesitated for a moment, then nodded. She needed to talk to someone, and Sarah was one of the few people who understood her.

They moved to the small seating area at the back of the store, where they settled into the cozy armchairs. Sarah waited patiently as Mia gathered her thoughts, sipping her tea as she watched her friend.

"I got an offer to go back to the city," Mia finally said, her voice tinged with uncertainty. "A promotion, better pay—it's everything I thought I wanted."

Sarah's eyebrows rose in surprise. "Wow, that's... big. What are you going to do?"

"I don't know," Mia admitted, feeling the weight of the decision pressing down on her. "I've been thinking about it all day, and I'm torn. Part of me wants to go back, to pick up where I left off. But the other part... the other part doesn't want to leave Willow Creek."

Sarah nodded, her expression thoughtful. "You've built something here, Mia. It's not just about the town or your writing—it's about the connections you've made, the growth you've experienced. Going back to the city might mean leaving all of that behind."

"That's what scares me," Mia said quietly. "I don't want to lose what I've found here. But I also don't want to pass up an opportunity like this. What if I regret staying?"

Sarah leaned forward, her eyes kind but firm. "What if you regret leaving? Opportunities come and go, but the things that really matter—the people, the relationships, the sense of belonging—those are harder to find. And from what I've seen, you've found all of that here in Willow Creek."

Mia felt a lump form in her throat. Sarah's words struck a chord deep within her, resonating with the feelings she'd been trying to ignore. She had found something special in Willow Creek—something that went beyond a job or a career. But was it enough to keep her here?

"I don't know what to do," Mia whispered, her voice shaky. "I'm so scared of making the wrong choice."

Sarah reached out and took Mia's hand, giving it a reassuring squeeze. "Whatever choice you make, it will be the right one for you. But don't make it out of fear. Make it out of love—love for yourself, love for this town, love for the people who matter to you."

Mia nodded, tears stinging her eyes. "Thank you, Sarah. I needed to hear that."

They sat in silence for a few moments, Mia absorbing Sarah's words. She still didn't have all the answers, but she felt a little more at peace. The decision was hers to make, and whatever path she chose, she would face it with courage and love.

Later that evening, Mia found herself sitting on her porch, watching the sun dip below the horizon. The air was cool, the sky painted in shades of pink and orange. Willow Creek was quiet, the town settling into the peaceful rhythm of the night.

As she sat there, lost in thought, she heard footsteps on the path. She looked up to see Ethan approaching, his expression warm and familiar.

"Hey," he said, sitting down beside her. "Mind if I join you?"

Mia shook her head, a small smile playing on her lips. "Not at all. I could use the company."

They sat in companionable silence for a while, the only sounds the rustling of the leaves and the distant chirping of crickets. Mia felt a sense of calm settle over her, the doubts of the day fading into the background.

Eventually, Ethan spoke, his voice soft. "You've got something on your mind, don't you?"

Mia sighed, leaning back in her chair. "I got an offer to go back to the city. A good offer."

Ethan was quiet for a moment, his expression unreadable. "And how do you feel about that?"

"Conflicted," Mia admitted. "Part of me wants to go back, to take the job and pick up where I left off. But another part of me... doesn't want to leave. Doesn't want to leave Willow Creek, or you."

Ethan looked at her, his eyes searching hers. "Mia, I want you to be happy. Whether that means staying here or going back to the city, I'll support whatever decision you make. But I'll be honest—I don't want you to leave."

His words hung in the air between them, heavy with meaning. Mia felt her heart ache with the weight of it all—the choices she had to make, the paths she had to choose between.

"I don't want to leave either," Mia whispered, her voice barely audible. "But I'm scared. Scared of making the wrong choice, of giving up something that could be good for me."

Ethan reached out, taking her hand in his. His touch was warm, grounding her in the moment. "There's no right or wrong choice here, Mia. There's only what feels right to you. And whatever you decide, you'll figure it out. We'll figure it out."

Mia looked at him, her heart full of emotion. Ethan had been her anchor, her constant, ever since she returned to Willow Creek. The thought of leaving him behind, of walking away from what they were building together, felt unbearable. But the city, her career, the life she once knew—it all felt so far away now, like a distant memory she wasn't sure she wanted to revisit.

As they sat there, hand in hand, Mia realized that the answer wasn't going to come easily. But for now, she was content to be here, with Ethan, in the place that had become home. And whatever the future held, she knew she would face it with the strength and courage she had found in Willow Creek.

As the stars began to emerge from the darkening sky, Mia and Ethan sat in quiet contemplation. The gentle breeze rustled the leaves around them, creating a soothing backdrop to their thoughts. Mia felt a sense of calm settling in, even though her mind was still a whirlwind of conflicting emotions.

Ethan eventually broke the silence, his voice thoughtful. "Have you had a chance to really think about what makes you happiest, Mia? Not just in terms of work or the city versus Willow Creek, but what truly brings you joy?"

Mia considered his question carefully. "I think I've been so focused on the logistics of making the decision that I haven't really taken a step back to think about what makes me happiest. I love Willow Creek, and I feel like I'm starting to build something meaningful here, both with my writing and with you. But the idea of returning to my old job—it's familiar, and there's a part of me that misses the challenge and excitement of that world."

Ethan nodded, his gaze steady. "Sometimes, we get so caught up in what we think we should do that we forget to listen to what we really want. Maybe it would help to take a step back and imagine your life in both scenarios. Picture yourself in the city, doing that job you're being offered. How does that feel? And then, picture yourself staying here, continuing your writing and your life with me in Willow Creek. What resonates more with you?"

Mia closed her eyes, letting Ethan's suggestion guide her thoughts. She imagined herself back in the city, returning to a high-paced job, surrounded by colleagues and deadlines. The excitement was there, but so was a sense of disconnection from what she had recently come to cherish.

Then, she imagined staying in Willow Creek. The quiet mornings, the sense of community, the slow but fulfilling pace of life. She saw herself finishing her writing project, contributing to the town's narrative, and building a future with Ethan. The sense of peace and belonging was palpable.

When she opened her eyes, she looked at Ethan with a soft smile. "I think I know what I need to do. I need to listen to my heart and follow what feels right for me, not just what looks good on paper."

Ethan's face lit up with a gentle smile. "Whatever you decide, I'm here for you. I believe in you and your ability to make the right choice for yourself."

Mia felt a renewed sense of clarity. The decision was still daunting, but she now had a clearer sense of where her true happiness lay. She knew that staying in Willow Creek felt right, even if it meant letting go of a secure opportunity in the city.

As the night deepened, Mia and Ethan continued to talk, their conversation flowing easily from one topic to another. The doubts that had plagued Mia earlier seemed to dissolve in the comfort of Ethan's presence and the familiarity of Willow Creek.

Eventually, Ethan stood up, stretching and yawning. "I should get going. It's getting late."

Mia rose as well, her heart lighter than it had been earlier. "Thanks for being here, Ethan. I really needed this."

Ethan reached out and pulled her into a gentle hug. "Anytime. I'm always here for you."

They shared a tender kiss goodnight, and Ethan walked down the path, disappearing into the soft glow of the streetlights. Mia watched him go, feeling a sense of peace settle over her. The decision was not entirely made yet, but she felt more certain about the direction she wanted to head.

She turned back to her porch, looking out at the tranquil night sky. The stars seemed to shine a little brighter, as if offering their own form of guidance. Mia knew that whatever path she chose, she would do so with the confidence that came from knowing her heart was in the right place.

She took a deep breath, ready to embrace the next steps in her journey with a renewed sense of purpose and clarity.

As Mia watched Ethan walk away, a sense of resolution began to form within her. The night had brought her clarity, but there were still practical considerations to address. She needed to decide how to formally respond to the job offer and how to communicate her decision to those who mattered most in her life.

The next morning, Mia woke early with a renewed sense of determination. She had decided that she would stay in Willow Creek, but she wanted to approach her decision thoughtfully and with respect to the opportunity she had been given.

She sat at her kitchen table, pen in hand, drafting a response to her former colleague. The words came slowly at first, but they began to flow as she expressed her gratitude for the offer and her regret at not being able to accept it. She carefully articulated her reasons, emphasizing that her decision was based on personal growth and a newfound sense of belonging in Willow Creek.

After sending the email, Mia felt a weight lift off her shoulders. She knew that her decision was the right one for her, but it was still difficult to let go of a familiar world that had once been a significant part of her life.

The rest of the day was spent in a flurry of activity. Mia met with Sarah to share her decision and to discuss the next steps for her writing project. Sarah was supportive and excited about the direction Mia was taking, and they brainstormed ideas for how Mia could integrate the town's history with her personal story.

Later, Mia visited the local library to continue her research. The project was starting to take shape, and she felt invigorated by the new energy she was channeling into her work. The library's cozy reading nooks and the knowledge contained in its shelves were a comfort, reminding her of why she had fallen in love with writing in the first place.

By the time evening rolled around, Mia felt a deep sense of satisfaction. She had made the right choice, and now she was ready to focus on her future in Willow Creek. But there was one more thing she needed to do—talk to Ethan about her decision and the future they were beginning to build together.

She decided to surprise him with dinner, preparing a simple but heartfelt meal. As she cooked, she thought about their conversation and the life they could build together. The aroma of the meal filled her kitchen, and she felt a sense of contentment wash over her.

When Ethan arrived, he was pleasantly surprised by the warm, inviting atmosphere of Mia's home. The table was set with care, and the smell of freshly cooked food was comforting.

"Wow, this looks amazing," Ethan said, taking in the scene with a smile. "You didn't have to go through all this trouble."

Mia smiled, her eyes meeting his with warmth. "I wanted to. I have something important to share with you."

They enjoyed their dinner together, the conversation flowing easily as always. Mia could see the genuine happiness in Ethan's eyes, and it made her heart swell with affection. As they finished their meal, Mia took a deep breath and prepared to share her decision.

"Ethan, I've made a decision about the job offer," she said, her voice steady but filled with emotion. "I've decided to stay in Willow Creek."

Ethan's eyes lit up, and he reached across the table to take her hand. "That's wonderful news, Mia. I'm so glad you're staying."

Mia felt a rush of relief and joy at his reaction. "I've realized that Willow Creek is where I belong right now. I want to finish my writing project and build a life here. And that means a lot to me."

Ethan squeezed her hand gently. "I'm really happy for you. And for us."

They shared a tender moment, their connection deepening with every word. Mia felt a renewed sense of hope and excitement about the future. She knew that there would be challenges ahead, but she was ready to face them with Ethan by her side and the support of the community she had come to cherish.

As they settled into the evening, talking about their plans and dreams, Mia felt a profound sense of peace. Her decision had been difficult, but it was the right one for her. And as she looked forward to the future, she knew that with each step she took, she was building a life filled with purpose, connection, and love.

After the heartfelt dinner with Ethan, Mia felt a sense of clarity and calm. The decision to stay in Willow Creek had brought her immense relief, but there were still a few conversations she needed to have to solidify her new path forward.

The next morning, Mia decided to visit her father, William Prescott. Their relationship had been strained, but she wanted to be honest with him about her decision and her new direction in life. It was time to bridge the gap between them and to share her plans.

She arrived at her father's house, a modest home on the edge of town. The familiar, weathered exterior brought a pang of nostalgia. Mia took a deep breath before ringing the doorbell. After a moment, William answered, his expression softening at the sight of her.

"Mia," he said, a hint of surprise in his voice. "It's good to see you."

"Hi, Dad," Mia replied, offering a tentative smile. "Can we talk?"

They settled in the living room, the space filled with the comforting hum of quiet domesticity. Mia felt a mix of apprehension and determination as she began to speak.

"I wanted to let you know that I've decided to stay in Willow Creek," Mia started. "I turned down the job offer in the city."

William's brow furrowed slightly, but he nodded, listening intently. "I see. And what does that mean for you?"

"It means that I'm focusing on my writing and this town," Mia explained. "I've started a project that combines my personal experiences with the history of Willow Creek. It's something I feel deeply connected to."

William's expression softened further, and he seemed to consider her words carefully. "That sounds like a significant undertaking. I'm glad to hear you're following your passion."

Mia took a deep breath, trying to find the right words. "Dad, I know our relationship hasn't been easy, but I want you to know that this decision is about more than just my career. It's about finding where I belong and reconnecting with my roots."

William's gaze met hers, and for a moment, there was a flicker of vulnerability in his eyes. "Mia, I may not always understand your choices, but I want you to be happy. I can see that this is important to you, and that's enough for me."

Mia felt a wave of emotion wash over her. The acknowledgment from her father, though understated, was meaningful. "Thank you, Dad. It means a lot to me."

As their conversation continued, they talked about their shared memories and the changes in their lives. It was a step towards mending their relationship, and Mia felt a sense of closure she hadn't anticipated. She left her father's house feeling lighter, with a renewed sense of hope for their future interactions.

The following days were a flurry of activity as Mia immersed herself in her writing project and continued to integrate her research into her work. The more she delved into the history of Willow Creek, the more she felt connected to the town and its people. She spent time interviewing locals, gathering stories, and piecing together the tapestry of the community's past.

Ethan continued to be a source of unwavering support. They spent their evenings together, often brainstorming ideas and discussing Mia's progress. The bond between them grew stronger, and Mia felt a deep sense of gratitude for his presence in her life.

One afternoon, as Mia was working on her manuscript, she received a call from Sarah. "Mia, I have some exciting news! The local community center is hosting a showcase for local authors, and they've invited you to present your project."

Mia's heart skipped a beat. The opportunity to share her work with the community was both thrilling and nerve-wracking. "That's amazing, Sarah. Thank you for letting me know."

Sarah's voice was encouraging. "You've worked so hard on this, Mia. I think it's a great chance for you to connect with others and showcase what you've been working on."

Mia agreed, feeling a renewed sense of purpose. She began preparing for the showcase, eager to share her journey and the story of Willow Creek with the people who had become such an integral part of her life.

As the day of the showcase approached, Mia felt a mixture of excitement and nervousness. She knew that presenting her work would be a significant step, but she was ready to embrace the opportunity and celebrate the progress she had made.

In the quiet moments leading up to the event, Mia reflected on her journey—from her return to Willow Creek to her decision to stay, and the personal growth she had experienced along the way. She had found a sense of belonging, purpose, and love, and she was excited to share that with the community.

With Ethan by her side, the support of her friends, and the sense of fulfillment that came from pursuing her passion, Mia felt ready to face whatever the future held. She had made her decision, embraced her new path, and was poised to take the next step in her journey with confidence and hope.

Chapter 15: A Heart Torn

The days after receiving the job offer were filled with a constant undercurrent of tension for Mia. Every waking moment, the decision loomed over her, pressing down on her with the weight of all the possibilities it represented. She found herself slipping into old habits—overthinking, analyzing every potential outcome, and imagining what her life might look like if she chose one path over the other.

Ethan noticed the change in her, though he didn't push her to talk about it. He respected her need for space, understanding that this was a decision only she could make. But his quiet support was ever-present, a steady reminder that whatever choice she made, she wasn't alone.

One afternoon, Mia found herself at the park where she and Ethan had shared their first kiss. The memory of that moment warmed her, bringing a small smile to her lips as she sat on a bench overlooking the lake. The water was calm, reflecting the clear blue sky above, and the peacefulness of the scene soothed some of the turmoil inside her.

She pulled out her notebook, the pages filled with scribbled notes and half-formed ideas for her writing project. But today, the words wouldn't come. Her mind kept drifting back to the offer, to the life she could have if she returned to the city. The familiar buzz of ambition tugged at her, reminding her of the satisfaction she once felt in her career.

But then she thought of Ethan, of the way he looked at her with such quiet understanding, of the warmth that spread through her whenever she was near him. She thought of the town, of the people who had welcomed her back with open arms, and the sense of belonging that had slowly begun to take root in her heart.

Mia closed her notebook, letting out a deep breath. She couldn't deny that a part of her was tempted by the offer, by the prospect of reclaiming the career she had once been so passionate about. But the thought of leaving Willow Creek, of leaving Ethan, filled her with a sadness that was hard to shake.

As she sat there, lost in thought, her phone buzzed in her pocket. She pulled it out and saw a message from her father.

William Prescott: *How are you holding up, Mia? I know you've got a lot on your plate. Just wanted to remind you that I'm here if you need to talk.*

Mia stared at the message, feeling a pang of guilt. She hadn't spoken to her father in days, too wrapped up in her own thoughts to reach out. But his message reminded her that she wasn't alone in this—her father had been trying to mend their relationship, just as she had been trying to find her way.

With a sigh, Mia typed out a response.

Mia: *I'm okay, Dad. Just trying to figure things out. Maybe we could talk later?*

His reply was almost immediate.

William Prescott: *Of course. I'll be here whenever you're ready.*

Mia slipped her phone back into her pocket, her thoughts drifting to her father. Their relationship had always been complicated, but in recent months, they had begun to bridge the gap that had grown between them. She knew he was trying, and that meant more to her than she could express.

Later that evening, Mia sat in her living room, the soft glow of the lamps casting a warm light over the room. She had decided to take her father up on his offer to talk, hoping that he might be able to provide some clarity—or at least a different perspective.

When she called, he answered on the first ring.

"Mia, it's good to hear from you," William said, his voice tinged with concern.

"Hi, Dad," Mia replied, her voice wavering slightly. "I, uh, I need some advice."

"Of course. What's on your mind?"

Mia took a deep breath, then told him about the job offer, about the conflict she felt between returning to the city and staying in Willow Creek. As she spoke, her father listened quietly, offering the occasional word of encouragement but mostly letting her work through her thoughts.

When she finished, there was a long pause on the other end of the line. Mia could almost picture her father sitting in his study, thinking carefully before he spoke.

"You know, Mia," William began slowly, "I've spent a lot of my life chasing after what I thought was success. I built a career, provided for my family, and achieved things I'm proud of. But in all that time, I lost sight of what really mattered—my relationships, my happiness. I don't want you to make the same mistakes I did."

Mia felt her heart tighten at his words. Her father had always been a man of few words when it came to emotions, but lately, he had been opening up more, showing a side of himself that she hadn't seen before.

"What are you saying, Dad?" she asked softly.

"I'm saying that you should follow your heart," William replied. "You've found something in Willow Creek that makes you happy. That's not something you should give up lightly. A career is important, but it's not everything. And from what you've told me, it sounds like you've built a life there that's worth holding on to."

Mia closed her eyes, tears prickling at the corners. "But what if I regret staying? What if I'm giving up a chance to be successful?"

"Success isn't just about what you do for a living, Mia," William said gently. "It's about finding fulfillment, about living a life that makes you happy. If that means staying in Willow Creek, then that's what you should do. And if it means going back to the city, then that's okay too. But whatever you decide, make sure it's what you want—not what you think you should do."

Mia nodded, even though he couldn't see her. "Thank you, Dad. I needed to hear that."

"Anytime, sweetheart," William replied, his voice full of warmth. "And whatever you decide, know that I'm proud of you. You've come a long way, and I'm honored to be your father."

After they hung up, Mia sat in the quiet of her living room, her heart full of conflicting emotions. Her father's words had given her some clarity, but the decision was still hers to make.

As she lay down to sleep that night, Mia found herself thinking about what her father had said. Success wasn't just about a career—it was about finding happiness, about building a life that was meaningful. And as she drifted off, one thought kept repeating in her mind: Willow Creek was where she felt most like herself. Maybe that was the answer she had been looking for all along.

The next morning, Mia woke up with a renewed sense of purpose. She had spent the night reflecting on her conversation with her father and the choices before her. The clarity she had gained helped to dispel some of the confusion and indecision that had plagued her.

With a deep breath, Mia decided to spend the day focusing on her writing project and the upcoming community showcase. As she worked, she found herself more immersed in her manuscript than she had been in days. The words flowed more freely, and she felt a sense of connection to her subject that was both comforting and invigorating.

Ethan noticed the change in her demeanor. She seemed lighter, more focused, and it was clear to him that she was making progress. One evening, as they sat together on her porch, Ethan decided to address the topic that had been lingering between them.

"Mia," he began gently, "you seem more at peace lately. Have you figured things out?"

Mia looked at him, her eyes reflecting a mixture of relief and determination. "I think I have," she said softly. "I've realized that staying in Willow Creek is what truly feels right for me. This town, the people, the life I'm building here—it's where I want to be. And it's not just about avoiding regret; it's about embracing the life I've found."

Ethan smiled, his relief evident. "I'm glad to hear that. I've always believed that you belong here, and I'm excited to see where your writing takes you."

They spent the rest of the evening talking about Mia's project and making plans for the community showcase. Ethan's support and enthusiasm made her feel even more confident in her decision. She knew that whatever challenges lay ahead, she had a solid foundation in Willow Creek and in her relationship with Ethan.

The day of the showcase arrived, and Mia was filled with a mix of nervousness and excitement. The community center was bustling with activity, and local residents filled the room, eager to see the work of their neighbors. Mia's heart raced as she prepared to present her project, but she also felt a deep sense of pride and accomplishment.

When her turn came, Mia took the stage and began to speak. She shared her journey, the inspiration behind her project, and the stories she had uncovered about Willow Creek. As she spoke, she felt a profound connection with the audience. Their interest and support were tangible, and she could see the impact her work was having on them.

After her presentation, Mia received warm congratulations and encouraging feedback from the community. It was a moment of validation, a reminder that she had made the right choice by staying in Willow Creek. The sense of belonging she felt was reinforced by the support of her neighbors and friends.

As the event came to a close, Ethan joined her, wrapping her in a comforting hug. "You did amazing," he said, his voice filled with pride. "I knew you would."

Mia smiled, her heart full. "Thank you, Ethan. I couldn't have done this without your support."

They walked out of the community center hand in hand, the night air cool and refreshing. Mia felt a deep sense of contentment and fulfillment. The decision to stay in Willow Creek had been a difficult one, but it had brought her to a place where she felt truly at home.

As they strolled through the quiet streets, Mia looked around at the familiar sights of her town, feeling a deep appreciation for the life she was building. She knew there would be challenges ahead, but she also knew that she was ready to face them with courage and determination.

With Ethan by her side and the support of her community, Mia felt confident in her path forward. She had found her place in Willow Creek, and it was here that she would continue to grow, to write, and to build a future filled with hope and happiness.

As the days went by following the showcase, Mia felt an undeniable shift within herself. The reassurance she had found in her decision to stay in Willow Creek had begun to settle into a deep sense of contentment. But even amidst this newfound peace, the echoes of her old life in the city still lingered, occasionally stirring up doubts and memories.

One afternoon, Mia found herself in the local library, sorting through old newspapers and town records for her writing project. The library's serene atmosphere was a welcome retreat from the bustle of the town, and Mia appreciated the quiet as she worked.

As she sifted through the stacks of papers, her eyes fell on a familiar face in an old photograph—an article about her former boss in the city, celebrating a major career milestone. The sight of the article brought a pang of nostalgia, and she couldn't help but wonder what her life might have been like had she stayed.

Lost in thought, she barely noticed when the librarian, Mrs. Thompson, approached her.

"Everything alright, dear?" Mrs. Thompson's voice was gentle, breaking through Mia's reverie.

"Oh, yes," Mia replied, looking up with a start. "Just reminiscing a bit."

Mrs. Thompson smiled kindly. "I understand. Sometimes, it's hard to leave behind what we once knew, even when we know we're making the right choice."

Mia nodded, feeling a bit embarrassed. "It's just that I keep thinking about my old job and what I left behind. I wonder if I made the right decision."

Mrs. Thompson sat down next to her, her eyes full of wisdom. "Change is always difficult. It's natural to question our choices. But remember, Mia, the heart often knows what's best even when the mind struggles. You've found something special here in Willow Creek. It's not just about what you left behind, but what you've gained by staying."

Mia's thoughts swirled as she listened to Mrs. Thompson's comforting words. It was true—her decision to stay had led her to rediscover parts of herself she had lost while pursuing her career in the city. She had reconnected with her roots, her community, and had started a new chapter in her life.

As Mia left the library that day, she felt a renewed sense of resolve. The doubts she had been wrestling with were still there, but they no longer seemed as overpowering. She realized that her decision wasn't just about choosing between two paths—it was about embracing the path that felt right for her now.

That evening, as she walked through Willow Creek's charming streets, she spotted Ethan sitting on a bench outside the town's quaint café. His presence was a comfort, a reminder of why she had chosen to stay.

"Hey," Mia greeted him, taking a seat beside him.

"Hey," Ethan replied with a warm smile. "How was your day?"

"Productive, but also a bit reflective," Mia said, her gaze drifting over the town's twinkling lights. "I've been thinking a lot about my decision lately."

Ethan took her hand, his touch reassuring. "It's normal to have doubts, Mia. Change is hard, and it's okay to question things. But you've done so much to build a life here. I can see how happy you are, and I believe in the path you've chosen."

Mia looked at him, her heart swelling with affection. "I know. And I'm grateful for your support. I've realized that while the city and my old job were important to me, they're not where I'm meant to be right now. Willow Creek is home."

Ethan nodded, squeezing her hand gently. "I'm glad you feel that way. And I'm here for you, no matter what."

They sat together in comfortable silence, enjoying the peaceful evening. As Mia looked around at the town she had come to love, she felt a sense of peace settle over her. The path she had chosen was hers, and though it had been difficult to get to this point, she knew that it was the right one for her.

The days ahead might bring new challenges and moments of doubt, but Mia felt ready to face them with the support of those she cared about and the newfound strength she had discovered within herself. As she and Ethan walked home, she knew that whatever lay ahead, she would embrace it with an open heart and a clear sense of purpose.

And as the stars shone brightly above Willow Creek, Mia felt a deep sense of belonging and contentment, knowing that she had made the choice that truly reflected who she was and what she valued most.

The days following Mia's conversation with Ethan were filled with a quiet determination. She had come to terms with her decision, but the transition was still a process. Each day, she found new ways to embrace her life in Willow Creek, deepening her connection with the community and continuing to work on her writing project.

One crisp autumn morning, Mia decided to take a break from her usual routine and visit the town's farmer's market. The market was bustling with activity, and the vibrant colors of fresh produce and handmade goods were a welcome sight. As she wandered through the stalls, she felt a renewed sense of appreciation for the simple pleasures of life in Willow Creek.

While browsing a stall of homemade jams, Mia bumped into Sarah, who was busy selecting some colorful peppers.

"Mia!" Sarah greeted her with a bright smile. "It's great to see you out and about. How's everything going?"

"Hi, Sarah," Mia said, returning her smile. "It's going well. I'm trying to make the most of my time here and really settle into my new life."

Sarah's eyes sparkled with understanding. "That's wonderful to hear. I've been meaning to catch up with you. How are things going with the writing project?"

Mia sighed, a mixture of satisfaction and frustration evident in her expression. "It's coming along. I'm still finding my rhythm, but I'm getting there. It's just been a bit challenging balancing everything and staying focused."

Sarah nodded sympathetically. "I can imagine. But knowing you, I'm sure you'll find a way to make it all work. You've always been so dedicated."

As they continued to chat, Sarah mentioned a new event the town was planning—a literary festival to celebrate local authors and their contributions to the community. Mia's interest was piqued. It seemed like the perfect opportunity to showcase her work and connect with other writers.

"Hey, that festival sounds amazing," Mia said with a grin. "I'd love to be involved. Do you know how I can participate?"

Sarah's face lit up. "Actually, I'm helping to organize it. We're looking for local authors to read their work and share their experiences. I think you'd be a great addition. Let me know if you're interested, and I can get you the details."

Mia's heart raced with excitement. The festival could be a significant step in her journey as a writer and a way to integrate even more deeply into the community she had grown to love.

"That sounds perfect," Mia said, her enthusiasm evident. "I'd love to be part of it. Just let me know what I need to do."

Sarah gave her a quick hug before they parted ways, and Mia continued her visit to the market with a renewed sense of purpose. The thought of participating in the festival filled her with a new energy and motivation.

Later that week, Mia received an invitation to discuss her participation in the festival with the planning committee. The meeting was held at the town hall, and as Mia walked in, she was greeted by familiar faces—Sarah, a few local authors, and other members of the community.

The meeting was productive and inspiring. Mia shared her ideas for her reading and discussed how she could contribute to the festival's success. She felt a deep sense of connection with the group, and their enthusiasm for the event matched her own.

As the meeting concluded, Sarah approached Mia with a warm smile. "I'm really glad you're going to be part of this. It's going to be a fantastic event, and having you there will make it even better."

"Thank you, Sarah," Mia said, feeling a surge of gratitude. "I'm excited to be involved. It feels like a great way to give back to the community that's given me so much."

With the festival on the horizon, Mia threw herself into her writing with renewed vigor. She worked on her reading selection, refining her work and preparing to share her journey with the town. The process was both exhilarating and nerve-wracking, but she felt a deep sense of fulfillment with each step.

As the day of the festival approached, Mia's anticipation grew. The community had rallied together to create a vibrant and celebratory event, and Mia couldn't wait to be a part of it. The festival represented not just a personal milestone but also a reflection of the new life she had built in Willow Creek.

One evening, as Mia sat at her kitchen table, reviewing her notes for the festival, Ethan joined her with a thoughtful expression.

"You've been working hard on this," he said, his voice gentle. "How are you feeling about it?"

Mia looked up, her eyes shining with a mix of excitement and nerves. "I'm feeling good. It's been a lot of work, but it's also been really rewarding. I think this festival is going to be a wonderful experience."

Ethan reached across the table, taking her hand in his. "I'm so proud of you. I know this means a lot to you, and I believe it's going to be fantastic."

Mia squeezed his hand, feeling a wave of affection. "Thank you. I couldn't have come this far without your support."

They shared a quiet moment together, their connection palpable. Mia knew that whatever the outcome of the festival, she had found something deeply meaningful in Willow Creek. The journey had been filled with challenges and doubts, but it had also been marked by moments of growth and discovery.

As the festival day dawned, Willow Creek was alive with activity and excitement. Mia stood on the stage, looking out at the crowd, her heart pounding with anticipation. The festival was a celebration of all she had achieved and a testament to the new chapter she was living.

As she began her reading, she felt a profound sense of gratitude and joy. The journey had been long and winding, but it had led her to a place where she truly belonged. And as she spoke her words to the audience, Mia knew that she had found her place in Willow Creek, and that her heart was finally at peace.

The festival day arrived with a crisp, golden autumn morning. Willow Creek was transformed into a lively hub of activity, with colorful banners fluttering in the breeze and the air filled with the aroma of freshly baked goods and brewed coffee. Booths lined the streets, showcasing local crafts, books, and art, while live music played in the background, adding to the festive atmosphere.

Mia walked through the bustling streets, taking in the sights and sounds with a mix of excitement and nervousness. She had spent weeks preparing for her reading, and now, as she approached the main stage, she felt a familiar flutter of anxiety in her stomach. The festival was not just a chance to share her work; it was a significant milestone in her journey of settling into Willow Creek and embracing her new life.

As she made her way to the stage, she noticed Ethan and Sarah among the crowd, their faces filled with encouragement and support. Ethan gave her a reassuring smile, while Sarah waved enthusiastically. Their presence was a comfort, reminding her of the strong support network she had built in the town.

The time for her reading approached, and Mia took a deep breath as she walked onto the stage. The sun was bright, casting a warm glow over the gathering crowd. She could see familiar faces from the community, their expressions filled with anticipation. Mia took her place at the microphone, her heart racing as she looked out over the audience.

She began her reading, her voice steady but tinged with emotion. As she spoke, she shared her journey of rediscovery and transformation, the challenges she had faced, and the profound impact Willow Creek had had on her life. Her words resonated with the audience, and she could see them nodding in understanding and connection.

Throughout her reading, Mia felt a deep sense of fulfillment. The festival was more than just an event; it was a celebration of her new beginning and the community that had welcomed her with open arms. The support and appreciation from the audience were overwhelming, and she knew that her decision to stay in Willow Creek was the right one.

After her reading, Mia mingled with the crowd, receiving heartfelt congratulations and compliments on her performance. She was touched by the warmth and kindness of the people around her, and she felt a renewed sense of belonging. The festival had been a beautiful affirmation of the life she had built in Willow Creek and the connections she had forged.

As the day turned into evening, Mia found herself standing beside Ethan, watching the sunset over the town. The sky was painted with shades of pink and orange, casting a serene glow over Willow Creek. Ethan reached for her hand, his touch warm and reassuring.

"You were amazing today," Ethan said softly. "I'm so proud of you."

Mia smiled, her heart full. "Thank you, Ethan. It was a wonderful day. I feel so grateful for all the support and love from everyone here."

Ethan looked at her with a tender expression. "I'm glad you're happy. I know how much this means to you."

They stood together in comfortable silence, savoring the peaceful end to a fulfilling day. The festival had been a success, and Mia felt a deep sense of contentment and clarity. Her heart was finally at peace, and she knew that she had made the right choice in staying in Willow Creek.

As they walked hand in hand through the town square, Mia reflected on the journey that had brought her to this moment. The doubts and struggles she had faced had been challenging, but they had also led her to a place of true happiness and belonging. She had found her voice, her purpose, and a love that made her heart whole.

In the glow of the festival lights and the warmth of Ethan's presence, Mia felt a profound sense of gratitude. The decision to stay in Willow Creek had been difficult, but it had also been the path to finding herself and creating a life that was truly fulfilling.

As they continued their walk, Mia glanced up at the starry sky, feeling a sense of wonder and possibility. The future was still uncertain, but for the first time in a long while, she felt ready to embrace whatever came next. With Ethan by her side and the support of her newfound community, Mia was confident that she could face any challenges that lay ahead.

And as the night settled over Willow Creek, Mia knew that she was exactly where she was meant to be. Her heart, once torn, was now whole, and her journey had led her to a place of peace and happiness that she had always dreamed of finding.

Chapter 16: A Glimpse of the Future

The next morning, Mia woke up with a sense of calm that had been eluding her for days. Her conversation with her father had lifted some of the weight off her shoulders, and she felt more at peace with the idea that whatever decision she made, it had to be based on what would make her truly happy.

She decided to take the day off from writing and go into town. The sun was shining brightly, casting a warm glow over the streets of Willow Creek. As she walked past the familiar shops and cafes, she couldn't help but feel a deep connection to this place. Every corner held a memory, every face she passed brought a smile to her lips. This town had embraced her when she needed it most, and now, it felt like home.

Mia stopped by the bakery and picked up a loaf of fresh bread before making her way to the park. She found a quiet spot by the lake, where she could sit and watch the water ripple in the breeze. As she tore off a piece of bread and nibbled on it, her mind wandered to the future.

What would it look like if she stayed in Willow Creek? She imagined herself continuing to write, finding inspiration in the everyday moments that this town offered. She pictured herself growing closer to Ethan, building a life with him that was rooted in love and trust. She could see herself becoming more involved in the community, perhaps even organizing events or workshops that brought people together.

And then there was the city. She could see that life too—a fast-paced, high-powered career that challenged her and pushed her to new heights. There would be excitement, ambition, and the satisfaction of achieving goals she had once set for herself. But it would also mean leaving behind the peace and simplicity that Willow Creek offered, and potentially losing the connection she had found with Ethan.

Mia sighed, feeling the familiar pull of doubt. It wasn't an easy decision, but she knew she couldn't keep putting it off. She needed to make a choice, and soon.

As she sat there, lost in thought, she heard footsteps approaching. She looked up to see Ethan walking towards her, a small smile on his face.

"Hey," he said, sitting down beside her. "Mind if I join you?"

"Not at all," Mia replied, her heart lifting at the sight of him. "What brings you here?"

"I was hoping to find you," Ethan said, his gaze steady on hers. "I wanted to talk."

Mia nodded, her stomach fluttering with nerves. She knew what was coming—Ethan had been giving her space, but she could tell that he was eager to know where her head was at.

"I've been thinking a lot," Mia began, her voice tentative. "About the offer, about Willow Creek, about us."

Ethan nodded, his expression serious. "And?"

"And... I'm still not sure what the right decision is," Mia admitted. "But I do know that I don't want to lose what we have. You're important to me, Ethan. More than I can put into words."

Ethan's eyes softened, and he reached out to take her hand. "You're important to me too, Mia. And I don't want you to feel pressured. This is your decision, and whatever you choose, I'll support you. But I have to be honest—I want you to stay. I want to build a life with you here, in Willow Creek."

Mia's heart swelled at his words. She could see the sincerity in his eyes, the depth of his feelings for her. And in that moment, she knew that she felt the same way. The thought of leaving him behind, of walking away from the love they were building, felt impossible.

"I want that too," Mia said softly, her voice trembling with emotion. "But I'm scared, Ethan. Scared of giving up everything I worked for, scared of making the wrong choice."

Ethan squeezed her hand, his touch reassuring. "I get it. But think about what you're gaining, not just what you're giving up. You're gaining a life here, with people who care about you. You're gaining a future that's full of possibilities."

Mia looked at him, her mind racing. He was right—she needed to focus on what she was gaining, not what she might be losing. Willow Creek had given her a sense of belonging that she hadn't felt in years, and Ethan had given her a love that felt real and true.

"I think I've already made my decision," Mia said, a smile slowly spreading across her face. "I just needed to say it out loud."

Ethan's eyes lit up with hope. "And what's that?"

Mia took a deep breath, feeling a sense of clarity wash over her. "I'm staying. I'm staying in Willow Creek."

Ethan's smile was radiant as he pulled her into a tight embrace. "I'm so glad to hear that, Mia. I can't imagine this place without you."

Mia held onto him, feeling a mix of relief and excitement. The decision had been a difficult one, but now that it was made, she felt a sense of peace she hadn't experienced in weeks.

They sat there together, the future suddenly seeming a lot brighter. Willow Creek was where Mia belonged, and with Ethan by her side, she knew that she could build a life that was meaningful, fulfilling, and full of love.

The next steps wouldn't be easy—there would be challenges, sacrifices, and moments of doubt. But as she looked out at the lake, with Ethan's arm around her, Mia knew that she had made the right choice. And whatever came next, she was ready to face it head-on.

The next morning, Mia woke up with a sense of calm that had been eluding her for days. Her conversation with her father had lifted some of the weight off her shoulders, and she felt more at peace with the idea that whatever decision she made, it had to be based on what would make her truly happy.

She decided to take the day off from writing and go into town. The sun was shining brightly, casting a warm glow over the streets of Willow Creek. As she walked past the familiar shops and cafes, she couldn't help but feel a deep connection to this place. Every corner held a memory, every face she passed brought a smile to her lips. This town had embraced her when she needed it most, and now, it felt like home.

Mia stopped by the bakery and picked up a loaf of fresh bread before making her way to the park. She found a quiet spot by the lake, where she could sit and watch the water ripple in the breeze. As she tore off a piece of bread and nibbled on it, her mind wandered to the future.

What would it look like if she stayed in Willow Creek? She imagined herself continuing to write, finding inspiration in the everyday moments that this town offered. She pictured herself growing closer to Ethan, building a life with him that was rooted in love and trust. She could see herself becoming more involved in the community, perhaps even organizing events or workshops that brought people together.

And then there was the city. She could see that life too—a fast-paced, high-powered career that challenged her and pushed her to new heights. There would be excitement, ambition, and the satisfaction of achieving goals she had once set for herself. But it would also mean leaving behind the peace and simplicity that Willow Creek offered, and potentially losing the connection she had found with Ethan.

Mia sighed, feeling the familiar pull of doubt. It wasn't an easy decision, but she knew she couldn't keep putting it off. She needed to make a choice, and soon.

As she sat there, lost in thought, she heard footsteps approaching. She looked up to see Ethan walking towards her, a small smile on his face.

"Hey," he said, sitting down beside her. "Mind if I join you?"

"Not at all," Mia replied, her heart lifting at the sight of him. "What brings you here?"

"I was hoping to find you," Ethan said, his gaze steady on hers. "I wanted to talk."

Mia nodded, her stomach fluttering with nerves. She knew what was coming—Ethan had been giving her space, but she could tell that he was eager to know where her head was at.

"I've been thinking a lot," Mia began, her voice tentative. "About the offer, about Willow Creek, about us."

Ethan nodded, his expression serious. "And?"

"And... I'm still not sure what the right decision is," Mia admitted. "But I do know that I don't want to lose what we have. You're important to me, Ethan. More than I can put into words."

Ethan's eyes softened, and he reached out to take her hand. "You're important to me too, Mia. And I don't want you to feel pressured. This is your decision, and whatever you choose, I'll support you. But I have to be honest—I want you to stay. I want to build a life with you here, in Willow Creek."

Mia's heart swelled at his words. She could see the sincerity in his eyes, the depth of his feelings for her. And in that moment, she knew that she felt the same way. The thought of leaving him behind, of walking away from the love they were building, felt impossible.

"I want that too," Mia said softly, her voice trembling with emotion. "But I'm scared, Ethan. Scared of giving up everything I worked for, scared of making the wrong choice."

Ethan squeezed her hand, his touch reassuring. "I get it. But think about what you're gaining, not just what you're giving up. You're gaining a life here, with people who care about you. You're gaining a future that's full of possibilities."

Mia looked at him, her mind racing. He was right—she needed to focus on what she was gaining, not what she might be losing. Willow Creek had given her a sense of belonging that she hadn't felt in years, and Ethan had given her a love that felt real and true.

"I think I've already made my decision," Mia said, a smile slowly spreading across her face. "I just needed to say it out loud."

Ethan's eyes lit up with hope. "And what's that?"

Mia took a deep breath, feeling a sense of clarity wash over her. "I'm staying. I'm staying in Willow Creek."

Ethan's smile was radiant as he pulled her into a tight embrace. "I'm so glad to hear that, Mia. I can't imagine this place without you."

Mia held onto him, feeling a mix of relief and excitement. The decision had been a difficult one, but now that it was made, she felt a sense of peace she hadn't experienced in weeks.

They sat there together, the future suddenly seeming a lot brighter. Willow Creek was where Mia belonged, and with Ethan by her side, she knew that she could build a life that was meaningful, fulfilling, and full of love.

The next steps wouldn't be easy—there would be challenges, sacrifices, and moments of doubt. But as she looked out at the lake, with Ethan's arm around her, Mia knew that she had made the right choice. And whatever came next, she was ready to face it head-on.

The next morning, Mia woke up with a sense of calm that had been eluding her for days. Her conversation with her father had lifted some of the weight off her shoulders, and she felt more at peace with the idea that whatever decision she made, it had to be based on what would make her truly happy.

She decided to take the day off from writing and go into town. The sun was shining brightly, casting a warm glow over the streets of Willow Creek. As she walked past the familiar shops and cafes, she couldn't help but feel a deep connection to this place. Every corner held a memory, and every face she passed brought a smile to her lips. This town had embraced her when she needed it most, and now, it felt like home.

Mia stopped by the bakery and picked up a loaf of fresh bread before making her way to the park. She found a quiet spot by the lake, where she could sit and watch the water ripple in the breeze. As she tore off a piece of bread and nibbled on it, her mind wandered to the future.

What would it look like if she stayed in Willow Creek? She imagined herself continuing to write, finding inspiration in the everyday moments that this town offered. She pictured herself growing closer to Ethan, building a life with him that was rooted in love and trust. She could see herself becoming more involved in the community, perhaps even organizing events or workshops that brought people together.

And then there was the city. She could see that life too—a fast-paced, high-powered career that challenged her and pushed her to new heights. There would be excitement, ambition, and the satisfaction of achieving goals she had once set for herself. But it would also mean leaving behind the peace and simplicity that Willow Creek offered, and potentially losing the connection she had found with Ethan.

Mia sighed, feeling the familiar pull of doubt. It wasn't an easy decision, but she knew she couldn't keep putting it off. She needed to make a choice, and soon.

As she sat there, lost in thought, she heard footsteps approaching. She looked up to see Ethan walking towards her, a small smile on his face.

"Hey," he said, sitting down beside her. "Mind if I join you?"

"Not at all," Mia replied, her heart lifting at the sight of him. "What brings you here?"

"I was hoping to find you," Ethan said, his gaze steady on hers. "I wanted to talk."

Mia nodded, her stomach fluttering with nerves. She knew what was coming—Ethan had been giving her space, but she could tell that he was eager to know where her head was at.

"I've been thinking a lot," Mia began, her voice tentative. "About the offer, about Willow Creek, about us."

Ethan nodded, his expression serious. "And?"

"And... I'm still not sure what the right decision is," Mia admitted. "But I do know that I don't want to lose what we have. You're important to me, Ethan. More than I can put into words."

Ethan's eyes softened, and he reached out to take her hand. "You're important to me too, Mia. And I don't want you to feel pressured. This is your decision, and whatever you choose, I'll support you. But I have to be honest—I want you to stay. I want to build a life with you here, in Willow Creek."

Mia's heart swelled at his words. She could see the sincerity in his eyes, the depth of his feelings for her. And in that moment, she knew that she felt the same way. The thought of leaving him behind, of walking away from the love they were building, felt impossible.

"I want that too," Mia said softly, her voice trembling with emotion. "But I'm scared, Ethan. Scared of giving up everything I worked for, scared of making the wrong choice."

Ethan squeezed her hand, his touch reassuring. "I get it. But think about what you're gaining, not just what you're giving up. You're gaining a life here, with people who care about you. You're gaining a future that's full of possibilities."

Mia looked at him, her mind racing. He was right—she needed to focus on what she was gaining, not what she might be losing. Willow Creek had given her a sense of belonging that she hadn't felt in years, and Ethan had given her a love that felt real and true.

"I think I've already made my decision," Mia said, a smile slowly spreading across her face. "I just needed to say it out loud."

Ethan's eyes lit up with hope. "And what's that?"

Mia took a deep breath, feeling a sense of clarity wash over her. "I'm staying. I'm staying in Willow Creek."

Ethan's smile was radiant as he pulled her into a tight embrace. "I'm so glad to hear that, Mia. I can't imagine this place without you."

Mia held onto him, feeling a mix of relief and excitement. The decision had been a difficult one, but now that it was made, she felt a sense of peace she hadn't experienced in weeks.

They sat there together, the future suddenly seeming a lot brighter. Willow Creek was where Mia belonged, and with Ethan by her side, she knew that she could build a life that was meaningful, fulfilling, and full of love.

As the days passed, Mia began to envision her new future with a growing sense of excitement. She started to explore opportunities to contribute to Willow Creek in new ways. She reached out to local organizations, offering to lead workshops and community events that would foster creativity and connection among the townsfolk. Her writing flourished as she found inspiration in the daily rhythms of her life and the stories of the people around her.

Ethan, too, was enthusiastic about the future. They spent weekends exploring the town and planning their life together. They talked about their dreams and aspirations, mapping out a future that blended their individual goals with their shared vision. The more they talked, the more Mia realized how much they complemented each other, and how their relationship had become a source of strength and inspiration.

One evening, as they walked hand in hand along the lake, Ethan turned to her with a thoughtful expression. "You know, I've been thinking. How about we make this place even more special? We could open a little bookstore here—something that brings people together, a place where we can host readings and meet-ups."

Mia's eyes lit up at the idea. "That sounds amazing! We could create a space that not only supports local writers but also fosters a sense of community."

Ethan smiled, his excitement evident. "Exactly. It could be our little project, something that brings us joy and gives back to the town that's given us so much."

Mia hugged him tightly, her heart full. "I love it. Let's do it."

The prospect of opening a bookstore filled Mia with a renewed sense of purpose. It was a project that would allow her to combine her love for writing with her desire to connect with the community.

The idea of creating a space where others could find inspiration and comfort was thrilling, and it felt like the perfect way to solidify her place in Willow Creek.

As the months went by, Mia and Ethan worked tirelessly on their new venture. The bookstore began to take shape, and with each passing day, it brought them closer together. Their dream was becoming a reality, and with it, their future seemed more promising than ever.

The journey ahead was filled with possibilities, challenges, and growth. But as Mia looked out at the lake, with Ethan by her side and their dreams unfolding before them, she knew that she was exactly where she was meant to be. Together, they were building a life that was rich in love, connection, and fulfillment—a life that embraced the best of both their worlds.

And with every step they took, Mia felt a deep sense of gratitude for the choices she had made, for the love she had found, and for the future that lay ahead.

The next morning, Mia woke up with a sense of calm that had been eluding her for days. Her conversation with her father had lifted some of the weight off her shoulders, and she felt more at peace with the idea that whatever decision she made, it had to be based on what would make her truly happy.

She decided to take the day off from writing and go into town. The sun was shining brightly, casting a warm glow over the streets of Willow Creek. As she walked past the familiar shops and cafes, she couldn't help but feel a deep connection to this place. Every corner held a memory, and every face she passed brought a smile to her lips. This town had embraced her when she needed it most, and now, it felt like home.

Mia stopped by the bakery and picked up a loaf of fresh bread before making her way to the park. She found a quiet spot by the lake, where she could sit and watch the water ripple in the breeze. As she tore off a piece of bread and nibbled on it, her mind wandered to the future.

What would it look like if she stayed in Willow Creek? She imagined herself continuing to write, finding inspiration in the everyday moments that this town offered. She pictured herself growing closer to Ethan, building a life with him that was rooted in love and trust. She could see herself becoming more involved in the community, perhaps even organizing events or workshops that brought people together.

And then there was the city. She could see that life too—a fast-paced, high-powered career that challenged her and pushed her to new heights. There would be excitement, ambition, and the satisfaction of achieving goals she had once set for herself. But it would also mean leaving behind the peace and simplicity that Willow Creek offered, and potentially losing the connection she had found with Ethan.

Mia sighed, feeling the familiar pull of doubt. It wasn't an easy decision, but she knew she couldn't keep putting it off. She needed to make a choice, and soon.

As she sat there, lost in thought, she heard footsteps approaching. She looked up to see Ethan walking towards her, a small smile on his face.

"Hey," he said, sitting down beside her. "Mind if I join you?"

"Not at all," Mia replied, her heart lifting at the sight of him. "What brings you here?"

"I was hoping to find you," Ethan said, his gaze steady on hers. "I wanted to talk."

Mia nodded, her stomach fluttering with nerves. She knew what was coming—Ethan had been giving her space, but she could tell that he was eager to know where her head was at.

"I've been thinking a lot," Mia began, her voice tentative. "About the offer, about Willow Creek, about us."

Ethan nodded, his expression serious. "And?"

"And... I'm still not sure what the right decision is," Mia admitted. "But I do know that I don't want to lose what we have. You're important to me, Ethan. More than I can put into words."

Ethan's eyes softened, and he reached out to take her hand. "You're important to me too, Mia. And I don't want you to feel pressured. This is your decision, and whatever you choose, I'll support you. But I have to be honest—I want you to stay. I want to build a life with you here, in Willow Creek."

Mia's heart swelled at his words. She could see the sincerity in his eyes, the depth of his feelings for her. And in that moment, she knew that she felt the same way. The thought of leaving him behind, of walking away from the love they were building, felt impossible.

"I want that too," Mia said softly, her voice trembling with emotion. "But I'm scared, Ethan. Scared of giving up everything I worked for, scared of making the wrong choice."

Ethan squeezed her hand, his touch reassuring. "I get it. But think about what you're gaining, not just what you're giving up. You're gaining a life here, with people who care about you. You're gaining a future that's full of possibilities."

Mia looked at him, her mind racing. He was right—she needed to focus on what she was gaining, not what she might be losing. Willow Creek had given her a sense of belonging that she hadn't felt in years, and Ethan had given her a love that felt real and true.

"I think I've already made my decision," Mia said, a smile slowly spreading across her face. "I just needed to say it out loud."

Ethan's eyes lit up with hope. "And what's that?"

Mia took a deep breath, feeling a sense of clarity wash over her. "I'm staying. I'm staying in Willow Creek."

Ethan's smile was radiant as he pulled her into a tight embrace. "I'm so glad to hear that, Mia. I can't imagine this place without you."

Mia held onto him, feeling a mix of relief and excitement. The decision had been a difficult one, but now that it was made, she felt a sense of peace she hadn't experienced in weeks.

They sat there together, the future suddenly seeming a lot brighter. Willow Creek was where Mia belonged, and with Ethan by her side, she knew that she could build a life that was meaningful, fulfilling, and full of love.

As the days passed, Mia began to envision her new future with a growing sense of excitement. She started to explore opportunities to contribute to Willow Creek in new ways. She reached out to local organizations, offering to lead workshops and community events that would foster creativity and connection among the townsfolk. Her writing flourished as she found inspiration in the daily rhythms of her life and the stories of the people around her.

Ethan, too, was enthusiastic about the future. They spent weekends exploring the town and planning their life together. They talked about their dreams and aspirations, mapping out a future that blended their individual goals with their shared vision. The more they talked, the more Mia realized how much they complemented each other, and how their relationship had become a source of strength and inspiration.

One evening, as they walked hand in hand along the lake, Ethan turned to her with a thoughtful expression. "You know, I've been thinking. How about we make this place even more special? We could open a little bookstore here—something that brings people together, a place where we can host readings and meet-ups."

Mia's eyes lit up at the idea. "That sounds amazing! We could create a space that not only supports local writers but also fosters a sense of community."

Ethan smiled, his excitement evident. "Exactly. It could be our little project, something that brings us joy and gives back to the town that's given us so much."

Mia hugged him tightly, her heart full. "I love it. Let's do it."

The prospect of opening a bookstore filled Mia with a renewed sense of purpose. It was a project that would allow her to combine her love for writing with her desire to connect with the community. The idea of creating a space where others could find inspiration and comfort was thrilling, and it felt like the perfect way to solidify her place in Willow Creek.

As the months went by, Mia and Ethan worked tirelessly on their new venture. The bookstore began to take shape, and with each passing day, it brought them closer together. Their dream was becoming a reality, and with it, their future seemed more promising than ever.

One chilly autumn afternoon, the bookstore's grand opening was met with an outpouring of support from the community. The walls were lined with books, the air filled with the comforting scent of coffee and baked goods, and the atmosphere buzzed with excitement. Mia and Ethan stood together at the entrance, welcoming visitors and sharing their vision for the new space.

The event was a resounding success. Locals and newcomers alike filled the store, engaging in conversations about literature, attending readings, and discovering new authors. The bookstore quickly became a hub of activity, a place where people could come together, share stories, and celebrate their love of books.

Mia looked around the room, her heart swelling with pride and happiness. This was the future she had envisioned—a life built on love, creativity, and community. The journey had been filled with challenges and uncertainties, but she had navigated it with courage and the unwavering support of those she loved.

As she stood beside Ethan, watching the bustling store and feeling the warmth of the community around her, Mia knew that she had made the right choice. Her decision to stay in Willow Creek had led her to a place of fulfillment and joy, and with Ethan by her side, she felt ready to embrace whatever the future had in store.

The future was now a tapestry of endless possibilities, woven together with threads of hope, love, and the promise of new beginnings. And as Mia looked out at the bright, smiling faces of those who had come to celebrate their new venture, she felt a deep sense of gratitude for the path she had chosen and the life she was building.

Chapter 17: Moving Forward

The decision to stay in Willow Creek gave Mia a renewed sense of purpose. The following days were a whirlwind of activity as she began to make the necessary arrangements to close the chapter on her city life and fully embrace her new path. There were calls to make, paperwork to fill out, and goodbyes to say. Each step felt like a weight lifting off her shoulders, bringing her closer to the life she truly wanted.

Mia's first task was to officially decline the job offer. Sitting at her desk, she drafted a carefully worded email to her former boss, explaining her decision. Her fingers hovered over the keyboard for a moment before she typed out the final line, expressing her gratitude for the opportunity but emphasizing her commitment to the life she was building in Willow Creek. As she hit "send," a sense of finality settled over her. There was no turning back now, but the thought didn't scare her anymore—instead, it filled her with a sense of freedom.

That evening, Mia met Ethan at the local diner, their favorite spot to unwind. The familiar hum of conversation and the clatter of dishes created a comforting backdrop as they sat in their usual booth.

"How did it go?" Ethan asked, his eyes full of concern and curiosity.

Mia smiled, feeling a rush of relief. "I did it. I turned down the job."

Ethan's face lit up, and he reached across the table to squeeze her hand. "I'm proud of you, Mia. I know that wasn't easy."

"It wasn't," Mia admitted, "but it was the right thing to do. I'm ready to move forward—here, with you."

Ethan's smile widened, and for a moment, they simply sat there, basking in the shared joy of Mia's decision. The future felt more tangible now, and the possibilities that had once seemed so far away were now within reach.

As the night wore on, they talked about their plans—about how Mia would continue her writing, about the projects Ethan was working on, and about how they could build a life together in Willow Creek. There was talk of weekend getaways, of planting a garden, and even of possibly getting a dog. The more they spoke, the more real their future became.

But even as they planned, Mia knew there were still things she needed to resolve—particularly her relationship with her father. The conversation they'd had before her decision had been comforting, but there was still much left unsaid. She wanted to move forward with a clean slate, and that meant confronting the past, no matter how painful it might be.

The next morning, Mia decided to visit her father. She hadn't been to his house in a while, and as she drove up the familiar driveway, memories of her childhood flooded back. The large, imposing house had always seemed a little too big, a little too cold, but today it felt different. Maybe it was because Mia herself had changed—she was no longer the unsure girl who had left this place years ago, but a woman who had found her way back to herself.

William Prescott greeted her at the door, a look of surprise on his face. "Mia, I wasn't expecting you."

"I know," Mia said with a small smile. "But I wanted to talk. Do you have some time?"

"Of course," William replied, stepping aside to let her in. "Come in, let's sit in the study."

The study was just as she remembered—dark wood paneling, shelves lined with books, and her father's large desk at the center of the room. But today, the room felt warmer, more inviting. Mia took a seat in one of the leather chairs, and William sat across from her, watching her with a mixture of curiosity and concern.

"I wanted to thank you," Mia began, her voice steady. "For the advice you gave me. It helped me make my decision."

William nodded, a faint smile on his lips. "I'm glad I could help. So, what did you decide?"

Mia took a deep breath. "I'm staying in Willow Creek. I turned down the job offer."

Her father's expression softened, and he leaned back in his chair. "I think that's a good choice, Mia. You've found something there—something real. I'm proud of you for making that decision."

"Thank you," Mia said, her heart swelling with emotion. "But there's something else I wanted to talk about. Something I've been avoiding for a long time."

William's brow furrowed slightly, and he nodded for her to continue.

"I know we've had our differences," Mia said carefully, "and I know that a lot of it was because of the way I left, the choices I made. But I don't want to carry that with me anymore. I want us to have a better relationship, Dad. I want us to be able to talk openly, to be there for each other."

William's eyes softened, and for a moment, Mia saw the vulnerability in him—the same vulnerability she had seen glimpses of in their recent conversations. "I want that too, Mia. I've made mistakes, and I know I haven't always been the father you needed. But I'm trying, and I'm willing to keep trying if you are."

Mia felt a lump in her throat, but she forced herself to speak. "I am. I really am. And I know it's going to take time, but I want to start fresh. Can we do that?"

William reached out and took her hand, his grip firm and reassuring. "We can, Mia. We can start fresh, and we can build something better. I'm here for you, now and always."

Tears welled up in Mia's eyes, and she blinked them back, squeezing her father's hand in return. "Thank you, Dad. That means a lot."

They sat in silence for a few moments, the weight of their conversation settling around them. But it wasn't an uncomfortable silence—rather, it was a silence filled with understanding, with the promise of a new beginning.

As Mia left her father's house later that day, she felt a sense of closure. The past was still there, but it no longer held her back. She had made peace with her father, and in doing so, she had made peace with herself.

Driving back to Willow Creek, Mia realized that she was finally ready to embrace the future. With Ethan by her side and her father's support, she knew that whatever challenges came her way, she would face them with courage and an open heart. The path ahead might not be easy, but it was hers to walk—and she was ready to take the first step.

The decision to stay in Willow Creek gave Mia a renewed sense of purpose. The following days were a whirlwind of activity as she began to make the necessary arrangements to close the chapter on her city life and fully embrace her new path. There were calls to make, paperwork to fill out, and goodbyes to say. Each step felt like a weight lifting off her shoulders, bringing her closer to the life she truly wanted.

Mia's first task was to officially decline the job offer. Sitting at her desk, she drafted a carefully worded email to her former boss, explaining her decision. Her fingers hovered over the keyboard for a moment before she typed out the final line, expressing her gratitude for the opportunity but emphasizing her commitment to the life she was building in Willow Creek. As she hit "send," a sense of finality settled over her. There was no turning back now, but the thought didn't scare her anymore—instead, it filled her with a sense of freedom.

That evening, Mia met Ethan at the local diner, their favorite spot to unwind. The familiar hum of conversation and the clatter of dishes created a comforting backdrop as they sat in their usual booth.

"How did it go?" Ethan asked, his eyes full of concern and curiosity.

Mia smiled, feeling a rush of relief. "I did it. I turned down the job."

Ethan's face lit up, and he reached across the table to squeeze her hand. "I'm proud of you, Mia. I know that wasn't easy."

"It wasn't," Mia admitted, "but it was the right thing to do. I'm ready to move forward—here, with you."

Ethan's smile widened, and for a moment, they simply sat there, basking in the shared joy of Mia's decision. The future felt more tangible now, and the possibilities that had once seemed so far away were now within reach.

As the night wore on, they talked about their plans—about how Mia would continue her writing, about the projects Ethan was working on, and about how they could build a life together in Willow Creek. There was talk of weekend getaways, of planting a garden, and even of possibly getting a dog. The more they spoke, the more real their future became.

But even as they planned, Mia knew there were still things she needed to resolve—particularly her relationship with her father. The conversation they'd had before her decision had been comforting, but there was still much left unsaid. She wanted to move forward with a clean slate, and that meant confronting the past, no matter how painful it might be.

The next morning, Mia decided to visit her father. She hadn't been to his house in a while, and as she drove up the familiar driveway, memories of her childhood flooded back. The large, imposing house had always seemed a little too big, a little too cold, but today it felt different. Maybe it was because Mia herself had changed—she was no longer the unsure girl who had left this place years ago but a woman who had found her way back to herself.

William Prescott greeted her at the door, a look of surprise on his face. "Mia, I wasn't expecting you."

"I know," Mia said with a small smile. "But I wanted to talk. Do you have some time?"

"Of course," William replied, stepping aside to let her in. "Come in, let's sit in the study."

The study was just as she remembered—dark wood paneling, shelves lined with books, and her father's large desk at the center of the room. But today, the room felt warmer, more inviting. Mia took a seat in one of the leather chairs, and William sat across from her, watching her with a mixture of curiosity and concern.

"I wanted to thank you," Mia began, her voice steady. "For the advice you gave me. It helped me make my decision."

William nodded, a faint smile on his lips. "I'm glad I could help. So, what did you decide?"

Mia took a deep breath. "I'm staying in Willow Creek. I turned down the job offer."

Her father's expression softened, and he leaned back in his chair. "I think that's a good choice, Mia. You've found something there—something real. I'm proud of you for making that decision."

"Thank you," Mia said, her heart swelling with emotion. "But there's something else I wanted to talk about. Something I've been avoiding for a long time."

William's brow furrowed slightly, and he nodded for her to continue.

"I know we've had our differences," Mia said carefully, "and I know that a lot of it was because of the way I left, the choices I made. But I don't want to carry that with me anymore. I want us to have a better relationship, Dad. I want us to be able to talk openly, to be there for each other."

William's eyes softened, and for a moment, Mia saw the vulnerability in him—the same vulnerability she had seen glimpses of in their recent conversations. "I want that too, Mia. I've made mistakes, and I know I haven't always been the father you needed. But I'm trying, and I'm willing to keep trying if you are."

Mia felt a lump in her throat, but she forced herself to speak. "I am. I really am. And I know it's going to take time, but I want to start fresh. Can we do that?"

William reached out and took her hand, his grip firm and reassuring. "We can, Mia. We can start fresh, and we can build something better. I'm here for you, now and always."

Tears welled up in Mia's eyes, and she blinked them back, squeezing her father's hand in return. "Thank you, Dad. That means a lot."

They sat in silence for a few moments, the weight of their conversation settling around them. But it wasn't an uncomfortable silence—rather, it was a silence filled with understanding, with the promise of a new beginning.

As Mia left her father's house later that day, she felt a sense of closure. The past was still there, but it no longer held her back. She had made peace with her father, and in doing so, she had made peace with herself.

Driving back to Willow Creek, Mia realized that she was finally ready to embrace the future. With Ethan by her side and her father's support, she knew that whatever challenges came her way, she would face them with courage and an open heart. The path ahead might not be easy, but it was hers to walk—and she was ready to take the first step.

In the weeks that followed, Mia threw herself into her new life with vigor. The bookstore project moved forward at a brisk pace, with Mia and Ethan making decisions about design, inventory, and community events. The sense of accomplishment as each milestone was reached was invigorating, and the project became a symbol of their shared dreams.

Mia's writing continued to flourish. She found that her newfound sense of contentment and purpose had a profound impact on her creativity. Her stories grew richer and more vibrant, reflecting the warmth and connection she felt in her life. She began to receive positive feedback from readers, which only fueled her passion further.

The bookstore's grand opening was a triumph, a celebration of everything Mia and Ethan had worked toward. The community embraced the new space, and it quickly became a hub of activity, just as they had hoped. Mia found immense joy in watching people engage with the books, attend events, and form connections with each other. The store was more than just a business; it was a testament to their commitment to Willow Creek and to each other.

One evening, after a particularly successful book signing event, Mia and Ethan walked home together, their hands intertwined. The sky was painted with the colors of sunset, and the crisp autumn air felt invigorating.

Ethan looked at Mia with a loving smile. "You know, I think we've created something truly special here. It's incredible to see how the bookstore has brought people together."

Mia squeezed his hand and smiled back. "It's more than I could have ever imagined. And it's all thanks to us—our hard work, our dreams, and our love for this town."

They stopped by the lake, a favorite spot of theirs, and watched as the last rays of sunlight danced on the water. Ethan pulled Mia close, and she rested her head on his shoulder, feeling a deep sense of contentment.

"I'm so grateful for everything we have," Mia said softly. "For this place, for our life together, and for the future we're building."

Ethan kissed her forehead and whispered, "Me too, Mia. Here's to moving forward, to embracing the future, and to all the wonderful moments yet to come."

As they stood there, wrapped in each other's arms, Mia felt a profound sense of peace. She knew that the journey ahead would be filled with both challenges and triumphs, but she was ready to face it all with the love and support of the people who mattered most. With Ethan by her side and a heart full of hope, Mia was ready to embrace the future and the beautiful life she was creating in Willow Creek.

In the weeks that followed, Mia threw herself into her new life with vigor. The bookstore project moved forward at a brisk pace, with Mia and Ethan making decisions about design, inventory, and community events. Each choice, from the color of the walls to the selection of books, felt like a small step toward the future they envisioned together. The project quickly became a symbol of their shared dreams, and the process of bringing their vision to life was both challenging and rewarding.

Mia's writing also continued to flourish. She found that her newfound sense of contentment and purpose had a profound impact on her creativity. Her stories grew richer and more vibrant, reflecting the warmth and connection she felt in her life. She began receiving positive feedback from readers, which only fueled her passion further. Her novel-in-progress began to take on a new life, inspired by the experiences and emotions she was living through.

The bookstore's grand opening was a triumph, a celebration of everything Mia and Ethan had worked toward. The event was well-attended, with the local community showing up in force to support the new venture. The bookstore quickly became a hub of activity, a place where people gathered to discuss books, attend readings, and participate in various events. It was more than just a business; it was a testament to their commitment to Willow Creek and to each other.

One chilly autumn evening, after a particularly successful book signing event, Mia and Ethan walked home together. The sky was painted with the colors of sunset, and the crisp air felt invigorating. They decided to take a detour to the park, where they could enjoy the peaceful surroundings and reflect on their recent successes.

As they strolled along the path, Mia glanced at Ethan and smiled. "I can hardly believe how much has changed in such a short time. The bookstore is thriving, and it feels like we've truly found our place here."

Ethan looked at her with a loving smile. "It's been incredible to see everything come together. I'm so proud of what we've accomplished, and even more proud of how we've done it together."

They found a bench overlooking the lake, and as they sat down, Mia felt a deep sense of contentment. The water's surface shimmered under the setting sun, and the tranquil setting provided a perfect backdrop for their conversation.

"There's something else I've been thinking about," Mia said, her voice softening. "With everything falling into place, I've been contemplating what our future might look like. I'm excited about what we're building here, but I also want to make sure we're thinking ahead."

Ethan turned to her, his expression thoughtful. "What do you have in mind?"

Mia took a deep breath. "I've been thinking about how we can continue to grow both personally and professionally. Maybe it's time to start thinking about some long-term goals. Things like eventually expanding the bookstore, or even thinking about other projects that might benefit the community."

Ethan nodded, his eyes reflecting his own thoughts. "I like the sound of that. We've already achieved so much, but there's always room for more growth and new ideas. And I agree—we should think about how we can make an even bigger impact."

They sat in companionable silence for a moment, the possibilities stretching out before them. The conversation shifted to their dreams and aspirations, and they discussed various ideas for how they might continue to contribute to their community and build a life that was both fulfilling and meaningful.

As the evening grew darker, they reluctantly left the park and headed home. The warmth of their shared dreams and plans enveloped them, and Mia felt a renewed sense of excitement about the future. The path ahead might be filled with challenges, but with Ethan by her side and the support of their community, she knew that they could navigate whatever came their way.

Back at their cozy home, they settled into their routine. The bookstore continued to thrive, and Mia's writing flourished. They made time for each other, balancing their professional commitments with moments of joy and relaxation. Whether it was a quiet evening spent at home or a lively community event at the bookstore, they cherished every moment.

One sunny morning, Mia and Ethan sat together on their porch, sipping coffee and enjoying the view of Willow Creek. The town had become their home, and they had woven themselves into its fabric. The future was bright, filled with possibilities, and Mia felt a profound sense of gratitude for the journey that had brought her to this point.

Ethan turned to her with a grin. "So, what's next on our list of dreams to tackle?"

Mia chuckled, her heart full. "I think we've got a lot of exciting things ahead of us. Let's take it one step at a time and continue building this amazing life together."

Ethan squeezed her hand, his eyes filled with love and determination. "Sounds like a plan. Here's to moving forward, embracing the future, and making every moment count."

As they sat there, basking in the morning sun, Mia knew that whatever challenges or triumphs lay ahead, she was ready to face them. With Ethan by her side and the community of Willow Creek as their foundation, Mia felt a deep sense of peace and excitement for the future. The path ahead was theirs to walk, and they were ready to take each step with hope, love, and unwavering commitment to their shared dreams.

As the leaves began to turn gold and crimson, Mia and Ethan settled into their new rhythm in Willow Creek. The days were filled with the joys and challenges of their growing bookstore, and their evenings were often spent dreaming up new ideas and plans. Each day brought a fresh sense of purpose, and the future seemed full of promise.

One afternoon, as Mia was arranging a new display in the bookstore, she received a call from Sarah. Her friend's voice was bright with excitement.

"Mia, I've got news!" Sarah said.

"What's up?" Mia asked, setting down a book.

"You're not going to believe it—there's an opportunity for us to collaborate on a community arts festival! They're looking for local businesses to participate, and I thought it would be perfect for the bookstore."

Mia's eyes lit up. "That sounds amazing! We'd love to be a part of it. What do we need to do?"

Sarah filled her in on the details, and Mia felt a rush of enthusiasm. The festival would be a great way to engage with the community, showcase local talent, and bring even more people into the bookstore. It was exactly the kind of event that aligned with their vision for the future.

Later that week, Mia and Ethan met with Sarah to discuss the festival. They brainstormed ideas for how the bookstore could contribute, from hosting author readings to setting up interactive book-themed activities. The possibilities were endless, and they were eager to get started.

As they worked on their plans, Mia found herself reflecting on how much her life had transformed since returning to Willow Creek. The decision to stay had not only allowed her to build a fulfilling career but had also deepened her relationships and provided her with a sense of belonging she hadn't experienced in years. Each day, she was reminded of the beauty and strength of the community she had chosen to embrace.

One evening, as they prepared for the upcoming festival, Mia and Ethan decided to take a break and go for a walk. The crisp autumn air was refreshing, and the colorful leaves crunched under their feet. They wandered down the main street of Willow Creek, chatting about their plans and enjoying each other's company.

"I'm really excited about the festival," Mia said, her eyes sparkling. "It feels like a perfect way to celebrate everything we've worked for and give back to the community that's welcomed us so warmly."

Ethan nodded, his arm around her shoulders. "Me too. It's amazing how far we've come and how much we've been able to contribute. And there's so much more we can do."

As they reached the edge of town, they stopped to admire the view of the rolling hills and the setting sun painting the sky in hues of orange and pink. Mia took a deep breath, savoring the peaceful moment.

"Do you ever think about what's next for us?" she asked, her voice thoughtful.

Ethan turned to her, his gaze tender. "All the time. I think about how we can keep growing, not just professionally but personally too. Maybe we'll start a family one day, or take on new projects that bring even more joy to our lives."

Mia smiled, feeling a warm sense of excitement about the future. "I'd like that. I'm looking forward to whatever comes next, knowing that we're in this together."

They shared a quiet moment of contentment, knowing that their journey was just beginning. The future was filled with possibilities, and they were ready to embrace each one with open hearts and minds.

As the festival approached, Mia and Ethan threw themselves into the preparations. The bookstore buzzed with activity, and the excitement in the air was palpable. The event was a resounding success, with the community coming out in full force to celebrate the arts and support local businesses. Mia felt a deep sense of fulfillment as she looked around at the happy faces and the vibrant atmosphere.

The festival was more than just a celebration; it was a testament to the power of community and the impact that they were making in Willow Creek. It also marked a new chapter in their lives—a chapter filled with continued growth, exploration, and love.

In the weeks that followed, Mia and Ethan continued to build their life together, savoring each moment and embracing new opportunities. Their relationship deepened, their business thrived, and their connection to Willow Creek grew stronger. They navigated the challenges and triumphs of life with a sense of optimism and resilience, knowing that they had the support of each other and their community.

One crisp winter evening, as they sat by the fire in their cozy home, Mia looked at Ethan with a sense of wonder and gratitude. "I can't believe how far we've come. It feels like we've truly found our place here."

Ethan smiled, taking her hand in his. "We have. And I'm excited about everything that's still to come. With you by my side, I know we can face anything and build a life that's full of joy and meaning."

Mia nodded, feeling a deep sense of contentment. The future was bright, and with Ethan by her side and the support of Willow Creek, she knew that their journey was far from over. As they looked out at the snowy landscape and the twinkling lights of their town, they felt ready to embrace whatever lay ahead with hope, love, and unwavering commitment to their shared dreams.

As the days grew shorter and the nights colder, Willow Creek transformed into a picturesque winter wonderland. Snow blanketed the town in a serene, sparkling white, and the holiday spirit was palpable. Mia and Ethan embraced the season with enthusiasm, finding joy in the simple pleasures that winter brought.

One Saturday morning, Mia and Ethan decided to take a break from their busy schedules and explore the local Christmas market. The market, held in the town square, was a charming collection of stalls offering handmade crafts, festive treats, and warm drinks. The smell of cinnamon and pine filled the air, and twinkling lights decorated every surface, creating a magical atmosphere.

As they strolled hand in hand, they admired the intricate ornaments, delicious baked goods, and the cheerful faces of their neighbors. Mia felt a profound sense of belonging. Willow Creek had become more than just a place to live—it was home, a community where she and Ethan were cherished and where their dreams could flourish.

At one of the stalls, they found a vendor selling personalized ornaments. Mia picked out a beautiful glass ornament with their names and the year engraved on it. It felt like the perfect symbol of their journey and the life they were building together.

"I think we should start a tradition," Mia said, holding up the ornament. "Every year, we should get a new one to mark our milestones."

Ethan's eyes sparkled with delight. "I love that idea. It'll be a great way to remember each year and the special moments we've shared."

They continued to explore the market, picking up a few gifts for friends and family, and savoring the festive treats. As they walked back to their car, Ethan stopped and turned to Mia, a thoughtful expression on his face.

"Do you ever think about how we got here?" he asked. "How everything seems to have fallen into place?"

Mia smiled, leaning into him. "I do. It's incredible to think about how our lives have intertwined so perfectly. I feel so grateful for everything that's happened and for the chance to build this life with you."

Ethan kissed her forehead gently. "I'm grateful too. We've come so far, and we have so much to look forward to."

As they prepared for the holiday season, Mia found herself reflecting on her relationship with her father and the progress they had made. They had been in touch more frequently, and their conversations were becoming more open and meaningful. Mia felt a renewed sense of hope that their relationship would continue to grow stronger.

One day, while she was working on a new manuscript at the bookstore, she received a text from her father. It was an invitation to join him for Christmas dinner. Mia felt a mix of excitement and nervousness. It would be their first major holiday gathering together since she had returned to Willow Creek.

She showed the message to Ethan, who offered her a reassuring smile. "It's a step forward. I think it's a good idea to go. It's an opportunity to strengthen your bond and create new memories."

Mia agreed, and they made plans to attend. On Christmas Eve, Mia and Ethan arrived at her father's house, their hearts full of anticipation. The house was beautifully decorated with twinkling lights and festive garlands, and the warmth inside was inviting.

William greeted them at the door with a warm smile. "Mia, Ethan, welcome. I'm so glad you could make it."

As they settled into the living room, Mia felt a mixture of nostalgia and hope. The room was filled with the aroma of a delicious Christmas feast, and the soft strains of holiday music played in the background.

Dinner was a heartwarming affair, filled with laughter and stories. Mia and her father exchanged smiles and meaningful glances, finding comfort in each other's presence. The evening was a testament to how far they had come and the potential for their relationship to continue healing and growing.

After dinner, William presented Mia with a small gift—a beautiful leather journal with a heartfelt note inside. It was a gesture of reconciliation and a symbol of new beginnings.

"I thought you might like this," William said, his voice soft. "For all the stories you'll write and the dreams you'll chase."

Mia was touched by the thoughtful gift. "Thank you, Dad. It means a lot to me."

As they exchanged holiday wishes and shared stories by the fire, Mia felt a sense of peace and joy. The evening had been a reminder of the importance of family, forgiveness, and the strength of their bond.

Back at their cozy home, Mia and Ethan reflected on the evening. The holiday season had brought them closer, and the sense of togetherness they felt was a beautiful gift.

"Tonight was special," Mia said, leaning against Ethan as they watched the snow gently fall outside their window.

"It was," Ethan agreed, wrapping his arm around her. "And it's just the beginning of many more special moments to come."

As they welcomed the New Year, Mia and Ethan embraced the future with optimism and love. They were ready to face whatever challenges and opportunities lay ahead, knowing that their shared dreams and unwavering commitment to each other would guide them through.

Together, they looked forward to a year filled with growth, new experiences, and continued joy. The future was bright, and with each other's support, Mia and Ethan knew they could build a life that was as beautiful and fulfilling as the snow-covered streets of Willow Creek.

Chapter 18: Homecoming

The days following Mia's conversation with her father felt like a breath of fresh air. She had shed the lingering doubts that had weighed her down, and now, she was fully focused on the life she was building in Willow Creek. There was an excitement in the air, a sense that she was finally where she belonged, and she was eager to see what the future would hold.

Mia spent her mornings writing, finding inspiration in the quiet beauty of the town. Her words flowed more freely now, as if the decision to stay had unlocked a creative wellspring within her. The novel she was working on began to take shape, and each day brought her closer to completing it. It was a story about love, about finding oneself, and about the power of second chances—themes that had become deeply personal to her.

In the afternoons, she would often meet up with Sarah for coffee or take long walks with Ethan, exploring the hidden corners of Willow Creek. They talked about everything—their hopes, their fears, their dreams for the future. Mia found herself opening up to Ethan in ways she never had before, sharing her deepest thoughts and feelings. And in return, Ethan did the same, revealing parts of himself that he had kept guarded for so long.

One afternoon, as they strolled along the riverbank, Ethan turned to Mia with a thoughtful expression.

"Do you ever think about what comes next?" he asked, his voice soft but serious.

Mia looked at him, her heart skipping a beat. "What do you mean?"

"I mean, now that you've decided to stay," Ethan clarified. "What do you see for us? For you? For Willow Creek?"

Mia considered his question, feeling the weight of it. She hadn't allowed herself to think too far ahead, focusing instead on the immediate decisions she had to make. But now, with the future stretching out before her, she realized that it was time to start thinking about what came next.

"I see us building a life together," Mia said, her voice steady. "I see myself continuing to write, finding my place in this community. I see us growing closer, supporting each other, and maybe even starting a family one day."

Ethan's eyes softened at her words, and he reached out to take her hand. "That's what I want too, Mia. I want a life with you, here in Willow Creek. I want us to build something that lasts."

Mia smiled, feeling a warmth spread through her chest. "Then that's what we'll do. We'll take it one step at a time, and we'll build the life we both want."

They continued walking, the sun casting a golden glow over the landscape. For the first time in a long time, Mia felt completely at peace with where she was and where she was going. She had found her home, not just in Willow Creek, but in Ethan's arms, and she was ready to embrace whatever the future held.

As the days turned into weeks, Mia and Ethan began to settle into their new routine. They found a rhythm that worked for them, balancing their work with their time together. Mia's writing flourished, and she felt more confident than ever in her ability to tell the stories that mattered to her.

Ethan, too, was thriving. His business was doing well, and he was taking on new projects that excited him. But more than that, he was happy—truly happy—in a way that Mia hadn't seen before. She knew that part of that happiness came from their relationship, and it made her even more determined to nurture what they had.

One evening, as they sat on the porch of Mia's cottage, watching the sunset, Ethan turned to her with a serious expression.

"I've been thinking," he began, his voice thoughtful. "About us, about our future."

Mia felt a flutter of nerves in her stomach. "What about it?"

Ethan took a deep breath, as if gathering his thoughts. "I know we've only just started building this life together, but I want you to know that I'm in this for the long haul. I don't want to rush you, but I want you to know that when you're ready, I'd like to take the next step."

Mia's heart skipped a beat. "The next step?"

Ethan nodded, his gaze steady. "I'm talking about marriage, Mia. I'm not proposing right now—I don't want to put any pressure on you. But I want you to know that I'm thinking about it, and when the time is right, I'll be ready."

Mia felt a rush of emotion at his words. Marriage—it was something she hadn't really thought about, not seriously, anyway. But now, hearing Ethan say it, she realized that it was something she wanted too. She could see a future with him, a life full of love and commitment. The idea of becoming his wife filled her with a warmth she hadn't expected.

"I appreciate that," Mia said softly, her voice thick with emotion. "And I want you to know that I'm thinking about it too. I'm not ready just yet, but when I am, you'll be the first to know."

Ethan smiled, a look of pure happiness on his face. "That's all I needed to hear."

They sat in silence for a moment, the weight of their conversation settling around them. But it wasn't a heavy silence—instead, it was filled with promise, with the anticipation of what was to come. They were building something real, something lasting, and both of them knew that they were in it together.

As the sun dipped below the horizon, casting the sky in shades of pink and purple, Mia leaned her head on Ethan's shoulder, feeling the steady beat of his heart beneath her cheek. This was where she belonged—in this town, in this life, in this moment.

And as the stars began to twinkle overhead, she knew that whatever the future held, she was ready to face it, hand in hand with the man she loved.

The days following Mia's heartfelt conversation with her father were filled with a sense of renewed purpose and clarity. Having released the lingering doubts that had previously weighed her down, she embraced her new life in Willow Creek with a vigor she hadn't known in years. The crisp winter air and the tranquil beauty of the snow-covered town seemed to echo her feelings of serenity and fulfillment.

Mia's mornings were devoted to her writing. The decision to stay had unlocked a creative floodgate within her, allowing her words to flow with newfound ease. Her manuscript, a reflection of her journey, began to take on a life of its own. It was a story of love, self-discovery, and second chances—each theme deeply resonating with her own experiences.

In the afternoons, Mia enjoyed simple pleasures. She and Sarah frequently met for coffee at the cozy local café, discussing everything from life's minor irritations to their grandest dreams. Ethan and Mia took long walks together, exploring the scenic trails around Willow Creek. Their conversations ranged from their hopes for the future to the small joys they found in their everyday lives. With each passing day, Mia and Ethan's bond grew deeper, built on trust, mutual respect, and a shared vision for their future.

One afternoon, as they meandered along the icy riverbank, Ethan turned to Mia with a thoughtful expression.

"Do you ever think about what comes next?" he asked, his voice carrying a weight of seriousness.

Mia looked at him, her heart fluttering. "What do you mean?"

"I mean, now that you've decided to stay," Ethan elaborated. "What do you envision for us? For your writing? For Willow Creek?"

Mia paused, the question making her reflect deeply. She had been focused on the immediate changes and settling in, but Ethan's question prompted her to think about the broader picture.

"I see us continuing to build a life together," Mia said, her voice steady. "I see myself immersed in my writing and becoming more integrated into the community. I imagine us growing closer, supporting each other, and perhaps even considering starting a family someday."

Ethan's eyes softened, and he took her hand in his. "That's what I want too. I want us to build something lasting, something meaningful."

Mia's heart warmed at his words. "Then that's exactly what we'll do. We'll take it one step at a time, and together, we'll create the life we both dream of."

The sun cast a golden glow over the winter landscape as they continued their walk. Mia felt a profound sense of peace and excitement. The future, once uncertain and filled with doubt, now felt full of promise and potential.

As winter deepened, Mia and Ethan settled into a new routine. Mia's writing thrived, and she felt increasingly confident in her storytelling. Ethan's business flourished as well, and he found joy in his work and in their life together. Their relationship was a source of mutual support and happiness, and Mia was grateful for every moment they shared.

One evening, while sitting on the porch of Mia's cottage, watching the sun set behind the snow-covered hills, Ethan broached a subject that had been on his mind.

"I've been thinking about us," he began, his tone serious but gentle. "About our future."

Mia's heart raced slightly. "What about it?"

Ethan took a deep breath. "I know we've just started building our life together, but I want you to know that I'm committed to this relationship. I'm not rushing you, but I want you to know that when you're ready, I'd like to take the next step."

Mia felt a flutter of emotion at his words. "The next step?"

Ethan nodded. "I'm talking about marriage. I'm not proposing right now—I don't want to put any pressure on you. But I want you to know that I'm thinking about it, and I'm ready when you are."

Mia's heart swelled with warmth and affection. Marriage had been something she hadn't seriously considered until now, but hearing Ethan's intentions made her realize how deeply she felt about their future together. The idea of becoming his wife was both exciting and comforting.

"I appreciate you sharing that with me," Mia said softly, her voice tinged with emotion. "I'm thinking about it too. I'm not ready just yet, but when I am, I promise you'll be the first to know."

Ethan's face lit up with a genuine smile. "That's all I needed to hear."

They sat together in a contented silence, the weight of their conversation settling around them. The future, while still unfolding, felt filled with hope and potential. They were embarking on a journey together, building a life grounded in love and mutual respect.

As the sun dipped below the horizon, painting the sky in shades of pink and purple, Mia leaned her head on Ethan's shoulder. The quiet of the evening and the warmth of Ethan's presence made her feel secure and loved.

With the first stars beginning to appear, Mia looked out at the winter landscape and felt a deep sense of belonging. This was her home—Willow Creek, with Ethan by her side. The future held countless possibilities, and she was ready to embrace each one, hand in hand with the man she loved.

The next chapter of their lives was just beginning, and as they faced it together, Mia knew they had everything they needed to build a life full of joy, love, and endless possibilities.

The days following Mia's heartfelt conversation with her father were marked by a newfound sense of clarity and purpose. She embraced her decision to stay in Willow Creek with a fervor that felt invigorating, as if she was finally aligned with her true path. The town, once a backdrop to her struggles, now felt like a warm embrace, welcoming her home.

Each morning, Mia's writing flourished. The creative block that had plagued her seemed to have lifted, replaced by a steady stream of inspiration. Her novel, a tapestry of love, self-discovery, and second chances, grew richer with each page. The themes of her story resonated deeply with her personal journey, turning her manuscript into a labor of love that mirrored her own transformation.

Her afternoons were spent exploring the town's hidden gems with Ethan or meeting Sarah for coffee. Their conversations often drifted from mundane topics to their dreams for the future. Ethan's presence was a constant source of comfort and joy, and their walks became a cherished ritual. The more they talked, the more Mia realized how deeply her feelings for Ethan had rooted themselves in her heart.

One crisp afternoon, while walking along the snow-covered riverbank, Ethan turned to Mia with a thoughtful expression.

"Do you ever think about what comes next?" he asked, his voice filled with a mix of curiosity and anticipation.

Mia glanced at him, her heart fluttering. "What do you mean?"

"I mean, now that you've decided to stay," Ethan said, "what do you envision for us? For you? For Willow Creek?"

Mia considered his question. She had been so focused on the immediate changes and settling into her new life that she hadn't fully allowed herself to imagine the broader picture. But Ethan's question nudged her to think about their future.

"I see us continuing to build a life together," Mia said, her voice steady. "I see myself growing more connected to this community and finding joy in my writing. I envision us supporting each other's dreams and perhaps even starting a family someday."

Ethan's eyes softened, and he took her hand in his. "That's exactly what I want too. I want us to create something meaningful and lasting."

Mia's heart warmed at his words. "Then that's what we'll do. We'll take it one step at a time, and together, we'll build the life we've always dreamed of."

As winter deepened, Mia and Ethan settled into a comfortable rhythm. Their days were filled with work and moments of shared happiness. Mia's writing continued to thrive, and Ethan's business was prospering. Their relationship grew stronger with each passing day, grounded in a deep sense of mutual respect and affection.

One evening, as they sat on the porch of Mia's cottage, wrapped in cozy blankets and watching the sunset paint the sky with hues of orange and pink, Ethan broached a subject that had been on his mind.

"I've been thinking about our future," he began, his voice serious but gentle.

Mia's heart skipped a beat. "What about it?"

Ethan took a deep breath. "I know we're still building our life together, but I want you to know that I'm committed to this relationship. I'm not rushing you, but I want you to know that when you're ready, I'd like us to consider taking the next step."

Mia's breath caught in her throat. "The next step?"

Ethan nodded. "I'm talking about marriage. I'm not proposing right now—I don't want to pressure you. But I want you to know that I'm thinking about it, and I'm ready when you are."

Mia felt a surge of emotion. The idea of marriage, once distant and abstract, now seemed real and compelling. She could envision a future with Ethan, a life filled with love and commitment. The thought of becoming his wife filled her with a sense of joy she hadn't anticipated.

"I appreciate you sharing that with me," Mia said softly, her voice thick with emotion. "I'm thinking about it too. I'm not ready yet, but when I am, I promise you'll be the first to know."

Ethan's face lit up with a relieved and happy smile. "That's all I needed to hear."

They sat together in the fading light, their conversation settling into a comfortable silence. The future, once clouded with uncertainty, now seemed bright and full of promise. They were building something real and lasting, and both knew they were in it together.

As the sun dipped below the horizon, casting long shadows across the snow-covered landscape, Mia leaned her head on Ethan's shoulder. The quiet of the evening and the warmth of his embrace made her feel content and secure.

Looking out at the tranquil beauty of Willow Creek, Mia felt a profound sense of belonging. This town, this life with Ethan—this was where she was meant to be. The future was full of potential, and she was ready to embrace it, hand in hand with the man she loved.

With each passing day, Mia's heart swelled with gratitude and anticipation. She knew that whatever challenges lay ahead, she would face them with courage and a heart full of love. The journey they were on together was just beginning, and Mia was eager to see where it would lead them.

The days following Mia's heartfelt conversation with her father brought a sense of renewal and anticipation. Willow Creek had transformed from a place of uncertainty into a sanctuary where she felt truly at home. Each morning, Mia greeted the day with a newfound clarity, her commitment to her life here fueling her every step.

Mia's mornings were dedicated to writing, and the creative flow she had longed for seemed to surge effortlessly now. The story of her novel unfolded with a natural grace, reflecting her personal journey of growth and self-discovery. Her characters came to life with renewed vibrancy, and she poured her heart into each chapter, finding solace and fulfillment in her work.

In the afternoons, Mia embraced the simple pleasures of life in Willow Creek. She spent time with Sarah, catching up over coffee and discussing their plans for the future. Their friendship had deepened, and Sarah had become an invaluable confidante and source of support. Together, they explored new places around town, discovering cozy cafes and hidden trails that added to the charm of their daily lives.

Mia and Ethan's walks became a cherished ritual. Each evening, they strolled hand in hand, taking in the beauty of the changing seasons. Their conversations flowed effortlessly, ranging from their dreams and aspirations to light-hearted musings about the quirks of their town. Ethan's presence was a constant source of strength and happiness, and Mia cherished the way their relationship had evolved into a partnership rooted in mutual respect and love.

One crisp afternoon, as they walked along a snow-covered path, Ethan turned to Mia with a contemplative expression.

"Do you ever think about what comes next?" he asked, his voice tinged with curiosity.

Mia paused, looking up at him. "What do you mean?"

"I mean, now that you've decided to stay," Ethan said, "what do you see for us? For you? For Willow Creek?"

Mia considered his question, her heart fluttering with a mix of excitement and apprehension. She hadn't allowed herself to fully envision their future, but Ethan's question prompted her to reflect on the possibilities.

"I see us building a life together," Mia said thoughtfully. "I see myself becoming more involved in this community, finding ways to contribute and connect. I imagine us growing closer, supporting each other's goals, and maybe even starting a family someday."

Ethan's eyes softened, and he reached out to gently squeeze her hand. "That's exactly what I want too. I want us to create something meaningful and lasting here."

Mia felt a warmth spread through her chest at his words. "Then that's what we'll do. We'll take it one step at a time and build the future we've always dreamed of."

As winter deepened, Mia and Ethan settled into their new routine with ease. Their days were filled with a balanced mix of work and shared moments of joy. Mia's writing continued to thrive, and Ethan's business prospered. Their relationship grew stronger, built on a foundation of trust, love, and shared dreams.

One evening, as they sat on the porch of Mia's cottage, wrapped in cozy blankets and watching the sunset, Ethan broached a topic that had been on his mind.

"I've been thinking about our future," he said, his tone serious but gentle.

Mia's heart raced with anticipation. "What about it?"

Ethan took a deep breath. "I know we're still in the early stages of building our life together, but I want you to know that I'm committed to this relationship. I'm not rushing you, but when you're ready, I'd like us to consider taking the next step."

Mia's breath caught. "The next step?"

Ethan nodded. "I'm talking about marriage. I'm not proposing right now—I don't want to pressure you. But I want you to know that I'm thinking about it, and I'm ready when you are."

Mia felt a surge of emotion at his words. The idea of marriage, once distant and abstract, now seemed real and attainable. The thought of spending her life with Ethan, of building a future together, filled her with a profound sense of joy.

"I appreciate you sharing that with me," Mia said softly, her voice thick with emotion. "I'm thinking about it too. I'm not ready just yet, but when I am, you'll be the first to know."

Ethan's face lit up with a relieved and happy smile. "That's all I needed to hear."

They sat together in the fading light, their conversation settling into a comfortable silence. The future, once filled with uncertainty, now seemed bright and full of promise. They were building something real and enduring, and both knew they were committed to each other.

As the sun dipped below the horizon, casting long shadows across the snow-covered landscape, Mia leaned her head on Ethan's shoulder. The quiet of the evening and the warmth of his embrace made her feel secure and content.

Looking out at the serene beauty of Willow Creek, Mia felt a deep sense of belonging. This town, this life with Ethan—this was where she was meant to be. The future was filled with potential, and she was ready to embrace it, hand in hand with the man she loved.

With each passing day, Mia's heart swelled with gratitude and excitement. She knew that whatever challenges lay ahead, she would face them with courage and a heart full of love. The journey they were on together was just beginning, and Mia eagerly anticipated the adventures and milestones that awaited them.

As winter continued to blanket Willow Creek in a serene layer of snow, Mia and Ethan's life together flourished. The cozy rhythms of their days wove a comforting tapestry of routine and spontaneity, each day blending seamlessly into the next. Mia's writing thrived in the tranquil atmosphere, and Ethan's presence provided an unwavering source of support and inspiration.

One snowy afternoon, Mia decided to organize a small gathering at her cottage to celebrate the season and the recent milestones in her life. She wanted to bring together the people who had supported her journey—Sarah, Ethan, and a few other close friends she had made since moving back to Willow Creek. It felt like the perfect way to mark this chapter of her life and share her gratitude with those who had been part of her story.

In preparation, Mia spent the morning decorating her cottage with twinkling fairy lights and setting up a table laden with seasonal treats. The aroma of cinnamon and pine filled the air as she put the finishing touches on her homemade apple cider. It was a labor of love, and she took great pleasure in creating a warm and inviting atmosphere for her guests.

When the afternoon arrived, the first to knock on her door was Sarah, bundled up in a bright red scarf. She entered with a cheerful grin and a bottle of homemade eggnog.

"This looks amazing, Mia!" Sarah exclaimed, taking in the festive decorations. "You've outdone yourself."

Mia laughed, feeling a rush of happiness. "Thanks, Sarah. I just wanted to do something special to thank everyone for being such a big part of my life."

As the evening progressed, more friends arrived, and the cottage quickly filled with lively conversation and laughter. Ethan was by Mia's side, proudly introducing her to his friends and family who had come to celebrate. The warmth and camaraderie in the room were palpable, and Mia felt an overwhelming sense of belonging.

Midway through the gathering, Ethan stood up and tapped his glass to get everyone's attention. The room quieted down, and Mia looked at him with curiosity.

"I just wanted to take a moment," Ethan began, his voice carrying a mix of emotion and sincerity, "to express how grateful I am for all of you. Mia and I have come a long way, and we're incredibly lucky to have each other and to have friends like you who have welcomed us with open arms."

A round of applause and cheers followed, and Mia felt her cheeks flush with warmth. Ethan's words were a reminder of how far she had come and how deeply she had integrated into this community.

Mia stood up, her heart full. "Thank you, Ethan. And thank you to all of you for being here tonight and for being such an important part of my life. This is truly a homecoming for me, and I couldn't have done it without your support and love."

As the evening wore on, the conversation flowed freely, and the atmosphere was filled with joy and connection. Mia and Ethan danced together to soft holiday music, their smiles reflecting the happiness that had become a constant presence in their lives.

When the party finally began to wind down, Mia found herself standing by the fireplace, gazing out at the snow gently falling outside. Ethan joined her, wrapping an arm around her shoulders.

"This has been perfect," Mia said softly, leaning into him. "Thank you for everything."

Ethan kissed the top of her head, his breath warm against her hair. "It's been perfect because of you, Mia. You've brought so much light into my life, and I'm grateful every day that we're building this future together."

As they stood there, the crackle of the fire and the quiet of the snow creating a peaceful backdrop, Mia reflected on the journey that had brought her to this moment. She had found her way back to Willow Creek, not just to a place, but to a sense of self and belonging she had longed for.

The future was no longer a distant concept—it was a canvas waiting to be filled with new experiences and shared dreams. Mia felt ready to embrace it all, knowing that she had a partner in Ethan and a community that supported her every step of the way.

As the night drew to a close, Mia and Ethan exchanged a tender glance, understanding that their journey was far from over. They had found their home, their place in each other's lives, and now, with a renewed sense of purpose and love, they were ready to face whatever came next, together.

Chapter 19: Unforeseen Turns

The peaceful rhythm of Mia and Ethan's life in Willow Creek carried on smoothly for several weeks. Mia's writing was progressing well, Ethan was diving into new projects, and their relationship continued to grow stronger. But as with any journey, life had a way of throwing unexpected challenges their way.

One afternoon, Mia received a phone call from Sarah, who sounded more serious than usual.

"Mia, I just heard something you should know about," Sarah said, her voice tinged with concern. "It's about your father."

Mia's heart skipped a beat. "What happened?"

"I don't know all the details, but it sounds like William's health might be worse than he's letting on," Sarah explained. "I overheard something at the clinic today—one of the nurses mentioned his name, and it didn't sound good. Maybe you should check in on him?"

Mia felt a wave of dread wash over her. Her father had always been a pillar of strength, rarely showing any signs of vulnerability. But Sarah's words left her feeling uneasy. She knew she couldn't ignore this, especially after they had worked so hard to rebuild their relationship.

"Thanks for letting me know, Sarah," Mia said, trying to keep her voice steady. "I'll call him right away."

After hanging up, Mia's mind raced. She dialed her father's number, and after a few rings, William answered, his voice as calm and composed as ever.

"Mia, this is a pleasant surprise," William said. "What's on your mind?"

Mia hesitated, unsure of how to approach the subject. "Dad, I just wanted to check in on you. How have you been feeling lately?"

There was a brief pause before William responded. "I'm doing just fine, Mia. Why do you ask?"

Mia could sense the subtle evasion in his tone. "I heard from someone at the clinic that you might not be feeling well. Is there something you're not telling me?"

Another pause, longer this time. When William finally spoke, there was a hint of resignation in his voice. "I didn't want to worry you, Mia. But the truth is, I've been having some health issues lately. The doctors are still running tests, but they think it might be something serious."

Mia's breath caught in her throat. "Serious? What do you mean?"

"I'm not sure yet," William admitted, his tone calm but heavy. "They're looking into a few possibilities, but I don't want to speculate until we have more information. I didn't want to burden you with this, especially after everything you've been through."

"Dad, you're not a burden," Mia said firmly, her voice trembling with emotion. "I'm your daughter—I want to be there for you, no matter what. Please, don't shut me out of this."

William sighed, and Mia could almost hear the weight of his emotions through the phone. "I'm sorry, Mia. I guess I'm not used to relying on anyone. But you're right—you deserve to know what's going on. I have another appointment tomorrow. If you'd like, you can come with me."

"I want to be there," Mia said without hesitation. "I'll be there, Dad."

After they ended the call, Mia sat in silence, processing the conversation. She had known something was wrong, but hearing her father admit it made it all too real. The thought of losing him, just when they had begun to rebuild their relationship, was almost too much to bear.

When Ethan arrived home later that evening, he immediately sensed something was wrong.

"Mia, what's going on?" he asked, concern etched across his face.

Mia recounted the conversation with her father, her voice faltering as she shared the details. Ethan listened quietly, his expression serious.

"I'm so sorry, Mia," he said softly when she finished. "I can't imagine how hard this must be for you."

Mia nodded, tears welling up in her eyes. "I'm scared, Ethan. I just got my dad back, and now this... I don't know what I'll do if something happens to him."

Ethan wrapped his arms around her, holding her close. "You don't have to go through this alone, Mia. I'm here for you, every step of the way. We'll get through this together."

Mia leaned into Ethan's embrace, drawing comfort from his strength. "Thank you, Ethan. I don't know what I'd do without you."

"You'll never have to find out," Ethan whispered, pressing a kiss to the top of her head.

The next morning, Mia drove to her father's house to accompany him to his appointment. The atmosphere was heavy with unspoken concerns, but Mia tried to stay positive, reassuring herself that they wouldn't know anything for sure until after the doctor's visit.

At the clinic, they waited in a small, sterile room while the doctor reviewed William's test results. The minutes dragged on, each one stretching Mia's nerves tighter. Finally, the doctor entered, holding a file that seemed to carry the weight of the world.

"Mr. Prescott, Mia," the doctor began, her expression professional but not without compassion. "I'm afraid the tests have confirmed our initial suspicions. Your father has early-stage cancer."

Mia felt as though the floor had dropped out from under her. The word echoed in her mind, heavy and foreboding: cancer.

"What kind of cancer?" William asked, his voice calm despite the gravity of the situation.

"It's lung cancer," the doctor replied gently. "Fortunately, we've caught it early, which gives us a better chance of treating it effectively. We'll need to discuss treatment options, but I'm optimistic that with the right approach, we can manage this."

Mia's mind spun as the doctor outlined the treatment plan, mentioning surgery, radiation, and possibly chemotherapy. She listened, but her thoughts kept drifting to the reality of the situation: her father was seriously ill, and their time together might be limited.

After the appointment, they drove back to William's house in silence. Once inside, Mia turned to her father, searching his face for any sign of fear or doubt. But William remained composed, his expression resolute.

"I'm going to fight this, Mia," he said, his voice steady. "I've been through worse, and I'm not about to give up now."

Mia's heart ached at his words, but she knew he was right. Her father was a fighter—he always had been. And if anyone could beat this, it was him.

"I'll be with you every step of the way, Dad," she said, her voice firm. "We'll get through this together."

As the days passed, Mia threw herself into supporting her father, balancing her time between writing, spending time with Ethan, and being there for William. It was exhausting, both physically and emotionally, but she knew she couldn't afford to falter. Her father needed her, and she was determined to be strong for him.

Ethan was her rock throughout it all, offering a steady presence and a shoulder to lean on whenever she needed it. Their relationship deepened as they faced this new challenge together, and Mia found herself leaning on him more than she ever had before.

Despite the uncertainty of the future, Mia knew one thing for sure: she wasn't alone in this. She had Ethan, she had Sarah, and most importantly, she had the strength to face whatever came next.

And as she looked out at the familiar landscape of Willow Creek, she knew that no matter what happened, this was where she was meant to be—surrounded by the people she loved, ready to face whatever life threw her way.

The peaceful rhythm of Mia and Ethan's life in Willow Creek continued for several weeks, punctuated by their shared joy and the steady progress in both of their professional and personal lives. Mia's writing flourished, Ethan's projects brought him satisfaction, and their relationship grew deeper. Yet, even in the midst of this harmony, life had a way of introducing unexpected challenges.

One chilly afternoon, the tranquility was disrupted when Mia received a phone call from Sarah. Her tone was uncharacteristically serious, and Mia's heart immediately sank.

"Mia, I've heard something that might be important," Sarah said, her voice laced with concern. "It's about your father."

Mia's pulse quickened. "What happened?"

"I'm not sure of all the details, but it sounds like William's health might be worse than he's letting on," Sarah explained. "I overheard something at the clinic today—a nurse mentioned his name, and it didn't sound good. You might want to check in on him."

The anxiety that surged through Mia was almost overwhelming. Her father, a figure of strength and resilience, had always kept his vulnerabilities hidden. The notion that he might be struggling was unsettling.

"Thank you for letting me know, Sarah," Mia said, trying to keep her voice steady. "I'll call him right away."

She ended the call and immediately dialed her father's number. The anticipation and worry were almost too much to bear. After a few rings, William answered, his voice as calm as ever.

"Mia, what a pleasant surprise," William said. "What's on your mind?"

Mia hesitated before speaking. "Dad, I just wanted to check in. How have you been feeling lately?"

There was a moment of silence before William replied. "I'm doing fine, Mia. Why do you ask?"

Mia sensed the evasion in his voice. "Sarah mentioned that you might not be feeling well. Is there something you're not telling me?"

There was a longer pause this time, and when William spoke, there was a trace of resignation in his voice. "I didn't want to worry you, Mia. But the truth is, I've been experiencing some health issues. The doctors are still running tests, but they think it might be serious."

Mia's heart clenched. "Serious? What do you mean?"

"I'm not entirely sure yet," William said quietly. "They're exploring a few possibilities, but I didn't want to burden you with this, especially after everything you've been through."

"Dad, you're not a burden," Mia said firmly, her voice trembling with emotion. "I'm your daughter. I want to be there for you, no matter what. Please don't shut me out."

William sighed deeply. "I suppose I'm not used to relying on anyone. But you're right—you should know what's going on. I have another appointment tomorrow. If you'd like, you can come with me."

"I want to be there," Mia said without hesitation. "I'll be there, Dad."

After hanging up, Mia sat in stunned silence, grappling with the weight of the conversation. The thought of her father being seriously ill was nearly unbearable, especially when their relationship had only recently begun to heal.

When Ethan arrived home that evening, he noticed the strain in Mia's expression immediately.

"Mia, what's wrong?" he asked, his concern evident.

Mia relayed the conversation with her father, her voice cracking as she spoke. Ethan listened intently, his face a portrait of empathy.

"I'm so sorry, Mia," he said softly once she finished. "I can't imagine how difficult this must be for you."

Mia nodded, tears welling in her eyes. "I'm terrified, Ethan. Just when I've finally reconnected with him, this happens. I don't know how to handle it."

Ethan enveloped her in a comforting embrace. "You don't have to go through this alone. I'm here for you, every step of the way. We'll face this together."

Mia leaned into Ethan's warmth, drawing strength from his presence. "Thank you. I don't know what I'd do without you."

"You'll never have to find out," Ethan whispered, pressing a kiss to her forehead.

The next morning, Mia drove to her father's house, her mind heavy with worry. The drive was a blur of anxious thoughts as she mentally prepared herself for the appointment.

At the clinic, the waiting room seemed to stretch on endlessly. Mia and William sat in tense silence until the doctor arrived, carrying a file that felt like it held the weight of their future.

"Mr. Prescott, Mia," the doctor began, her expression sympathetic. "I'm afraid the tests have confirmed our initial suspicions. Your father has early-stage cancer."

The word "cancer" hit Mia like a punch to the gut. It reverberated through her mind, heavy and chilling.

"What kind of cancer?" William asked, his voice calm but laced with concern.

"It's lung cancer," the doctor replied gently. "Fortunately, we've caught it early, which gives us a better chance of effective treatment. We'll need to discuss options, including surgery, radiation, and possibly chemotherapy. With the right approach, we can manage this."

Mia's mind spun with the implications of the diagnosis. Her father was facing a serious battle, and the prospect of treatment, uncertainty, and recovery loomed large.

After the appointment, they returned to William's house. The drive was quiet, each of them lost in their thoughts. Inside, Mia turned to her father, seeking any sign of despair or fear. But William remained composed, his resolve evident.

"I'm going to fight this, Mia," he said, his voice steady. "I've faced challenges before, and I'm not giving up now."

Mia's heart ached, but she saw the determination in her father's eyes. If anyone could face this battle, it was him.

"I'll be with you every step of the way," Mia said firmly. "We'll get through this together."

In the days that followed, Mia juggled her time between supporting her father, continuing her writing, and spending time with Ethan. The demands were exhausting, but she knew she had to be strong. Her father needed her, and she was determined to be there for him.

Ethan remained a pillar of support, his unwavering presence and understanding helping Mia navigate this challenging period. Their relationship grew even stronger as they faced this new adversity together, their bond deepening with each shared moment of vulnerability and strength.

Despite the uncertainty, Mia found solace in the fact that she wasn't alone. She had Ethan, Sarah, and a growing sense of resilience. As she looked out at the snowy landscape of Willow Creek, she knew that no matter what the future held, she was ready to face it with the people she loved by her side.

The days following the appointment were a blur of activity and emotions. Mia found herself caught in a whirlwind of doctor's visits, treatment plans, and conversations about her father's health. Despite the heaviness of the situation, she tried to maintain a sense of normalcy in her life, knowing that her father needed her strength now more than ever.

Each morning, Mia visited William, helping him with daily tasks and accompanying him to his medical appointments. The treatments began to take their toll, and the once vibrant man who had always been a pillar of strength now seemed fragile and weary. Mia's heart broke seeing him like this, but she remained a constant source of support, determined to be there for him through every step of his journey.

Ethan, ever the supportive partner, made sure to balance his work with his role as Mia's emotional anchor. He took on additional responsibilities around the house and provided a steady presence during the difficult moments. His gestures of support—whether it was preparing meals, managing household chores, or simply being there to listen—were a lifeline for Mia, helping her navigate the challenges she faced.

One evening, as Mia sat by her father's bedside, she noticed a shift in his demeanor. William had been quiet and introspective for days, but tonight, he seemed unusually reflective.

"Mia," William began, his voice soft but resolute, "I've been thinking a lot lately about the past and the choices I've made."

Mia looked up from the book she had been reading aloud to him. "What do you mean, Dad?"

"I've had regrets," William admitted, his eyes searching hers for understanding. "Not about you—never about you—but about the way I lived my life. There are things I wish I'd done differently, ways I wish I'd been more present."

Mia's heart ached at his words. "You've done the best you could, Dad. No one is perfect. What matters is that we're here now, trying to make things right."

William nodded slowly. "I know. But it's hard not to look back and wish for more time, more chances to make things right."

Mia took his hand, squeezing it gently. "We still have time, Dad. We're going to focus on getting you through this, and we'll make the most of the time we have."

The conversation left Mia feeling reflective. She spent the rest of the evening with Ethan, sharing her thoughts and feelings. They talked about the complexities of life, the challenges of facing mortality, and the importance of cherishing every moment.

Ethan listened intently, his hand resting on hers. "It's tough to see someone you love going through this," he said softly. "But you're doing an amazing job, Mia. Your strength and dedication are incredible."

Mia smiled faintly, her eyes misting with tears. "I couldn't do it without you, Ethan. Your support means everything to me."

As the weeks went by, Mia noticed that the strain of the situation was beginning to take a toll on her. Despite her best efforts to stay positive, the constant worry and stress were wearing her down. She found herself increasingly exhausted, both physically and emotionally.

One day, Sarah visited, sensing that Mia might need a break. She showed up with a care package of comforting treats and a warm smile.

"Mia, you look like you could use some time for yourself," Sarah said, handing her the package. "Why don't you take a few hours off? I can sit with your dad while you get some rest."

Mia hesitated, reluctant to leave her father's side, but she knew Sarah was right. She needed to recharge if she was going to be the support her father needed.

"Thank you, Sarah," Mia said, her voice filled with gratitude. "I'll take you up on that offer."

As she took a rare afternoon off, Mia found herself wandering through Willow Creek. The quiet beauty of the town was a soothing balm for her frayed nerves. She visited some of her favorite spots—a cozy café, a tranquil park—and allowed herself to relax for the first time in weeks.

During her break, Mia had a chance to reflect on her life, her relationship with Ethan, and her father's illness. She realized that while she had been so focused on being strong for her father, she had neglected her own needs. The brief respite was a reminder of the importance of self-care and balance.

When she returned to her father's house, she felt renewed, ready to face the challenges ahead. Sarah had been a wonderful support, and Mia was grateful for her friend's kindness.

William's treatment continued, and while the journey was arduous, there were moments of hope and progress. The doctors remained optimistic, and William's determination to fight the illness inspired Mia daily.

One evening, as Mia and Ethan sat together on the porch, watching the sun dip below the horizon, Ethan turned to her with a thoughtful expression.

"You've been incredible through all of this," Ethan said softly. "But remember, it's okay to lean on others, too. You don't have to carry this burden alone."

Mia nodded, her heart swelling with appreciation for Ethan's unwavering support. "I know. I'm learning that every day. Thank you for being here for me."

Ethan took her hand in his, their fingers intertwined. "We'll face this together. No matter what happens, we'll get through it."

As the stars began to emerge in the twilight sky, Mia felt a renewed sense of hope. The future remained uncertain, but she knew that with Ethan by her side and the support of her friends and family, she was equipped to face whatever lay ahead.

In the midst of the challenges and unforeseen turns, Mia found strength in the love and connections she had nurtured. And as she looked out over Willow Creek, she felt a profound sense of gratitude for the journey she was on, ready to embrace the future with courage and resilience.

The days rolled on, each one blending into the next as Mia juggled her responsibilities and emotions. Despite the ever-present weight of worry about her father's health, life in Willow Creek continued its steady rhythm. The support from Ethan, Sarah, and the community had been a beacon of light in the darkness, helping Mia navigate the storm.

One crisp autumn morning, as the leaves began to fall and the air turned chilly, Mia received an unexpected call from her publisher. They had read a draft of her novel and wanted to discuss it further. The timing felt surreal—amidst the chaos of her personal life, the possibility of her book being published seemed both like a distant dream and a welcome distraction.

Meeting with her publisher in the city was a welcome change of pace. Mia spent the day discussing her book, revisions, and potential release dates. The excitement of the conversation provided a temporary escape from the constant worry about her father. By the end of the meeting, she felt invigorated, with renewed energy and focus on her writing.

Returning to Willow Creek that evening, Mia was greeted by Ethan with a warm embrace. He could see the spark in her eyes and the bounce in her step, signs that her day had been a positive one.

"You look like you've had a good day," Ethan said, his voice filled with curiosity.

Mia smiled, her eyes shining. "I did. My publisher is excited about the book. We're making some revisions, and it looks like it could be published soon."

Ethan's face lit up with genuine happiness. "That's amazing, Mia! I'm so proud of you."

As they celebrated this small victory, Mia felt a sense of balance return to her life. Despite the ongoing challenges, moments like these reminded her of the good things she had worked hard to achieve. She cherished these reprieves, using them as fuel to keep moving forward.

But the tranquility was short-lived. A few days later, another unforeseen turn arrived. William's condition had taken a sudden decline. The treatment wasn't progressing as hoped, and a new round of tests revealed that the cancer had spread more aggressively than initially anticipated.

The news hit Mia like a freight train. She spent hours at the hospital, navigating the whirlwind of medical jargon and treatment options. Each conversation with doctors seemed to bring more uncertainty, more questions than answers.

Ethan was by her side through it all, his unwavering presence a source of comfort. He took charge of logistical details, ensuring that Mia had everything she needed while she focused on her father's care. Their shared strength became a pillar of support for Mia, allowing her to stay grounded despite the emotional turmoil.

One night, after a particularly draining day at the hospital, Mia sat with Ethan on the porch of her cottage. The quiet of the night was a stark contrast to the chaos of the past few days.

"I don't know how much more I can handle, Ethan," Mia admitted, her voice breaking. "It feels like every time we start to see a glimmer of hope, something else happens."

Ethan took her hand, his gaze steady and reassuring. "You're stronger than you know, Mia. And no matter what happens, you're not alone. We're in this together."

Mia leaned into him, drawing strength from his words. "I'm scared, Ethan. I can't imagine losing him, not after everything we've been through."

Ethan wrapped his arms around her, his touch a reassuring anchor. "We'll face whatever comes next, one step at a time. And no matter how tough it gets, we'll find a way to get through it."

As the days turned into weeks, Mia and Ethan continued to face the challenges head-on. The treatments were harsh, and William's health fluctuated, but there were still moments of hope and connection. Mia cherished the quiet conversations with her father, the shared memories, and the love they had always shared.

Amidst the ongoing struggles, there were moments of profound clarity. Mia realized that life was unpredictable, filled with both joy and sorrow, and that strength came from facing each moment with courage and grace. Her father's illness, while devastating, had also brought her closer to those she loved and reminded her of the importance of cherishing every day.

One evening, as she sat by William's bedside, he reached out and took her hand.

"Mia," he said softly, his voice filled with a mix of gratitude and sadness, "I want you to know how proud I am of you. You've been amazing through all of this."

Mia's eyes filled with tears. "I'm just doing what I can, Dad. I love you, and I want to be here for you."

William smiled faintly. "I know. And that means more to me than you can imagine."

The days continued to be a blend of hope and uncertainty. Mia found solace in the small victories, the moments of connection with her father, and the unwavering support from Ethan and Sarah. They had become her anchor in the storm, guiding her through the turbulent waters of the past few months.

As winter approached, the landscape of Willow Creek transformed into a frosty wonderland. The beauty of the season was a reminder of the cycles of life, of endings and new beginnings. Mia looked out at the snow-covered town, feeling a mix of sadness and hope.

In the midst of the trials, she knew one thing for certain: she was surrounded by love, by the strength of her relationships, and by the resilience she had found within herself. And as she faced each new turn, she did so with the knowledge that she was not alone, ready to embrace whatever the future held with courage and grace.

Winter's chill deepened as the holidays approached, and Willow Creek was blanketed in a layer of snow, transforming it into a picturesque winter wonderland. For Mia, however, the season brought a bittersweet mix of holiday cheer and ongoing challenges. The festive decorations and the warmth of the community provided a stark contrast to the worry and exhaustion she felt as she continued to care for her father.

One cold December morning, as Mia prepared to visit the hospital, Ethan approached her with a concerned look. "Mia, there's something I need to talk to you about."

Mia looked up from the pile of papers she was organizing. "What is it?"

Ethan hesitated, choosing his words carefully. "I've been thinking a lot about us and our future. I know things have been really tough lately, and I don't want to add more stress, but I need to be honest with you. I've been offered a major project in another city—one that could mean a big opportunity for me."

Mia's heart sank. She had been so focused on her father's health and the challenges of her own life that she hadn't considered the implications of Ethan's career. "Another city? When would this be?"

Ethan nodded, looking pained. "It's a big opportunity, but it would mean being away for several months. I don't want to make this decision without talking to you first. I know things are difficult right now, and I don't want to make it even harder for you."

Mia took a deep breath, trying to steady her emotions. The thought of Ethan being away during such a critical time was overwhelming. Yet, she understood the importance of his career and the opportunity before him.

"Ethan, I appreciate that you're considering how this will affect us," Mia said, her voice steady but filled with concern. "But right now, with everything going on with my father, I don't know how

I'd manage if you were gone. It's not just about the practical aspects—it's about the emotional support I need."

Ethan's expression softened, and he took her hands in his. "I understand, Mia. This is a huge decision for both of us. If you need me to stay, I will. I want to be here for you and for your father."

Mia looked into his eyes, feeling a mixture of gratitude and sadness. "I need you here, Ethan. I need you now more than ever. Let's talk about this again when things settle down, but right now, I can't handle the idea of you being away."

Ethan nodded, squeezing her hands gently. "I'll turn down the project. My priority is being here for you. We'll face this together."

The conversation left Mia feeling both relieved and conflicted. She appreciated Ethan's willingness to stay, but the weight of his unfulfilled career opportunity lingered in her mind. She knew that their relationship would be tested in new ways as they navigated these challenges together.

As Christmas approached, the town of Willow Creek held its annual holiday festival. Despite the ongoing difficulties, Mia decided to participate, hoping that the festive spirit might provide a temporary reprieve from the stress.

The festival was a beautiful distraction, with twinkling lights, festive music, and the scent of cinnamon and pine in the air. Mia and Ethan joined Sarah and some friends from the community in setting up a booth for local crafts and homemade treats. The joy and laughter of the festival provided a much-needed escape, even if only for a few hours.

That evening, as Mia and Ethan walked home through the snow-covered streets, Mia felt a sense of tranquility that had been elusive for weeks. The sight of the holiday decorations, the sound of carolers, and the warmth of the community created a moment of peace amidst the chaos.

"Thank you for today," Mia said, her voice soft but sincere. "It meant a lot to me. I needed this break."

Ethan wrapped an arm around her, pulling her close. "I'm glad we could be a part of it. We needed this, too."

They walked in silence for a while, taking in the beauty of the season. As they approached Mia's cottage, Ethan stopped and turned to her.

"Mia, there's something else I want to say," he began, his voice serious. "With everything going on, I want you to know that no matter how tough things get, I'm here for you. We've faced a lot already, and I believe we can get through anything as long as we're together."

Mia's heart swelled with emotion, and she felt tears prick at her eyes. "I know, Ethan. I couldn't do this without you. Thank you for everything."

They shared a tender kiss, their love a beacon of light in the midst of uncertainty. The snow continued to fall gently around them, a reminder of the beauty that could still be found in the midst of hardship.

As the New Year approached, Mia and Ethan continued to face the challenges of her father's illness with courage and determination. Each day brought new obstacles, but also new moments of connection and hope. Their relationship grew stronger as they navigated these trials together, their love a source of strength in the face of adversity.

Mia knew that the future remained uncertain, but she was ready to face it with the support of those she loved. The road ahead would be difficult, but with Ethan by her side, she felt a renewed sense of resilience and hope. As the first snowflakes of the New Year fell gently over Willow Creek, Mia looked forward with a cautious optimism, ready to embrace whatever the future might hold.

Chapter 20: A New Beginning

The next few weeks were a whirlwind of appointments, treatments, and emotional highs and lows. Mia found herself on an emotional rollercoaster, one moment feeling hopeful as her father responded well to treatment, and the next overwhelmed by the gravity of the situation. But through it all, she remained steadfast, determined to be there for her father in every way possible.

Ethan continued to be her anchor, always knowing when to offer comfort or when to give her space. Their relationship, though tested by the stress of William's illness, grew stronger with each passing day. Mia found solace in their quiet moments together, whether it was a simple walk along the river or an evening spent talking on the porch. Ethan's unwavering support was a constant reminder that she didn't have to face this battle alone.

One afternoon, after another grueling round of treatment, Mia and William returned to his house. They sat in the living room, the weight of the day hanging over them like a cloud. William, looking tired but determined, broke the silence.

"Mia, I've been thinking a lot lately," he began, his voice soft but resolute. "About life, about everything we've been through."

Mia turned to her father, sensing the seriousness in his tone. "What's on your mind, Dad?"

"I've spent so much of my life focused on work, on building a legacy," William continued, his gaze distant. "But now, facing something like this... it makes you realize what's truly important."

Mia listened, her heart aching for her father. She had always known him as a strong, determined man, but now, she could see the vulnerability beneath that exterior.

"What's important is the time we have with the people we love," William said, his voice thick with emotion. "And I don't want to waste any more of it. I want to make the most of whatever time I have left."

Mia felt tears welling up in her eyes. "We'll make the most of it, Dad. I promise."

William smiled, a hint of sadness in his eyes. "I know we will, Mia. And I'm so proud of the woman you've become. You've shown more strength than I ever imagined, and I'm grateful for every moment we've had together."

Mia reached out and took her father's hand, squeezing it gently. "I'm proud of you too, Dad. You've always been my hero."

They sat in silence for a moment, both of them lost in their thoughts. Then, William cleared his throat, breaking the quiet.

"There's something else I've been thinking about," he said, his tone shifting slightly. "I want to make sure that when I'm gone, you're taken care of. I've been working with my lawyer to get everything in order, and I want you to know that I'm leaving the house to you."

Mia's eyes widened in surprise. "Dad, you don't have to—"

William held up a hand, stopping her. "I want to, Mia. This house... it's been our family's home for generations. And I want you to have it. I know you'll take good care of it, and I hope it brings you as much comfort as it brought me."

Mia was overwhelmed by her father's generosity. The house had always been a symbol of their family's history, and the thought of it becoming hers was both comforting and bittersweet.

"Thank you, Dad," Mia said softly, her voice trembling. "I'll cherish it always."

William nodded, his expression one of quiet contentment. "That's all I need to hear."

As the days turned into weeks, William's condition remained stable, though the reality of his illness was never far from Mia's mind. She continued to balance her time between writing, spending time with Ethan, and caring for her father. The novel she was working on became an outlet for her emotions, and she found herself pouring her heart into the story, using it as a way to process everything she was going through.

One evening, as Mia sat at her desk, staring at the blinking cursor on her screen, she felt a sudden surge of inspiration. The story she had been working on—the tale of love, loss, and second chances—had taken on new meaning in light of her father's illness. She realized that the characters in her novel, much like herself, were searching for a way to reconcile the past with the present, to find hope in the face of uncertainty.

Mia began to type, the words flowing from her fingertips as if they had been waiting for this moment. The scenes unfolded in her mind, vivid and clear, and she wrote late into the night, driven by a sense of urgency she hadn't felt before. It was as if the story was writing itself, guiding her toward a conclusion that felt both inevitable and deeply personal.

By the time she finished, the sun was beginning to rise, casting a soft glow over the town. Mia leaned back in her chair, exhaustion tugging at her eyelids, but she felt a sense of peace that had eluded her for so long. She knew that the novel was far from finished, but she had reached a turning point—both in her story and in her life.

The following morning, as Mia and Ethan sat on the porch, sipping their coffee, Mia told him about the breakthrough she had experienced the night before.

"It feels like everything's finally coming together," she said, a small smile playing on her lips. "The story, my life here... it's all starting to make sense."

Ethan reached out and took her hand, his thumb brushing gently over her knuckles. "I'm so proud of you, Mia. You've been through so much, and yet you've found a way to turn it into something beautiful."

Mia's smile widened, her heart swelling with gratitude. "I couldn't have done it without you, Ethan. You've been my rock through all of this."

Ethan leaned in, pressing a soft kiss to her lips. "And I'll continue to be, for as long as you need me."

As they sat together, watching the world wake up around them, Mia felt a sense of contentment that she hadn't experienced in a long time. Despite the uncertainty of her father's illness, despite the challenges they still faced, she knew that she was exactly where she was meant to be.

In Willow Creek, with Ethan by her side, Mia had found her home. And no matter what the future held, she knew that together, they could face anything.

The next few weeks unfolded with a blend of determination and introspection for Mia. As winter's cold deepened, so did the sense of urgency in her life. The hospital visits and treatments became a routine she navigated with a sense of purpose, yet each day was punctuated with moments of emotional intensity. Her father's resilience in the face of his illness became a source of inspiration, and Mia drew strength from his unwavering courage.

Ethan continued to be a steadfast presence, his support never faltering. Their shared moments of quiet reflection and togetherness became a sanctuary from the chaos that surrounded them. Whether they were taking peaceful walks through the snow-covered streets of Willow Creek or enjoying the simple pleasure of shared meals, their bond grew stronger. Ethan's patience and understanding provided Mia with a sense of stability, and she found solace in their deepening connection.

One afternoon, after another round of treatment, Mia and William returned to the house. They sat together in the cozy living room, the warmth from the fireplace a stark contrast to the chill in the air outside. William looked more at ease than he had in weeks, a subtle sign of the hope that had begun to surface amidst the uncertainty.

"Mia," William began, his voice soft but steady, "I've been thinking about the future. I know this has been a difficult time for both of us, but I want to make sure that we're looking forward with hope, not just holding on to what we've lost."

Mia nodded, her gaze focused on her father. "What are you thinking, Dad?"

William took a deep breath, his eyes reflecting a mix of determination and vulnerability. "I want to make sure that we're not just surviving this, but truly living. I've always been so focused on the practicalities, on making sure everything is in order, but I want to take a step back and appreciate the moments we have."

Mia's heart swelled with emotion. "What do you have in mind?"

"I'd like us to create some new memories," William said, his voice gaining strength. "I've arranged for us to take a short trip together—a chance to get away from everything and spend some quality time as a family."

Mia's eyes widened in surprise. "A trip? Where are we going?"

William smiled, a glimmer of excitement in his eyes. "I thought we could visit a cabin in the mountains. It's a place we used to go when you were younger. I remember how much you loved it there. It's a chance for us to reconnect and make some new memories together."

Mia felt a surge of warmth at the thought. The cabin in the mountains held cherished memories from her childhood, and the idea of returning there with her father was both comforting and invigorating. "That sounds wonderful, Dad. I'd love to do that."

As the plans for the trip began to take shape, Mia felt a renewed sense of purpose. The prospect of spending quality time with her father in a place that held so much significance for them both was a beacon of hope amidst the ongoing challenges.

In the days leading up to the trip, Mia poured her heart into her writing, using the novel as a way to channel her emotions and experiences. The story she was working on began to reflect the themes of resilience and renewal that were so present in her own life. Writing became a form of therapy, a way for her to navigate the complexities of her feelings while finding solace in her creativity.

Ethan remained a supportive presence, helping Mia prepare for the trip and ensuring that everything was in order. Their relationship continued to flourish, and the bond they shared became a source of strength for both of them. They took comfort in their shared moments of quiet reflection, finding joy in the simple pleasures of life.

The day of the trip arrived, and Mia, William, and Ethan set out for the cabin in the mountains. The drive was filled with anticipation, and as they approached the cabin, Mia's heart swelled with nostalgia. The familiar sight of the cabin, nestled amidst snow-covered trees, evoked a sense of peace and tranquility.

The cabin was as charming as Mia remembered, with its cozy interior and crackling fireplace. They spent the first evening settling in, reminiscing about past visits, and sharing stories. The atmosphere was warm and inviting, a stark contrast to the cold outside.

Over the next few days, they explored the surrounding landscape, enjoying the beauty of the winter scenery. The time spent together was filled with laughter, heartfelt conversations, and a renewed sense of connection. The trip became a cherished memory, a testament to the strength of their family bonds and their ability to find joy amidst adversity.

As they packed up to leave, Mia felt a deep sense of gratitude for the time they had spent together. The trip had provided a much-needed respite from the challenges they faced, and it had allowed them to focus on what truly mattered—each other.

Back in Willow Creek, as the New Year approached, Mia found herself reflecting on the journey she had undertaken. The trials she had faced had been difficult, but they had also brought her closer to the people she loved and had given her a renewed sense of purpose.

Ethan's support had been unwavering, and their relationship had grown stronger as a result. The novel she was working on continued to evolve, becoming a reflection of her personal growth and the love she had found in her life.

Mia knew that the future remained uncertain, but she felt a sense of hope and resilience that had carried her through the challenges. With Ethan by her side and the support of her father, she was ready to embrace whatever came next.

As the first light of the New Year dawned over Willow Creek, Mia stood on the porch, watching the snowflakes fall gently from the sky.

She felt a renewed sense of optimism and determination, ready to face the future with courage and love.

In the quiet of the early morning, Mia knew that she had found her place in the world. Surrounded by the people she cherished and guided by the lessons she had learned, she was ready to embrace a new beginning—a future filled with hope, love, and endless possibilities.

As the first light of the New Year dawned over Willow Creek, Mia felt a profound sense of renewal. The crisp winter air was invigorating, a fresh start symbolized by the untouched snow covering the ground. The previous year had tested her in ways she hadn't imagined, but it had also revealed the strength within her and the depth of the relationships she cherished.

Mia had spent the final days of the year reflecting on the journey she had undertaken. The trip to the cabin had been a turning point, providing her with the clarity and peace she needed to move forward. Each day had been a step towards healing, not just for her father but for herself as well.

The morning after their return from the cabin, Mia woke up with a renewed sense of purpose. She had spent the night before working on her novel, the story flowing effortlessly as if it were mirroring her own journey. The characters in her book were finding their way, much like she was, and the novel was beginning to take shape in ways she hadn't expected.

Ethan, ever perceptive to Mia's needs, had planned a quiet New Year's celebration for just the two of them. They had spent the day relaxing, cooking a simple meal together, and talking about their hopes for the future. The evening was marked by a peaceful dinner and a shared resolution to face whatever the coming year might bring with optimism and courage.

As they sat on the porch, the twinkling lights of their home casting a warm glow in the darkness, Mia turned to Ethan with a thoughtful expression. "I've been thinking a lot about what comes next for us. I feel like this year is a blank slate, full of possibilities."

Ethan smiled, his eyes reflecting the warmth of the moment. "I feel the same way. This past year has shown us how strong we can be together. I'm excited to see where this new beginning takes us."

They shared a tender kiss as the clock struck midnight, the start of a new year marked by their embrace. The promise of new beginnings hung in the air, and Mia felt a surge of hope and excitement for the future.

In the weeks that followed, Mia continued to focus on her writing and supporting her father through his treatment. The novel became a therapeutic outlet, and she found herself pouring her heart into the pages, channeling her experiences and emotions into the story.

William's health remained stable, and the treatments were proving effective. He was determined to fight his illness with every ounce of strength he had, and Mia admired his resolve. Their time together at the cabin had rekindled their bond, and they continued to share meaningful conversations and moments of connection.

One evening, as Mia and Ethan sat together in their cozy living room, Ethan broached a subject that had been on his mind. "Mia, I've been thinking about the future, not just for us but for your writing as well. Have you thought about publishing your novel?"

Mia looked up, surprised by the question. "I've thought about it, but I wasn't sure if it was the right time. My focus has been on getting through this year and supporting my family."

Ethan took her hand, his gaze steady. "I think it's the perfect time. Your story is incredible, and it's a reflection of everything you've been through. It deserves to be shared with others."

Mia's heart swelled with gratitude for Ethan's encouragement. The idea of publishing her novel had always been a distant dream, but now, it felt like a tangible possibility. "Thank you, Ethan. Your support means more to me than I can say."

With Ethan's encouragement, Mia began exploring options for publishing her novel. She reached out to literary agents and attended workshops to refine her manuscript. The process was both exciting and daunting, but Mia approached it with the same determination she had applied to every challenge she faced.

As spring approached, the town of Willow Creek began to awaken from its winter slumber. The snow melted, giving way to budding flowers and green shoots. The changing season mirrored Mia's own sense of renewal and growth.

Ethan and Mia continued to build their life together, finding joy in the small moments and savoring the time they spent with each other. Their relationship deepened as they faced the uncertainties of the future with optimism and resilience.

One sunny afternoon, Mia received a phone call that would change everything. It was from a publishing house interested in her novel. The excitement was palpable as she shared the news with Ethan, who was overjoyed for her.

"I can't believe it!" Mia said, her voice trembling with emotion. "This is really happening."

Ethan pulled her into a tight embrace. "I knew you could do it. I'm so proud of you."

The following months were filled with preparations for the book's release. Mia worked closely with editors and designers to bring her novel to life, and the anticipation built as the publication date approached.

The day of the book launch arrived, and Mia found herself standing before a crowd of friends, family, and supporters at a local bookstore. The room was filled with a sense of celebration and accomplishment as she signed copies of her book and shared her journey with those who had come to support her.

As she looked out at the faces of those gathered, Mia felt a profound sense of gratitude. The challenges she had faced had shaped her, but they had also brought her to this moment of triumph. She had found her voice, both in her writing and in her life, and she was ready to embrace the future with open arms.

Ethan stood by her side, his presence a constant reminder of the love and support that had carried her through the past year. Together, they looked forward to the future, ready to face whatever came their way with courage and hope.

In the heart of Willow Creek, amidst the changing seasons and the promise of new beginnings, Mia knew that she had found her place. Surrounded by the people she loved and guided by the lessons she had learned, she was ready to embark on the next chapter of her life—one filled with endless possibilities and the promise of a brighter future.

As the first light of the New Year dawned over Willow Creek, Mia felt a profound sense of renewal. The crisp winter air was invigorating, a fresh start symbolized by the untouched snow covering the ground. The previous year had tested her in ways she hadn't imagined, but it had also revealed the strength within her and the depth of the relationships she cherished.

Mia had spent the final days of the year reflecting on the journey she had undertaken. The trip to the cabin had been a turning point, providing her with the clarity and peace she needed to move forward. Each day had been a step towards healing, not just for her father but for herself as well.

The morning after their return from the cabin, Mia woke up with a renewed sense of purpose. She had spent the night before working on her novel, the story flowing effortlessly as if it were mirroring her own journey. The characters in her book were finding their way, much like she was, and the novel was beginning to take shape in ways she hadn't expected.

Ethan, ever perceptive to Mia's needs, had planned a quiet New Year's celebration for just the two of them. They had spent the day relaxing, cooking a simple meal together, and talking about their hopes for the future. The evening was marked by a peaceful dinner and a shared resolution to face whatever the coming year might bring with optimism and courage.

As they sat on the porch, the twinkling lights of their home casting a warm glow in the darkness, Mia turned to Ethan with a thoughtful expression. "I've been thinking a lot about what comes next for us. I feel like this year is a blank slate, full of possibilities."

Ethan smiled, his eyes reflecting the warmth of the moment. "I feel the same way. This past year has shown us how strong we can be together. I'm excited to see where this new beginning takes us."

They shared a tender kiss as the clock struck midnight, the start of a new year marked by their embrace. The promise of new beginnings hung in the air, and Mia felt a surge of hope and excitement for the future.

In the weeks that followed, Mia continued to focus on her writing and supporting her father through his treatment. The novel became a therapeutic outlet, and she found herself pouring her heart into the pages, channeling her experiences and emotions into the story.

William's health remained stable, and the treatments were proving effective. He was determined to fight his illness with every ounce of strength he had, and Mia admired his resolve. Their time together at the cabin had rekindled their bond, and they continued to share meaningful conversations and moments of connection.

One evening, as Mia and Ethan sat together in their cozy living room, Ethan broached a subject that had been on his mind. "Mia, I've been thinking about the future, not just for us but for your writing as well. Have you thought about publishing your novel?"

Mia looked up, surprised by the question. "I've thought about it, but I wasn't sure if it was the right time. My focus has been on getting through this year and supporting my family."

Ethan took her hand, his gaze steady. "I think it's the perfect time. Your story is incredible, and it's a reflection of everything you've been through. It deserves to be shared with others."

Mia's heart swelled with gratitude for Ethan's encouragement. The idea of publishing her novel had always been a distant dream, but now, it felt like a tangible possibility. "Thank you, Ethan. Your support means more to me than I can say."

With Ethan's encouragement, Mia began exploring options for publishing her novel. She reached out to literary agents and attended workshops to refine her manuscript. The process was both exciting and daunting, but Mia approached it with the same determination she had applied to every challenge she faced.

As spring approached, the town of Willow Creek began to awaken from its winter slumber. The snow melted, giving way to budding flowers and green shoots. The changing season mirrored Mia's own sense of renewal and growth.

Ethan and Mia continued to build their life together, finding joy in the small moments and savoring the time they spent with each other. Their relationship deepened as they faced the uncertainties of the future with optimism and resilience.

One sunny afternoon, Mia received a phone call that would change everything. It was from a publishing house interested in her novel. The excitement was palpable as she shared the news with Ethan, who was overjoyed for her.

"I can't believe it!" Mia said, her voice trembling with emotion. "This is really happening."

Ethan pulled her into a tight embrace. "I knew you could do it. I'm so proud of you."

The following months were filled with preparations for the book's release. Mia worked closely with editors and designers to bring her novel to life, and the anticipation built as the publication date approached.

The day of the book launch arrived, and Mia found herself standing before a crowd of friends, family, and supporters at a local bookstore. The room was filled with a sense of celebration and accomplishment as she signed copies of her book and shared her journey with those who had come to support her.

As she looked out at the faces of those gathered, Mia felt a profound sense of gratitude. The challenges she had faced had shaped her, but they had also brought her to this moment of triumph. She had found her voice, both in her writing and in her life, and she was ready to embrace the future with open arms.

Ethan stood by her side, his presence a constant reminder of the love and support that had carried her through the past year. Together, they looked forward to the future, ready to face whatever came their way with courage and hope.

The book's success was just the beginning. As Mia embarked on a new chapter in her career, she also looked forward to continuing her journey with Ethan by her side. They had weathered the storms of the past year, and now, with the dawn of a new year, they were ready to embrace the possibilities that lay ahead.

In the heart of Willow Creek, amidst the changing seasons and the promise of new beginnings, Mia knew that she had found her place. Surrounded by the people she loved and guided by the lessons she had learned, she was ready to embark on the next chapter of her life—one filled with endless possibilities and the promise of a brighter future.

As winter slowly receded, the first hints of spring began to stir in Willow Creek. The once-frozen landscape started to thaw, and the town awakened to the promise of new beginnings. Mia and Ethan found solace in the changing seasons, using the opportunity to refresh their outlook on life and their future together.

The release of Mia's novel was met with enthusiastic praise from both critics and readers. The book's raw emotional depth and authentic portrayal of personal growth resonated with many, and Mia found herself immersed in a whirlwind of book signings, interviews, and promotional events. It was a new and exhilarating experience, one that allowed her to share her story with a wider audience while continuing to work on her craft.

Ethan was her constant support throughout this process. He attended every event by her side, cheering her on and celebrating her successes. Their bond grew even stronger as they navigated this new chapter together, finding joy in each accomplishment and comfort in each other's presence.

One sunny Saturday afternoon, as the first daffodils began to bloom, Mia and Ethan took a break from their busy schedules to enjoy some quiet time together. They decided to visit the local park, where they strolled hand in hand, taking in the beauty of the emerging spring.

The park was alive with families, children playing, and couples enjoying the sunshine. Mia and Ethan found a secluded spot under a large oak tree and sat down, savoring the peaceful atmosphere.

"I've been thinking a lot lately," Mia said, her voice soft and contemplative. "About where we are and where we're headed."

Ethan looked at her, his eyes filled with curiosity and affection. "What's on your mind?"

Mia took a deep breath, gathering her thoughts. "I think about how much has changed over the past year. It's been a time of incredible growth for both of us. We've faced so many challenges, but we've come through stronger."

Ethan nodded in agreement. "It's been a journey, hasn't it? And through it all, we've learned so much about ourselves and each other."

Mia smiled, her heart swelling with emotion. "I feel like we've reached a turning point. We've found a way to balance our dreams and our reality, and it feels like we're finally on the path we were meant to be on."

Ethan took her hand, his touch gentle and reassuring. "I feel the same way. This past year has shown me how important it is to cherish the moments we have and to embrace the future with open hearts."

Mia looked out at the park, watching as children ran around and couples shared quiet moments. "I've been thinking about our future, about what we want to build together. I want to make sure we're creating a life that reflects our dreams and values."

Ethan's gaze was steady and loving. "I'm excited about the future with you, Mia. I want to build a life filled with love, laughter, and new adventures. I want us to continue growing together and supporting each other in everything we do."

Mia felt a wave of warmth and contentment. "Me too, Ethan. I want to continue writing, to explore new creative projects, and to make a difference in the world. And I want to do it all with you by my side."

As they sat together, basking in the gentle warmth of the spring sun, Mia realized that this was the beginning of a new chapter not just in her writing but in her life. She felt a deep sense of peace, knowing that she had found a balance between her personal and professional aspirations.

The weeks that followed were filled with exciting developments. Mia continued to work on her writing, exploring new ideas and projects that inspired her. She also began to collaborate with local schools and community groups, sharing her passion for storytelling and inspiring others with her journey.

Ethan, too, was making strides in his own career, taking on new projects that aligned with his goals and values. Their shared commitment to personal and professional growth created a strong foundation for their relationship, and they continued to support each other in every endeavor.

One evening, as they sat together in their cozy living room, Ethan took a deep breath and looked at Mia with a thoughtful expression. "Mia, there's something I've been meaning to ask you."

Mia's curiosity was piqued. "What is it?"

Ethan reached into his pocket and pulled out a small, velvet box. He opened it to reveal a beautiful ring, its simplicity and elegance capturing Mia's attention. "I've been thinking about how much we've been through and how much I want to continue building our life together. Would you marry me?"

Mia's eyes filled with tears as she looked at the ring, then back at Ethan. The depth of her emotions was overwhelming, and she felt a surge of love and gratitude. "Yes, Ethan. I would love to marry you."

They embraced, their hearts full of joy and anticipation for the future. The engagement marked a new chapter in their lives, one filled with promise and excitement.

As they planned their wedding and continued to build their life together, Mia and Ethan embraced the new beginnings that lay ahead. They knew that their journey would be filled with both challenges and triumphs, but they faced it with a sense of hope and commitment.

In the heart of Willow Creek, surrounded by the beauty of spring and the love of those who mattered most, Mia and Ethan began a new chapter, one defined by the strength of their bond and the promise of a bright future. They were ready to face whatever came their way, knowing that they had each other and the unwavering support of their loved ones.

With the first buds of spring blooming around them, Mia and Ethan embarked on their new journey, ready to embrace the adventures and joys that awaited them. Together, they looked forward to a life filled with love, laughter, and endless possibilities, knowing that their story was just beginning.

As the sun dipped below the horizon, casting a golden hue over Willow Creek, Mia and Ethan stood hand in hand at the edge of the small town's central park. The air was crisp with the promise of spring, and the gentle rustling of leaves seemed to echo the excitement and hope that filled their hearts.

The past year had been a whirlwind of challenges and triumphs, but it had also brought them closer together than they had ever been. They had navigated through trials of health, uncertainty, and personal growth, and now, with the dawn of a new season, they were ready to embrace their future.

Mia looked around at the familiar landscape, her heart swelling with gratitude. The park, once a place of quiet reflection, had become a symbol of new beginnings for her and Ethan. It was where they had shared countless moments of joy, found solace in each other's company, and built the foundation of their life together.

Ethan's arm wrapped around her shoulder, pulling her closer. "It feels like everything is falling into place," he said softly, his voice filled with warmth. "I'm excited for what's ahead."

Mia nodded, her eyes shining with determination. "Me too. We've come so far, and I know we're ready for whatever the future holds."

Their engagement had been met with joy and celebration from their family and friends, and they had begun planning their wedding with enthusiasm and love. Every detail was a reflection of their journey—simple, heartfelt, and deeply personal. They wanted their wedding day to be a celebration of their love and the life they were building together.

As they walked through the park, Mia's thoughts turned to her father. William's health had stabilized, and while the journey ahead would still have its challenges, his strength and resilience had inspired her more than ever. Their relationship had grown even deeper during this time, and Mia was grateful for the opportunity to share these moments with him.

Ethan's voice broke through her thoughts. "What do you think about the wedding location? We could have it right here in the park, surrounded by the beauty of spring."

Mia's eyes lit up at the idea. "I love that. It feels so right—like it's a part of our story."

The park's charm and serenity would indeed provide the perfect backdrop for their special day. They envisioned a ceremony beneath the blooming trees, with the gentle rustle of leaves as their backdrop and the warmth of their loved ones surrounding them. It would be a celebration of love, resilience, and new beginnings.

In the weeks that followed, Mia and Ethan immersed themselves in the preparations for their wedding. They chose flowers, crafted invitations, and designed every aspect of the event to reflect their journey and their love. Each decision was made with care, and they were grateful for the support of their family and friends.

As the day of the wedding approached, the excitement in Willow Creek was palpable. The town had embraced Mia and Ethan's love story, and the park was transformed into a picturesque setting for their vows. The ceremony was filled with laughter, tears, and heartfelt promises, and as they exchanged their vows, Mia and Ethan felt a profound sense of connection and joy.

Their wedding day was a testament to their love and their journey—a celebration of the challenges they had overcome and the future they were building together. The park, bathed in the soft glow of twilight, provided the perfect backdrop for their vows, and the presence of their loved ones made the day even more special.

As they shared their first dance as a married couple, Mia looked into Ethan's eyes and felt a deep sense of contentment. The future was bright, filled with endless possibilities, and she knew that with Ethan by her side, she was ready to embrace whatever came their way.

The night ended with laughter and dancing, and as the stars twinkled above, Mia and Ethan walked hand in hand through the park, savoring the joy of their new beginning. They were surrounded by the beauty of the spring night and the love of those who mattered most, and they knew that their journey was just beginning.

As they looked out at the night sky, Mia and Ethan felt a profound sense of peace and excitement. They were ready to face the future together, knowing that their love would guide them through whatever challenges and joys lay ahead.

With their hearts full of hope and their spirits buoyed by the promise of new beginnings, Mia and Ethan embarked on their new journey, ready to embrace the adventures and opportunities that awaited them. Together, they faced the future with love, courage, and an unshakable belief in the power of their shared dreams.

And so, beneath the twinkling stars and the soft whispers of the spring breeze, Mia and Ethan stepped into their new life, ready to write the next chapter of their story—a story filled with love, laughter, and endless possibilities.